The Beast
of Gévaudan

The Beast of Gévaudan

(LA BÊTE DE GÉVAUDAN)

Élie Berthet

TRANSLATED BY

Gerald Briggs

WILDSIDE PRESS

For Élie Berthet, a 19th century author whose exceptional writing deserves to be better known in the 21st century.

Acknowledgements

Whether you are an author or a translator, your work is only as good as your proofreader, and I have been very fortunate in that regard. Cynthia Berresse Ploski, a good friend (and pod mate) who has published three books herself, has been a superb proofreader, and even better, a grammar teacher and general advisor who also occasionally corrected my rusty syntax and twisted vocabulary. I also wish to thank Sally (Sarah) Imberti, another good and patient friend here in France, who provided me with useful counsel, especially on matters pertaining to the Catholic church.

Special thanks to John Betancourt of Wildside Press LLC for accepting this manuscript and making its publication possible. John had also published my translation of *Maître Bernard* by the same author.

A Note to the Reader

I translated this particular work because it was the most famous in a collection of over 100 books written by my Great-Great-Grandfather, Élie Berthet (1815-1891) who was one of the leading novelists of the 19th century. I found it to be a fascinating book, providing a fictionalized version of real historic events during the 1700s in France that generated a legend and a mystery still unsolved today.

The Beast of Gévaudan (*La Bête de Gévaudan*) is the historical name associated with a real animal, most probably a monstrous wolf, that terrorized a part of France called the Gévaudan (today part of the *département* of Lozère) in the south-central region of France between 1764 and 1767. Between100 and 300 persons were reportedly killed by the monster, often by having their throats torn out. The entire Kingdom was alerted and thousands of hunters were encouraged with rewards to find and destroy the beast. Public hysteria at the time contributed to widespread myths about the beast. Louis XV himself sent professional wolf hunters to slay the animal, but they failed. The beast was reportedly killed several times, before the attacks finally ceased in 1767.

The rampage of the beast of Gévaudan became one of the first international news stories reported by a local newspaper in nearby Avignon in 1764 and later taken up by the Paris press. From there the story spread abroad. Over the following years a dozen books have been written about the subject, and most recently a number of films and TV documentaries have been produced on the Beast of Gévaudan and the various theories concerning it.

Élie Berthet was the first to write a romanticized version based on these historic events. This work appeared in serialized form in a Parisian weekly newspaper in 1858. The series was a great success and added to Berthet's growing reputation as a leading French novelist. It was later published in book form to further acclaim.

What impressed me the most in this fictionalized version of the legend of the *Beast of Gévaudan* is the accurate historical depiction of the times. The religious wars had ended over a century earlier, but tension between the Protestants and Catholics remained and are intertwined with this story. The characters are vividly described and the atmosphere and countryside descriptions come alive under Berthet's pen. As I worked on translating this novel, I fell in love with the colorful images I discovered with every chapter.

I hope that you will as well!

—Gerald Briggs
September 2021

CHAPTER I

THE PUBLIC WAY

Langogne, a small town in the ancient province of Gévaudan which now defines the limits of the departments of Lozère and the Ardeche, is situated in a region of rugged mountains and forests which render access difficult. Although it had been a disputed fortification at the time that the religious wars devastated the Cevennes, notably after the revolt of the Huguenots following the revocation of the Edict of Nantes[1], its situation in this infertile region without resources and commerce, had always prevented it from any form of development. Even to this day, Langogne remains a small town in a department lacking large population centers and whose county seat would have less importance than certain villages in the outskirts of Paris.

However, one day in the early autumn of 1764, the small number of inhabitants remaining in Langogne to work the fields were in a state of extreme agitation. The bailiff, accompanied by a drummer, was circulating in the township to provide its citizens with a proclamation which generated great interest. The bailiff, draped in his black cloak, wearing an ample wig and squared cap, marched with the appropriate solemnity, holding a scrolled parchment. At each square, at each intersection, they halted; the drum roll was executed, then the bailiff, unrolling his parchment amid a deep silence, began to read, in a nasal voice, the official act which he was charged with proclaiming. This pronouncement was made in two languages: first in French, then in the local dialect, an indispensable precaution since French was not prevalent in the region, and the bailiff risked not being understood by some in the audience.

So, here is the subject of the solemn proclamation which had the groups of Langognais citizens murmuring, as it had in all the villages of the province,

Over the past several months, the surrounding countryside had been ravaged by a ferocious animal that was thought to be a monstrous wolf and which had already been named *the beast of Gévaudan*. It had devoured a great number of persons, men as well as women and children. Each day

---

1   Edict of Nantes: Signed by King Henry IV in 1598 granting Protestant Calvinists religious freedom. It was revoked by King Louis XIV in 1665 creating a period of racial intolerance.

brought news of another of its misdeeds; some families had been decimated; farmers no longer dared go out to the fields unless armed and in numbers; and, in spite of these precautions, incidents continued to multiply without interruption. Hunts had been ordered, and all the huntsmen in the area had united to track down, then trap or kill the enraged monster. Searches were organized in the woods it frequented, but to no avail. As cunning as it was vicious, it succeeded in evading its ardent pursuers, and the same evening of these grand hunts, young shepherds, or lone travelers, would be torn to pieces in in exactly the same area that the hunters had just left.

This state of affairs had generated such widespread complaints and the terror in the countryside was so great, that the provincial authorities had finally been moved to take serious action. The proclamation read by the bailiff announced that a sum of two thousand pounds would be granted by the Languedoc authorities to the individual who succeeded in killing *the beast of Gévaudan*. To this sum, the local authorities of Mende and Viviers added five hundred pounds, not counting certain exemptions or municipal immunities that would be given to the slayer, or slayers, of the *beast*. In addition, all persons of good will were invited, armed or not, to meet the next day at the Chateau de Mercoire, located a few leagues from the town, to take part in a new hunt organized by Sire de Laroche-Boisseau, the official wolf hunter for the Province and one of the barons of Gévaudan.

The bailiff, as we said, having visited each square and intersection of Langogne, which did not take long, returned to read his proclamation one final time on its main thoroughfare, just opposite an inn where all travelers were likely to stop, since there was no other. His task completed, the bailiff dismissed the drummer, then without answering questions from the assembled crowd surrounding him, which included many of the village notables, he returned to his lodging with majestic strides.

However, his departure did not result in the dispersal of the group gathered in front the inn's portal, and they continued heated discussions of the day's events.

"Two thousand five hundred pounds!" repeated a small, slender man who was the town's clothier; "the Mende syndicates and the Languedoc authorities have done things well, and it is said that the king will add four or five thousand pounds to this sum from his personal funds. One would have to measure many yards of cloth and ribbon to gain such an amount of money! By my faith! If my wife permits it, I will take down my grandfather's old arquebus, and join the others at the Chateau de Mercoire to try my luck."

"In that case, the beast had better behave, neighbor Guignard," chuckled the feudalist magistrate[2] from the Langogne Abbey. "I would willingly

2   Feudalist magistrate: a jurist specialized in feudal law as regards the rights

wager that little mother Guignard would risk the life of her husband, if you are willing to risk it yourself... Well, since you are so brave, why not go ask Sire de Laroche-Boisseau for a favorable position to give you a chance to benefit from this windfall?"

The clothier suddenly wore such a pitiful expression that the group burst out laughing.

"To tell you the truth, Sire," replied Guignard; uncomfortably, "the arquebus is not in a very good condition, and has not been used since the days of Jean Cavalier[3], and I doubt that the smith would be able to repair it by tomorrow. Moreover, I doubt that Sire de Laroche-Boisseau would deign to reserve favorable positions for the common folks like us; everything is reserved for the nobility these days, and you shall see, it will certainly be one of our rich gentlemen that Sire Baron will have win!"

"And why would he not try to win the prize himself?" replied the Abbey's jurist with a mocking smile: "he is the most capable huntsman, the most expert marksman in the province; why would he concede the honor and the benefits to someone else? Despite his pride, I guarantee that he would not disdain receiving those two thousand five hundred pounds. Everyone knows that his affairs are in difficulty...."

A lovely thirty-six-year-old brunette, coquettishly dressed, wearing a golden cross at her neck and a ring on each finger, interrupted the feudalist magistrate:

"Shame! Sire Blindet," she said effusively, "Dare you speak in my presence and in this manner of a handsome and gallant gentleman who always stays at my inn when he passes by Langogne? That Sire de Laroche-Boisseau has some debts, where is the harm? Important nobles like him, are they not obliged to have debts to maintain their status?... But perhaps it might not be too difficult to understand the reason for these nasty remarks. Despite your hopes, he did not wish to select you as his financial advisor, and it was that old pinch-penny de Legris to whom he confided his interests. Moreover, since becoming the feudalist magistrate for the town's convent, you almost consider yourself part of the church, and these Laroche-Boisseaus are suspected to be covert Protestants.... I am not sure about this; but I can affirm that Sire Baron has never eaten meat in my place on Fridays; he normally orders a trout omelet for lunch and a bottle of my old Saint-Péray. He is a civil and good-natured Lord, with always a kind word for his hostess...

"....and always ready to pay his note with a kiss, is that not true, Madam Richard?" completed the clever magistrate.

The lovely innkeeper blushed up to her ears.

---

and responsibilities of nobility in their fiefdoms.

3   Jean Cavalier (1680-1740): was the most famous of the Huguenot leaders.

"You have a wicked tongue, Sire Blindet," she replied with an embarrassed smile; "but for God's sake, do not speak so loudly, who knows who might hear us. I must tell you that Sire de Laroche-Boisseau is coming to Langogne today on his way to the Chateau de Mercoire, and will undoubtedly stop at my inn to freshen up and rest his horses.... Your slanderous remarks could harm him. You are aware," she said, lowering her voice, "that there is question of his marriage to Miss de Barjac, the rich and beautiful mistress of Mercoire?"

"So it is said, but I do not believe it. On the contrary, I heard..."

These two persons were speaking in such low tones that it was no longer possible to hear them; on the contrary, the discussions between the other members of the group was becoming louder and more animated.

"Well, finally! Is it a wolf or is it not?" demanded the town's barrel maker with a perplexed expression. "The authorities must know, but the proclamation does not say. It only mentions a beast that it calls *the beast of Gévaudan*.... Morbleu![4] This is not very clear. We are not lacking in beasts around here!"

The man had not intended being sarcastic, and was surprised at the hilarity his remark generated.

"Brother Grivet's observation is not lacking in good sense as one might think," said the village notary with some authority; "under normal procedures, the State should define the species of animal to be destroyed... and this is precisely the problem; and I, who have twice served as scribe in the investigations of these events, I would have the greatest difficulty in saying whether the perpetrator is human or animal."

"What is your understanding, then? Explain yourself, Sire Florisel!" they cried from all sides.

The notary seemed pleased with the impression that he had obtained and he graced them with a confident look.

"Listen well," he continued: "the first time it was Guillaume Patureau, the son of a Combeville farmer. Guillaume, who is sixteen years old, was returning from the fair in Mende, with ten ecus in his pocket, when, around ten o'clock in the evening, while travelling through the Villaret forest, he was apparently attacked by the beast. The next morning, the unfortunate Guillaume was discovered, half devoured, at the bottom of a ravine. The Provost Lieutenant, who was in charge of the investigation, stated that there were traces of both claw scratches and teeth marks, but noted that the claw marks were more spaced, and on the contrary, the teeth marks were closer together, than for any animal known in our forest. Moreover, the poor boy's clothing was more or less intact and the money that he was known to have on him had disappeared.... Since I do not believe that any

4   Morbleu! exclamation, expressing annoyance

ferocious animal is capable of eating three and six-pound ecus, I say these facts are extraordinary."

The assemblage seemed to agree; but the feudalist jurist, who had just interrupted his quasi-confidential conversation with Madam Richard to listen to Notary Florisel's narration, shook his head disdainfully.

"Well! Is that your conclusion, naïve and credulous young man?" He continued; "when you have attained a greater experience in judicial affairs, you will know that a wise magistrate must look for the simplest and most natural explanations, because they are almost always true. Thus, in this case, would it not be possible that a passer-by might have searched the pockets of the victim before your arrival? I would wager that the one who first discovered the body and notified the authorities took that wise precaution."

This lesson provided by an old practitioner, in front of so many commendable persons, disconcerted master Florisel; However, he soon resumed with irony:

"You are a clever man, Sire Blindet, and it is regrettable that the Provost office does not often have the benefit of your experience. No evildoer on two or four feet would escape you. However, since you have so much wisdom, give me also an explanation for the events which were the object of the second investigation in which I took part. This time, the bailiff of Chateauneuf was charged with preparing the official report; it concerns a four-year old child, whose mother, a farmer's wife in Gabriac, had left alone in his crib, when she went out to the fields. The farm is isolated and located on the edge of the forest; when the mother returned about an hour later, she found the child dead and horribly torn a short distance from the crib. However, the most inconceivable aspect of all this is that the mother swore by all the Gods that when leaving, she had closed the latch on the door, and when she returned, the latch was still in place. Twenty times, the bailiff questioned her, and twenty times he obtained the same response. If it is a wolf that is ravaging the countryside in this way, one must admit that this wolf has a special talent for knowing how to open and shut latched doors…. What do you say about this Sire Jurist?"

The group's curiosity had risen to its highest level, and all turned towards Blindet to hear his opinion on this embarrassing situation. The magistrate himself was scratching his ear, hidden under his voluminous hemp wig:

"I would not easily imagine," he replied gravely, "that a wolf would have sufficient instinct to open a door closed with a latch, although we have all seen dogs and cats execute the same maneuver. I would not tell you that a ferocious beast, attracted by the cries of an infant, would not have leaped against the door, and pushed by chance on the latch, lifting the toggle. I prefer thinking that the farmer's wife was mistaken, and to excuse her grave error...."

"Once again, she swore under oath, that she had done nothing to reproach herself, but even if she had unwittingly left the door ajar; how is it possible that the door was found latched upon her return?"

"Nonsense, a gust of wind could have..."

"These gentlemen and ladies will judge," interrupted Florisel, addressing his audience who, indeed, seemed dissatisfied with the jurist's explanations. "As for me, in spite of my deference to the superior wisdom and extensive experience of Sire Blindet, I persist in the idea that the beast of Gévaudan is perhaps not what we think it to be."

This was said with the tone of an oracle which weighed heavily on his audience. There was a moment of silence:

"In your opinion, what is it then, Sire Florisel?" asked the lovely innkeeper; "Sire de Laroche-Boisseau insists that it is a wolf, and he must know what he is talking about, I imagine!"

"I have heard say that it is a lynx... an animal that can see through walls," said the barrel maker.

"And I a lion which has escaped from the zoo in Montpelier," added the clothier.

"I think more likely that it is an elephant," rejoined the jurist with exaggerated coolness.... "An elephant, you know, can execute all kinds of manipulations with its trunk, and this would explain that the beast in question could open and shut doors as Sire Florisel has indicated."

An explosion of laughter greeted these words. Only Madam Richard took the jest seriously.

"Ah, it could be an elephant," she said naively, "Sire de Laroche-Boisseau, who is such a capable huntsman will get him, I assure you!"

However, Florisel keenly felt the jurist's sarcasm; he replied with pursed lips:

"Each is free to attribute these tragedies to a lynx, a lion, or even an elephant, as suggests Sire Blindet with his usual astuteness; as for myself, even if I am the only one to think so, I maintain that the supposed beast of Gévaudan is..."

"It is a wolf, of course!" said a rough voice coming from the back of the crowd. "I am certain because I have seen it; and as recently as last evening."

This new speaker, a large and vigorous looking peasant, seemed to have just arrived from some neighboring village. He carried in one hand his vest and clogs, and in the other a long staff at the end of which was fixed an old knife, forming a sort of lance. At his heels was an enormous mastiff with a hanging red tongue and a collar with metal spikes. The animal must have been a solid travelling companion.

Florisel, irritated by this interruption at the moment he was about to divulge his own theory on the scourge of the countryside, glared at the traveler and asked in a disdainful tone:

"You have seen the beast of Gévaudan, have you? And who are you, friend, to interrupt our conversation without ceremony?"

"With all due respect, Sire," replied the peasant confidently, "I am Jean Godard, shepherd for Miss de Barjac, over in Mercoire. I have been sent by my mistress to see the bailiff and ask that he urge the people of Langogne to participate in the hunt tomorrow as it is getting urgent. Yesterday, at dusk, as I was saying, the beast had hurled itself upon our Jeanette, who was bringing her turkeys up the path to the farm, and was already dragging the poor girl away when I was running towards her cries. My dog, here, leaped on the wolf, which is not common, as other dogs would flee at the sight of a wolf; but my Médor knows no fear, and between the two of us, we were able to free Jeanette. She was crazy with fright, but escaped with severe abrasions, the dear girl"

This account, so precise, cut short the more or less acceptable suppositions that had been put forward a few moments earlier. Notary Florisel appeared totally confused.

"And you are certain, completely certain, that this beast is a wolf?"

"Yes, I am certain," replied Jean Godard. "I saw him just as I see you, Sire; I was even able to snatch a fistful of its hair while it was rolling on the ground with my brave Médor.... Yes, it was a wolf, but on my honor, it was as big as a donkey. It was grey in color, and I struck at its side with my knife without being able to pierce its hide. It carried off Jeannette, who is generous in size, like I could carry a one-year old child, and it tossed Médor twenty paces away with a shake of its head. To tell the truth, I do not know how we would have survived if the people from the farm had not come running to help us, which decided the wolf to return into the forest.... But my excuses to everyone," said the peasant, "but I must hasten to complete my mission with the bailiff, because I am anxious to return to the chateau; I believe it would not be a good idea to be in the Mercoire forest tonight where the wolf has settled itself!"

At the same time, Jean Godard whistled for his dog and went on his way. His departure was so rapid that he did not hear, with the noise of the crowd, a new voice which was saying with horror:

"The beast is in the Mercoire forest? May the Virgin saint protect us! And we must travel through it to reach the chateau of Miss de Barjac!"

The preceding conversations had been held in the local dialect, and this last observation had been made in French. Surprised by this change, the crowd turned to see that two travelers, mounted on their mules, had approached the group without being noticed and had been listening to what was being said.

The older of the two travelers was a Benedictine monk wearing the white and black colors of his order. His hood, thrown back, revealed hair trimmed in the form of a crown, and intelligent features animated by eyes which were both bright and soft. He was no more than forty-five years old, but the first signs of plumpness indicated a life of study with perhaps an appreciation of good food, a weakness of the clerics of that time. This rounded his form and slightly spoiled the otherwise perfect regularity of his florid face. Moreover, the fineness of his clothes, the harness of his mule and the luxurious quality of all their equipment indicated more than a simple monk; and indeed, the silver cross, hung around his neck on a wide ribbon, were indications of a high-level ecclesiastic personage.

His companion, a young man in his twenties, dressed in black with a severity that did not exclude elegance, wore long blond hair tied in a knot but without powder which was the custom at the time. He did not carry a sword, but swords no longer characterized being a gentleman, as the humblest of functionaries believed they had the right to usurp this sign of nobility. His features were handsome, expressive, and his gaze, when animated, did not lack audacity. Lithe, and well-built he must have excelled in all types of physical exercises. However, the stranger did not appear to be conscious of his favorable appearance. The delicate nature of his face would lead one to suppose that study and reflection occupied more of his free time than games and other youthful activities. Something in his modest composure revealed an adolescent only recently freed from the discipline of an austere education. But one could guess from some of his brusque movements, and sudden pinching of the eyebrows and firm intonations of his voice, that here was an energetic and intelligent man who would no doubt reveal himself at the first favorable moment.

In the meantime, the young rider imitated, with a submission no doubt originating from long habit, the monk's movements, all the while showing respect and affection. He had halted when the cleric had halted, and listened with him to the frightening news brought to Langogne by Jean Godard. However, he did not seem to share his older companion's alarm at the news. An ironic smile, without being disdainful, crossed his face, slightly shadowed by a nascent beard.

As soon as the good people of Langogne had taken a proper look at the travelers, hats and bonnets disappeared like magic: a respectful silence fell on this meeting which a few moments earlier had been so noisy and animated.

It was Madam Richard, the lovely innkeeper, who was the first to recover her wits.

"It is the Reverend Father Bonaventure, the Prior of the Frontenac Abbey!" she said, addressing the monk with her most gracious curtsy "and also Sire Léonce, his Reverence's nephew...." (Here a new curtsy, acknowledged by the young man, who blushed.) "Welcome to our town Reverend Father and give us your blessing."

"You have it, my child, you and all Christians who hear us," replied the monk distractedly. "But, good God, Madam Richard, did I just hear that wretched animal, the beast of Gévaudan..."

"Ah," interrupted the innkeeper, adopting her most caressing tone, "you would not pass through Langogne without resting a moment at my lodging? Your presence would bring joy to my humble inn. If, as I suspect, you are going to Mercoire, you will be obliged to make a stop somewhere, and this will be the best of all places to do so."

"I would like to, my child," replied the Prior Bonaventure; but you heard for yourself that we should not tarry before crossing the forest."

"You will surely arrive at the chateau well before nightfall; Agree to dismount, and I will offer you refreshments that will not displease you. You know that I have succeeded in serving you in accordance with your tastes."

The Prior appeared extremely tempted.

"Yes, yes, you are incomparable, I agree, in your preparation of pigéon with mushrooms and trout omelets, my dear lady; but perhaps this is not the moment to allow ourselves something perhaps sensually reprehensible... So, what do you think, Léonce?" he asked turning towards his nephew. "Should we stop over at the inn?"

"Your wish is my command, my uncle," replied Léonce modestly. "We have been travelling four hours over the mountains, and you ate very lightly at the abbey; you must need some food and rest. In addition, our mules could probably enjoy a short stop."

"So be it," resumed the Prior, whose appetite was struggling with suggestions of fear. "We will stop here for a moment.... You heard that, Madam Richard? A moment only; Do not let us languish; the lightest offering will help us regain our strength. It is a pity, my child, that we are such slaves to our miserable bodies!"

"Trust me, Reverend Father," she exclaimed. What joy for our house!... Come, come, everything is ready. Thank heavens that I was not caught unprepared."

She seized the bridle of the mule that the Prior was riding, and led it in triumph towards the inn, while Léonce followed indifferently.

"Ha!" said the magistrate, chuckling, "I feel sorry for the poor devils that will be staying at widow Richard's. Their only dinner will be stories about the prior's prowess."

But no one heard the sarcastic Blindet's observation.

The moment the curious observers had seen the travelers disappear into the inn, they spread far and wide to announce that the prior of Frontenac had just arrived in Langogne, that they were staying with widow Richard and that they were both going to the Chateau de Mercoire; and from there, the little town could begin developing an unlimited number of suppositions that we will spare the reader.

Chapter II

THE INN

To understand the profound excitement created in Langogne by the arrival of Prior Bonaventure, it is important to know that the Abbey of Frontenac, to which he belonged, was the largest, the richest, the most powerful religious community of the entire province. This Abbey, situated in the vicinity of Florac, had immense possessions which included well-cultivated fertile land with numerous and loyal tenant farmers. In addition, thanks to its religious foundations and faithful followers, it exercised a considerable influence over a certain number of domains and fiefs that it did not directly own. The priests of Frontenac were considered to be very learned, and their abbey, over the past few centuries, was a breeding ground for theologians, scholars and historians, several of whom had made their mark on the world. Their Abbot had the rank of prelate with the right to add *Dom* to his name. He was one of seven representatives of the clergy of the province of Gévaudan who met each year, either in Mende or Marvejols, for a session presided by the cardinal of Mende. In other words, he was as much a power in secular affairs as he was a prince of the church in spiritual affairs.

At that time, the Abbot of Frontenac, because of his age and infirmities, found himself incapable of managing the convent by himself, and his authority was passed on to the prior in its entirety. Thus, the Prior Bonaventure was vested with the total confidence of his superior and that of the assembly of Frontenac, giving him a controlling say in affairs within the community, which he ruled with a firm hand internally and represented with dignity externally. Studious, well-educated and a fervent priest, the prior had been the pride of the abbey before becoming its true leader. In addition to these qualities, clerical in nature, Prior Bonaventure also had a good business sense and a worldly wisdom that was very necessary in a country where ancient religious conflicts were far from being resolved, and the Protestant opposition, though muffled and contained, often created obstacles for the clergy. Through prudence, he succeeded in triumphing over secret hatreds, grudges and jealousies generated by Frontenac's wealth; and one could say that his adroit and conciliatory governance served to increase that prosperity.

One could judge the pride and pleasure that Mistress Richard took in receiving in her small village inn such a powerful personage accompanied by a young relative reputed for his spirit and knowledge. However, now she was in a frenzy. After having introduced her guests into a small salon next to the kitchen, she seized a white apron and began running from oven to oven commandeering the servants. Much had been prepared in advance to receive distinguished guests. The small salon, lined with chestnut wood panels, was scrupulously clean, which was rare in inns in southern France. The settings were in place, and on the tablecloth, white as snow, one could see baskets filled with luscious fruit, bowls of appetizing cream, pyramids of ripe strawberries and platters of cold poultry which was golden in color. This joyful tableau was indeed of a nature to distract the prior from his concerns about the beast of Gévaudan. However, after having thrown a caressing look at the table, the good father said to the hostess, in a regretful tone:

"Remove the poultry, my child, although Léonce and I may invoke the privilege of travelers, we cannot forget that today is a day of fasting... We will content ourselves with your trout omelet and some fruit... which looks most appetizing."

Madam Richard obeyed and took away the rejected dishes. As promised, she sped up the preparations and a few minutes later, the famous omelet made its entrance to the salon on a pewter dish that shone as if it were silver. The monk, napkin tucked under his chin, hastened to satisfy his hunger and Léonce, the exercise and fresh air of the mountains also having worked up his appetite, did his best to follow suite. Several glasses of excellent wine reinvigorated the spirits and the bodies of the travelers, such that both uncle and nephew, especially the uncle, were much less eager to depart.

The innkeeper scampered back and forth between them, having kept for herself the right to serve the distinguished guests, she did her best to skillfully obtain information about the purpose of their trip. "It is truly a miracle, a real miracle," she was saying, "to see the Reverend Prior of Frontenac; but no doubt the Prior Bonaventure and the young gentleman, his nephew, are going to Mercoire to participate in the great hunt which will take place tomorrow?"

"Do I look like a huntsman?" asked the priest good humoredly, and Léonce, does he look like one of these idiots who galop twelve consecutive hours over mountain and dale to see a poor beast torn apart by dogs? This time, no doubt, the hunt will have a nobler and more useful objective, since its purpose is to rescue the country from the ravages of a ferocious beast. However, Léonce and I do not fit very well in this affair; my nephew has not touched a firearm in his life, and I... Finally, my child, and it is not a secret, I am going to Mercoire to assist Miss de Barjac, a ward of our convent, with any difficulties which might come from the crowd expected tomorrow.

The chateau will be overrun by hunters, some of whom may be too brazen in their words, or too disrespectful in their manners. My presence will weigh on these turbulent guests, and this is why I undertook this voyage."

Perhaps the monk had other motives than those he chose to give her, but he spoke with such ease and so naturally that he left no room for doubt. Madam Richard smiled knowingly.

"Well, my Reverend Father," she continued, "if what they say around here is true, your mission will be easy. Miss de Barjac knows very well how to take care of herself. I would not wish to speak ill of a noble lady, a ward of the sainted Abbey of Frontenac, but it is said that the young damsel is of an independent nature and does not have the normal timidity of us poor women.... In truth, I would hardly dare repeat to you half the stories which are told about her."

The Prior Bonaventure stopped eating and looked coolly at the innkeeper.

"Explain yourself Madam Richard," he responded with authority; "I order you... I must know *everything* that is said about Miss de Barjac."

"My goodness, Reverend Father," replied the innkeeper, intimidated, as she served her guests more wine. "These were certainly slander, no doubt; people are so mean! Moreover, they were not attacking the honor or reputation of your ward. She is a proud damsel, and this is known. And the suitors who come prowling around her do not have the best of intentions... but they gossip about her lively way of living; her abruptness and her whims, which are sometimes excessive. It is said that she dresses like a man to ride across the countryside on horseback, that she is sometimes heavy-handed when punishing those who offend her, and in those moments of impatience, is not afraid of swearing. Our forage supplier, who in reality is a Huguenot, assures that he has heard her swear."

A sudden blush appeared on the cheeks of Léonce.

"Good woman," he said, in a restrained manner, "spare us from these shameful lies and learn to better respect a lady of quality..."

He interrupted himself, and lowered his eyes when he saw his uncle staring at him.

"Once again, worthy sire," replied Dame Richard, humbly, "I have only reported things that are being said and I have no reason to believe them. Miss de Barjac is known to be an excellent person, generous, helpful towards the unfortunate and making best use of her wealth. Her most admirable traits are cited; only the unconventional and impulsive side of her character is questioned."

Prior Bonaventure had shown neither surprise or irritation upon learning of the unfavorable opinion of the rich ward of the abbey. After having calmly finished his glass, he said in measured tones:

"That suffices, my child; avoid repeating these absurdities as this would be a sin against Christian charity and the spirit of justice. Miss de Barjac, as everyone knows, was cruelly neglected during her childhood. Brought up by her father, an inveterate hunter, surrounded only by men in an old chateau lost in the middle of mountains and forests, she grew up with no one concerned about nurturing her heart and spirit, or even giving her the slightest notions of the needs and obligations of her sex. It was only at the hour of his death that the father regretted her abandoned state, and bequeathed to us the care of this poor child, and to guide her in the ways of the world and in the ways of God. This task has not been easy. Christine de Barjac, despite her generous heart, has developed a rebelliousness, which has caused us a number of problems. However, thanks to the perseverance of our efforts, and the devotion of certain pious and intelligent persons now surrounding her, we will eventually succeed in dominating her rebellious spirit and her impatience with rules and restraint… This is why, my child, we must be indulgent with her; soon she will become a sweet woman, modest and reserved as one encounters in the world. It would be unjust to have her pay for the faults of her parents."

Dame Richard promised to conform to his instructions. While she was again trying to apologize for her excessive freedom of words, several horsemen had pulled up in front of the inn's entrance. At the same moment, a maid ran up, flustered, and whispered a few words in her ear, which caused the innkeeper to turn pale.

"Saint Virgin!" murmured the pretty hostess with horror, "what will he say? Good Lord, I had completely forgotten about him!"

And she immediately left with the servant, undoubtedly to greet the new arrivals.

Soon the noise of spur-clad boots resounded in the front hall; then the sound of a loud kiss and a male voice that was saying in French:

"Yes, it is I, my dear…. Morbleu! My valets who passed by here this morning must have announced my arrival. Is everything ready?"

"Excuse me, Sire Baron, I was no longer expecting you," replied the hostess, mortally embarrassed. "I had prepared everything to receive you, but…"

"No matter! You know, my beauty, the least item prepared by your delicate hand will suffice for me. Provide some refreshments to my lancers, and in the little salon, serve *my* trout omelet and my bottle of Saint-Péray. You will come and keep me company, charming one, as your pretty face whets the appetite like a fresh breeze."

At the same time, the one who was speaking seemed to want to go further, but was put off.

"Sire Baron," resumed the innkeeper in an almost tearful voice, "I told you that I was no longer expecting you, and so, other travelers..."

"Ah! You have other travelers here? Very well; I can get along with them providing they are gentlemen and enjoy good living."

Brusquely opening the door, the stranger entered the room where sat the Prior Bonaventure and Léonce.

This unceremonious personage was a young and robust cavalier in his thirties, of proud stature, with a curled moustache and a self-assured look. He wore the rich uniform of the Louveterie;[5] a blue velvet jacket trimmed with silver braid, white breeches, knee-high boots, a powdered wig and a three-cornered hat. A hunting knife, with a chiseled silver handle, completed the outfit, which showed off the superb height and fitness of the newcomer. He held a whip in his hand and balanced it it with confidence as if he were ready to use it on all comers.

The Baron de Laroche-Boisseau, for that was the name and title of the gentleman, was one of the eight barons entitled to sit at the State councils of Languedoc and Gévaudan. His family was a minor branch of the ancient house of Varinas, extinct for some years, but once the most illustrious of the Province. The counts of Varinas, at the time of the last of the Valois[6] had adopted the religious reform and until the revocation of the Edict of Nantes were the leaders of Protestantism in this part of the Cevennes. At the time of the insurrection of the Huguenots at the beginning of the 18th century, a lord of the Varinas, the great-grandfather of the current baron, held off for a long period the Catholic forces led by Berwick and Villars. However, defeated in this unequal struggle, abandoned by his friends, the partisan Huguenot was reduced to hiding. It is said that he lived for several years in a remote cave where he died, a martyr to his religious faith. The locals, to this day, point to this cave, remarkable by its vastness and the magnificent stalactites that decorate it. It is now called the *Grotto de Varinas* for its old occupant.

In any event, his descendants did not go as far in their pursuit of their religious convictions. Frightened by the rigorous measures that were taken following the insurrection, they ostensibly renounced their faith in order to retain their possessions and aristocratic privileges. However, this renunciation was not sincere for many of them, and they remained Protestant in their hearts. The father of the current baron was never known for his Catholic fervor, and the Baron himself was seen as a man who was skeptical, derisive and denigrating, or as described at the time of Agrippa d'Aubigné,[7] *uncomfortable in his faith.* He showed a taste for new ideas, and liked to show

---

5   Louveterie: Wolf hunting guild
6   Valois: The house of Valois was the royal house of France from 1328 to 1589.
7   Agrippa d'Aubigné (1552-1630): French poet, soldier, propagandist and chronicler

off his lack of religion. Moreover, he led a crazy, dissipated and luxurious life, to the detriment of his fortune, which was already compromised, imitating that thoughtless nobility whose errors were presaging the revolution.

Prior Bonaventure had known the Baron de Laroche-Boisseau for a long time, and was aware that his hunting skills had resulted in the king naming him Wolf hunter for the province of Gévaudan. They had met several times at the state assemblies where the prior was known for his wisdom and moderation, while the Baron for his flippancy and quarrelsome temperament; and following from there, an enmity was aggravated by circumstances that we shall soon discover. In the meantime, either the monk had chosen to forget past conflicts, or he simply wished to keep up appearances. He rose upon seeing the Baron and greeted him politely. Léonce, in deference to his uncle, greeted him as well, but with noticeable repugnance.

Sire de Laroche-Boisseau appeared not to notice these signs of deference. He remained standing on the threshold, frowning, his head covered. He had undoubtedly recognized the prior of Frontenac; but judged it not appropriate to manifest it, and half turning towards Dame Richard, who was behind him, distraught and trembling, said to her harshly:

"Ha! Mordieu! My beauty, I begin to understand your simpering. By the devil! You gave my lunch to these monks!"

The widow was full of excuses and lamentations; it was not that food was lacking, thanks be to God: and she could offer the Baron a meal worthy of him. But the trout omelet that had been prepared for Sire Baron..."

"You needed something to satisfy the taste of these good clerics," added Laroche-Boisseau, "and you gave them the preference.... Bravo, my lovely hostess! But if they had been gentlemen instead of men of the church, I would have troubled their digestion in a most unpleasant way, I assure you!"

This menace brought a flush to the cheeks of Léonce; however, a look from his uncle sufficed to have him lower his eyes. Prior Bonaventure, who had thus far remained calm and smiling, began to speak:

"Now, Sire Baron," he said with a slightly ironic politeness, "be indulgent with this poor woman. As was mentioned to you, the trout omelet was not the only food available in the inn. There is plenty of room at this table, and if I can believe certain reports, you would have no scruples about feasting on cold ham and poultry available here on a day of fast."

This allusion to the secret beliefs of his family seemed to increase the Baron's irritation; however, he controlled his temper with some effort, and with a peal of laughter, said to his hostess:

"Poor Dame Richard, look how distraught she is!... Well, that there no longer be any question of this. I am a huntsman, and therefore not too difficult in my tastes. Bring me what you wish, my beauty; as long as I do not have to wait for it. I am in a hurry."

The innkeeper, joyful at the change of situation, hastened out saying that Sire Baron will be served immediately. As for the Baron, he threw his hat and whip on a piece of furniture and went to sit at the available place at the table while Prior Bonaventure and Léonce regained their seats to finish their meal.

Chapter III

THE DECLARATION OF WAR

There was a moment of embarrassed silence. Obviously, Sire de Laroche-Boisseau felt a real desire to enter into a more personal discussion with the prior and his nephew, but pride kept him from making the first move. The Prior Bonaventure, sensing his intentions, remained prudently quiet. The Baron, his legs crossed, began drumming on the table with the tips of his fingers. Finally, he asked in a brusque tone:

"Ah, Reverend Father, I hope that you will not bear a grudge for my vivacity of a short time ago? Nothing leads to bad humor like an empty stomach. The only culprit in this affair is our thoughtless hostess who shamefully served you the lunch prepared for me."

The monk, while carefully pealing a juicy pear, replied that he was unaware of the circumstances, but that he was sufficiently Christian to forgive a bad mood.

"I am delighted, Reverend Father, though there exists between us other motives of mutual dissatisfaction, I would be pleased if this encounter could provide us with the opportunity to bury ancient differences.... What would be your opinion on this, Sire Prior?"

Bonaventure replied with the same composure and the same humility that he was always ready to use if it was compatible with his duty to obtain the good graces of the Baron. The latter did not seem to be very satisfied with these vague and conservative words. He reconsidered the thoughts that he was about to put forward, and said distractedly:

"Undoubtedly, Reverend, you are going to Mercoire to be with Miss de Barjac?"

"Indeed, Sire Baron, and yourself...?"

"You are well aware, and the entire province knows it, I am going as a champion to exterminate a monster that is creating havoc on the land of a beautiful chatelaine."

"And do you think, Sire Baron," asked the Prior with marked interest, "that you will triumph over this enraged beast?"

"I am sure of it," replied Laroche-Boisseau with the complacency of a huntsman. "This wolf, according to the latest reports, has taken refuge in the Mercoire forest, and it is doubtful that it will leave it. Tomorrow, it will be tracked, flushed out, hunted, and inevitably, killed before the day ends. You can count on it."

"That is fine for tomorrow: but today, in your opinion, could peaceful travelers cross the forest without danger?"

This time, Prior Bonaventure allowed his fear to show so clearly that the Baron could not resist the malicious pleasure of tormenting him further.

"Hmm!" he said coldly, "this beast is colossal in size and of an inconceivable audacity.... I would be worried."

The prior let out a sort of moan and looked at his nephew wo remained calm. At this moment Dame Richard came in, accompanied by her servants, who brought the Baron his lunch. All normal conversation became impossible. However, Laroche-Boisseau, as if he had been anxious to resume the conversation, soon dismissed the hostess and the servants, assuring drily that he no longer needed anything. The Prior, increasingly alarmed as the hour of departure approached, resumed with a caressing tone:

"Come now, Sire Baron, since we are also going to Mercoire, could you not do us the honor of travelling with you? Your bravery is known, and your people provide a formidable escort. Allow us, then, to travel in your company, and certainly Miss de Barjac, our ward, will be appreciative of your gesture."

This direct request seemed to have cost the good father some effort; however, the Baron did not seem in a hurry to accept this proposal. He excused himself on the basis that he needed to travel very rapidly, as that evening he would have to give many orders and make many arrangements for the hunt the next day.

"Our mules are not so bad," replied the, Prior, the obstacle irritating his secret fears, "and your fine horses will not be able to travel faster than they on the difficult mountain paths.... Really, Sire Baron, would it be a sign of generosity to refuse us a favor that would cost you so little?"

Laroche-Boisseau smiled in a distinctive fashion, then he suddenly drank one after the other several glasses of the Saint-Péray wine, for which he had a special preference and, undoubtedly, encouraged by the generous beverage, he replied in a more expansive tone:

"Well Reverend Prior, perhaps I might be more disposed to serve you, but at least, I would need to know if you are my friends or my enemies?"

"Your enemies Sire Baron? You have no enemies among the Reverend Fathers of Frontenac."

"But are you friends? That is another question, is it not, worthy prior?... Here, let us put our cards on the table; and since chance, or Providence, if you prefer, has brought us here together, let us take advantage of this favorable opportunity. I believe," continued Laroche-Boisseau, turning towards Léonce, "that I can speak freely in the presence of this young man?"

"He is my nephew," replied the monk with eagerness; "he is my secretary, my confidant, my alter ego."

"That is fine, moreover, I am not in the habit of making a mystery of my projects. Listen, then, and be frank like me. You have not forgotten, my Reverend Father, my legitimate grievances against your abbey, and in particular, against yourself who is the soul of the convent, since you have total authority."

"Against me, Sire Baron?"

"Please do not interrupt me... These grievances, are now old, those of my family as well as mine. People think of me as flippant and scatterbrained, interested only in leading a joyous life. They imagine that I am incapable of reflection; they assume that I am indifferent to the interests and dignity of my name. They would rapidly learn that this is not the case. Whatever the obstacles, I would know how to overcome them, if one had the imprudence to push me too far."

While speaking, he was frowning and clenching his fists menacingly; but Bonaventure remained impassive. The Baron resumed in a calmer tone:

"Let us go back, if you will, Reverend Father, to the events which occurred sixteen or eighteen years ago. My father was still alive as was my uncle, the Count of Varinas, Lord of the magnificent domain which carried his name. There was not a great friendship, I admit, between my father, the Baron de Laroche-Boisseau, and his older brother, the Count of Varinas. My father was, like me, a joyful gentleman, bon vivant, careless about his affairs, enjoying pleasure and good food. Varinas, on the contrary, was of a somber disposition and sickly. Towards the end of his life, he became both miserly and devout beyond reason. Following the death of his wife, instead of living on his land, he spent all his time at the Frontenac Abbey, where he had lodging, and it is said that you, Reverend Father, then a simple monk, exercised a great influence on his enfeebled spirit."

"Nevertheless, the relationship between the two brothers had never been hostile: at each formal occasion, they exchanged expressions of mutual respect as befits close relatives in an honorable family. At that time, neither my father nor I imagined that we would ever request to be the beneficiaries of the Count's succession. He had a three or four-year old son who carried the title of Knight of Verinas, and was expected to inherit his name and his domain. However, the child died in an accident, and less than six months later, the Count himself breathed his last at the Frontenac Abbey. Upon learning of the sad news, my father, despite the coolness that existed between him and his brother over recent years, was deeply affected and travelled immediately to the Abbey to pay his last respects. This done, he wished to claim, on my behalf as well as his, the family possessions, and notably the Varinas domain, as the closest relative and natural heir of the deceased Lord. But imagine his indignation when he was shown a will in which my uncle bequeathed the ownership of his lands and his chateaus to the Frontenac abbey!"

"This was a revolting iniquity. Obviously, there was, in this act, deceit and intrigue. They had taken advantage of the count's weakness of spirit in his last moments to deprive the family of its heritage. Trickery had been used, force perhaps, to have obtained this absurd result. Therefore, my father, with his fiery and hot-headed temperament, was enraged by this. He spoke harshly to your abbot and his chapter; then he left Frontenac swearing that he would obtain justice."

"Indeed, he filed a lawsuit against the Abbey through the parliament in Bordeaux in an attempt to obtain an annulment of this absurd will. However, the advantage enjoyed by a monastic order in this province rapidly became apparent. The cause of the Abbot of Frontenac became the cause of the entire clergy. Important ecclesiastics, even cardinals, intervened on his behalf. They brought up the old accusation of Protestantism which appears every time we attempt to claim our rights. You in particular, my Reverend Father, were, if my memory serves me well, as I was quite young at the time, the most effective and intelligent champion of the Abbot's cause. Thanks to your efforts, my father had his demand rejected and was condemned to pay heavy court costs while the convent retained possession of our patrimony…. Tell me Reverend Father, the events that I have just rapidly described, are they not the exact truth?"

The muted hatred, the hostile insinuations contained in this narrative did not alter in any way the serenity of the prior. He had quietly listened, arms folded on his chest and a smile on his face.

"The facts, as well as the assessment, are absolutely accurate, Sire Baron," he replied; "I will not deny that I played an important role in loss of your father's lawsuit, and if I acted wrongly, I will be accountable to God, and my conscience. However, you omitted one little condition that could change everything…. It is that the donation made to our revered Abbot by your deceased father, may he rest in peace, was not definitive; it must be considered provisionally as a trust. A codicil of the Count of Varinas' will has been kept in the archives of our Abbey, and by the express wishes of the deceased, the codicil may only be opened on a certain date, which will be in a few months' time from now. Therefore, in only a few months, the true wishes of your uncle will be known. Until then, you must abstain from denouncing his will. Moreover, we have never considered ourselves as having acquired the estate of Varinas; we satisfied ourselves with managing it with wisdom, and we will restore it to whomever it may concern the day that the definitive will reveals to us our duty."

"This supposed codicil is another shameful trick!" exclaimed the Baron impetuously, "and I am certain that it will not seriously modify the intentions of the original will. I have guessed, Father Prior, the purpose of the clever maneuvers by which your community intends acquiring full control over the Varinas domain. Fearing, no doubt, that a simple and immediate donation of such a rich property might raise general indignation, you have decided to make it conditional in an effort to avoid the odious image of the detrimental effects on the legitimate heirs. You thought that it was a good idea to buy time to accustom, little by little, public opinion on this outrageous exploitation. While waiting for the codicil to guarantee you the ownership of my uncle's estate, you can say that you are simply its custodian, and over the past sixteen years you have not been troubled in this fraud. You are hoping that with the long delay, this illegal acquisition will have been forgotten, passions will have calmed, and you will be able, without noise or bother, to definitively add our heritage to the vast possessions of the Abbey…. It may not turn out that way, Sire Prior; I make no secret of the fact that regarding this old affair, I will be back as soon as the opportunity arises. My father died grief-stricken, almost ruined by your intrigues and your chicanery; but I still exist, and I will find the way to reclaim the rights of my family… Come the moment that the codicil is opened, and if it allows you to succeed in your maneuvers, you may rest assured that I will not remain idle. Times have changed over the past sixteen years. The century has moved on. The clergy does not retain the omnipotence it once had. There is talk of chasing from France the richest, the most powerful religious orders, like the Jesuits. Thanks to the philosophy and progress of the people, the winds are turning against you. Beware; next time your power may not be sufficient to allow an iniquity to triumph."

Laroche-Boisseau expressed himself with great vehemence, and Léonce himself was struck by the apparent legitimacy of his claims. The young man, elbow on the table, studied his uncle with an air of pained astonishment, as if his honest soul could not believe the indignities of which the Frontenac community was being accused and awaited an explanation. However, the Prior Bonaventure continued to remain impassive; he smiled, all the while using the back of his white and chubby right hand to smooth the folds of his monastic robe.

"Well, Sire Baron," he resumed, "You will not have to wait very long for that opportunity. As I told you, the date fixed for the opening of the codicil is very near. You will act in accordance with your interests or your feelings. As concerns the Frontenac Abbey, we will firmly uphold, without fear, the wishes of the Count of Verinas, whatever they may be."

The attitude of the prior was open and natural; the Baron was undoubtedly intimidated, as he resumed more calmly:

"Let us not go too rapidly nor too far, my Reverend Father; I still have hope that I will not have to go to those extremes. My only objective in awakening memories of this ancient conflict was to establish the reality of the damages I have suffered and the claim I might have for a compensation from your community. If such compensation is granted me, I would solemnly commit to cease contesting the Abbey's ownership of the Varinas domains."

"A compensation, Sire Baron. I do not understand you."

"On the contrary. I think you understand me very well, my Reverend Father; but listen again: In the aftermath of the lawsuit we filed against your convent, and also perhaps due to some inconsiderate squandering of funds, my current financial situation, as everyone knows, is badly compromised. My revenues have been reduced, and my lands mortgaged, and without the interested help of Master Legris, my financial advisor, I would be hard put to maintain my status with dignity. So, I can see only two ways I might recover from this painful situation: either I take advantage of every opportunity to repeatedly reclaim the lands of Varinas that have been denied me, or, that I re-establish my fortune through an advantageous marriage.... And it is on this second project, Reverend Father, that I would ask that you facilitate its accomplishment."

"I still do not follow you, Sire Baron."

"You normally demonstrate more perceptiveness," resumed Laroche-Boisseau drily, but I will explain more clearly. Your convent, which collects large heritages so willingly, shows the same particular taste for rich heiresses. You currently have an opulent ward over whom you watch with jealous care. You surround her with spies, you scrutinize her most innocent actions and you take offense at everyone who approaches her. Without understanding the objective of the intrigue which surrounds Miss Christine de Barjac, I would like to believe that you do not intend turning her into a nun and convert her superb domain into a convent for women."

The monk, over the past few moments, seemed to support with increasingly less patience the rather outrageous expressions used by the Baron. A crimson flush had come to his cheeks.

"Sire Baron," he replied in a slightly trembling voice, "in spite of my desire to remain within the limits of moderation, I cannot tolerate any further your insulting suppositions towards the sainted house to which I belong. If this conversation is to continue, I invite you to speak with less bitterness and more fairness.... The Abbot and Chapter of Frontenac have never had the idea of guiding Miss de Barjac towards a religious career, and they will persist in this resolution unless our ward shows a persistent interest for that vocation, though that seems unlikely. The task of looking after a young girl who is strong-willed, uncontrollable and resistant to all advice is not easy. The Ursuline nuns from Mende attempted to teach her the basic elements of their instruction; but her progress was mediocre, and she left the convent after two years, leaving the poor sisters completely frustrated by her insubordination and turbulence. Since her return to the Chateau de Mercoire, we have placed in her company a brave and loyal gentleman as well as an elderly nun whom we have known for a long time for her patience, devotion and virtue. Each has written us at least twenty times begging that we end the mission of trust that we assigned them. You see, Sire Baron, that with a ward with that sort of character, it would be quite a challenge to impose our will. Therefore, if Miss de Barjac wishes to remain in the outside world and marry, we would not think of opposing her choice… providing that he be not unworthy of her and the noble house from which she came."

"Is this really true, my Reverend Father?" exclaimed Laroche-Boisseau, excitedly. "Would there be no opposition on your part if the suitor had the misfortune of displeasing you, or one of the dignitaries of your Abbey?... Just suppose that I, who is speaking to you, conceived of the idea of taming this little lioness, and that I had succeeded in making a favorable impression on her, and I wished to take the risk of marrying her in spite of her fierce character; tell me frankly, would you not try by any means to prevent such an alliance?"

This direct question seemed to greatly trouble the prior; Léonce, himself, waited anxiously for his response.

"What! Sire Baron," asked Bonaventure, "did you manage to attract the favorable attention of Miss de Barjac? Until now, the young lady has remained intractable towards anyone who dared approach her with gallantries...."

"And it would have been the same with me if I had been foolish enough to make the mistake of trying to impress her with musical phrases which she despises. No, I did not once express one word of love, but on the occasions that the hunts brought me to Mercoire, Miss de Barjac took greater pleasure in my company than that of any other gentleman of the Commune. This is undoubtedly little, perhaps; but coming from a young lady so different from the ordinary, it is sufficient to provide a certain optimism. Thus, if I had the hope of not being impeded in my plan, I would not lose courage. Therefore, I implore you to tell me what to expect. Are you my friends or my enemies?"

"And I will not tire of answering that the priests of Frontenac are not the enemies of anyone. Is not love for everyone recommended even towards those who wish us harm?"

"You shall not escape so easily, Sire Prior…. Would you deny, for example, that your visit has, as its principal objective, to counter my progress towards the affections of Miss de Barjac? Did you not have knowledge of the preferences towards me expressed by your ward? And, having learned of my upcoming arrival at the Chateau de Mercoire, did you not immediately undertake the journey; you the principal counsel and leader of your community, in order to block all my efforts by your presence? Come now, my Reverend Father, in spite of your worldly guile, I am confident of your sincerity; give me a simple reply, and I will believe you without hesitation."

Thus pressured, Prior Bonaventure could no longer evade the question.

"Well!" he resumed, "I do not deny that my presence in Mercoire seemed necessary to impose a control over possible suitors that were constantly attracted by the riches and beauty of Miss de Barjac. We fulfill the parental obligations towards this young girl. Could we leave her without protection amidst a turbulent society that meets within her home?"

"Very well," said the Baron in a dry tone while getting to his feet. "Finally, it has been made clear, my Reverend Father. You do not approve of my presence near your ward and you will combat my efforts with all your might?"

"I have already had the honor of assuring Sire de Laroche-Boisseau that Miss de Barjac will remain absolutely free in her choice. However, the Fathers of Frontenac will retain, by their responsibilities, the right to give advice, to present warnings...."

"Better and better," replied the gentleman with irony as he paced back and forth, his silver spurs jingling. "Unfortunately for you, my Reverend, it is said that your warnings are not often listened to by this undisciplined child.... But could you please explain to me the root of these unfortunate prejudices that you have against me?"

"Ah! Sire Baron," exclaimed Prior Bonaventure, impatiently, "is it necessary to look elsewhere than at your disorganized life, the degradation of your fortune and worst of all, your secret attachment to the heresy of Protestantism?"

"My ruin was thanks to you," responded Laroche-Boisseau with energy. "My life is that of every gentleman who is aware of his nobility. As for that old accusation of Protestantism that one is always throwing in my face like they used to throw in the face of my ancestors, not to mention the devoted and fervent Catholic, the Count of Varinas, I could ask on what it was based. But even if there were some truth in it, would it not be better to be Protestant deep in one's heart than not have any religion, like so many others?"

"And is that not also your case, Sire Baron?" said the monk with severity. "They say that preaching... Enough!" he interrupted himself with an effort. "One cannot scrutinize a conscience without being formally invited to do so. God will judge us all!"

They were quiet again; the Baron continued to pace back and forth. Finally, he stopped in front of the prior.

"Thus, my Reverend Father," he asked with restrained anger, "you do not accept the means that I have offered to repair a gross injustice? I had wished to erase the past and establish peace with you, with Miss de Barjac as the guarantee; you prefer war, and I will wage it, ardently and relentlessly, I swear.... To begin with, I declare that I will marry your ward in spite of you!"

The prior replied with a smile at this special challenge. But Léonce, mutely quiet until now, if not almost indifferent to the altercation, exclaimed while getting to his feet as if he were reacting to an irresistible sentiment:

"What! Sire Baron, you are certain that Miss de Barjac loves you?"

Laroche-Boisseau turned around abruptly. The Prior himself appeared stupefied, but not irritated by the boldness of his nephew.

"Now! Now! What is your problem, little one?" asked the Baron in a scoffing tone, looking scornfully at the adolescent. "Are these the subjects the convents give to little monks like you to keep them occupied? Chivalry must not be in the curriculum; you would be better off reading your prayer book, and undoubtedly the Father, here present, will give you a penitence for having involved yourself in a non-religious conversation without permission."

"Sire," replied Léonce, "I do not belong to the church. I am secular, as are you, and I will not support..."

He stopped speaking, as if shocked by his own audacity.

"What will you not support, my boy?" asked Laroche-Boisseau, in his insulting ironic tone: "that Miss de Barjac expresses a preference for me? I do not understand why this is any of your concern, nor what you can do about it."

"It is not that," stammered Léonce, whose anger struggled with his embarrassment, "I meant to say that the outrageous manner that you have just been treating my venerable uncle and the Revered Fathers of Frontenac...."

"Ah! my dear child, is it your intention of becoming their champion and challenging me to a duel on their account? That is wonderful because I have no intention of retracting my statement or apologizing.... I would even add, to whoever wishes to listen, that the priests of Frontenac are, without exception, hypocrites, schemers and greedy; that they robbed me of my heritage, and that they undoubtedly hope to utilize an innocent ward as an instrument to acquire additional riches and influence. But I will be watching and I will foil their evil maneuvers. I love Miss de Barjac, and perhaps I am loved by her: we shall see who will dare throw himself in my way!"

"You love her?" exclaimed Léonce, his eyes sparkling; "you love with a worn heart and a withered soul...."

"I see, my good young man, that they have given you a horror of mundane men like me; fortunately, there are better examples!... Yes, by my faith! Whatever one can say, I love this brave girl. She is not an ordinary woman, and I find in her zestful qualities...: but, Morbleu!" he interrupted himself and said with disdain: "and what have you to do in all this? And myself, am I not above answering indiscreet questions from a hot-headed choirboy!"

"Sire!" exclaimed Léonce in a menacing tone, "I will no longer tolerate your insolent remarks, and I will..."

"You will do what, my valiant cavalier?" replied Laroche-Boisseau, laughing uproariously, "Provoke me? That should be amusing. As you wish, master. Ready for battle!... Here I am, ready to receive you...."

And he placed himself in an on-guard position and pretended to parry an imaginary thrust with the handle of his whip.

"What? You do not advance?" He persevered, still laughing, "but, God forgive me, I think that you have forgotten your rapier, my frisky gentleman, of the sacristy.... What has become of your rapier?"

"I can combat you with the weapon of your choice!" exclaimed Léonce, beside himself.

He seized his whip which had remained on a nearby chair, and ran, arm raised, towards the Baron.

During this violent altercation, Prior Bonaventure had retained his totally unexplainable calm. One would have said that he wanted to see how far the legitimate indignation of Léonce would carry him and measure the degree of courage and energy of this young man whom he had seen since his infancy as gentle and peaceful. Perhaps this test made a good impression on the monk because Bonaventure smiled at each repartee of his champion. However, when he saw that the two adversaries were about to come to blows, he ran forward with a vivacity unusual for him, and threw himself between them, shouting:

"Fie upon you! Léonce, have you already forgotten your lessons? Are you going to adopt the habits and passions of ferocious duelists? Do reason and religion allow such disputes?... And you, Sire Baron," he continued, now speaking to Laroche-Boisseau, who was still in a defensive stance; "are you not ashamed of yourself, for engaging in provocations of an inoffensive child?"

As soon as his uncle began speaking, Léonce, ashamed of his actions, had dropped his whip and returned to his seat. He was hiding his face with his two hands despondently, without speaking. The Baron, on his side, changed expression and resumed in a light tone:

"By the devil!" he said, "you are right this time, Reverend Father, I should have disregarded the affronts of your nephew.... However," he added with a disdainful superiority, "the young man has fire in him, and will not be easy to control, until perhaps he begins to grow a beard…. But let us leave that subject; time passes and I must resume my journey…. Since you have rejected my proposal for accompanying you, each shall follow his own path, and the victory will be for the strongest, or the most cunning."

He opened the door to the kitchen, and cried out:

"On your horses, my people… everyone, mount your horses."

Immediately there was a great movement in the front room, as if there was a hurry to obey the master's orders.

"So, Sire Baron," asked the prior with a humility far different from the firmness he had just shown, "you will not allow us to take advantage of your escort to travel to Mercoire in security? In spite of the differences between us, you would regret it, I am sure, if an accident…"

"You are giving me too much credit for being generous or charitable," replied Laroche-Boisseau in his mocking tone. "Good God! If the beast gobbled you up, do you think it would be doing me a disservice? From within the Frontenac Abbey, you are perhaps the only person capable of hindering my plans. I have everything to fear from your insight, vigilance and vigor. I would not light-heartedly abandon the favorable opportunity which has presented itself. We are at war, Sire Prior, and all means are good to attain victory…. Besides," he added, looking at Léonce, who remained lost in his thoughts, "do you not have with you an intrepid defender, perfectly capable of defeating the famous beast of Gévaudan? He will protect you, and his fiery courage would be best served against a wolf than against a gentleman…. We will meet again tonight at the Chateau de Mercoire, where you will arrive safe and sound… which is my wish for you. So be it. Go with God."

He put on his cap and went out, whistling a hunting tune.

A few moments later, one could hear the noise of horses galloping away.

Prior Bonaventure, goaded by the fear of lingering in the dangerous forest that he had to cross, also hurried to ask for his mules; he had hoped to follow the Baron at a distance, thus putting them under their protection in spite of themselves. But the inn was in a state of confusion due to the excess of travelers and the mules were not ready; then they had to listen to the profuse thanks of Dame Richard, for the honor that the prior had bestowed upon them by staying there, and then her lamentations about the mix-up with Laroche-Boisseau, who had held it against her and left without paying his bill, which, by the way, did not particularly upset the pretty widow. Much time was lost in this manner. By the time Bonaventure and Léonce finally left Langogne, amidst bowing and genuflections by the town's residents, they could perceive neither the Baron nor his people, looking as far as the eye could see.

Chapter IV

THE ATTACK

It had already been an hour since the prior of Frontenac and his nephew Léonce had left Langogne, and except for some minor difficulties along the path, nothing had troubled their journey. In truth, in spite of their attentive efforts, they had never been able to catch sight of the horsemen who preceded them; but they sometimes heard the sounds of a horn in the distance, and the rare travelers whose path they crossed assured them that the hunters were not more than a quarter league[8] in front of them. The Prior Bonaventure continually prodded his mule hoping to see, around the next bend, the brilliant costumes of the Baron and his lancers, and Léonce imitated him without thinking, but the proddings did not produce much of an effect on the reluctant mules, such that apparently the distance between the two travelers and the more favorably mounted cavaliers increased rather than decreased.

After many turnings, they arrived at one of those limestone plateaus called *causses*, surrounded by vast uncultivated plains encircled by mountains that were even higher. This plain was sterile, bare, bereft of vegetation; and in the far distance stood a few chestnut trees, partly damaged by the violent storms common in that area; their yellow leaves brightening the surrounding drab land. The plateau ended where the path led down into a wooded canyon; however, with at least a half-league view before them, there was no sign of the hunters.

Moreover, the route did not, for the moment, present any difficulties. The terrain was even, open, and even lacking brush, which reduced fears of an ambush or the sudden appearance of ferocious animals. In addition, a deep calm reigned in this immense arena; the weather was excellent, and the sun, still high over the horizon, gave hope that they might cross the woods before nightfall. Also, the prior seemed to have acquired some patience with the situation; he stopped torturing his mule, which was breathless, not from obeying, but from resisting, and he made a sign to Léonce to rejoin him.

Since they had left the town, the young man had not uttered a word; his head bent forward as if in deep thought. However, he hastened to obey

8   League: a former measure of distance, usually about three miles.

and was now trotting next to the monk, made possible by a widening in the path.

"I believe, my child," said the Prior, "that we can give up thoughts of catching up to that arrogant gentleman... May God protect us! Perhaps we should have brought a few brave souls from Langogne to accompany us, but we left so hurriedly.... Therefore, we should not be more than two leagues away from the chateau by now, and that would be about two hours of travel. Truthfully, the route will be much less beautiful in the heart of the Monadière".

And he indicated, with a slightly worried look the path at the end of the plateau.

Léonce only replied with a distracted shrug. Gentle and communicative in nature, he had been brought up with a mistrust of himself but had great respect for those who had authority over him. Normally reserved and quiet, he was willing to speak but waited until he was asked questions. However, his current silence, after his headstrong scene at the inn, surprised the Prior.

"Ah, my dear Léonce, what is the matter?" he asked in a friendly tone as the two mules ambled together. "Are you ill, or are you also afraid of that cursed beast, may God protect us?"

"Neither one or the other, my uncle; only, I was thinking..."

"About what, my child?"

"Nothing, my Reverend Father."

And the handsome adolescent let out a profound sigh. Bonaventure glanced at him discreetly.

"Léonce," he resumed with gravity, "I owe you both praise and a reprimand. Praise because of the generous enthusiasm, a short time ago, with which you took the defense of myself and your dear protectors, the Fathers of Frontenac; and a reprimand for having been carried away to the point of provoking a gentleman whose faults did not excuse yours."

"And what?" asked Léonce with ill-contained irritation, "Should we quietly put up with the insolent statements of this Laroche-Boisseau? Must one listen without protest to his slanderous boasts concerning Miss de Barjac?"

"And what is Miss de Barjac to you, my boy?"

Léonce leaned forward as if to tighten a strap of his saddle, but in reality, to hide that he was blushing.

"My uncle," he stammered, "I thought... Miss de Barjac is the ward of the abbey; your ward; we are going to receive her hospitality in her home. Could I allow her to be treated with such outrageous flippancy? But I must admit," he added in animated tones, "every word coming from this odious Baron affects my brain like the vapors of an alcoholic drink. I do not know what instincts have been awakened in me; but I feel an irresistible desire to throw myself upon him and smash his face.... If I had had a sword, I would have attacked him on the spot, in spite of your presence! But I did not have a sword, and I am not a gentleman. I am only a humble and peaceful student with the Benedictine Fathers of Frontenac, and I had to swallow the affront."

At the same time, Léonce, releasing long pent up emotions, suddenly broke down in tears. The prior did not appear to be too surprised by these sudden emotions; he understood, perhaps better than his nephew did himself, what was happening to his innocent soul. However, he resumed with a mixture of gentleness and severity:

"What! Léonce, you are crying? Is that what I should expect from a young man so sensible and steadfast in his faith, my beloved student, the child of my affections, the son of my sister? From where do these foolish passions that have suddenly erupted, come? Have I not told you a hundred times, Léonce, that reasonable creatures, made in the image of God, should never have recourse to force and violence, the weapons of beasts? It is intelligence and persuasion that a Christian must seek. Do not imitate the turbulent youth of our times, and especially the corrupted, like the Baron de Laroche-Boisseau, always ready to use the point of his sword against reason, truth and justice. Should you have, one day, rank and fortune that you value, remember that anger and hate are horrible vices which are not worthy of you."

Léonce wiped his eyes.

"Pardon me this show of weakness, my uncle;" he said, strengthening his voice. "I still do not understand my failure.... But since we are discussing my role in this world, allow me to request some clarifications which my respect prevented me from questioning you about until now, and which with every passing hour become more important for my peace of mind."

"The moment is badly chosen for an explanation," said the monk, looking around; "however, if you have something on your mind, my child, do not delay in telling me."

"Perhaps my dear uncle, I should have revealed my state of mind, to you; my mentor and my best friend. In recent days I have been gripped by a dark sadness. I have been obsessed day and night with ambitious dreams of pleasure and worldly glory. This uneasiness of spirit, which sometimes becomes a real anguish, is undoubtedly caused by my deep uncertainty of the future which awaits me. My thoughts wander in a vacuum and get lost for lack of direction.... Listen to me, my beloved guide; and I beg of you, do not reject the request I am about to make. I lost my father and mother at an early age and never knew them, but I have never lacked for tender and loving attention. Bless you, my worthy uncle, for the unfailing care you have provided for a poor orphan! You welcomed me to your peaceful cloister, you committed yourself to guiding my heart and my spirit; you taught me with doctrine and example. Each of the excellent Fathers of Frontenac, your friends and brothers, have assisted you in this generous mission. The most scholarly and wisest made every effort to instill in me their science and their knowledge. I include you all in a feeling of respect and gratitude; I consider myself your child and I question whether I will ever have the strength to leave you."

"However, my Reverend Father, in recent times, either by chance, or premeditatedly, you seem to be making every effort to distance me from the cloister where I have spent my youth; you seem to take pleasure in interrupting my studies and you do not miss an opportunity to put me into contact with the outside world. Take today, for example, you insist that I be a participant in the noisy and tumultuous spectacle of a great hunt. These demands, awakening new ideas and instincts, are creating a moral confusion for me. I can easily get carried away by impulsive moments, my uncle, as you witnessed a short time ago with the Baron de Laroche-Boisseau, and their energy frightens me…. It is up to you to put an end to this senseless training…. If I am to renounce the world, I am sure to succeed with your counsel and encouragement. I therefore implore you, my uncle and Reverend Father, allow me to return to the abbey as soon as possible, put on the robes of a novice and after the usual procedures, take the vows. I wish to live and die there, among friends who will always be dear to me."

The Prior Bonaventure was expecting such a proposal, as he showed no surprise; However, numerous creases appeared on his wide and bald pate.

"Léonce," he asked thoughtfully, have you really thought this through? This vocation for a monastic life, is it frank and sincere?"

"I… think so."

"And I, who can read into your soul like an open book, I am sure of the contrary. These impulsive moments that you were describing prove clearly to me that you are not born for the cloister. Do you think that under those priestly vestments that this proud soul, that boiling blood, those irritable nerves will suddenly calm down? No, that robe would burn you like Nessus' tunic[9].… Moreover, my son, there are elements which you will learn about later which will absolutely prevent you from entering the cloistered life."

"What are you saying, my uncle?" exclaimed Léonce at the height of astonishment. "Would they refuse me the consolation promised to all wounded souls…"

"Your soul is not wounded, but if it were, the wound would not be too serious at your age. Do not question me; you can no longer think about tak-

---

9   Nessus tunic: In Greek mythology, was the poisoned shirt used to kill Heracles.

ing your vows, either in Frontenac, or at any other religious facility... or at least not until circumstances have changed and you are fully aware of the ramifications of such a sacrifice."

Léonce was distraught.

"My Father," he resumed, "I will wait patiently until you judge it appropriate to explain to me this strange refusal, but if you push me out of the cloister, well good Lord! what will be my destiny? I had always believed, seeing you prepare me with so much care against the agitations and storms of the outside world, that your secret wish was to create in me an aversion to it...."

"If this had been the case, my child, the Reverend Fathers of Frontenac and I would have gone beyond the objective we wished to attain. Our only desire was to make of you a man who is educated, steadfast, open and a Christian who would later be a model for society.... But listen, Léonce," added the monk, with a touch of severity, "I think I have understood the reasons behind this supposed vocation that came to you so suddenly. It has as its origin a wounded pride, a frustrated ambition.... You are beginning to glimpse the brilliant theatre of the outside world, and like all young persons, you begin to want to play an important role in it, to achieve glory and to share its joys. However, in the middle of all these dreams, you are struck by your impotence and your humility. You tell yourself that the paths that lead to important positions in society are not available to you; poor plebeian, you the simple nephew of a country monk.... Reply honestly, Léonce, is this not true?"

"My dear uncle, could you have thought..."

"There are, perhaps, other reasons," continued the Prior, throwing one of those looks in his direction which seemed to reach right down into the soul of the young man, "but the one that I have just explained is the main one. Well!! Léonce, I do not want to give you unreasonable hopes, unattainable in their juvenile exaggeration; but rest assured, the future has reserved for you sufficient advantages for a moderate ambition. Have confidence in yourself and move forward boldly, counting on reason and justice. God will do the rest!"

Concerned that these words, even with reserve with which they were expressed, could have had too strong an effect on his nephew, the prior continued immediately:

"Once again, Léonce, do not allow your spirit to launch itself impudently in the pursuit of foolish dreams and try to understand me.... I am dead to this world, and I have nothing further to search for on earth for myself. But you are my student, my friend, my son by adoption; I have watched you grow up. I guided you in the development of your good habits, I know that your heart has many virtues in the midst of a world of human imperfections. The ambitions I no longer have for myself, I have for you. I live again in my beloved disciple. I have conceived numerous projects for your earthly happiness and your development, to which the Fathers of Frontenac, who idolize you, will add their support. Our efforts, our energy and our influence will all go towards assuring you a great and joyful destiny."

One could have said that these explanations had generated in Léonce a feeling of distrust: instead of thanking his uncle, he remained somber and constrained.

"I would like to believe," he finally said, "that these projects could no longer be interpreted badly, and that the intrigues of which the Baron de Laroche-Boisseau was accusing the monks of Frontenac…"

"Ah! Here are the results of the venomous words of that gentleman!" interrupted the Father Bonaventure with pained astonishment. "But you, Léonce, should you turn these poisonous remarks against your friends, your benefactors?"

There was so much reproach in the tone of the prior that Léonce jumped nimbly down from his mule, which halted, and ran to his uncle taking his hand and covering it with kisses and tears.

"Pardon me, pardon me," he said in a voice intermingled with sobs. "If you only knew how I suffer! I think that God has abandoned me!"

The sincerity of this suffering touched Prior Bonaventure.

"I willingly pardon," he replied, smiling with tenderness. "Poor Léonce, do you not think that I have guessed the reason for this sudden strange change your behavior, formerly so calm and steady, the reason for this mournful sadness, or these actions which explode suddenly like a storm in your soul…. But this is not a good time to discuss these matters…. Re-mount your mule, Léonce, and let us continue our voyage."

The young man obeyed with his usual submission, and they trotted side by side for a time.

"My child," soon resumed the monk in a kindly tone, "although I have forgiven your offense, I wish to impose a penitence…. We are going to find the Baron de Laroche-Boisseau in Mercoire and I would be very satisfied that you avoid any new discussion with him. I have some particular reasons for wishing that there no longer exist between you either hate or anger, and you would undoubtedly regret later not having followed my advice…. Well, Léonce, what do you say?"

"I can disregard an insult that has been addressed to me, my uncle, but can I allow an offense, in my presence, against a person who has my affection and my respect?"

"I require your unconditional promise; and by your exactitude in keeping it, I will judge if you sincerely regret your inconceivable behavior."

"So be it, my uncle, I give you my promise, but, my God! what ordeals you are continually putting me through!"

"Ordeals? Léonce, I no longer understand you."

"I hardly understand myself…. My poor head is in chaos, where everything runs together in total confusion…. Ah! my uncle, why did you insist that I return to Mercoire?"

"First, my boy, because I could not have found another traveling companion as dependable and pleasant as you. Moreover, as you have noticed, I wished to familiarize you with the world that you are about to enter and I took advantage of this excellent occasion to bring you with me when the elite of Gévaudan nobility were gathered. Finally, I had another reason. I noticed, dear Léonce, that you had a particular influence on Miss de Barjac. Our imperious ward, appears, in your presence, to rediscover some traces of timidity and reserve that befit well-born ladies; it would seem that your gentle and tender nature, full of good sense and reason, has an influence on her haughty, uncultivated, but spontaneous character. This impression was already visible a few years ago. Do you remember our first visit with Miss de Barjac when she was with the Ursulines in Mende? That unruly student had been at the convent some six months and the poor sisters had not been able to get her to learn her alphabet; she tore apart her works of sewing and embroidery and she insulted her teachers. She would show up in the visiting room with her clothing and hair in disarray, and yet was charming as an angel in revolt. She listened to my reproaches impatiently, and maintained a sullen silence. I was frustrated by this hardening of her behavior, and while I was talking on the side with the Mother Superior, we noticed that you had approached Christine de Barjac. Almost a child yourself, you seemed to sympathize with the sadness of this untamable child; she listened to you, at first with astonishment, then with deference. We could not hear your conversation, but we continued to watch both of you. A book was laying there, and you opened it randomly and you began to explain to her the mechanics of the grammatical construction of words to an attentive student. Soon, she seized the book in turn, and hesitated, then stammered, and you had to give her further explanations. Finally, she took back the book, and lo, the miracle! She read almost the rest of the page by herself without error…. What the teachers had not been able to accomplish after six months of effort, you had been able to do in minutes…. I was speechless with admiration and the Mother Superior cried with joy, while the student herself remained amazed by her marvelous success."

"This is true, my uncle, this is true," replied Léonce, excitedly; "but what is the use of recalling these old memories?"

"Since that time," continued the monk, "I have had numerous examples of the influence you had over her. Upon each of my visits to the chateau, I noticed the favorable changes in her when you accompanied me. When you were there, she was modest, kind, and suppressed the behavior which upset the servants and her friends. She finally increasingly resembled the person we wanted her to be. I frankly admit, my dear Léonce, that I am acting in the interest of our ward in bringing you to her. The ungrateful child does not always show herself as respectful towards myself and the other Fathers of Frontenac; by that alone, it is our duty is to counsel her and reduce the effects of her fiery character. Under the present circumstances, I would be disconsolate if Miss de Barjac were to create a bad impression. You have heard some of the bad opinions some of the country folk have of her.... I had therefore hoped, my son, that by your mere presence, you would help maintain our ward within the limits of strict decorum amidst the people of quality who will be coming to Mercoire."

"And you, my uncle, so prudent and wise," exclaimed Léonce, with a sort of desperation, 'have you ever thought of the risks for me in such a situation? But you are mistaken; the influence you credit me for does not exist. The events you described were the result of chance. Miss de Barjac, a young lady of high birth and great fortune, never paid me the slightest attention. She has never shown so much coolness and remoteness. When she sees me, she only expresses discomfort and unease. She is so lively and energetic that to please her one would have to resemble that brilliant and frivolous Lord de Laroche-Boisseau, who had boasted, a short time ago, of the preference she accords him.... I am nothing to her, I assure you! So, my uncle, I beg of you, do not make me stay for long in Mercoire, and when we have left the chateau, have pity on me, and make sure that I never have to return there!"

These words seemed to have been torn out of him by a terrible torture; it was a heartfelt cry that this time had to be understood. Moreover, as one might have guessed, the prior had not waited for the increasingly clear confessions of his nephew to understand the secret sentiments of this naïve soul. He was about to open his mouth, either to give Léonce his condolences, or to reproach him, when a look around him changed the direction of his thoughts.

The travelers had, indeed arrived at the extremity of the *causse*; before them a dark passage plunged between two mountains covered with trees that grew to their summit. The path became difficult and uneven with enormous boulders, fallen from above, which left just enough space for the passage of a rider. The sun, which had lowered considerably during this last conversation, gilded the highest peaks, but no longer penetrated into this deep canyon, where an intense mist was beginning to accumulate. As far as one could see, there were trees lost in dark green vegetation; one would have said that it was an immense and interminable forest, enveloped in a network of leaves, hills and mountains.

This sudden change of scene, the savage aspect of the isolation, and most of all, the knowledge that they were entering the area where the beast was ravaging the countryside, were of a nature to greatly affect both uncle and nephew. The prior spoke with a slight alteration in his voice:

"I would have a lot to say about what you just expressed, my child; but here I am lacking the concentration to do so, and we will take this up again later. We are approaching the heart of the Monadière, which is where it is said the beast attacked its victims yesterday.... Do not speak, and remain as close as possible to me. May God and the Virgin protect us!"

Léonce did not share his uncle's fears, but perhaps he was not unhappy at not finishing the discussion that he had himself provoked. There was still a modesty in the heart of this adolescent that made him reluctant to give light of day to his first loves. Therefore, the young man was not sad about this interruption and submitted willingly to the prior's suggestion.

They moved on fairly rapidly for several minutes, but the more they advanced, the more the obscurity became dense around them. The forest was made up of oak and fir trees as well beech trees, known as *fayards* in that area. These trees, close together and leafy, did not let in enough light to read even at noon on a clear day; therefore, at that hour of the evening, in the depth of a forest surrounded by foreboding mountains, hardly a pallid ray of light came through from the sky. Their eyes could not distinguish anything in the somber depths. The undergrowth and brambles pushed a garland of thorns across their path. Moreover, since they were still traveling downward, the fog was spreading an increasingly thick veil across the countryside. The peaks of the mountain, the tips of the rocks, the indentations in the ground, all the sign posts, had disappeared. However, the travelers were aware that a number of routes crossed the forest, and a mistake might be dangerous.

They were initially guided by ruts that had been dug into the clay soil by the wagons and oxen on their way to Mercoire. This was a sure sign that they were on the main road of communications between Mercoire and the neighboring towns, the majority of the other pathways through the forest not being practicable for the wagons. However, soon these useful markers began to disappear. The nature of the soil changed; it was now dry, gravelly and too hard to retain the traces of wheels. They vainly hoped for a clearing in the forest, a land feature or a familiar object which might indicate the proper direction to follow. However, the fog enveloped everything in a distressing haze, and the two travelers, in spite of their proximity, could only see each other as vague and phantom-like figures.

Finally, they arrived at a fork in the route, and Léonce stopped his mount. The Prior, who was reciting his rosary, perhaps to calm his secret fears, also reigned up on his bridle.

"My uncle," said the young man with embarrassment, "after some quick observations, I had thought that we had arrived at Saint Paul's cross, but I am mistaken.... We must have passed without seeing it. Do you have any idea where we are? I have no recollection of being here."

"And I, the same, my child," replied the prior in a plaintive voice. "Saint Virgin! Are we lost?"

"In any case, not by much, but I would like to move to higher ground. It must still be daylight on the mountain ridges. What do you say, my uncle? Let us take the route on the left, which appears to go towards the summit of the Monadière? Once I have a little open space, I should be able to rediscover the road to the chateau."

"I trust your judgment, my boy," the Prior Bonaventure timidly replied; "I readily admit that right now your counsel is better than mine.... This, I hope," he added, attempting to jest, "will not affect our future!"

Léonce himself did not appear too certain, when suddenly, interrupting the silence, the distant sound of a horn sounded to their left.

"Over here, my uncle," he exclaimed, "we will certainly find some people in this direction.... We will move up the mountainside and head ourselves in the right direction. Come on, then, we must not be surprised by nightfall while still in these impenetrable thickets."

The prior followed passively, but the expectations of Léonce were proven wrong. The new route, after climbing a small hill; plummeted steeply towards the deep thickets they wished to avoid.

The lost travelers were obliged to halt again to deliberate. During this short stop, the horn was heard once more, but this time from another direction.

"I just do not understand," resumed the monk anxiously: "the sound comes from our right this time."

"There are strange sound effects in the mountains," replied Léonce reflectively; "the layout of the land and this heavy fog can create extraordinary illusions. The person holding the horn is probably not where he seems to be. We sometimes hear it one place then the other, and he might be just two hundred steps in front of us!"

"In that case, my child, why would we not try to simply call for help?"

Combining their two voices, they both began yelling loudly at different moments, then stopping to listen if someone was responding. But it seemed that their cries had been absorbed by the heavy atmosphere, unmoving and almost cotton-like. They repeated their cries, followed by a vague distant echo, but a silence would fall again.

The Prior had by now definitively abdicated the authority that his age and experience normally gave him over his young companion.

"What will we do, Léonce?" he asked.

"In truth, my uncle, I have no idea. I seem to see some animal tracks on the ground, and perhaps this path does lead towards some dwelling…. Let us continue to follow it."

"So be it!" said the Prior Bonaventure. "Should we not still be in the hands of God?"

The perseverance of the travelers was finally rewarded. The path began going up again as though it wanted to lift itself up the side of the mountain, and the air seemed to have less particles of humidity. Although the trees still provided a thick cover above their heads, more daylight was seeping through; and the sounds of a horn were becoming more distinct and closer. They could begin to imagine that they were finally going to escape the embarrassing and perhaps dangerous situation they were in, when an event suddenly changed their vague apprehension to that of downright terror.

They were moving forward with caution, when a savage scream came from the thickets a short distance away. The mules froze in place, their ears perked and their legs trembling, as happens with timid animals that sense danger nearby. The Prior and his nephew looked at each other.

"The beast of Gévaudan!" said the monk, turning pale; "May God forgive our sins…. All is lost!"

Léonce was searching for an object that he could use as a weapon, as he only had his whip for protection against an adversary that announced itself in this manner.

"Courage, my uncle," he replied. "If it is the wolf, perhaps it might hesitate to attack two persons mounted on mules…. If only I had some kind of bludgeon…."

The howling had ceased; but now they could hear a noise of a large body violently forcing its way through the brambles towards them, but the brushwood was heavy, the light was dim and the fog still so thick that they could not yet see anything.

Suddenly they could again hear the screeching howl; but this time the animal it came from seemed only paces away from them.

This was too much for the poor monk; feeling his bones already cracking between the monster's fangs, he began yelling out cries of distress. Léonce, on the contrary, was searching for the enemy, ready to repel it the best he could; but his courage served no purpose. The mules, terrified by howls so near to them, reared up, spun around, and each fled in opposite directions. The Prior's mount carried away its rider, hanging on to its mane and continuing to cry out. Léonce's mule, finding no space in front of it, plunged blindly into the bush and was thrashing frantically in the middle of vines and thorned vegetation.

All that the young man could do was to remain on his steed for a few moments in spite of its violent and jerky leaps. But his riding talents did not prevent him from finally being thrown off. Caught by a low hanging branch of a beech tree, he was hurled precisely in the direction of the most recent howling.

The landing was a hard one. Léonce was stunned, his face turned facing the ground. Immediately, a low and guttural growling sounded next to his ear, a heavy body fell on his, and he felt formidable teeth tear at his shoulder, while sharp claws penetrated his flesh through his clothing.

The atrocious pain and imminent danger brought Léonce back to his senses; and he attempted to turn himself over and free his arm in order to push away the ferocious beast that was attempting to devour him, but the thorny plants entangled him in their spiny knots and the weight on him hampered his movements. He managed to turn on his side and one of his hands attempted to push away the monster that he could not see. However, it was not the head of a ferocious beast that his hand encountered, but what appeared to be coarse, unkempt and bristly hair belonging to a human head.

In that terrible moment, when the instinct of self-preservation dominated all rational thinking, Léonce was not searching for an explanation of this inconceivable discovery. He continued his struggles against the embrace and the bites of his adversary, and reacted convulsively without knowing what he was doing.

Suddenly, the combat ended just when the unfortunate young man, exhausted, out of breath, almost fainting with pain and terror, was about to give up all resistance. The claws and the teeth had ceased their attack. He felt the release from the weight that was crushing him. Reanimated by this unexpected change, he struggled into a sitting position. Then, leaning on one elbow, he gave a dazed look around him.

All traces of his formidable aggressor had disappeared, though one could still hear a sort of shuddering in the neighboring foliage, but one could see nothing. Moreover, Léonce's attention was drawn by other sounds coming rapidly towards him from the path. It was the perfectly clear sound of a horn and the barking of a dog, and especially the sound of the Prior calling in anguished tones.

Léonce was incapable of answering. He remained in the same position, still doubting his own existence. Finally, he saw, vaguely through the mist, two persons, one on foot, the other mounted, who seemed to be looking for him, and he heard his uncle saying:

"Léonce, where are you? Léonce, in God's name, if you are still alive, please reply!"

The poor Léonce finally recovered sufficiently to respond:

"Over here, my uncle, on this side…"

"Ah!, we finally found him!" exclaimed the monk, dismounting from his mule. "Well, my boy, are you hurt?"

"I... I do not think so, my uncle."

"Thanks be to God! Thanks be to God"'"

As the Prior Bonaventure went to disengage Léonce from the vines and nettles, his companion spoke to him in the local dialect:

"Be careful, Reverend Father, the beast is not far from us as my dog is growling. Here Castor! Stay here, we will perhaps need you."

However, his fears did not stop the Prior, overjoyed at having found his adoptive son, he climbed over some obstacles without worrying about his monastic robe, and hugged poor Léonce, who passively received his caresses.

It was only after the young man, with the help of his uncle, was able to get back on the path so that they could get an idea of the extent of the deplorable state he was in. His hat was crushed, his clothes were torn, his hands and face covered with blood. One could see a large open wound on his left shoulder as if a strip of flesh had been torn out by a claw slash or teeth.

Horrified, the Prior Bonaventure hastened to bandage the wound with his handkerchief and that of Léonce. The newcomer helped with this charitable task as well as he could.

"Mercy!" said the man, with horror, in his dialect, "you really had a close call. Another minute, and you would have been devoured!"

The speaker who had so effectively helped the endangered travelers was, as you have undoubtedly guessed, Jean Godard, the shepherd from Mercoire. After leaving Langogne, he had taken a short-cut usable only by travelers on foot. Upon arriving at the section of the forest where the beast had been active, he had the idea of using his shepherd's horn, which he always carried, hoping this might protect him from the fierce animal's attack. He had finally heard the yelling of the uncle and nephew, and guessing that they came from persons lost in the fog, he had the humanity to go search for them. But the cries of terror at the moment of the catastrophe sent him in the proper direction and he was almost trampled by the fleeing mule and its rider. After a quick explanation, they hurried to help Léonce who they supposed correctly was in great danger.

The young man, miraculously rescued, was at first, unable to answer any questions, and only slowly regained his senses.

"My uncle," he finally said in a strained voice, "did you see him? He must have passed near you."

"Who?" replied the Prior in astonishment.

"That man.... The lunatic who attacked me."

"A man! Are you dreaming?... The poor child must have received a violent blow to his head.... Think about what you are saying, my dear Léonce.

It was not a man that attacked you, but a monster that we call the beast of Gévaudan!"

"The beast of Gévaudan! Are you sure, my uncle?" asked Léonce, whose head was clearing bit by bit. "In truth, I cannot be sure of anything, as I am not even sure where I am…. However, I cannot believe that it was a ferocious beast that assaulted me."

"Eh, Good Lord, what was it, then?" said the shepherd. If you could see the gash that you have on your shoulder, you would have no doubts about it. What a set of teeth!... It is a horror. But let us depart, Sires, it is not a good idea to stay here. Night approaches, and the beast is diabolically persistent; if it decides to attack us again, we might not end up being the strongest. There is nothing to be gained in staying in the forest after sunset!"

"This brave man is right," said the prior. Now reassured about the safety of his nephew, he began to worry about his own. "Let us depart immediately…. What a sinister and dismal place; and Léonce, my child, you need immediate care…. Take courage, and let us to get to the chateau as rapidly as possible."

It was not difficult to find Léonce's mule. After the fall of its rider, it had fallen and remained enmeshed in the bushes and could not extricate itself. It was with considerable effort that Jean Godard succeeded in getting it back up on its legs and hurried to bring it to its master. But after only a few steps, they realized that Léonce was incapable of remaining in the saddle: his head was swaying back and forth, and his damaged arm could not handle the reins; So, Jean Godard did not hesitate. Without ceremony jumping up on the mule's back, using one arm to hold Léonce against his chest, and seizing the reins with the other, he called out:

"On our way! When we arrive outside of the forest, we can make better arrangements, but this is not the moment to dawdle. You see Castor is picking up his ears and gnashing his teeth…. On our way!... and you Castor, hold firm!... in a quarter of an hour, we will be out of danger!"

He urged the mule forward and Bonaventure followed him while the mastiff trotted behind, growling and frequently turning its head….

Chapter V

THE CHATELAINE

The Chateau de Mercoire, now the home of Miss Christine de Barjac was located in the center of the immense forest where the Prior and his nephew had experienced such dangers. It had been built at an epoch when it was generally considered unnecessary to fortify the residences of country nobility; but in the province of Gévaudan, thanks to the antagonisms between religions and the ensuing hatreds that resulted, it had never been sufficiently calm to not take such precautions. Therefore, the home of the Lords of Mercoire was medieval in appearance. It was built on rolling terrain above a small village of about thirty dwellings. Large round towers with slate roofs were positioned at each corner. It was surrounded by a moat and walls, equipped with a drawbridge. In truth, the moat was lacking water, the walls had many gaps and the drawbridge remained immobile for lack of chains. But one had to be very near to recognize the ravages of time. Seen from afar, the chateau, with its pointed spires, its somber mass of volcanic stone and its magnificent enclosure of grey walls had an imposing air which gave an impression of the power its masters.

On the day that the events that we have just described occurred, the area which surrounded the domain, normally empty and silent, was bustling with activity. All the routes arriving in Mercoire disgorged individuals or groups of travelers, some on foot, others on horseback, all coming to participate in the great hunt for the wolf the following day. The majority were going to the village where they hoped to find lodging for the night; others were headed for the principal portal of the chateau. Among them, one could see gentlemen, who were neighboring huntsmen, richly mounted and followed by their lancers on foot, leading several dogs on leashes. Some of these gentlemen were ridding double with either their wives or their sisters, who hid their fearless way of straddling by wearing a form of skirt called a *horse apron*. However, the ladies did not appear to be numerous at this reunion, either because of the dangers of the voyage, or they were not willing to face the whims and brusqueness of the eccentric chatelaine. A few of the more intrepid ones, bored in their manors, anxious to break the deathly monotony of their existence, had dared come to this gathering, where fatigue might be more likely than pleasure.

The travelers, after having crossed the drawbridge, entered a courtyard of the chateau where nothing indicated elegant or attentive hospitality. This courtyard, adapted to rural activities, was cluttered with broken carts, split barrels, pieces of manure and in the middle of all this a legion of chickens, pigeons and ducks hopped, cackled and fluttered. The dilapidated buildings which surrounded it seemed equally diverted from their original purpose; one supposed from the broken windows without glass, that they were now used as storage for forage.

It was in this first courtyard that the cavaliers dismounted, as well as those on foot that had not received an invitation from the lady of the manor. Two farmhands, dressed up for the occasion in formal jackets trimmed with gold braid, as once was worn by the lackeys of royal houses, were permanently stationed there to welcome new arrivals. They helped the ladies dismount, untied the luggage and took the horses to the stable. The guests of inferior standing were shown into a large low-ceilinged hall where there were improvised tables on tresses containing ample provisions of bread, wine, cheeses and chestnuts. They could sit down, eat, and drink wine without further ceremony; and then more easily take advantage of this abundance in that, once satiated, the partakers had only to push open a door and find themselves in a hay-loft, their future bedroom. As for the guests of more noble status, one of the substitute lackeys would lead them to a second courtyard which was surrounded by buildings occupied by the chatelaine.

This portion of the chateau was much better maintained; everything was in its proper place and exquisitely clean. A building with two wings formed the three sides of the square courtyard with a lovely fountain in the center. The fourth side was made up of an iron grill with a monumental gate crested by a shield with the coat of arms of the de Barjac family. This gate opened out to a good-sized park which was once separated from the forest by a wall and a moat, but time had used the wall to fill the moat, and for a long time, the grill had been the chateau's only protection against the mixed society which inhabited the forest of Mercoire; a society which was particularly noisy on long winter nights.

At one of the corners of this courtyard, a small stone stoop gave access to the reception apartments. Standing on that stoop, an old man, tall in stature, thin, stiff, with a haughty expression, performed the function of master of ceremonies. He was dressed in black, with a whip, cuff links and ponytail. He had his cap under his arm and one of his hands leaned with laughable seriousness on the handle of his long sword. He was the Knight de Magnac, gentleman of an honorable house, but youngest of the family, therefore very poor. The brave cavalier, after having served with distinction in the armies of the king, would have fallen on bad times if the Prior of Frontenac, who had known him for a long time, had not had the idea of placing him as steward, gentleman in waiting and in reality, chaperone to the ward of the convent. Under the current circumstances, Sire de Magnac seemed over-imbued with the importance of his responsibilities. His tall figure expressed a combination of dignity and embarrassment. As soon as guests appeared, he would take three steps toward them, kiss the hand of the lady, then speak profound words of welcome to the husband; then would lead them to a vast dining hall already occupied by a large number of guests. There, he would bestow upon them a speech prepared in advance; always the same, by which he would present the excuses for the absence of lady of the manor who "had been detained," he said, but who "would be with them soon."

"In the meantime," he would continue, "my noble mistress, invites you, through my words, to make use of everything that is hers as though it were yours. Her home is yours and her servants are at your service."

Then, the Sire Knight de Magnac would bow once again and return to his post on the stoop. Perhaps he feared that he had not sufficiently compensated, by his exaggerated politeness, for the indifference of his mistress towards so many distinguished guests, because, finding himself alone, he let out a deep sigh and sent an anguished look towards a portion of the chateau where the windows remained carefully closed.

The guests, on their side, might have taken offense that Miss Christine de Barjac would let her steward take the responsibility of receiving them in her home; but the joyful hunters and country neighbors who were arriving each moment, did not seem to mind. They were used to the whims of the pretty chatelaine, and no one was feeling offended. Moreover, a good fire burned brightly in the chimney; the table was heaped with cold meats, delicacies of all kinds and exquisite wines; comfortable tapestried chairs were in place; alert servants were hurrying back and forth to satisfy all needs; what could the visitors complain about? Therefore, most of them, without worrying about what might have been lacking in the ceremonial correctness in the reception, had joyfully settled themselves around the hospitality table and taken literally the knight's invitation to make themselves at home.

So, while the guests continued to arrive in Mercoire, what was the serious matter which was "detaining" the chatelaine? Hidden in a small garden which served as a riding stable, accompanied by Sister Magloire, her governess, and Maurissot, an old servant to her father, she was doing dressage exercises with a small horse she intended to ride at the hunt the next day.

Christine de Barjac, then eighteen years old, was straight and slender as a willow. Each of her movements was graceful, but also supple and vigorous. Her features had a bold look, her mouth with red lips disdainful, her dark eyes almond-shaped, altogether formed a combination of remarkable beauty. However, her beauty had not yet attained its definitive character. Her complexion, slightly tanned by the sun, did not yet presage feminine delicateness, and her eyes did not yet know how to lower, or half close, under their lids fringed with long lashes. One would have described her as an impish, spoiled and headstrong child in the body of an attractive young girl. Her gestures were firm, often arrogant and the least vexation would bring light creases to her brow.

The clothing that she was currently wearing, which was her outfit of preference, added to her virile external appearance. It consisted of a loose-fitting green silk dress with slit sleeves and cut much like our amazons of today. Her magnificent black hair, which she did not allow to be powdered, contrary to the style of the day, was held by a silk knot. On her head she wore a small three-cornered hat with curled white feathers and gold braid. Her semi-masculine costume was perfectly adapted to the life style and determined character of Christine de Barjac. This led the locals to comment that she dressed like a man, and in truth, except for the skirt, the lower hem of which could be tucked into the belt, one could mistake her for a little gentleman, more disposed to becoming a musketeer than a seminarian.

We already know some of the circumstances which had influenced Christine, and had made her so different from other girls of her age. Deprived very early of her mother, she had lived among men in this isolated chateau. Her father and her uncle were great hunters, but ignorant and fairly coarse and only received other hunters like themselves. They had taken some unknown pleasure in seeing the poor child adopt the same free style and uncontrolled behavior which she now found difficult to change. During the joyous dinners which followed hunting parties, Christine was brought in and these inebriated souls enjoyed having her repeat the latest swear words, teaching her cavalier gestures and even listening to her chirp out drinking songs. Her father, who before she was born, had hoped for a son, was now overjoyed with her performances. Her uncle, even more impudent, did all he could to teach her new mischief. However, both adored this innocent creature, and it never occurred to them that they might be corrupting her young imagination. With a dreadful lack of foresight, they only saw her as an amusing toy.

Such was Christine's earliest education. Thanks to Miss Barjac's instincts for imitation, inherent in human nature, she molded herself to fit the tastes, customs and language of those who surrounded her. She only thought about running, jumping and riding. Her uncle had died as a result of a marsh hunting accident, but her father never ceased encouraging her capricious and turbulent behavior. However, a short time before his own death, Sire de Barjac had apparently recognized the dangers of his actions and repented. To repair his errors, he bequeathed the guardianship and education of his daughter to the monks of Frontenac, whom he felt would be the most trustworthy for such a mission. Unfortunately, it was much too late to erase the traces of that first vicious education; Christine was almost twelve years old, and at that age, it was already difficult for her to accept new ideas, to surmount certain inclinations and habits. In addition, the efforts of the good Fathers, at that epoch, were perhaps less than perfect, and the noble damsel was not yet an example of gentleness, patience and modesty.

At that moment, as we have said, Miss de Barjac, without worrying about the numerous guests arriving at the chateau, was taking pleasure in training little Buch, her favorite horse. It was not the easiest of tasks: Buch, a handsome black steed, energetic, bright eyed and alert, seemed, despite his small size, to be as obstinate and capricious as his young mistress. He was being ridden by Maurissot, who, despite his seventy years, considered himself to still be an excellent horseman. Christine, whip in hand, was standing in the middle of the riding area and ordering the movements to be executed. Sometimes the animal was perfectly docile in responding to the intentions of the rider; however, at other times it would balk or rear up on its hind legs. Then, Christine would crack her whip, or would become furious, either with the horse, or with the cavalier. At other times she would become impatient and order the rider to dismount; and though Buch's harness consisted only of a bridle and a light rug, she would jump up on its back and oblige it to execute the desired movements. She would then dismount and recovering her whip, say to Maurissot:

"Morbleu! You old scoundrel, are you not ashamed of your clumsiness? Buch is impish, but not mean, and you do not know how to control him. You are too brusque, instead of giving him a little time to think about what you want of him.... The more reasonable of the two of you is not obvious!"

Each time she let escape a curse word from her lovely mouth, a plaintive voice would cry out behind her:

"Saint Virgin! Miss, in spite of you promises you are using swear words again!... What will the Fathers say when they see that I am bringing you up so badly? I could be excommunicated for less."

"Alright! Alright! Sister Magloire," replied Christine with disdain. "Do not worry yourself about what those nasty old monks will do or say!"

"Nasty old monks?" but that is impiety, it is sacrilege.... Ah! my dear child, do you want to lose your soul? My God forgive your sins!"

Sister Magloire, who was speaking, was sitting in one corner of the riding area, protected from Buch's escapades by flower boxes. She was knitting a woolen stocking, as was her custom. Miss de Barjac's governess wore the robe of an Ursuline nun while at the chateau. She was a woman of about fifty years, whose mannerisms indicated that she had once lived in the secular world. She appeared to be very well educated, but what had specifically qualified her to become Christine's tutor was her great patience and deep piety which permitted her to put up, with resignation, injustice, harshness and even insults. Sister Magloire's virtues were often rudely put to the test. Indeed, the nun shared with the Knight de Magnac the management of the chateau, and they constantly relayed each other the task of guiding their student towards adherence to appropriate social behavior. Within the chateau, it was the sister who had the upper hand; she did a lot of preaching which included pleading and compassion. Outside, it was the cold and phlegmatic Knight de Magnac who followed his young mistress, either on foot or on horseback. Less eloquent, and especially less talkative than Sister Magloire, he accompanied each of his instructions with a short and absolute precept, like an axiom; but once determined, he would let himself be battered, or torn to pieces before ceding, and his cold stubbornness usually succeeded better with the young girl than the endless sermons of the nun.

However, as one can imagine, Miss de Barjac suffered considerably under this double surveillance. She had a good heart, in spite of her regrettable early education, and enough good sense to recognize the excellence of their objective, but their obsession soured her mood and irritated her pride. One could not say that she hated her over-zealous protectors, but she took pleasure in confounding their jealous vigilance by tricking them by some kind of joyous mischief. In summary she attempted to torture them in a thousand ways. This conduct distressed the honest knight and poor Sister Magloire, and although the other aspects of their life at the chateau were quite pleasant, there were many times when they were ready to give up on this mission which was producing such negative results.

While Miss de Barjac was contemplating the circular travels of Buch, the nun was being kept up to date as to what was happening in the other part of the chateau. From time to time, a young woman dressed in picturesque local attire appeared on the sill of a nearby doorway, whispered a few words in the ear of the doleful nun, and left immediately. This messenger had been sent by the knight to tell the governess which noble guests had arrived and to urge their joint mistress to come as soon as possible to fulfill her duties of hospitality.

The nun could not have hoped for better, and she had wished on several occasions to shorten the riding exercises, but her vexing student did not hear her prayers, and the sister, afraid of irritating her by prolonged requests, was waiting for the proper occasion to renew her efforts.

That occasion soon presented itself. The horse was showing signs of fatigue, and the old retainer, more courageous than robust due to his age, had his brow bathed in perspiration. Christine therefore suggested that Maurissot take a moment to rest, then she came over to sit on a bench next to her governess. Taking off her cap, she began to nonchalantly rearrange her disorderly hair.

"My child," said Sister Magloire, quick to take up the subject, "Would it not be a good time to go in? Quite a number of persons are waiting for you in the salon, and you owe some respect to these gentlemen who are here to rid your domain of a terrible animal that is ravaging it."

"Bah! What a lot of noise for a wolf!" replied the young girl, shrugging her shoulders; "I still remember that my father and Uncle Hilaire would kill six in one hunt. I participated in the kill at the hunt in the Lozère, encumbered by snow.... Ah! Sister Magloire!" she continued, with a tenderness which was rare for her. "You never knew my good father and my poor uncle Hilaire! What men they were, and what hunters! If they were still alive, they would not need all those little gentlemen braggarts that create more noise than results. They would have mounted their horses with their lancers followed by a dozen eager hounds, and would have rapidly taken care of that cursed wolf which is so fond of human flesh.... But times have changed. Poor father! Poor Uncle Hilaire!"

And she turned her head aside as if to hide a tear.

"I am aware, my child," coolly resumed the nun, "that the Sires de Barjac were honorable Lords and experienced hunters. However, they cruelly neglected certain responsibilities towards you. Nevertheless, you owe some recognition to your good neighbors who are helping under the current circumstances, and you should go yourself."

"Ah! Morbleu! Is not the Knight de Magnac there? We have provided them with everything they need, I hope?"

"No doubt; however, certain persons of distinction could take your prolonged absence the wrong way.... There is, for example, the young Count de Laffrenas, Brigadier in the king's armies...."

"Well, give Sire Laffrenas a mirror. He will not get bored as long as he can see his face in it. He can pass an enjoyable evening that way."

"There is the Marquis of Brenneville?"

"Have him visit the kennels; he enjoys himself in particular in the company of dogs."

"There is also the Baron and Baroness of Florac."

"Seat them at a table and be careful to continually refill their glasses and their plates; I guarantee that they will never notice my absence; at least as long as the wine and the food is to their liking."

"Finally, Miss," continued the nun, sounding a little irritated, "there are some guests who will be arriving any time now, and for these you should really show some love and respect...."

"Alright! I see where you are going with this, Sister Magloire: you are certainly expecting those cursed prie... I mean some monks from the Abbey?"

"You should speak much more warmly of your pious benefactors and spiritual fathers," replied the nun with bitterness. "Well, yes, we have prepared lodging for one or several Reverend Fathers."

"So, Devil take the..."

"Miss!"

Christine bit her lip, while stamping a small morocco-leather booted foot on the ground.

Sister Magloire sighed and lifted her eyes to the sky, sign that she was about to start a long sermon on the transgressions of her student, when the same young woman returned and announced the arrival of the Baron de Laroche-Boisseau. This news suddenly changed Miss de Barjac's attitude.

"Laroche-Boisseau," she exclaimed; "Good! He is a joyful companion, that one! We will enjoy ourselves... like old times. Well, Sister Magloire," she continued, getting up hastily, "you are right, and I would like to go inside."

However, the teacher did not share Christine's high opinion of the Baron, and she remained immobile on her chair.

"In truth, I do not understand your marked preference for Sire de Laroche-Boisseau. It is said that he is a spendthrift, lecherous and perhaps even an enemy of our sainted religion...."

"He is an excellent huntsman, a perfect cavalier and good company. I have never asked about the rest," replied Miss de Barjac with unconcern; "and he does not try to overwhelm me with banalities and compliments like the rest.... But do you want me to tell you, Sister Magloire, where your prejudice against him comes from? It is from my liking him. You are always against anyone I like; but morbleu! I will act as I please."

She began to walk, with a deliberate step, towards the squire, who, with the arm entwined with the horse's bridle was catching his breath.

"We should go in, Maurissot," she said, "But since you are tired, I will finish the lesson myself."

Without effort she mounted the frisky animal which began executing graceful bows as if to express its joy. For several minutes the lovely young amazon had the horse practice some of the most difficult movements, brusquely changing its pace, and stopping short while in full galop. Finally, satisfied with the docility of her mount, she made a mysterious sign to the old retainer.

"And now, *the last grammar lesson*!" she said, smiling.

"Miss, would you like me to bring you..."

"Shh!" said the malicious child.

And she nodded towards Sister Magloire, who had taken up her knitting.

Maurissot understood her thoughts and gave a sly smile as he did not like the sister who reprimanded him constantly. He then went to a corner to get two dueling pistols which he presented in silence to his mistress. Christine began galloping in circles around the riding area, and as she next passed in front of the nun, she placed one of the pistols between Buch's perked ears and fired.

At the loud sound of the explosion, Sister Magloire gave a sudden start, crying out woefully "Jesus! My God!" while the merciless girl burst out laughing.

"Well! Well! Dear sister," she exclaimed, "will you never get used to loud noises?... By my soul, I think that even Buch flinched a little. I will not stand for that Sire Buch! I will do it again and if you react... Do not be afraid, Sister Magloire; you know it is not dangerous!"

Taking the second pistol, she shot again, the flame from the powder singeing Bush's mane; however, this time the animal did not seem to notice, and nothing troubled the rhythm of his pace.

"Thank goodness!" said Christine triumphantly.

She jumped to the ground and as she caressed the glistening neck of her mount, the squire approached to take the bridle.

"I treated you harshly, my poor Maurissot," said Miss de Barjac in a friendly tone. "The education of Buch was perfect; I was wrong, pardon me.... Do not let me forget that I owe you a few Louis[10] to drink to my health."

The old retainer was thanking her profusely when the strange girl turned her back to him and approached Sister Magloire. It was only then that she realized that the nun was in tears.

Surprise and sadness immediately replaced the joyful expression on her face.

She threw her arms around the neck of her governess and said to her with emotion:

"What is the matter, dear sister? Do you take a jest so seriously?... Pardon me, I will not do that again.... Come now, give me a kiss, I want you to give me a kiss!"

"Miss," said the poor nun, gently pushing her away, "you treat me cruelly; I have reached the end of my patience and courage. I have done my best, but you do not love me; you hate me...."

"This is not so, I love you," replied Christine, with her usual impetuosity; "Yes, I love you, my dear; but you are good, and I am wicked. I have

10   Louis; also called Louis D'Or, a gold coin circulated in France before the Revolution.

tried a hundred times to stop doing this mischief, and I do not know what devil... Do not hold a grudge against me for this.... I will change, I promise you. Come now, is it over? Give me a kiss!"

She seized both hands of the pale and wrinkled face of the nun and placed several kisses. Sister Magloire could not help but smile through her tears, seeing Christine admit her faults so frankly.

"Ah! Miss, you take advantage of my indulgence, my weakness... but think sometimes that..."

"Are you going to start again? You forgave me.... Look, as a reward, you will see how I will be polite and friendly with the people in the dining hall. You will not recognize me. You would not find a lady as sweet as I, even at the Court. I promise to be really welcoming, even with... your monks. Did you not say that you expected the visit of Father Jerome, the Treasurer of the convent?"

"No, Miss, in all probability, his Reverence the Father Prior himself wished to assist you on this solemn occasion."

"The Prior? He is the least strict, yet he is the one I fear the most.... And do you think, my sister," she continued, with a feigned indifference, "that he is coming by himself?"

"Perhaps he will be accompanied, as usual, by his nephew, the excellent Sire Léonce."

"Léonce!" replied Christine with a start.

She almost immediately added, with vivacity:

"Let us go in now, dear sister! If you let my promises get cold, I cannot be held responsible!"

And she wanted to pull the nun up from her seat.

"I am coming, my child," said Sister Magloire, folding her knitting; but you cannot present yourself in riding clothes to the noble guests who are waiting for you at the chateau. You must first go to your apartments, and allow yourself to be properly dressed and coiffed, as befits a young lady of your standing."

"Well," said Miss de Barjac, pouting, "Letting a handful of white flour be thrown on my hair, and being obliged to put on a dress with a large hooped skirt that they sent me from Paris? I do not want to. I could not walk, or talk, or even move freely.... I am fine the way I am dressed now, because I will be at ease; they will take me the way I am."

"But Miss..."

"Ah, Morbleu!! And you, Sister Magloire, why would you not change your outfit?"

"My child, I am a nun, and without the specific permission of my superior, I cannot remove the clothing of my order."

"Well! I do not wish to remove the clothing of my riding!

And the obstinate child, perching her cap over one ear with a mutinous air, headed towards the dining hall at such a rapid pace that Sister Magloire had trouble keeping up.

Chapter VI

THE ARRIVAL

Night was falling and many candles, along with the flames of the vast fireplace, illuminated the large salon occupied by guests in the chateau. Some were still eating and drinking around the table to which servants were continually bringing new dishes. Others were recovering from their fatigue in front of the hearth. The rest had gathered into joyous and animated groups. However, when Miss de Barjac made her appearance, everyone hurried towards her. Christine would have preferred entering alone and unnoticed, but Sire de Magnac had other ideas. The honorable Knight did not want to miss this excellent opportunity to perform his duties in the presence of such a distinguished audience. At the entryway, seizing the hand of his young mistress, his arm held away from his body, a smile on his face, the tip of his foot in advance, he led Christine forward with a slowness and studied respect that must have greatly irritated the short-tempered and spoiled child.

However, she put up better than we would have thought with the compliments, the affectations and the caresses that were heaped upon her. She allowed herself to be kissed and fussed over by women who called her "my sweet one and my adorable one." She did not cut short the bland comments of the old gentlemen who dated from the Régence,[11] and old gallants from the royal Courts of Marly and Versailles. She even found gracious words for some of the guests, and politely thanked everyone for the favor they would be doing her by purging her domain of the terrible beast of Gévaudan. In fact, she was so different from her usual self that several of her guests hardly recognized the bizarre young girl who was the subject of so many extraordinary stories. However, no one was as surprised by this unexpected change as the Knight de Magnac and Sister Magloire. They were standing several steps behind their mistress, and watched her with a mixture of admiration and delight.

"Perfect! my sister," murmured the knight, inhaling a dose of Spanish tobacco.

"An angel, Sire," said the nun, lifting her eyes to the sky.

---

11   Régence; The Régence was the period in French history between 1715 and 1723, when King Louis XV was a minor and the country was governed by Philippe d'Orléans, a nephew of Louis XIV as prince regent.

They were less satisfied with what happened next. Laroche-Boisseau had proved the most attentive towards Miss de Barjac, who had greeted him in a friendly manner. Soon she distractedly took a seat between the Baron and a young elegantly dressed man with intense eyes and ingratiating manners. It was said that he was Laroche-Boisseau's confidant, and followed him everywhere.

This young man, whose name is Legris, will play a fairly important role in this story. He was the son of a rich former public prosecutor who, in recent years, had earned the good graces of the Baron by lending him money. Undoubtedly, Legris Senior had found this arrangement to his advantage and rumor had it that he was named the beneficiary of the greater part of the lavish Baron's patrimony as a collateral. Nevertheless, apparently the best of relations existed between Laroche-Boisseau and the Legris, father and son. The latter, though quite villainous, had wished to mix with nobility. Laroche-Boisseau had complied with this desire and introduced the young bourgeois into the world of certain nobles as dissolute as he, and also not particularly selective in the choice of their companions. Thanks to this patronage, the young Legris had been accepted on an equal basis among these gentlemen of decadence, and since he always had a few Louis in his pocket to lose on gambling, dressed elegantly and, as long as he did not take to heart some more or less subtle mocking comments about his humble origins, he was tolerated at these aristocratic reunions. Moreover, the Baron, leader of the group, while sometimes mocking of his protégé, would not put up with anyone else taking that liberty, and no one was brave enough to risk animosities that they knew could be fearsome.

Now, was Laroche-Boisseau's interest in the son of his money lender sincere? Many doubted that it was. Some felt that Legris was simply attached to him as a spy and ordered to observe all his activities. Others were convinced that on the contrary, Laroche-Boisseau's sole objective was to please the old prosecutor and that he was using the son to obtain the largest sums of money possible from the father. Moreover, the young Legris played his role as a friend in such a manner as to never hurt the pride of his irritable master; in fact, he habitually showed him so much deference that it approached servility. Laroche-Boisseau could not say a word, perform an action no matter how insignificant, but that the other would praise him outrageously and overwhelm him with flattery. Moreover, Legris proved himself quite skillful at missions that a less devoted companion would have found repugnant. For a man of the Baron's character, it was not impossible that a friend of this sort could become increasingly useful. Perhaps Laroche-Boisseau had even developed a sort of affection for him, providing he was capable of loving anyone other than himself.

These two intimates had been separated several days, and Legris thought himself dishonored at not being able to participate in the activities at Mercoire, but the gentleman, thinking that he might need the help of his faithful protege, had not failed to have him sent an invitation. They were thus reunited at the chateau and Christine de Barjac, gracious with the Baron, could not help but favorably receive Legris who presented himself under the Baron's auspices.

The conversation between the three of them became increasingly animated. However, neither the knight, nor Sister Magloire were happy with this situation. Laroche-Boisseau, with his haughty demeanor and elegant velvet jacket trimmed with silver braid, displeased them greatly. The knight's long features became even longer, and the sister, who a short time ago, was having such pleasant dreams, had resumed her sighs of despair.

Both approached the privileged group imperceptibly to listen to their conversation.

"Morbleu! Miss," the Baron was saying, with more charm than usual, "I am ashamed to think that I, humble huntsman, when compared to the ancient Lords of Mercoire, will lead a hunt for a wolf on their domains! It gives me the impression of desecration; and if your wish, and my duty did not oblige me to fulfill this task, I would have declined in respect to those great huntsmen of renown."

This tribute to the memory of her parents greatly impressed Miss de Barjac, and her eyes sparkled more than usual.

"Ah! you have judged well my beloved father and excellent Uncle Hilaire!" she exclaimed; "In their day, never had a wild beast become so fearsome in our forest as the one that is now causing so much trouble. It would have been captured or killed within twenty-four hours after its first misdeed.... But," she continued, tempering the tenderness in her tone, "since those of whom we speak are no longer here to protect their property, they could not be replaced by a more fearless and capable huntsman than Sire de Laroche Boisseau."

In spite of the suitability of this reply, the knight and the nun seemed less and less satisfied with the progress of their student. It got much worse when she added:

"Besides, being the daughter and niece of famous huntsmen, I will not remain idle while so many distinguished persons put themselves in my service. You can count on me, gentlemen, to be by your side, sharing your fatigue and your dangers... if there are dangers," she concluded, smiling with disdain.

"Spoken like the worthy daughter of the brave Count de Barjac!" exclaimed the Baron. "Well! Miss, since you wish to be with us, you will certainly allow the leader of the hunt to be your cavalier for the entire day tomorrow and not leave you for an instant?"

"Gladly, Sire Baron," replied Christine simply, "The most favorable position, I believe, will be next to you."

"And I too," said Legris in a simpering manner, "I request the favor of being among the guard of honor of Miss de Barjac."

"As you wish, Sire Legris," she replied indifferently.

Magnac, upon learning of the arrangements for the next day which would have deprived him of his usual functions, pursed his lips, shook his head and murmured between his teeth so as to be heard only by the governess:

"Hmm! Sire Gallants, we shall see!"

In the meanwhile, the conversation had become more general.

"Well Baron," asked Sire de Laffrenas, "do you think we will be done rapidly with this cursed beast which has installed itself without permission in the forest of our charming hostess?"

"I am sure of it, my dear Count."

"And if my noble friend, the Baron, says this," responded Legris, with deference, "one can have no doubt about it."

"On the subject of hunting, one is never certain of anything," replied Christine; "and my father, who was an authority on the subject, was in the habit of saying…"

"Miss de Barjac is right," interrupted Laroche-Boisseau; "No one really knows how a hunt will end. However, we will do everything necessary to assure the desired result. I have brought Badineau, my favorite bloodhound, and I plan to visit the forest myself at the light of day tomorrow to rout out the beast, if possible…. Have we heard about any other escapades by our evil wolf since yesterday's incident?"

"None that I know of," replied Miss de Barjac. "It is still confined in the depths of the Monadière, one or two leagues from here…. But," she added, with a slight note of concern in her voice, "it is an hour when it can still be dangerous, and I still have not seen some friends we are expecting to arrive."

The knight and Sister Magloire quickly exchanged a few words in low voices. However, before they could share their thoughts with Christine, Laroche-Boisseau suddenly exclaimed with a snigger:

"Good Lord, you just reminded me! I have not yet seen those poor travelers from the Frontenac abbey, that I had left in Langogne at the hotel of Widow Richard…. They should have departed shortly after us. Could they have, by any chance, been eaten by the wolf they were so worried about?"

"Saint Virgin! What is he saying?" murmured Sister Magloire, clasping her hands.

"Sire Baron," Magnac asked stiffly, "Is he talking about the respectable monks from Frontenac who have been delayed on the way…"

"Ah! undoubtedly," replied Laroche-Boisseau lightly. "There were two of them, a young one and an old one, and they left Langogne a short time after me. My goodness, it would be amusing if they got lost in the heavy fog in the valley and were obliged to sleep in the middle of the woods. If this were the case, what a night those poor wretches would have! They would recite their *paters* and *aves* to purify the forest soiled by of all the swearwords from hunters past and present. I wager that in spite of their frocks and robes, we will find them perched at the very top of some birches among the birds' nests and squirrels."

Legris burst out laughing.

"And to say," he resumed mockingly, "that if they are blocked in their tree by the wolves, like the musician from Quinsac, they would not have the resources as he did, of throwing an accordion bloated with air down on the middle of the pack to scare them away!"

His audience laughed in turn at the refence to this anecdote well known locally, but fell quiet immediately upon seeing the mistress of the house frown.

"Baron," she asked, with ill-concealed agitation, "do you know these two monks that you saw in Langogne, and do you know their names?"

"I believe," replied Laroche-Boisseau with an indifferent air, "that one was Father Bonaventure, the Prior of the abbey, and the other... by my faith! was, if I am not mistaken, a relative, a valet, or the secretary of the Prior; something like that."

"There is no longer doubt," cried out Christine, "it is Léonce!"

"Léonce! yes, it seems to me that the Prior addressed the young lad this way in my presence."

The chatelaine had stood up impetuously.

"Knight de Magnac, Sister Magloire," she said, "give orders that my people immediately begin a search for my missing guests; have them enter the forest with flaming torches, have them cry out, sound horns... but on further reflection, I will go out myself on horseback. Have Maurissot take the chestnut mare to accompany me."

"Marvelous! My child; you have a good heart," murmured Sister Magloire.

Everyone was surprised by the change in the young chatelaine.

"Really, Miss," resumed Laroche-Boisseau gayly, "I do not understand your generosity. What is the great harm in these devout persons spending the night nestled in the leaves or perched in a tree? It would be an opportunity for them to meditate or pray, without risking more than a head cold."

"Peace, Sire Baron," interrupted Christine drily. "I will not put up with such pleasantries. Prior Bonaventure is the best and the wisest of the monks in the abbey and he has always treated me with great kindness. His nephew,

Sire Léonce, is my childhood friend; I would never forgive myself if something happened to either of them.... What? Sire de Magnac, are you still here?" she continued, turning towards her honorable Knight.

"I am leaving, Miss; but allow me to tell you in all humility that leaving such honorable guests to search the forest would really not be proper."

"Proper! Proper!" repeated the proud young girl. "What a great word to throw at me, Sire.... Are my orders to be questioned? Am I not the mistress here? If everyone refuses to obey me, I will mount my horse and go out alone, if necessary...."

"Miss," exclaimed the Baron, "allow me to accompany you.... Morbleu!" he added in a low voice, "I have often tracked deer, but never monks. It will be like tracking a new species."

"I also request the honor of accompanying Miss de Barjac!" said Legris, taking, as usual, Laroche-Boisseau as his model.

"And I too! I too!" came the cry from all the hunters around the room.

"My thanks, Sires," said the chatelaine. "At least I will not be accused of abandoning my guests.... But let us hurry; it is late and night has fallen, and I fear..."

Suddenly a weak voice came from the doorway:

"May the peace of God be upon you...."

Miss de Barjac and those following her stopped abruptly. And they saw Prior Bonaventure, in a pitiful state, enter supporting Léonce who was walking with great difficulty. Both were covered by a shepherd's cloak.

The Mercoire guests erupted with exclamations of surprise, and in some cases, relief, as a nighttime sojourn in the woods was not particularly appealing to them. Miss de Barjac showed great satisfaction.

"Ah! my Reverend Father, it is you at last?" she cried out, running towards the travelers; "welcome to Mercoire, you and Sire Léonce. We were getting very worried and were about to set out to... But, good Lord! what happened to you?"

Christine had just noticed the dishevelment of the poor monk, the paleness, exhaustion and weakness of Léonce.

"You will know soon," my child," said the Prior, "but first, allow me to get a chair for this boy.... I do not know why we were bought in here to trouble this joyous reunion, instead of simply taking us to our rooms.... Well, thanks be to heaven, for God has certainly helped us in our moment of peril."

While speaking, he had led Léonce towards an armchair that Sister Magloire had hastened to bring forward. The young man was looking more embarrassed than unwell, and the attention that he was getting was bringing a temporary redness on his cheeks. This redness became more marked when his eyes met those of Miss de Barjac.

"Sire Léonce," cried Christine, incapable of moderating her impatience, "what is the matter with you? Are you hurt?... Yes, my God! Your clothes are torn.... You are covered with blood!"

"It is nothing, Miss, almost nothing," replied Léonce, forcing a smile, "a mere scratch from the beast of Gévaudan."

"The beast! Once again, the beast!" cried Christine, tapping her foot on the ground in frustration.

"It is a miracle, my child, that we are still alive," said the Prior, who had also collapsed in a chair while murmuring; "the poor boy was almost devoured by the ferocious beast."

"Léonce! my dear Léonce, is this true?" asked Miss de Barjac.

And everyone noticed the distinctive tone used by this strange girl, who was not good at hiding her feelings, when she said the words: "my dear Léonce."

The young man continued to smile feebly.

"My uncle is exaggerating the harm," he stammered, "and tomorrow, one will probably see nothing."

"Bah!" said the Baron in a scornful tone, "this animal is better at frightening than biting, and the people he devours seem to be doing quite well."

Léonce did not reply to this comment and simply turned his head the other way; but the Prior reacted sharply:

"Ah! Sire de Laroche-Boisseau, it is you? Well, your hope in letting us travel unarmed through the Mercoire forest by ourselves was partially fulfilled.... May God forgive your lack of charity."

"This undoubtedly means, my Reverend Father," replied the Baron sarcastically, "that you do not forgive me, yourself? So be it! I am in the habit of not fearing anything."

At the insistence of Miss de Barjac, Bonaventure explained briefly how the heavy fog had caused them to lose their way in the forest, how the mules had been frightened by the howling of the beast and bolted in two directions and finally, how Léonce had been thrown off his mule and would have certainly perished had it not been for the arrival of Jean Godard and his dog.

"Jean Godard shall be rewarded!' exclaimed Miss de Barjac. Do you hear Sire Knight? I shall name him henceforth Chief Herdsman of all my domains.... But let us examine your wound, Léonce; Sister Magloire and I have some knowledge of medicine. We can properly treat it while waiting for the doctor that we will bring in from the town."

"What? Miss, you would do this yourself, in front of all these people?"

"Come now, do not be childish, Mordieu! Do you take me for a silly prude? I insist!"

At the same time, with irresistible authority, she pushed aside the coarse cloak which enveloped Léonce. The velvet jacket, as we know, was torn, and through the tear protruded the white and delicate shoulder of the adolescent. When the bloody handkerchiefs which had served as first bandages came off, blood began flowing in abundance again from a wide and deep gash, which was perhaps less serious than it appeared.

"What a horrible wound!" said Christine who paled and seemed to steel herself against her own emotions; "Sister Magloire, right away, some dressings and fresh water…. Then bring me some gauze and our family balm…. What are those stupid peasant servants doing?... The flesh is cruelly torn."

"That?" interrupted the Baron, who had slid in among the curious who were each in turn examining the wound. "That, a toothmark from a large wolf? On my honor as a gentleman, I cannot accept this conclusion…. An animal like the beast of Gévaudan would crush a bone with one clamp of his jaw, and the trace of its claws on flesh would leave two-inch deep furrows. Here, however, there are no signs of the enormous fangs and the claws of steel that have ravaged so many victims in our countryside recently. I call upon all huntsmen who can hear me, to all those who have seen the terrible wounds on the hounds following a wolf when it is cornered, to bear witness."

The suspicion implied by these words caused Léonce to react, in spite of his feebleness and suffering.

"Sire," he responded, "I admit that I was stunned by my fall, and entwined by the thorns and undergrowth, I could not turn to see…"

"Ah! ah! ah!" exclaimed Laroche-Boisseau, "You are now much less sure of yourself. And what wolf would pre-announce its attack by howling. This cannot be the beast of Gévaudan! From all reports, it hurls itself upon its victims and drags them away in silence. Once again, I call upon the experienced hunters present, is it believable that a ferocious animal…"

"But Sire Baron," resumed the Prior impatiently, "with your expertise on this subject, can you tell us at least what animal could have frightened the mules and torn the flesh of this unfortunate child? The wound exists and it was not a dream!"

"Who knows," said Laroche-Boisseau, snickering, "Fright does strange things. A broken branch could have caused the hurt on the rosy shoulder of our young friend. If one must absolutely attribute this scratch to some animal in the forest, my opinion would lean towards a wild cat, or perhaps an ill-tempered weasel, or worst case, a wolf cub still suckling its mother; but certainly, not an old wolf like the beast of Gévaudan."

This opinion, so clearly expressed, generated considerable controversy and heated whispering among those present. The Prior himself seemed shaken in his convictions.

"It is true that I, nor anyone else actually saw the animal, but it seems impossible to me…"

"You hear that, gentlemen?" interrupted the Baron, triumphantly, "We end up with no one having seen an animal. I need not ask further. Decidedly, the Reverend Father and his nephew were too anxious to present themselves as martyrs, and this lovely story is reduced to that of a fall from a mule."

These hateful remarks, though seemingly frivolous, merited a strong response from the Prior, but Bonaventure merely shrugged his shoulders and gave Laroche-Boisseau a contemptuous smile.

Meanwhile, Miss de Barjac, who had taken no part in this contestation, was totally absorbed in taking care of the victim and seemed to not have heard anything. After having cleaned the wound, she applied the bandages prepared by Sister Magloire, well experienced in this task. The dressing completed, Léonce had wanted to thank the charming chatelaine, but either some secret emotion affected him too strongly, or the loss of blood had caused his system to react negatively, because as he tried to speak, his eyes closed and he lost consciousness.

This event had everyone murmuring, but no one was as upset as Christine, normally so courageous and superior to the feebleness of her sex.

"Good heavens, he is dying!" she cried. "Does he have another wound which is more serious? Sister Magloire… Reverend Father…. Help! Help! He will die!"

The servants were running back and forth, not knowing what to do.

"Bah! It is only a fainting spell," said Laroche-Boisseau quietly; throw a glass of water on his face; that generally suffices to bring little ladies back to their senses."

But even after the usual treatments, he remained unconscious.

"Léonce, my childhood friend!... my beloved brother!" wailed Christine, leaning towards him.

Finally, the friendly voices seemed to have a salutary effect and the young man gave a sigh and half-opened his eyes.

"He is alive! cried out Christine.

Léonce, indeed, was beginning to recognize the people surrounding him.

"We must now transport him up to the room we prepared for him," said Sister Magloire…. "Calm and sleep will help him recover."

"Yes, yes," resumed Miss de Barjac. "This noise and movement must overwhelm him…. Pierre," speaking to one of the robust valets who was posted near the door, "take Sire Léonce in your arms and carry him to the green room…. Léonarde will lead the way with a torch…. Walk carefully, you see that he is hurt."

Pierre obeyed; as he was carefully picking up Léonce, the latter let out a cry of pain. Christine bounded forward like a panther and raised her hand as if to strike the clumsy servant:

"Imbecile! Oaf!" she exclaimed. "Did I not tell you... Wait, I will help, and woe upon you if it happens again!... You, Léonarde, precede us!"

While speaking, she had put her arms around Léonce's waist, and placed his head on her shoulder. One would have said a mother carrying her sleeping child.

This action, so contrary to their idea of etiquette, horrified Sister Magloire and the knight. At the moment that their mistress was about to leave the room, Magnac thrust himself forward, with the courage of desperation:

"Miss," he said hurriedly, "Think, please! It is not seemly... allow me to..."

Christine did not deign respond, but turning her head towards her unfortunate counselor, she sent him a look which was so imperious and menacing that the poor man stopped as if petrified.

"Gads! That was a abduction!" said Laroche-Boisseau, who was badly hiding his spite with forced humor; "yes, that was a definitely an abduction. Well, Father Prior, now what do you think of your timid pupil?"

"Do not have bad thoughts about them, Sires," said the priest, speaking to those present, "These poor children are as innocent as Adam and Eve when they left the hand of God!"

He made a sign to Sister Magloire and the two left hurriedly to rejoin the young pair.

One hour later, the guests at the Chateau de Mercoire had retired, and the Baron de Laroche Boisseau was pacing meditatively in his room, reflecting on the day's events.

"Yes, yes," he murmured, "this young bird, this failed young monk loves Miss de Barjac; I did not doubt it this morning after seeing the warmth with which he spoke of her; they saw each other during their childhood; and love which thrives on opposites and contrasts... but, could she also love him? That is the problem. She almost compromised herself for him this evening, and from another person, this imprudent action would have been significant; but with this savage creature, always extreme in her impressions as with her desires, can one be sure of anything? If, however, she loved him? That is absurd, therefore possible. In that case, such a love could not escape the attention of the wily Prior. However, the Prior does not seem to disapprove of this nascent intimacy, and one could think... may God damn me! that he is protecting her. Does he have the idea... the Devil! I may be on to something."

He accelerated his pacing as if to help his intelligence to function.

"There is no longer any doubt about it," he resumed, tapping his brow; "it is the abbey's plan, patient and tortuous, like a serpent.... That ambitious monk thought up the project of making his relative rich by giving him the hand of the wealthy heiress. He is all-powerful in Frontenac, he has the experience and has marvelous subtlety. He must maneuver to obtain this result, and he kindles the flames, when he can, of the mutual affection of these two children.... Morbleu! If this is so, then I will have a hard task, and I will only be able to win with a master stroke!... a rapid stroke, which would strike like lightning!"

He continued pacing in silence; soon a bitter smile played on his lips.

"So," he continued, "I can have my turn. Christine received me tonight with pleasure and cordiality, a distinction which escaped no one and generated some jealousies. Why would the balance not tilt again in my favor? A favorable occasion will present itself, and I will make it happen.... Yes, I will not hesitate. I will abduct this charming creature from them, so seductive with her whims and follies.... She has a total confidence in me; and perhaps she loves me.... Therefore, she must be mine!"

Chapter VII

THE WOLF HUNT

The next day, during the early morning hours, an immense crowd converged on Mercoire. The proclamation by the authorities, the enormous bounty promised to the fortunate huntsman who succeeded in killing the beast of Gévaudan and above all, the ardent desire to rid the country of the monster that had caused so much harm and decimated so many families, had generated an extraordinary competition. According to historians, over thirty parishes in Gévaudan, Rouergue and Auvergne had risen, en masse, to participate in this hunt. Entire village populations were constantly arriving, led by their Lords or even by their parish priest; As each group arrived, one could also see women and children. Among the huntsmen, some carried rifles, pistols and even ancient muskets. These were the ones that wished to have the role of *shooters* in the planned hunt. The others, much more numerous, simply had sticks with which to strike the undergrowth, or ox horns, rattles, trumpets, drums, or even old kettles; any instrument useful for making an infernal noise. These persons were satisfied with the more modest roles of *trackers* or *beaters*. Moreover, the hunters from both categories were obliged to follow the strict orders of Laroche-Boisseau, who, in his role as Lieutenant of the Louveterie, was in command of all the maneuvers; keeping the silence until the time for action; assuring that no cry, or sound of hunting horns nor barking of hounds alert the savage beasts in the depths of the forest.

One can easily understand that this multitude of persons had not been able to find shelter either in the village of Mercoire or in the chateau, already crowded from the previous evening. Only certain gentlemen were invited to rejoin the persons of distinction who were receiving the hospitality of Miss de Barjac. The other hunters camped in groups, either under the large trees on the main fare, or on the sort of esplanade which extended in front of the manor. Forest guards and lancers, wearing the blue uniforms of the Louveterie, strolled among the colorful crowd to maintain order. As these good people, most of whom had come from afar, had brought provisions of food, cutlery and plates that were spread on coats, and lunch was being enjoyed with as much gaiety as appetite.

The weather was good, but hazy, and the sun was having trouble piercing through the mist. One could barely make out the form of the nearest mountains. Such conditions could cause a hunt to fail in that it could allow the wolf to escape the view of the shooters. Nevertheless, no one despaired; each boasted about what he would accomplish if luck came his way. Trackers and beaters, motivated by tales of the beast's evil exploits, awaited with extreme impatience the order to move forward.

However, time passed, and the order did not come. This lack of action worried the less experienced, unable to understand that success of the attack depended on the preliminary operations. Laroche-Boisseau had been gone since early that morning, with an excellent bloodhound and several capable hunters, to *do the forest*, that is to say, to ascertain that the beast is still in the Mercoire forest and to identify in which part of the forest it has taken refuge at daybreak. However, neither the Baron, nor those who accompanied him, had yet to appear, and as long as they had not returned, it was impossible to try anything as this might compromise the result of the whole enterprise.

Finally, around nine o'clock, about the time that some were beginning to think that the hunters and hounds had been devoured by the terrible beast, a small group of three or four persons on foot, one of which held a magnificent dog straining at its leash, emerged from the woods and headed towards the chateau. Immediately there was a murmur from the crowd; they had recognized the Lieutenant of the Louveterie by his colorful uniform. They surrounded him and pressed him with questions. Had he found the beast? In what part of the woods is it hiding? Will the hunt be successful? However, the Baron did not seem to have the time nor the willingness to answer. He restricted himself to giving brief instructions to the lancers and guards, who immediately began to transmit them to the huntsmen. As soon as he saw everyone on their feet, he rapidly continued on towards the chateau without paying heed to the salutations and marks of respect from those around him.

At that moment, the noble company at Mercoire were agreeably occupied with their lunch. There were vast tables set in both the salon and the dining hall; the hunters, already in hunting clothes, some standing, some seated, were doing noisy honor to the meal. Miss de Barjac, still in her amazon outfit, bare headed, was moving from one table to another, to the great desperation of the Knight de Magnac and Sister Magloire, who could not keep up. Christine appeared proud and happy with all this activity, of all this noise. She chatted, she laughed; her rosy cheeks expressed pure pleasure. She did not appear to remember the unfortunate wounded young man, who, only a few hours earlier, had been the cause of so many tears, and whom she had carried in her arms; however, she only expressed some confusion if, by chance, someone mentioned her hasty departure the previous evening.

As soon as the Baron de Laroche-Boisseau appeared, his brow bathed in sweat and his clothes damp from the morning dew, all eyes turned towards him and everyone asked questions at once.

"Good news, my charming Chatelaine!" he exclaimed in greeting to Christine who was approaching with the others; "good news, my fellow huntsmen!... You have ten minutes to finish your lunch, retrieve your arms and take your positions at Bois-Brûlé, in the heart of the Monadière."

"You have located the beast?" they asked eagerly.

"By the grace of God and Saint Hubert, the patron saint of huntsmen," replied the Baron; "at Bois-Brûlé, a small forest of about thirty acres of shrubs and trees, I learned of a wolf, which according to someone who saw it, is of enormous size. After making sure that the animal had not left the area, I had it encircled in silence to ensure that it does not make its escape. Now the trackers and beaters are on their way, and once there, my chief hunting assistant, old Laramée, will place them downwind.... And as I said, we must be on our way to our firing positions in ten minutes, as the beast, frightened, might be capable of slipping out on us before we have the time to attack and destroy it."

Cheers and congratulations greeted the report; most of the hunters present left immediately, hastening to the meeting point indicated, hoping, undoubtedly, that the first arrivals would get the best placed positions. As for the Baron, a man who appreciated the value of time, he reached over the head of an obstinate guest, seized a piece of bread and some ham, and began his lunch standing up, all the while distractedly answering questions being rained upon him. As this military-style lunch came to its end, Miss de Barjac approached, holding in her hand a glass of Muscat wine.

"You will allow the lady of the house to offer you one for the road, my dear Baron?" she said, offering him the glass with a smile; "you have valiantly toiled in her service this morning, and the day will be difficult, I think."

Laroche-Boisseau bowed profoundly, and in recognition of Christine's gesture, he emptied the glass in one swallow.

"Another would imply that our gracious chatelaine would intoxicate her guests with love and wine," he continued, "but she would not allow such gallantries; I would therefore prefer asking if she still remembers her promise of last evening?"

"Morbleu! Of course, I remember! Is it not my duty as mistress of this domain, to follow the leader of the hunt? I am attaching myself to you, Baron. I will not leave your side."

Laroche-Boisseau was delighted with this persistence, which fulfilled his secret wishes; however, he took great care not to let this show.

"Miss, my station will always be at the head of the front line of shooters, and under cover, accidents are unfortunately not infrequent; however, I will do my best to protect you from any risk.... Moreover," he added, with a mocking smile, "you will undoubtedly be under the protection of your intrepid bodyguard?"

And he indicated, with a nod of his head, the Knight de Magnac, who was standing rigid and aloof on his long legs, four steps behind his mistress.

"Pshaw on bodyguards!" pouted Christine in a low voice.

Laroche-Boisseau winked as though planning some mischief towards the knight and Christine smiled her approval.

"Well, Miss!" resumed the Baron in a light tone, "you have not spoken about the little lamb that so happily escaped the fangs of the wolf and who seems to inspire so much pity from you.... How are his scratches this morning?"

"I... I do not know," stammered Christine, whose face flushed.

"I would have thought that you would have been eager to inform yourself about him. Yesterday, you treated him with an affection that made us all jealous. Good Lord! we would let ourselves be torn apart not only by a wolf but by all the lions of Arabia, to merit the right to lay our heads for an instant on your shoulder!"

"I do not understand.... I do not know what happened; the sight of blood troubled my mind.... But you just made me realize that this morning I failed to inform myself about the state of the poor young man; yes, by my faith, in the middle of all that is going on, I forgot, completely forgot!"

As she was saying this, she was turning to the right and to the left with an embarrassed air, to escape the piercing eyes of the Baron.

At that moment, Father Bonaventure entered the room, where there remained only a few ladies and guests, too attracted by the charm of the offerings on the table. The Prior, with the help of Sister Magloire and the ladies of the chateau, had repaired the damage to his clerical clothing. Aside from a slight paleness of his benevolent features, nothing betrayed the fatigue and emotions of the previous day.

Christine ran over to him.

"Good day, Reverend Father, I see with pleasure that you are fresh and rested this morning.... But here is Sire de Laroche-Boisseau who would like to have some news about your young nephew, and I could not give him any."

"If this sudden interest is to make amends for the affronts to my nephew and me," replied the prior dryly, "then I thank Sire Baron.... Aside from a brief period of fever, the state of the poor child has greatly improved, and the doctor assures that in a few days he will be fine.... But you, Miss," he continued softly, addressing Christine, "you cannot be unaware of the favorable news; our dear Sister Magloire, who has already been three or four times to the patient's room must have told you...."

"Do I pay attention to what Sister Magloire says?" replied the young girl impatiently.

"You are wrong, Miss, as the sister is a wise and discreet person who loves you with all her heart…. However, I thought I recognized your voice this morning in the gallery that leads to Léonce's room. A person watched for the nun and at each of her exits from the room and made interested inquiries."

"It was not I, it was not I," replied Christine; but let us go Sire de Laroche-Boisseau, they are just waiting for us…. I will get ready and rejoin you in just a moment."

She saluted and ran out, as if happy to evade moral discomfort.

The Baron and Prior Bonaventure remained, facing each other; the Father a little pensive, the Baron, radiant and triumphant.

"Well, Father," resumed the Baron, in a mocking tone, "It would seem that the wind has turned since last evening?... *Women are fickle*, as said François 1er."

"*And who trusts them is a fool*," replied the monk with a smile on completing the proverb:[12] "are you certain, Sire Baron, that the wind has really turned?"

Laroche-Boisseau became pensive as well.

"Sambleu! Reverend Father," he asked finally in anger, "what role are you playing in all this, you, a man of the Church?"

"That of a humble instrument of Providence, Sire; an instrument who God undoubtedly wishes to use to protect the pure and simple in heart against the evil and the arrogant."

The Prior left the room to rejoin his dear nephew. Laroche-Boisseau followed him with his eyes, shaking his head.

"He is perhaps right," he murmured, "it is possible that this sudden change was simply caused by a reaction of an excess of modesty compared to her exaggerated show of emotion yesterday evening…. Decidedly, I must not lose any time and play it carefully."

He was about to go out himself when saw, in a corner of the room, now almost deserted, his friend Legris, who appeared to be waiting for him.

"Legris," he said to him in a low voice, "have you brought me the two hundred Pistoles[13] that I need for gratuities to the lancers and the guards?"

"My dear Baron," replied the moneylender's son, in embarrassment, "I

---

12   Proverb: *Souvent femme varie, Bien fol est qui s'y fie*—accredited to François 1er (1545) and supposedly engraved on a window at Chateau de Chambord, which was never found.

13   Pistoles: Gold coins also called Louis d'Or

must admit that my father..."

"Is a miser and a skinflint," interrupted Laroche-Boisseau with spite.

"Please, do not be angry. You already owe him so much money!... However, if you are in need, my friend, am I not always at your service? My father gave me for my minor expenses, around forty Louis d'Or which I offer you with pleasure."

"All right, I understand," said Laroche-Boisseau, with a slightly contemptuous smile; finally, I accept, Master Legris. You will turn over this sum go my lancer, Laramé, and I will repay you the next time I win at cards.... I must admit that you are not a bad fellow, Legris, and you do not at all resemble your... Good, I will once again give you proof of my confidence by asking you for another service."

"Speak, dear Baron, what does it concern?"

"Well, you committed yourself to remaining as close as possible to Miss de Barjac during the hunt, did you not?"

"That is true, it is an honor..."

"Which you will renounce. I request, on the contrary, that for today, you remain as far away as possible from our lovely savage and myself."

"If you so wish...."

"And that is not all; you will have to prevent that unbearable Knight de Magnac or other unwelcome intruder to rejoin Miss de Barjac and myself. Can you promise me this, *my friend*?"

"This is truly a sacrifice that you ask of me, Laroche-Boisseau, as our hostess is a ravishing creature! Well, I will devote myself to pleasing you.... However, take care, my dear Baron! Although I do not know your intent, it seems to me that you are playing a dangerous game.... Miss de Barjac is surrounded by powerful people and loyal servants. Notably, this Knight de Magnac, with his sullen demeanor and ridiculous manners, would not tolerate any mischief, and if he has any suspicions?"

"He does, and that is why your help is necessary. You have long proven to me your friendship, Legris, I know how fertile your mind can be for solutions. I am therefore counting on you to amuse this Cerberus[14] during the hunt, and I am certain that I will not be disappointed."

These flatteries, deftly calculated, had the objective of igniting the zeal of the young bourgeois-gentleman: therefore, Legris, despite his earlier hesitations, now promised to do whatever he was asked, and the two friends separated.

A short time later, Laroche-Boisseau and Miss de Barjac were on horseback in the courtyard of the chateau; he, mounted on a fine animal raised in the Limousin region, and she, on her favorite, Buch. Christine carried on a shoulder strap an elegant rifle, inlaid with gold, that had belonged to

14 Cerberus: A three-headed monstrous dog, guardian of the Greek underworld.

her father. The Baron, other than his hunting knife in a blue velvet sheath decorated with silver wolf heads, was armed with a large rifle from Saint-Étienne, more remarkable for its precision and range than by the richness of its decorations. Moreover, since this was not a chase with hounds, but a simple hunt with beaters, the order had been given that the huntsmen were to travel to Bois-Brûlé on foot, except for the Lieutenant of the Louveterie and the lady of the chateau. Further, they should both dismount when they approach the line of shooters, to avoid any chance of an accident. This order appeared to disconcert the poor Knight de Magnac, who, for reasons known by him, did not want to lose sight of his mistress. As she was about to leave with the gallant wolf hunter, he ran over, alarmed, a cane in his hand, his thin legs encased in leggings too large for him, and asked in a grim, almost sad tone:

"Miss, where shall I rejoin you?"

"By my faith, I have no idea," replied Christine, who was doing her best to restrain the impatience of her frisky mount; "Sire Baron will tell you."

The knight asked the same question to Laroche-Boisseau, who answered distractedly:

"Somewhere in the direction of Bois-Brûlé, and everywhere there is a need."

This response was not of a nature to satisfy Sire de Magnac, and he was about to insist that he be given more precise indications, but they did not give him the time to do so. The Baron gave a sign to Christine, and after giving a vague salute, the two of them gave their horses free rein and left in a gallop. Further, the honorable squire had the chagrin of hearing the malicious young girl emit a peal of mocking laughter.

The poor man sighed; however, he was not discouraged and resolved to put all his efforts into catching up to the fugitive as rapidly as possible. He had started walking with that intention, when Legris, gallantly equipped as a hunter with a rifle on his shoulder, approached him.

"Sire Knight," he said courteously, "you are certainly in a hurry, as am I, to rejoin our noble hostess and Sire Lieutenant of Louveterie. We will meet inevitably at Bois-Brûlé, but as I am not familiar with the countryside, and as I can easily lose my way in the immense forest, would you grant me the honor of your company until we reach the meeting point?"

Magnac was not lacking in reasons to be wary of Legris, knowing that he was the henchman of Laroche-Boisseau, but since after all, this was a natural request, he replied in a formal tone:

"The honor is mine, Sire…. I am at your service. Let us proceed."

And to give the example, he moved forward with enormous strides.

They left the chateau and entered the forest, where every trail, every footpath, was familiar to Sire de Magnac. The majority of hunters had already arrived at the spot where the chase was to begin. One met only a small number of stragglers, and as an absolute silence at been imposed on everyone, the Mercoire forest had regained its normal solitude.

The route was long and the knight, in spite of his zeal, no longer had the vigor of his youth; therefore, his pace soon slowed. Legris, who was waiting for the opportunity, tried to engage him in conversation. At first, Magnac was on his guard and only replied with glacial courtesy; but his travelling companion, as we know, was not lacking in guile and tenacity, and he imperceptibly succeeded in getting his man to be more communicative.

They were entering an alley of oak trees, dark and somber, where the sun seems to have never penetrated, when Legris resumed speaking in his most insinuating tone, said:

"In truth, Sire, I have always admired that a gentleman of such high distinction such as yourself, a former officer of the king's army, had accepted the inferior position that you occupy at the Mercoire chateau."

"Inferior position!" repeated the Knight with majesty, stopping in his tracks and straightening his tall figure; "what do you mean by such terms; unsuitable? In what way is my position inferior to that of my rank as a gentleman? Do I not have absolute power over the household staff of the chateau? Is there anyone in the entire breadth of this domain who would dare speak to me with irreverence? As for my functions with Miss de Barjac, is there any shame in serving a young lady of standing, who in all circumstances shows me her friendship and esteem? By my faith! Young man, if you had a little royal blood in your veins, I would teach you the respect that is my due!"

Legris realized that he had taken the wrong approach, and he hastened to appease the irascible squire.

"You have misunderstood me, Sire," he said in a honeyed tone, "heaven forbid that I would ever demean Sire Knight de Magnac! It is only that I do not understand how, after years of war and harvesting laurels in the battles of Flanders[15], how you, one of the bravest soldiers of Maurice de Saxe[16], could have gotten used to the quiet life of this chateau. They speak of you often in high places, Sire de Magnac, and I am aware that you valiantly conducted yourself at the battle Fontenoy, some twenty years ago."

This battle of Fontenoy, the memory of which Legris had just mentioned, was, as everyone in Mercoire was aware, a subject on which the normally reserved knight, never tired of expressing himself with satisfac-

---

15   Flanders: the Flemish region of Belgium
16   Maurice de Saxe: Maurice, Count of Saxony was a noble officer and famed military commander of the 18th century.

tion. Upon hearing the name, de Magnac gave a start, his face brightened, and he launched himself into a response:

"In that case, Sire, I am angry that a misunderstanding... we are hot-headed in our family; but this time, I am wrong, I must admit.... Yes, young man, what was said was true; I was indeed at Fontenoy, and few have seen what I saw as it was a terrible affair, and of those who were there, few are still alive today."

At the same time, he launched an interminable narration of the attacks and counter-attacks of the French during the battle, on the importance and capabilities of Maurice de Saxe and on the decisive role of the royal house in the successes of the day. The glorious epic was far from complete when they attainted a sort of clearing. Several men armed with rifles were hiding behind the shrubs: They had finally found the line of shooters.

The knight immediately interrupted himself and was now thinking only about his duty towards his mistress. As he was searching with his eyes for someone who could inform him, a guard, who seemed to be responsible for that portion of the forest, politely approached him:

"Sires," he said in a low voice, "you should not remain here in full sight, you might alert the beast which may be somewhere in this under-brush."

"Yes, yes, Pierre," replied the knight, stepping back several paces; "we are searching for Miss de Barjac and Sire Baron de Laroche-Boisseau; where are they now?"

They crossed the firing line a short while ago, and they must be at Quatre-Coins."

"That suffices."

And Magnac made a sign to Legris and was about to follow the edge of the forest to attain the location indicated, when the guard stopped him.

"Not that way, Sire Knight," he said, "you might trouble the shooters and risk being shot.... Sire Baron has specifically forbidden crossing this line.... You must go by way of Bute-Rouge."

Magnac stifled a sigh; but he understood all too well the wisdom of these instructions to infringe on them; returning on their steps, they took the direction indicated.

The detour was a fairly long one. After a moment, Legris asked in an almost prayerful tone:

"Well, Sire Knight, will you not continue your narrative which I find absolutely fascinating? You were at the moment where your regiment, the regiment of Navarre, was about to attack the defenses of Moulin-à-Vent."

Thus, reminded of the memories of his exploits, the knight continued his recital, However, now he was distracted; preoccupied, he constantly looked around him and interrupted himself to listen. These distractions were probably the reason he lost himself in uninteresting and useless details; therefore, in his story, the enemy were still defending when they arrived at the crossing in the forest called Quatre-Coins.

There, they found themselves again at a line of shooters. At the junction itself was a lancer and several servants who were guarding the horses of the Baron and Miss de Barjac; however, the leader of the hunt and the lovely chatelaine had gone ahead on foot about a half hour earlier, according to the retainers.

"In which direction did they go?" asked the knight.

"By my faith, I am not too sure," said the lancer, in what seemed to be a mocking tone. "but it seemed to me that they were headed for the slopes of the Monadière."

And he nonchalantly pointed towards a nearby mountain. The knight looked attentively in that direction. On the side of the mountain, the trees became less numerous and stopped well below the summit which was bare and crowned with rock formations. Unfortunately, a white cloud enveloped the upper part of the mountain and it was not possible to distinguish any human forms at that distance.

"Hmm!" said Legris to his guide, after a few moments of observation, "I think that our hunters better hasten…. That mist which is gathering on the mountain surely presages a storm for tonight. You are familiar with the local saying:

> *"When the Monadière covers its chapel,*
> *"Shepherd, take your cloak…."*

But the knight was not worried about these prognostics; he had other concerns. He had no idea as to what direction he should continue his search, when suddenly, a gunshot was heard coming from the Monadière, just at the edge of the white cloud, which the local inhabitants called its *chapel*.

"That is the signal," the lancer said in a low voice; "Sire de Laroche-Boisseau has just fired his rifle…. Attention! now the hunt begins."

Indeed, from the depth of the valleys, a distant sound rose up, but strange, discordant, savage, always increasing, which finally took the proportions of a formidable tumult. The beaters had moved forward to drive the beast out of the thickets where it had hidden and pushed it towards the quieter but much more lethal line of the shooters.

The latter, eyes and ears on alert, fingers on the trigger of their rifles, huddled in silence behind bushes and tree trunks; Only the knight and Legris remained standing in the middle of the clearing. The lancer spoke to them impatiently:

"You cannot remain here, Sires; your presence may result in the wolf returning into the brush and heading back towards the trackers. We are dealing with cunning animal which knows all the tricks of its evil trade; hide yourselves, or…"

"We are leaving," said Magnac, "I have noted the part of the mountain from where Sire de Laroche-Boisseau gave the signal, and I know where to find my young mistress. Are you coming Sire Legris, or do you wish to stay here and take your chance at having a shot at the terrible beast of Gévaudan?

Legris was extremely tempted, but remembering the insistent request of his friend, the Baron, he showed no hesitation.

"I will not abandon you," he replied, "however perhaps we should…"

A gesture at once imperious and supplicating by the lancer interrupted their conversation, and they hastened to enter the woods.

They then followed a small trail that wound upward towards the crest of the Monadière. Gradually as the forest lightened, the path became steeper and more rugged. The taller plants became undergrowth and brush, and finally they arrived at an open space where they had a clear view of a large portion of countryside around them; but this did not help. Below them, the mountain and valleys were hidden by luxuriant foliage; above their heads, like a dome, was the white and luminous cloud through which they could barely distinguish the irregular and craggy crest of the Monadière.

During their climb, the din at the foot of the mountain continued. At times, it seemed less loud and sustained; undoubtedly because the poor trackers were often too entangled in the underbrush to concentrate on their instruments; but then the fracas would resume with a new vigor. These were the sounds of an infernal hunt resounding through the forest like a tempest. The somber roll of kettles, the duets of oxen horns, the rhythm of rattles and drums, were all sufficient to render the deaf even more so. On the contrary, everything remained calm on the side of the shooters; not a rifle shot, not a cry of *tayau*, or *harloup*[17] was to be heard. Undoubtedly the beast, if it had not already left the area, had guessed, with the fine instinct common to wild animals, the tactic of its enemy and was using its cunning to avoid their deadly fire.

Sires de Magnac and Legris had stopped for a moment to catch their breath on a small plateau covered with heather and blueberries which was about two thirds the way up the mountain. It was there that began the cloud which we have mentioned, and where trails of mist were constantly gathering from the gorges below. A half-league below was the tip of nearest part of the forest, and one could see, huddled in a tuft of evergreen shrubs, the last shooter of the line. Aside from this lone shooter, motionless in his ambush, there was no one on the mountain; there was no indication as to

17   *Tayau and harloup:* cries used during the hunt to excite the hounds

where the Baron and Miss de Barjac had gone.

Suddenly, the feeble noise of human voices came through the haze. The knight turned suddenly, and pointed his finger towards a sort of overhang on the side of the mountain, slightly above their current location:

"Over here!" he said hurriedly, "I had forgotten about the ravine of Creux-aux-Sangliers, where Jeannot has her hut.... We will find them there, as I have recognized the voice of my young mistress."

And he began walking up the path with the speed of his long legs.

"But where are you taking me?" asked Legris, who was having trouble keeping up.

"You will see.... They are there, I tell you...."

Soon, they had arrived at the edge of the ravine, which was hardly visible from below, but now plunged at their feet like an abyss. It seemed to have been formed by the rainwater coming from the peaks of the Monadière and the bottom was strewed with fragments of rocks. However, the slope bristled with ferns which would allow them to descend without difficulty. Legris, in particular, was astonished that a human creature would have established a home in such a wretched place. On the opposite side of the ravine, a sort of cave had been dug into the hillside. It was enclosed by several tree trunks in which a door and two small openings for windows had been roughly carved. Nothing could be as sad and miserable as this dwelling located far from where anyone lived and in a region of storms and birds of prey.

As Legris examined the strange construction which more closely resembled a bear den than a human habitation, the sound of voices that had alerted them was heard once more, and this time, it came from the mysterious dwelling.

"I was right," said the knight, "it comes from there, I am certain.... Let us hurry, quickly! It sounds like a cry for help!"

Taking Legris by his arm, he dragged him onto the grassy slope of the ravine. They had reached the bottom where there trailed some heavy layers of mist. Before they had the time to turn around, an enormous animal, its jaws gaping, its eyes blazing, and emitting loud growling sounds, leaped upon them, the shock knocking both to the ground; then, without doing them further harm, continued on his way towards the end of the ravine. Hardly had the ferocious animal disappeared from sight that suddenly an astounding burst of laughter came from somewhere, as if some malicious demon was celebrating their misadventure.

However, it was only a little later that the knight and Legris remembered this last occurrence. Stunned by the impulsive charge of the animal, which they had involuntarily disturbed in its hideaway, they remained sprawled on the ground unable to move. Legris was the first to come his senses and he rose to recover his rifle had which had been thrown some ten paces from them.

"It is the beast of Gévaudan!" Legris was saying, his voice muffled by emotion; "we must protect ourselves…."

"Yes, it is indeed the beast," replied the night, bringing his hand up to his bruised face, "and the devil take him!... I took a real blow…. But how is it that no hunter was there to protect this passage?"

He was interrupted by piercing cries, closely followed by a heart-rending scream, which came from the hut which we have described. Magnac and his companion flinched.

"That is the voice of my mistress!" exclaimed the knight.

"I also recognized the voice of the Baron," said Legris.

The door to the hut suddenly opened, and Miss de Barjac appeared on the threshold. Christine was bareheaded, her hair in disarray and her face flushed; she held in her hand a hunting knife, the blade covered with blood.

Finding herself face to face with Magnac and Legris, she showed neither surprise nor fear; but she maintained a somber expression, and said almost distractedly:

"You have come too late…. I have killed him…. Go on inside, and you will find your wonderful master of the hunt!"

And she threw the bloodied knife at the feet of the two horrified companions, and she began to run down the mountainside like a madwoman.

Chapter VIII

The Wild Boar Ravine

Let us see now what happened between Laroche-Boisseau and Miss de Barjac, after they had left the Chateau de Mercoire together.

Christine could hardly contain her joy as she galloped on her spirited little black horse along the wide avenues of the forest. She thought herself back in the happy days of her childhood, when her father and her uncle were still enjoying the boisterous pleasures of the hunt in these same woods. Her tanned face glowed with the colors of health: her pink nostrils dilated as if to better breathe in the fresh air of the countryside. It was not only the absence of her usual mentors that delighted her; she burst out laughing at the manner that she had escaped her honorable squire; she abandoned herself without constraint to all the whims of her capricious nature; Sometimes she would release the bridle of little Buch, and its mane waving in the wind, the horse would devour the space before it; sometimes she obliged it to prance in place, letting it gnaw on its silver bit. Using the strands of her whip, she amused herself by cutting down low overhead branches or little flowers in the grass. When she passed a hunter on her path, she gave him a friendly greeting or a smile; happiness seemed to flow from her.

The elegant gentleman who accompanied her was the personification, for her, of all this liberty, this excitement, this satisfaction. Moreover, it seemed to Laroche-Boisseau that she had never shown him as much graciousness. She approved his projects and applauded at his witticisms. A sister would not have acted differently with a well-loved brother. They advanced, side-by-side, easily exchanging malicious observations; and passers-by, witness to this charming union, drew the most favorable conclusions about the lovely chatelaine changing her name.

But as much as Christine was acting with candor in her manner with the Baron, he employed astuteness and dissimulation. His cheerfulness was false, his apparent ease, calculated. He analyzed each frivolous phrase, each gesture, each smile of the over-confident child, and noted it in his memory. However, he had too much experience in this area to take a perhaps temporary attraction seriously. He suspected that a too direct approach could easily shock this spirited soul and put her on her guard. He therefore put on an air of levity and nonchalance and let his imprudent companion safely intoxicate herself with the fresh air and sun; however, he covertly watched the progress of this intoxication and made his plans to take advantage of it.

As long as he was watching over the immense preparations of the hunt, it was impossible for him to have intimate chats with Miss de Barjac, but it was noted that on that day, the ease with which the Baron de Laroche-Boisseau, normally so fastidious in matters of the hunt, accepted all the arrangements made by the people to whom he had given orders that morning. One would have said that he was in a hurry to get things over with. He hardly listened to what was said and answered in monosyllables and an air of impatience. Finally, when Christine and he had reviewed on horseback the entire line of shooters and confirmed that everyone was in place, they left their mounts at Quatre-Coins, as the reader is already aware, and began their climb up the Monadière, from where the signal should come to begin the hunt, in accordance with the plan.

Miss de Barjac, the hem of her long dress hitched to her belt, her rifle thrown over her shoulder, walked with agility and freedom. The Baron wanted to offer her his arm, but she thanked him with a slightly disdainfully air, and truly, she did not require any assistance to overcome all the difficulties of the terrain. She was sure-footed, breathed easily and moved like a young wild goat: her clear eyes calmly measured the depth of the crevasses. Laroche-Boisseau himself had difficulty in following her. With an admiration mixed with cruel satisfaction, he observed her; light-hearted, joyful and confident, heading for the most deserted portion of the mountain. However, he was no longer speaking to her; he seemed embarrassed and preoccupied by some secret plan. Christine, left to herself, became dreamy as well. The calm and the solitude which reigned around them began to give her reflections a melancholic turn.

"Baron," she said suddenly, stopping to catch her breath, "I am doing my best to use my imagination, but this is not how things were done in the time of my poor father. What kind of hunt for penitent Béguines[18] have we here? We do not hear either the baying of the hounds or the neighing of the horses, or the cries of the lancers, or the joyful fanfare of the horns. The hunters lay huddled in the bushes like hares in their lairs, and even the most ardent risk falling asleep at their posts…. Good Lord! we functioned differently in those times. When we hunted in Mercoire, twenty horns sounded in all directions, a hundred hounds howled while following the traces of the beast, gentlemen in colorful uniforms galloped through the forest on their horses, gunshots were heard everywhere; It was a fracas, a movement, an

---

18   Béguines: Christian lay religious order of the 13th-16th century in Europe whose members lived in semi-monastic communities but did not take religious vows, which perplexed their contemporaries and created problems for the Church.

outburst which made you shiver with pleasure…. Oh! my poor father, my dear uncle Hilaire, where are you?"

And a tear trembled like a dew drop on the tip of Christine's long black eyelash.

"A plague on these memories which come at the wrong time!" thought the Baron.

However, smilingly, he resumed:

"Patience, Miss! You forget that this is a simple hunt, not a mounted hunt with hounds as in your honored father's Day…. However, if you like that style of hunting and its diversions which once provided such animation in Mercoire," he continued, moving closer to her, "have you thought Miss, that it only depends on you to see the rebirth of those wonderful days?"

"And how so, my dear Baron?" asked Christine, whose freedom of spirit, allowed her to pass quickly from one sentiment to another.

"Well, by God! By marrying a hunter!"

Miss de Barjac pouted.

"Ah, Baron," she said with humor, "you, whom I do not distrust, are you going to tease me too?"

"You would therefore have a certain repugnance to marrying a brave gentleman, bon vivant, intrepid hunter who loves you with all his heart and…"

"I just do not know."

"Perhaps," resumed Laroche-Boisseau with irony, "perhaps you might prefer a pale young man, a smooth talker, confined in his books and his devotions, who had never touched a rifle or a hunting knife, and spent his time making beautiful speeches on many subjects? Young damsels are often smitten with tenderness for these timid *lambs* who have escaped from the jaws of a wolf…"

Christine interrupted him impatiently:

"Sire Baron," she said proudly, "I will not pretend to misunderstand you. Why do you attribute me with sentiments of preference for… for the person to whom you have just alluded?"

"Do not become angry, Miss; God is my witness that I hope that I am mistaken; however how else can one interpret the extraordinary emotion you displayed at the arrival of Prior Bonaventure's nephew, your grief at the sight of a few miserable scratches, the sentiment which pushed you to carrying the young man in your arms and all this in full view of everyone at the chateau?"

"Ah!" resumed Miss de Barjac, with agitation, "is this how people judge a simple humanitarian reaction? I thought as much, and for this reason, this morning I… Listen, Baron, I will be frank with you. I feel towards this young man, who is for me a childhood friend, respect and friendship which I do not need to hide. One may think what one wishes, but one should consider that he is not of my rank, and that he is the protégé of persons whose domination I have always impatiently accepted. That said, forget the absurd suppositions and the stupid remarks. I worry about them like last year's snow."

"Decidedly, she does not love him!" thought the Baron.

However, almost immediately the idea came to him that Christine could be lying to him, or more likely, to herself.

"However, yesterday I obtained some information about Sire Léonce," he resumed with insistence, "and I am assured that your manner towards him is strange…. Your affectation of not informing yourself about his condition after taking such a compromising interest…."

"Eh! Was I not right that one could interpret against me this innocent action?... However, it is true, Laroche-Boisseau," added Christine, with a sort of abandon, "that in the presence of Léonce, I feel an embarrassment, a discomfort that no other person in the world generates in me. He has always shown me a great affection; but he is so reasonable, so rigid, that I am more afraid of death than his disapproval."

This naïve confession was not to Laroche-Boisseau's liking, and he responded in a pitying tone:

"I see it, Christine, poor child, you are already suffering under the influence of the powerful intrigues which surround you and the importance of which perhaps you do not suspect! These monks, who appropriated for themselves an absolute control over you, wish to sacrifice your happiness for their ambitious projects, and they have surely hatched some secret plot where your inexperience will entrap you. It is not without a good reason, believe me, that this young man, their creature, finds himself continually in your path; They have cleverly used the impressions that he could have on you and this dark conspiracy seems to be approaching success. This nephew of the astute Prior Bonaventure has found a place in your heart which is greater than you think; he knows it and I can bear witness to his smugness."

"What are you saying, Baron?" she asked; "has Léonce boasted, in your presence, of a preference… of a preference on my side? I beg of you, on your honor as a gentleman, to answer me frankly."

"I cannot affirm that he boasted in an outright manner," replied Laroche-Boisseau hypocritically, "but I could observe that this insolent commoner holds, towards you, audacious hopes, which your indulgence towards him seem to justify."

Miss de Barjac remained quiet; she felt a violent internal agitation. Finally, she dominated her feelings, and replied drily:

All these suppositions do not make sense…. Mordieu? One does not use me without my consent, and if someone dared… but really, Baron," she continued, turning her anger towards Laroche-Boisseau himself, "how can you allow yourself to torment me on such a subject? How can this concern you, please?"

The Baron thought the occasion suitable to take one more risk.

"Christine, Christine," he said, making his voice and gaze as passionate a look as possible, "how can you ask me this?"

This time, Miss de Barjac lowered her eyes and blushed. After a brief silence, she exclaimed:

"The hell with all this sentimental foolishness!... Are we here to discuss sentimentalities? A Lieutenant of the Louveterie who interrupts a great hunt to utter a stream of nonsense to a woman!... Let us go after the wolf! Sambleu!... We have already wasted too much time."

She resumed climbing the mountain at a rapid pace, and the Baron followed, satisfied, and full of hope. First, Christine had not been angered by his relatively clear confessions; furthermore, his malicious insinuations regarding Léonce made quite an impression on the proud young girl. As he was celebrating his success, Miss de Barjac asked:

"Baron, did you take care to post one of your best shooters at the Creux-au-Sangliers?[19]"

And she pointed with her hand to a profound crevice in the side of the mountain.

"I… I do not believe so," replied Laroche-Boisseau.

"That is a mistake, then. My people should have told you that this ravine is a known refuge for all the animals hunted in Bois-Brûlé when they want to escape to the main forest; it was one of the most important places to watch. My poor father knew it well. For all the shooting hunts, he reserved this spot for himself. He killed several wild boars there which is why this ravine bears that name.

"You could, dear Christine, teach a thing or two to many hunters who think themselves quite capable," replied the Baron. "However, at the time that Creux-les-Sangliers had such importance, perhaps the layout was a little different. For example, perhaps the forest came up to the edge of the crevice, whereas now there is an open space of a hundred or so paces. A large animal trying to reach the ravine would inevitably be seen by the shooters at the fringe of the woods."

"Well, do you not think that a clever wolf, as this beast is said to be, might have the idea of crawling on its stomach, taking advantage of the fog, as a means of reaching Creux-aux-Sangliers. I assure you that it has accomplished things more difficult than that."

Laroche-Boisseau examined the countryside carefully in order to evaluate the soundness of Christine's theory.

---

19   *Creux-aux-Sangliers*: translation—Wild Boar Ravine.

"In truth, Miss," he resumed, with real or feigned admiration, "your wisdom astounds me…. Indeed, it is not impossible that the wolf executed such a maneuver, and I should have thought earlier about thwarting it…. Unfortunately, it is too late; all our shooters are in place and await impatiently for my signal. Unless you and I, we take the post of guarding Creux-aux-Sangliers…."

"Yes, yes, that's it," exclaimed Christine, clapping her hands with the joy of a child; "what joy, my dear Baron, if you succeeded in killing this terrible beast of Gévaudan which is ravaging my domain these past three months, harming and killing my retainers and friends…"

"And who almost devoured the *lamb* of the good Fathers!" said the Baron laughing as he completed Christine's phrase.

Miss de Barjac could not help smiling; however, she lifted her finger to keep Laroche-Boisseau from pursuing that subject, and rapidly resumed:

"Well, let us hurry; I know of an excellent position, a sort of hut, built in the ravine by one of my old herdsmen who we called Jeannot Grandes-Dents. This man, overwhelmed by poverty, was one of these mountain dwellers from Mézenc, whose character, as we both know, is intractable and fierce. However, he was happy in this dreadful lair, where he lived like a savage; He barely travelled down to the chateau more than once a year. This perpetual solitude final affected his reason and he almost lost his ability to speak. The flock that we had entrusted to him wandered on its own. Each day, several animals were lost or had strayed. Moreover, Jeannot Grandes-Dents was so bad-tempered that he could not meet with our people without mistreating them. Things went so far that he became a local terror. Tired of hearing continual complaints and lamentations about him, I decided to get rid of him. Jeannot was not born on my land so I did not owe him any special considerations. Finally, about three months ago, after I was told about another of his acts of brutality, I came up here with two of my guards, since the cowards did not dare handle the matter without me. We chased Jeannot out of his hut, with a warning not to return, or even set foot again in my forests. He left, snarling, but since then I have heard nothing further about him. However, we are going to the miserable dwelling he built for himself, and, if I am right, it is admirably placed for the execution of my plan."

"And you do not know whatever became of that lout?"

"Bah! He certainly returned to his Mézenc mountains, which should never have left…. We are much more peaceful since he left, except for the cursed wolf. By the Devil! "Christine interrupted herself, radically changing her tone. "What is this?"

This sudden exclamation was torn from her by an unexpected discovery.

During the preceding conversation, they had arrived at the edge of the ravine, precisely opposite the hut previously occupied by Jeannot Grandes-Dents; and imagine the surprise and the anger of Miss de Barjac upon seeing the entry of the hut open and on the sill, the individual that they were just discussing!

Jeannot Grandes-Dents was a robust peasant, around fifty years old, whose exterior appearance inspired disgust and fear. He was of colossal size, but gaunt and emaciated; his face bony and swarthy with scaly patches giving it a bestial air. His large mouth, which was always open, with a hanging lower lip revealed long pointed yellow teeth which were at the origin of his name. His wild and haggard eyes were half hidden under bushy eyebrows; his coarse grey hair was disheveled as was his unkept beard. His only clothing was a shirt made of burlap and pants of the same cloth that did not cover his legs which were hairy, black and rough-skinned. He represented a hideous degradation of the human species, and any other woman than the courageous Christine de Barjac would have fled in terror at the sight of this dreadful brute, perhaps as dangerous as his appearance was repugnant.

At the moment that the chatelaine and Laroche-Boisseau appeared on the opposite side of the divide, Jeannot Grandes-Dents was, as we said, at the entry of the hut. His two hands were on the ground, in the well-known posture of the larger species of apes. He remained motionless, his eyes fixed on the other end of the ravine which ran down towards Bois-Brûlé. At the sound created by the arrivals, he raised his head; however, his initial movement did not seem to come from fear. On the contrary, he shook his immense crop of hair defiantly and made a low growling sound similar to that of an angry bulldog.

Christine, on her side, showed no signs of alarm at these menacing demonstrations. The horror inspired in her by this hideous creature as well as the sentiment of unrecognized authority excited her entire nervous system. She responded with energy in speaking to Jeannot Grandes-Dents:

How do you dare, you scoundrel, to appear again before me, despite my orders? What are you doing here? Did I not tell you that if you had the audacity to set foot on my domains again, I would treat you like an enraged beast?... I will find out which of my guards tolerated your presence in my forests and did not alert me; it is probably Fargeot, that cursed drunkard! Fargeot will pay for this. Well! Did you not hear me? Leave at once! I order you, and do not return!"

However, Jeannot did not move; one would have said that Christine's words did not get through to his intelligence or that his intelligence was too slow to understand. He continued to emit low growls and appeared to prepare an attack on the courageous young girl. Laroche-Boisseau hurriedly loaded his rifle.

"Take care, Miss," he exclaimed; "this peculiar character is the most dangerous looking individual I have ever seen, and he could be capable…"

"Stay out of this, Baron," responded Christine with authority, while still also arming her rifle. "For God's sake, let me handle things…. This scoundrel will not intimidate me, and I know how to be mistress of my lands."

Then once again addressing Jeannot Grandes-Dents:

"Go away!" she said in an irritated tone; "you have done too much damage here for me to consider you for any indulgence or pity…. Go away and that I never see you again…. Bloody Hell! Is it to defy me that you look at me this way?"

And she brought her rifle up to her cheek.

The sight of the weapon aimed in his direction stirred Jeannot Grandes-Dents out of his immobility. He began leaping from place to place with prodigious agility without coming nearer. While he was proceeding with these strange gymnastics, he spoke in a mountain dialect:

"All the hunters came here… all of them… all!... But the wolf is not afraid! The wolf will tear them up with its long teeth…. The wolf is clever, the wolf is powerful…. The wolf is not afraid of the hunters!"

He accompanied these words, barely intelligible, with a halting and compulsive laugh. Christine could not help feeling a slight shiver; however, she resumed with her rifle still at her cheek:

"Do not abuse my patience, and run…. Run away, now! Or by the Devil, I will kill you without mercy!"

This time, the madman seemed to understand what was expected of him. He slowly retreated, but without turning his back, and said with his strange accent:

"The wolf goes away when the hunters arrive, but it will return, at night, when the others are sleeping…. It will devour the young girl…. It likes it when there are many dead and there is much blood, the wolf!"

He added, after a short pause:

"Here they come! Here they come!... Into the forest, quickly, into the forest!... Here they come!"

And he began following the edge of the ravine to enter the main forest. He was making enormous leaps, travelling with as much ease on his hands as on his feet. It was difficult to recognize a human creature in this agile body that seemed to fly over the rocks and shrubs. Christine, obeying an undefinable feeling, pressed the trigger of her rifle just as Jeannot was about to round a bend in the ravine. The shot went off, but a peal of laughter accompanied this hostile act, and when the smoke from the explosion cleared, the maniac was no longer in sight.

"You missed him," said the Baron; "the fact that the wretch was travelling at such a speed…"

"Do you really think I was aiming at him?" replied Christine impatiently. "What would have been the use of killing the poor fool…. No, no, I just wanted to instill enough terror in him to prevent his ever approaching me again; he gives me the same impression as that of a venomous reptile… But," she added, trying to listen, "what is that?"

A deafening noise had exploded from below.

"That is the hunt which has begun," replied Laroche-Boisseau. "They took your rifle shot as the signal that I was to give precisely from this place, and our people have begun to move forward…. Let us go, it is all for the best."

"Let us hasten to take our position!" said Christine impetuously; "now that that dreadful Jeannot has left the hut, we can place ourselves in ambush; and if anyone shoots the beast, I have the hope that it will be you."

While speaking, she lightly descended the bank of the ravine and headed for the hut. Laroche-Boisseau hesitated at first, as if the confidence which this innocent child showed towards him had awakened certain scruples; but this hesitation did not last long. Soon, a mocking smile crossed his lips, and he hurried to rejoin Miss de Barjac.

The hut, in reality, was a cavity in the rock, on which had been fabricated a rough façade made of mud and tree trunks. The interior did not contain any furniture except for a wooden chopping block destined to be used as a chair. No household utensils, no garments hanging on the walls were there to indicate a permanent residence. A carpet of ferns emitted a pleasant odor, but this rustic layer had not been used yet judging from the freshness and condition of these plants which most probably adorned the sides of the mountain a few hours earlier.

The hut, despite its bareness, was not repugnant in character; however, one unusual item struck the Baron and Christine. Laroche-Boisseau noticed, in a dark corner, a relatively voluminous object, the nature of which he could not identify. He pushed aside the material that hid it with his foot; it was a quarter of lamb, still covered by its wool.

"What?" he said, hurriedly pushing the bloody flesh into a fissure in the rock. "Is our friend Jeannot sharing the meals of the beast of Gévaudan?"

"Indeed, it is not impossible that this man has been living on the remains left by the wolf," said Christine, averting her eyes; "He is almost as ferocious as the animal itself…. "But," she added hastily," we have spent too much time on that vagabond…. The beaters are beginning to approach us; the beast is likely to pass by soon if it is fleeing their charge. I will therefore reload my rifle; and from the hut's window will be on the lookout for it."

"Do you really hope that with that child's toy you will kill the formidable wolf whose traces I found this morning? I guarantee that a bullet from that cute weapon would be flattened by its thick hide. If it is your great desire is to shoot the beast, then I will gladly pass you my large-gauge rifle that I loaded myself with a double charge."

"Thank you, Baron," exclaimed Christine, seizing the massive weapon that she had trouble lifting; "this is a hunter's devotion whose price I truly appreciate…. All my life, I shall never forget this sacrifice!"

She half-opened the hut's little window and placed the rifle so as to be able to easily fire upon anything coming down the ravine. Laroche-Boisseau contemplated her with passionate admiration.

"Dear Christine," he finally said, "nothing presses. The forest is vast with much undergrowth, and the beast will not leave it until it reaches its furthest extremity. Moreover, if it decides to break through, we will be alerted by the sounds of shooting and the cries of the hunters. Count on my experience and do not tire yourself by standing in front of that window and agree to rest yourself a bit. This race on horseback, the climb up the mountain must have fatigued you. For goodness sake, so sit down, if only for an instant."

Christine, indeed, did feel some weariness, and, furthermore, did not dare refuse the kind entreaties of her companion. Therefore, leaving the rifle leaning against side of the opening, she said with a mischievous air:

"Alright, I believe you, but if I miss the occasion to shoot the beast, I will not forgive you."

Laroche-Boisseau took her hand and led her to the wooden block, the only seat in the hut. As for himself, he settled at her feet on the aromatic ferns, and began contemplating her with impassioned eyes.

Miss de Barjac was not alarmed by this. She had removed her hat, and negligently rearranged the curls on her forehead that had been disturbed by the climb. After a short silence, the Baron spoke:

"Christine, dear Christine," he said, now carried away; "do you know that you are the most beautiful, the most fearless, the most courageous of women?"

Miss de Barjac, in turn, looked at him with good humor.

"Well, well! what has gotten into you?" she asked maliciously; are you also courting me with words? That is treason!"

"Oh, do not speak to me in such a mocking tone, Christine, charming girl!" exclaimed Laroche-Boisseau, covering her hands with kisses; "and since fate, or rather, my good star, has reunited us without witnesses, allow me to express how much I love you!"

Christine attempted, in vain, to free herself.

"Morbleu! Baron," she replied impatiently, "let me go…. I am not a prude; but I insist that one speaks to me from a distance, and one does not hinder my movements."

"You will not escape me, adorable girl.... Once again, it is my good star that places you in my power, in this solitary hut, far from any intruders or the indiscreet!"

"A thousand Devils! release me or I swear…"

"Do you think that you scare me with this hummingbird wrath? It makes you even more charming!... Christine, I love you!"

And he tried to kiss her. Miss de Barjac, outraged, attempted to push him away and cried out with her might, but her screams seemed to be drowned out by the din coming from the plains below.

Finally, however, she was able to free one of her hands and while attempting to push away this obsessed person who was attempting to violate her, she felt, under her fingers, the hilt of the hunting knife that he carried on his belt. Drunk with fury and fright, she pulled it from its sheath, and plunged it into the chest of Laroche-Boisseau.

The Baron gave a cry of pain. Horrified by her action, Christine stepped back several paces, still holding the bloody weapon. The colorful uniform of the Louvetier suddenly took on a crimson hue. Laroche-Boisseau was leaning against the wall of the hut.

"Well done, by my faith," he gasped with a bitter smile, "that is what comes of attacking a heroine!... I think, however, that I received what I deserved."

And he sagged onto the floor; Christine fled.

We know how, on leaving the hut, she encountered the Knight de Magnac and Legris, still shaken up by the charge of the beast of Gévaudan, and one can explain the words she spoke to them.

Magnac first had the thought of following his young mistress who was fleeing down the mountain with the speed of the wind, but Christine's bewildered look, her disturbing words, the bloody knife that she had thrown at his feet, made him think that it was perhaps more useful for him to find out exactly what happened. Therefore, he hastened to pick up the knife and rejoined Legris who had just entered the hut.

They found Laroche-Boisseau huddled on the floor trying with a handkerchief to staunch the blood that was flowing abundantly from the wound. While the knight was taking an investigating look around the hut, Legris had leaned towards his friend and asked with horror:

"Good Lord! my dear Baron, what happened? Did that damned girl…"

"As you see, my poor Legris" replied Laroche-Boisseau, "many go out for wool and come home shorn.... Upon my soul, I have been nicely served!"

Legris helped him as much as was within his power.

In the meantime, the Knight de Magnac continued his investigation. Upon seeing Miss de Barjac's hat, which remained on the floor, guessed the truth, and murmured while shaking his head:

"I knew that sooner or later something like this would happen.... If you do not flee trouble, you can expect to be troubled.... Well, maybe now *she* will believe me!"

Legris had managed to bandage the Baron's wound. The latter resumed speaking, still trying to jest:

"Morbleu! Master Legris, you are taking care of me as if you knew that if I were dead, your father would have a difficult time getting himself reimbursed of my letters of credit.... Speak of a creditor to be treated and pampered wonderfully!"

"Your wound must not be too serious, Laroche-Boisseau, because you still have the strength and courage to laugh about it.... But in the name of humanity, Sire Knight" continued Legris addressing Magnac, "will you not help bring comfort to my unfortunate friend? The hunt is a failure, and the beast must now be out of reach. Hasten to find the nearest hunters; among them should be some surgeons; have them warned without delay.... Come, Sire, abandon your apathy, if this is possible; the circumstances are worth the effort. What the Devil! Is it not for you to repair the damage caused by your arrogant mistress; that Devil in skirts, that..."

"Silence! Master Legris," interrupted the knight in a menacing tone; "are you forgetting of whom you are speaking, and to whom you are speaking?"

He continued after a pause:

"I will go get some help, and we will transport Sire Baron to the chateau, as we cannot act otherwise without giving rise to disagreeable conjecture. However, first, let us agree please. Sire Baron was wounded by NO ONE: Sire Baron wounded HIMSELF by falling on his hunting knife.... Provide the details as you wish, but anyone giving another cause of this accident will be contradicted by me in a clear and categorical manner."

"Eh, how can we possibly admit..."

"Sire Knight de Magnac is right," said Laroche-Boisseau in a weak voice; "we must tell the story as he wishes. I will be too ridiculed if the truth is known on this stupid affair."

"Perfect, Sires," resumed the knight coldly, "this point resolved, we have to agree on another issue. I dare hope that the Sire Baron's wound is not a mortal one, and the day that he is healed, I will ask him the honor of joining me on the *pré*,[20] so that we can settle certain affairs in the manner of persons of quality. It should be easy to find pretext to avoid denigrating

---

20   Sur le *pré:* term used at that time meaning go to the meadow to do battle, or fight a duel.

anyone of honor and worthy of respect. I make this request in advance, so that Sire de Laroche-Boisseau, the moment arrived, will accord me this privilege in preference to another."

The Baron himself, could not help smiling in receiving this impetuous challenge to a duel.

"If you insist," he replied. "I will not deny you this pleasure in due time and place, be assured.... However," he added immediately, holding back with difficulty a groan, "I fear that you may never have the satisfaction of having me before you with sword in hand."

"I would infinitely regret that, Sire Baron."

"Ah!" exclaimed Legris with impatience, "is there any sense in proposing a duel to an unfortunate wounded man?"

Magnac turned towards the young bourgeois, and deserting the forms of politeness, which to his thinking, could only be used with a gentleman, he resumed in a disdainful tone:

"As for you, Master Legris, we should also meet again. I will give you all the time necessary to look after for your friend; however as soon as your aid is no longer needed, I count on your coming to see me to ask for the continuation of the story on the battle of Fontenoy.... I have interesting information to communicate to you on the manner, in the marshal's army, we rid ourselves of the insolent bourgeois who slipped in among us.... Until then, take care to not get in my way; this is charitable advice which I offer you."

He left with a majestic stride, leaving Legris subject to a double anxiety, for the Baron, and for himself.

Several moments later, a throng of hunters, informed about the alleged accident that had just occurred, arrived at the hut in the Creux-des-Sangliers. Laroche-Boisseau was now unconscious, and the doctors who examined his wound all declared it to be extremely serious.

After having bandaged the Baron better than Legris had been able to do, he was placed on an improvised stretcher and they began the task of transporting him to the chateau.

However, the Knight de Magnac, having given the first orders, did not further concern himself about the Baron; all his attention now was on his young mistress as he remembered her distress and bewilderment. He descended to the Quatre-Coins, where Christine had left her horse; the servants told him that she had returned and taken it a few moments earlier, and that she had plunged into the forest without allowing anyone to accompany her. Magnac then went to the chateau; Miss de Barjac was not there, but Buch had just entered the stable, by itself, with its bridle dangling. Increasingly concerned, Magnac ran into the woods asking for news from the numerous hunters who were dispersing after this useless and ill-fated event.

None had seen Miss de Barjac. The poor knight was besides himself; time was passing, night was already falling, a storm was imminent and Miss de Barjac was nowhere to be found.

Chapter IX

THE GUARD FARGEOT

The morning of the same day, Léonce awoke refreshed and without fever in the room he occupied in Mercoire. Thanks to the attentive care by the house staff, and especially that of the worthy nun, his wound was well on the way to healing, and except for the loss of blood, he was hardly feeling the effects.

But if his body was in a satisfactory condition, the same could not be said for his spirits. The strangeness of the situation, the revelations of his uncle, and on top of all that, certain recent memories, were keeping the young man in a constant state of agitation. At times he remained silent and dreamy; then he would overwhelm his care-givers with inconsequential questions, but which must have had some hidden purpose. Perhaps this purpose was not a mystery for the Prior and for Sister Magloire herself, as they exchanged knowing looks each time Léonce posed a question which was too direct. The latter noticed this, and it only increased his agitation. Soon, he spoke of getting up, of going down to the salon, of participating in the hunt. In vain, they explained to him the danger of all movement before the wound was seriously healed, but he did not want to hear it. Finally, to calm him, they agreed to let him get dressed provided he agree not to leave his room and that he would remain in a chair in front of a window that faced out on the main courtyard of the chateau.

They found a change of clothing in Léonce's bag as those that he had worn had suffered greatly during his misadventure in the forest. The good Prior offered to serve as valet for his adopted child, and when the young man was dressed, and Sister Magloire had fashioned a sling for his arm, they installed him near the window. He appeared pleased to look out at the movements of the crowd below.

Prior Bonaventure and Sister Magloire took advantage of this moment to descend to the salon where other urgent duties required their presence, and they left Léonce to his peaceful observations.

When the Prior returned alone an hour later, his nephew, an excited expression on his face, was pacing back and forth emotionally. Upon seeing the Prior, Léonce ran over to him and said in a choked voice:

"My uncle, my dear uncle, I beg of you, take me away from here....

I am well now; I can travel…. Please, do not retain me any longer in this place, if you do not wish to see me die of anger and grief!"

And he collapsed in tears.

Prior Bonaventure, as surprised as he was distressed by this unexpected reaction, forced Léonce to return to his chair.

"What has happened, my child?" he asked with kindness. "You were so calm a short time ago! Where does this violent and sudden reaction come from?"

The young man opened his mouth as if to confess something, but a secret sentiment prevented him from doing so, and he lowered his head, sobbing. The Prior sat down next to him:

"Come now, Léonce," he continued. "Speak frankly. Have you lost confidence in me, your uncle, your best friend? Who spoke with you during my absence?"

"No one, my uncle."

"Then, what did you see out this window to upset you so?"

"Nothing, nothing, my uncle, I assure you."

Prior Bonaventure gazed at him with a mixture of kindness and inquiry; Léonce submitted to this examination with visible discomfort.

"Alright, I understand!" finally resumed the monk, smiling, "you saw that young scatter-brained girl, Miss de Barjac, leave with the Baron de Laroche-Boisseau, and you were shocked by the apparent familiarity between them; is that not so?"

"And why would I be surprised or angry at what the Lady of the chateau is doing?" asked Léonce in a dry tone without lifting his eyes; what do I care if it pleases Miss de Barjac to flirt and traipse through the woods in the company of a lecher as the Baron is said to be?... However, my uncle," he continued in a different tone, "should the ward of the abbey of Frontenac conduct herself in such a compromising manner? Do you not have complete authority over this impudent young lady until the time of her marriage? And can you accept…"

"Now, now! my child," interrupted the Prior softly, "do not forget that this poor Christine cannot be judged under the common rules. She committed an impropriety yesterday evening which was even greater in carrying you in her arms in spite of the barely hidden smiles of all the habitants of the chateau, and you have not thought of complaining about that. Miss de Barjac is an honest person, full of righteousness and energetic enough to impose the respect of anyone attempting to bother her."

"Do you think so, my uncle? Are you forgetting the threats he made yesterday when he said that in spite of you, in spite of the whole world, he wanted to make himself loved by Miss de Barjac? Did he not openly defy you to prevent him from doing this? And he was right, Reverend Father;

yes, he was right, as she already loves him.... She loves him, I assure you. I can attest to the caressing looks she was giving him a short time ago, there, under my window: I can also attest to the pride and joy I saw on the facial expression of that insolent gentleman!"

Hiding his brow in his hand, he once again gave way to sobs. The monk seemed torn between indulgent pity and sentiments of a different nature.

"Come now, my dear Léonce," he resumed with embarrassment, "do not torment yourself this way.... As you said yourself a while ago, what is the importance of the way Miss de Barjac acts?... But no," he added, immediately retracting his words, "it is very important to you, I am sure; you convince me that I should tell you things that perhaps I should not say.... Do not be discouraged; whatever inexperience I have in such matters, I believe that Miss de Barjac does not love the Baron de Laroche-Boisseau...."

He stopped. Léonce was struck with surprise; his tears suddenly dried.

"My uncle," he exclaimed, while his heart pounded, "explain yourself, I beg of you!"

"I cannot explain myself further," replied the Prior; I can only repeat that in spite of the frivolous appearances, Miss de Barjac does not love Sire de Laroche-Boisseau, and even if she did, the detestable behavior of the Baron, the lamentable state of his fortune and especially his religion presents between them unsurmountable obstacles. No, never will our beautiful and rich ward become the prey of such a man; and this suitor eliminated, the field is open to all the other reasonable pretenders."

"And among these reasonable pretenders," asked Léonce breathlessly, would you include a poor child, without a birthright, a stranger to this world, who dared raise his sights to this noble and rich heiress?"

"And why not, Léonce," said the Prior Bonaventure calmly.

The young man threw his arm around the neck of the Prior.

"Would this be possible, my friend, my benefactor, my father?" he exclaimed, carried away; "is it truly you, always so prudent, so wise, who is speaking in this manner? The thought came to me yesterday, I do not quite know why, that my love was not a secret for you, and that perhaps you had seen it develop without anger.... My uncle, tell me the truth, what can I hope for? What can I believe? Could I, indeed, aspire, without impertinence, to the hand of this charming Christine?"

"Well, yes, Léonce," replied the monk with practice, "you have not wanted to understand until now my hints and my reluctances, but since you are pressuring me this much, know this; there is not as much distance as you think from my nephew to the only child and heiress of the Count de Barjac."

"Then, it is true? It is you, you my uncle, who encourages me in these absurd and audacious hopes?"

"Do not have any illusions, my child," replied the Prior, shaking his head, "and again be careful before going too far.... Everything depends on certain events, and in particular the will, the capriciousness perhaps, of Miss Christine. Indeed, we can prevent our intractable ward from making the wrong choice, but we do not have the right to impose on her the choice which we have made. It is for those who deem themselves worthy to inspire in her sentiments of esteem and affection; and if one must admit it, Léonce, in my opinion, you have a better chance than anyone to succeed."

"On this single hope, my uncle, I am prepared to risk all my future, all my happiness; I believed that Miss de Barjac felt a remoteness for me and I thought... But I was wrong, no doubt. I take your word, certain that you cannot be mistaken, that you would not lie to me.... Oh! Christine, dear Christine! I am thus allowed to love you, without fear and without remorse."

The Prior, in his smooth and persuasive voice, attempted to calm the young man and bring him back to a more reserved state of mind in his thinking. He made him understand that there could be a number of difficulties that could hinder the realization of his wishes. Léonce hardly listened. The new day which enlightened his naïve love, after so much obscurity and so many secret fears, delighted him. However, his uncle had begun to have him envisage, in a calmer manner, the possible consequences of this passion, when someone knocked softly at the door, and Sister Magloire, to Léonce's great regret, interrupted their discussion.

The nun seemed embarrassed.

"My Reverend Father," she said, almost in a hushed voice, "there is downstairs a man named Fargeot, an old tenant from Varinas, whom you named chief guard of the forest of Mercoire.... He should have participated with the others in the hunt, but he excused himself because wanted to speak with you about an affair which he says is extremely urgent. I argued in vain that you were overwhelmed by other activities, that you had our accounts to review and that the illness of your nephew was taking all your available time; but he would not hear of it, and he took an almost menacing tone with me. He so intimidated me that I could not help but put him in the yellow salon, where he awaits you."

"You have done well, my sister," replied the Prior rising suddenly; indeed, it is necessary that I see Fargeot.... Tell him not to be impatient. I will come straight away."

Sister Magloire was greatly astonished by the deference given by an important dignitary of Frontenac to a forest guard; but she made no comment; and after having bowed deeply, she left to carry out the Prior's orders.

"Léonce," he resumed, "I was just telling you that there would be many obstacles to the execution of our projects; and perhaps here is a new one I had not counted upon.... Do not hasten to build up exaggerated hopes; the task of your happiness may be difficult.... Take courage, however, and let us place our confidence in God."

And he left the room with visible concern.

Léonce, now alone, indulged himself for a few moments, in his pleasant thoughts despite the concerned warnings of the Prior, then he returned to his observations out the window; however, now the courtyard was deserted and the chateau itself seemed abandoned. A feverish impatience overtook Léonce.

"She is not returning," he murmured; "where can she be?... Undoubtedly with the Baron who is overwhelming her with compliments and flattery!... What if my uncle has misjudged the feelings that Miss de Barjac has for that proud seducer? The Prior is very experienced, but I doubt that in such a matter... "Oh! if this was true."

He paced around the room with rapid strides.

"Ah!" he exclaimed, as if stuck by an idea, "why would I not go myself and judge what is going on? I feel well and my strength has returned.... It should be easy for me to approach the lovely and capricious Christine without being seen! Yes, yes, that is it; I am going! My uncle will not be back soon; moreover, if he does not find me, he will certainly guess where I could be.... I want to see again that dear Christine, whom I am finally allowed to love!"

He descended the main staircase without being seen, and reached the inner courtyard which served as a riding arena. On that side, the grill's gate facing directly into the woods was wide open to facilitate passage for the hunters, and Léonce, trembling with impatience, joy and perhaps jealousy, plunged rapidly into the forest.

In the meantime, the Prior went to the salon where the guard was waiting. This room, furnished with old pieces of furniture and covered with velvet colored in Utrecht yellow, which gave it its name, served as an office for keeping the accounts of the domain. It was filled with labeled storage boxes and registers with copper latches, well known to the farmers who were late in their payments. Here were normally found the Knight de Magnac and Sister Magloire who shared the administration of the chateau when their services were not required by Miss de Barjac.

The attention of the Prior was first focused on the person whose visit had been announced. Fargeot, the chief guard of the Mercoire forest, was reaching sixty; he was fat, short and his corpulence seemed about to cause his handsome green uniform with gold shoulder strap, worn for the occasion, to explode. His bloated face, covered with pimples, attested to the habits of a drunkard; however, his grey eyes did not yet indicate the stupor that this passion often brings, and were sometimes sparkling with intelligence. Without taking notice of the nun, who in the hierarchy of the cha-teau, had a rank much higher than his own, Fargeot had installed himself in an armchair which threatened to break under his enormous weight, and he negligently played with an ivory-headed cane.

In spite of his shameless manners, the guard, upon seeing the Prior, attempted to get up on his elephant-like legs, but he fell back heavily; a second similar effort was equally fruitless. Bonaventure smiled and made him a sign to remain sitting.

"Good day, Fargeot," he said in a friendly tone; "you seem to be flour-ishing, if I am right… God forgive me! You seem to have gained weight since the last time I saw you, and I did not think that would be possible!"

He took a seat opposite the guard; the latter gave up on his desperate attempts to stand up.

"Well! my Reverend Father," he replied in a hoarse voice, "since you allow…. I am no longer very spry. There is so much work here! One must run night and day after those poachers and wood thieves; the constant exer-cise fortifies one more than one might want."

"I would have thought," said Sister Magloire, bitterly, "that idleness rather than fatigue would have produced such a result. Whatever you say, Master Fargeot, the poachers and the thieves do not keep you from sleep-ing. You are always crammed into the Cransac wine tavern, and your poor daughter, Marion, remains alone in the lodge in Mare. Even at this moment, you do not appear sober, and the Reverend Father can observe it as I do; I leave it to him to judge if this is a behavior suitable for chief guard of the Mercoire forest."

Fargeot, indeed, had stopped at the tavern prior to coming to the cha-teau, and drunkenness, as well as his corpulence, prevented him from standing on his legs; however, perhaps Bonaventure had his reasons for not addressing the conduct of the guard, and he simply shook his head with indulgence. On the other hand, Fargeot showed great irritation over the criticisms of Sister Magloire; his face went from red to a deep crimson. He breathed in a large gulp of air, at the risk of splitting his ceremonial uniform thanks to the dilation of his vast chest.

"And how does this concern you, you *beguine*?" he asked in his dull and furry voice; "what do you care about the conduct of the guards? I take my orders only from Miss de Barjac, our mistress, and the Reverend Father, here present; as for the others, knights or nuns, I could not care…"

"Peace!" interrupted the Prior; "what is this! Fargeot, are you lacking in respect for the good Sister Magloire?... And you, my sister, are you for-getting that one must forgive much to an old retainer like Fargeot?"

"Jesus, my God!" replied Sister Magloire in an unctuous tone, "I will forgive all that you wish. Your Reverence knows only too well how one must act, and as you rule against me, I have nothing more to say. However, if we had rid the domain of a slacker, a drunkard, who is a subject of scandal…"

"Enough! Sister Magloire, a little charity…."

"Get rid of me!" exclaimed the large Fargeot, thrashing about in his chair like a man possessed.; "you hear her Reverend Father? Tell her that one does not dismiss me in such a manner; that I will be here on the lands of Mercoire long after she has been chased away herself…. Yes, yes, tell her that, Father Prior; I *insist* that you tell her!"

"What?" said the Prior, throwing him a fearsome look.

Intimidated, the guard stammered some excuses.

"That suffices," resumed Bonaventure; "dear sister, leave me a moment with Master Fargeot. As you have noticed, he is not quite himself today, and this must excuse, up to a point, his misuse of words; but I will speak with him, and undoubtedly will inspire in him repentance for his error."

"God willing! my Reverend Father," replied the nun in a sullen tone.

She left the room. As soon as she had gone, Prior Bonaventure pulled closed the latch on the door; then, returning to his seat, said with severity:

"What is the meaning of this conduct, Master Fargeot? How do you dare raise your voice in this manner? Are you incorrigible? Age cannot surmount these terrible vices which have already caused your misfortune and that of your family? This is bad, Fargeot, very bad; if you do not mend your ways, I shall withdraw my favors!"

Initially, the guard had lowered his head in confusion listening to these merited reproaches, but the menace produced a completely different reaction.

"Withdraw my favors, my Reverend Father? He replied twisting his mouth in a sarcastic manner; "you should think twice before using harshness on an old friend!"

"Do not rely on it, Fargeot, for some time now, numerous complaints have been coming in about you, and if these continue, despite the memories of your good wife, and despite my interest in your innocent daughter, who I know you upset greatly, I will send you out of the domain, and you will be on your own."

"So! Is that the way it is Reverend Father?" replied the guard, puffing out his chest, "you should not be so hard with a man who knows what I know! On my side, I have been wanting to speak with you in person for a long time, but each time that you have come to Mercoire, one would think that you made a point of hiding from me…. Today, at least, this will not be the case, and now that I have you, you will not escape me.!"

"Hide from you? Escape you? Ah! hear this, my man, have the wine spirits obscured your mind to the point that you have forgotten who you are speaking to?... However," added the monk in a calmer tone, "I must not let you think that the Prior of Frontenac is avoiding you due to fear or any other sentiment unworthy of him.... What is it that you have to say to me, Fargeot? Speak boldly, I am listening."

He straightened himself majestically. The guard, in spite of his assurance, looked uneasy:

"Now, now! my Reverend Father, let us not get angry," he said, finally, with a little friendly laugh. "What am I asking for? Only that we continue to get along, as in the past. And if I find you a little co-operative, you will never have to complain about me. Finally, you have always given me and mine your protection; continue to be good to us, and I will not be ungrateful, I assure you."

"This protection, how have you merited it, you personally? Your vices have only gotten worse with age, and if I had consulted my own indignation, I would have abandoned you to their consequences. However, you had long been in the services of the Count of Varinas; your wife, Marguerite, had been the wet-nurse of the young Viscount who died at such a young age under unfortunate circumstances; your daughter Marion was the foster sister of that poor child; for all these reasons a friend of the family of your old masters had to make some efforts to rescue you from disgrace and misery. Therefore, after the death of your wife, I had you leave Varinas where your actions had created universal feelings of contempt, and brought you here to be chief guard of the forest of Mercoire. I had hoped that, retired to the little chalet in the middle of the woods, far from your comrades in debauchery, you would change your life style, that you would flee bad influences. Instead, you persist in your disastrous habits. In spite of your monstrous corpulence which you owe to your incurable laziness, you travel a long distance each day to Cransac where you spend the money you have earned in its tavern. Your poor daughter is always alone in your lodge, and often, I am told, she is missing in necessities.... In good conscience, Fargeot, do you think that there is any consideration that would make me tolerate this for long? There is a moment when such indulgence becomes a crime."

"All right, all right you will continue to be indulgent. So be it; my Reverend Father, I give you this advice in your own interest.... I admit my faults; I am a good companion liking to laugh and drink; I am worthless as a guard, and I am bored to death in my lodge where one sees nothing except for wolves and boars. This cannot go on any longer. You would not refuse me an honest dowry for my daughter, Marion, who indeed is not very happy with me, the poor little one; this would assure me an income that I could use where I want; or rather pay me a one-time sum that I can dispose of as I wish, and you will no longer have to worry about me, I promise you."

"That is fine, Fargeot; you come directly to the point, I see.... Now, on what basis do you claim such favors?"

"Of course! I am, as you said a short time ago, an old retainer of Varinas; is it not just that the heirs to this beautiful domain help us meet our needs, mine and those of my family, now that old age and infirmities prevent me from working?"

Fargeot had a mocking tone and an impudence that was absolutely offensive. Nevertheless, the Prior answered with simplicity:

"It is not for me to either accept or reject your request; in my capacity as a monk, I possess nothing, and it is impossible for me to make a determination on an affair of this type without the opinion of the Chapter of the Frontenac Abbey, of which I am an just an unworthy member."

"Now, Reverend Father," replied the guard impatiently, "everyone knows that you manage the Chapter as you wish; with your airs of neutrality, you are now, thanks to your wardships and heritages, almost as powerful as the king in this province!... But I see where you are going; you want to gain time, then you will say that the Chapter rejected my request.... That will not work, I warn you."

"I have absolutely no intention of gaining time, Fargeot, and to prove it, I will tell you on the spot how the Chapter will function and how I would function myself; If you had always been irreproachable, perhaps the current owners of Varinas would have taken your distress under consideration; but handing out money that could be used for charity to a slacker and a drunkard who has been a bad husband, and is still a bad father..."

The guard made a furious shudder.

"A thousand devils!" he exclaimed, "do not push me too far! I may be all that you say, however at least I have not committed any CRIMES, like the saint personages that I will soon unmask if they do not show themselves more lenient with me."

Prior Bonaventure could not hide his discomfort.

"Crimes?" he repeated, growing pale; "Have you completely lost your senses, Master Fargeot?"

"Not in the least, Reverend Father, and to prove it, I will remind you of a little story which you seem to have forgotten.... However," he added, looking around him in a mocking manner, "I am a rather bad story-teller when I have nothing to humidify my throat and to facilitate flow of my words.... Is there nothing to drink here?"

The Prior remained stone faced.

"All right, no matter," resumed Fargeot, after a moment. "If one gives me nothing to refresh myself while I am speaking, I will be sure not to forget anything before I finish.... So, listen to me."

"You will remember, my Reverend, the circumstances that accompanied the tragic death of the little Viscount de Varinas, about sixteen or seventeen years ago. At that time, his father, Sire Count de Varinas, our Lord, was seriously ill with languor[21] disease, from which he later succumbed. He became somber, gloomy, morose; he no longer allowed himself to be approached by friends or his family, and finally, he retired to your abbey in Frontenac, where, according to what was rumored, he was carefully protected. The Count never did have a strong character, and now that he was exhausted, almost dying, exposed night and day to your solicitations, you had no problem in taking over his mind; it is said that even when his son was alive, he had ceded a part of his holdings in favor of your abbey, which was already so rich and powerful. But that portion did not seem to you to be sufficient, as one can later understand."

At this point, the Prior, indignant, rose suddenly and raised his arm to protest against these assertions being expressed with such rudeness; but a reflection, no doubt, stopped him short, because he sat back down, and let drop his arm while. smiling disdainfully. Fargeot continued untroubled:

"While the Sire Count lived in Frontenac, and they were waiting day-to-day for the fatal issue of the malady which was reputedly incurable, his only son, the little Viscount de Varinas, remained at the chateau, under the care of my wife Marguerite, his wet-nurse. The child was of weak and sickly temperament like that of his father. When he was three years old, people thought he was half that age. My wife, to whom the Countess had entrusted this innocent creature, did not leave him either night or day. She adored the infant, who had already begun stammering her name and following her tottering on the paths of the garden. However, on one occasion, her watchfulness failed her, and that negligence cost her all the tears in her eyes, and the results were truly disastrous."

"Marguerite has told the story of this tragedy so many times in my presence, that in spite of the fact that I was not at the chateau, where I was not greatly appreciated, I can tell the story in the most minute detail. It was a summer evening, in sweltering heat, near nightfall. My wife had allowed Babet, the sweet child, to go down to the village to visit her family. She had remained alone with the young Viscount in the little garden which leads to the terrace of the vegetable garden. You know as I do, Reverend Father, the layout of the Varinas chateau. It is built on a plateau which on one side is bordered by a chasm at the bottom of which flows a raging torrent. This chasm, is of a frightful depth, with walls spiked with crystals of basalt and forms the limiting edge of the garden. One of the ancient Lords had built a parapet over which one can peer to watch the frothing water. It is best not to go look over the edge if one has drunk a little too much, or if one suffers

---

21 Languor: a depressive state of the body or mind caused by exhaustion or disease and characterized by a languid feeling: lassitude. from Latin: *languor* (faintness, languor)

from vertigo, because the noise of the cascade, the turbulence of the foam, the points of the rocks which seem to move and dance, make your head spin; finally; sober or not, I stay away from that spot like the plague."

"Therefore, on the day of which we speak, Marguerite had chosen that garden for the child's recreation, hoping that on that hot evening, that the breeze from the nearby cascade would bring a little freshness. Besides, there was little risk on an accident; the soil had been carefully sprinkled with sand or covered with grass and flowers, and the parapet which bordered the abyss was in good condition and too high for a delicate child who barely walked to climb. Thus, Marguerite, sitting on a stone bench, did not lose sight of her young master while the latter, dressed in a white jacket, amused himself looking in the grass for pretty glowing bugs that shone like fire."

"Suddenly, a man, dressed like a local peasant, but who was not a member of the local domestic staff of the chateau, and who had never been seen before by Marguerite, appeared next to her in the garden, and spoke to her in a strange accent:

"Nurse, your little Marion just fell down over there in the courtyard; I heard her cries in passing; you had better go see how she is."

"Then, this man continued rapidly on his way and disappeared in the mist of the evening."

"Marguerite was very troubled; she wanted to pick up the child and bring him with her, but the Viscount, attached to his favorite game, started screaming; she put him back down on the grass, and he immediately quieted down. What to do? She was a mother first; Marguerite reflected that she would only be gone a minute or two, that her young master was busy with his fireflies, would not move; moreover, what danger could there be in this enclosed terrace. She no longer resisted these motherly concerns and went to the part of the chateau where she had been told that her own daughter had suffered an accident."

"Upon arriving, all out of breath, at the courtyard, she found Marion quietly playing with other children; she had not been hurt; she hardly took the time to kiss her little girl. What did this mysterious warning that she received signify? Seriously alarmed, without being sure why, she hastily returned towards the little Viscount."

"It was now getting dark. When she entered the garden, Marguerite thought that she heard a feeble cry that came from the other extremity. She quickened her pace and called out as loudly as she could; she received no response. She ran to the grassy spot where the child should have been, or where the whiteness of his jacket could have been seen from afar; the child was nowhere to be seen. Almost crazed with fright, Marguerite ran across the terrace, calling all the while; she found no trace of the dear little creature. However, at the foot of the parapet which borders the chasm, was the cap that the child had been wearing. No longer doubting a tragedy, the poor woman let out a wail and fell in a faint; she remained unconscious on the sand until the servants, worried by her absence, came to rescue her."

"You know as well as I do, my Reverend Father, what followed. The authorities came to the chateau; everyone was questioned and searches were launched. Finally, three days later, a small body was recovered from the torrent, mutilated and disfigured by being smashed against the rocks. By his white garments, they recognized the young Viscount de Varinas. It was declared that the unfortunate child had been thrown purposely into the abyss during the brief absence of his nurse."

While listening to this narrative, the Prior did not betray any sign of emotion. He soon resumed with a perfect calm:

"Ah! my friend, where are you going with this old story which is known by the entire community and with which I am more familiar than anyone? We were relatively easy on your wife in spite of her culpable negligence. On the contrary, we had pity on her suffering and her repentance; She, as well as yourself and your daughter, Marion, were granted many favors!"

"Aha! Perhaps we should have not been so grateful, my Reverend Father, as perhaps you had good reasons for that…. Initially, no one dared say what they thought about this extraordinary event; Marguerite herself, either because sadness troubled her mind, or that she feared some powerful hostility, kept quiet like the others. She confided her doubts to no one on the subject of the death of her young master, or at least I had no knowledge of any at that time; it was only later, when she had information not known by the authorities, that she dared explain before her death, that she could no longer resist the pangs of her conscience which obliged her to reveal the truth."

"What are you saying, Fargeot?" demanded the Prior, shuddering, "Are you speaking of revelations made by your wife only now? You had hidden from me until today information that was so important?"

"You would have known it already, my Reverend Father, if, since moving to Mercoire, I had been able to approach you as I have today; however, you kept me at a distance and I could not speak to you in front of strangers. However, remember that I made several allusions in your presence, and if I am not wrong, they had an effect on you…. Also, when I have finished, good Father Prior, you will see that you are particularly concerned in this villainous affair."

"I, Master Fargeot?" said the Prior, trying to smile.

"Patience! You will not laugh in a while, my Reverend Father; allow me to finish."

"When Marguerite calmed down sufficiently to reconsider this dreadful event, she became convinced that it was the result of a crime. A hundred times I heard her affirm that during her short absence, there had not been enough time for the little boy to reach the parapet, and besides that, the parapet was much too high for such a young infant to climb. She therefore did not have any doubt that an abominable murder had been committed by the unknown person who had given her false information to draw her away. As far as that man, she could not provide any information; the darkness and the broad brimmed hat which he wore did not permit her to see his features, and when speaking, he seemed to disguise his voice."

"All this is very vague, and Marguerite's conclusion had been based on suppositions, until an unexpected discovery confirmed it."

"At that epoch, I worked a tenant farm belonging to the Varinas domain and I had, as a farm helper, a mountaineer from Mézenc, whose brutality obliged us to send away later. His name was Jeannot; he was an uncouth fellow who frightened me, but Marguerite, thanks to her sweetness and patience, was the only one able to tame him at times. One day, long after the accident, Jeannot, seeing poor Marguerite lamenting again the loss of the unfortunate child entrusted to her care, confessed to her some singular information. The same evening that the young Viscount perished, Jeannot was returning from the fields, on the path leading to the small gate of the chateau. Tired by the day's work, he had lain down behind a bush to catch his breath, when he heard two persons who were rapidly approaching on the path below him, speaking in low voices. One of them had a large peasant's hat like the person that Marguerite had seen in the garden. In addition, he was completely enveloped in a large coat. His companion was dressed similarly; however, my helper recognized him; he was a monk from Frontenac who came often to Varinas, and it is not necessary to name him, my Reverend Father."

The Prior turned pale.

"You are telling me," he resumed, "that I, Prior of Frontenac, was recognized?"

"You were then a simple monk, my Reverend Father; but my helper had seen you several times at the chateau, and he was not mistaken. When you passed in front of the bush where he was hiding, he distinctly heard the other who was saying: "yes, yes, the infant must disappear; it is safer." Jeannot, who is of a dull nature and a bit stupid, did not at first understand the seriousness of these words; he did not move, and I suspect that he fell asleep. However, soon he was alerted by the new sound of steps on the path. It was you who was returning with the man wearing the large hat. You were walking very rapidly and no longer speaking. He tried again to examine you, but night had fallen and observation was becoming difficult. However, with the natural curiosity of a peasant, Jeannot got up and took several steps to see where you were going. At the bottom of the hill was a third person who was waiting with some horses. You each hastened to mount them and after a few minutes you were lost in the darkness.… This is what my helper, Jeannot, told me, and, certainly, there is nothing there which gives a favorable opinion of your saintliness."

Bonaventure seemed struck by consternation and dismay. After having reflected for a moment, as if measuring the extent of the danger, he resumed while trying to control the trembling of his voice:

"And this farm helper, this Jeannot, who recounts these marvelous and unbelievable things, does he still exist? You just said, I believe, that you had to send him away from your farm?"

"Indeed, we did send him away, and for several years we had no news about him, but I found him again nearby, and I see him frequently at my lodge; unfortunately, I must admit, the poor Jeannot has completely lost his reason."

"He is insane" exclaimed the Prior; and it is on the testimony of a madman that you attack a community which is powerful and respected?"

"However, Jeannot was sane when he spoke of his encounter with you; and Marguerite, who was educated and astute in writing and spelling like a bourgeoise, had the excellent idea of writing down all this affair on a paper which she signed. While she was dying of the malady which killed her, she wanted to destroy the note, but I, who knew what it contained, obtained it for future use."

At the same time, Fargeot flaunted a greasy wallet, which he immediately plunged into a pocket of his uniform.

"Now," he resumed, "you must be starting to understand, my Reverend Father, what this is all about. The declaration of my wife, my testimony and especially, that of my helper, Jeannot, although at this time, one cannot get much out of the poor devil, would surely interest certain judges.… It is said that times are not favorable for monks, and if we do not remain friends, we will perhaps see some havoc at Frontenac!"

And the guard began laughing with maliciousness.

"Is that all, Master Fargeot? asked the Prior, "You do not have any other accusations against me or the holy institution of which I am a member?"

"Eh! well my good Father, does it not seem to you that this is largely sufficient?"

"What? Do you persist in thinking that the abominable suppositions of a woman undoubtedly anxious to be forgiven for her negligence, or the testimony of a farm helper who became insane, and that of a lazy drunkard, could be used against so many men recognized for their virtue and piety?"

"Yes, I do think so, my Reverend Father; you have the reputation and the wealth to do some dirty tricks to impose my silence.… But if things become difficult, I intend addressing myself to an individual, who I am sure, can stand up to you!"

"And who would that be, Master Fargeot?"

"Ah, pardieu! Sire de Laroche-Boisseau, who just happens to be in Mercoire at this moment. He is the closest relative to the Count de Varinas, from whom he should have inherited the Domaine, if you had not interfered. His father had launched a lawsuit against your abbey, and he is not any more favorably disposed towards you. He belongs to the Protestant religion and he will not have any reason to proceed lightly against monks. If I told him one single word about Marguerite's confession or the testimony of Jeannot, he would not worry about rewarding a few hundred crowns to a poor man who could bring him such proofs. Moreover, it will not be easy to enforce his silence; he is one of the barons of the grand council, and he fears neither God nor Devil; he will sing you a psalm like you have never heard in the choir loft of your church…. Ah! ah! ah! my Reverend Father, I think that this is beginning to upset you!"

Indeed, the name of Laroche-Boisseau seemed to maximize the anguish of the Prior. Nevertheless, after taking a moment to collect himself, he resumed with a mixture of sadness and dignity:

"I know exactly where you are going with this, Fargeot. You want to take a chance on a scandal, and indeed no one can help you more than the Baron de Laroche-Boisseau in this vicious scheme. However, perhaps you believe in good faith, that in attacking us, you are seeking justice; I affirm to you then, by the most solemn oaths, that neither I, nor any other priest of Frontenac, have taken any part in the murder of that poor child; We have been deceived by misleading appearances and a series of fateful circumstances, but the day will surely come when our innocence will be as clear as the sun…. You will be inexcusable if you persist in these odious allegations, and you risk the punishment cited in the Gospels[22] which says; "Woe to him by whom scandal comes!"

Fargeot blinked his eyes.

"My God! Reverend Father," he resumed, "I am not as harsh as you may think. I am perfectly ready to believe that you are innocent, you and the other monks; I ask no better than to give you Marguerite's note, to burn it if you wish; I can promise to silence Jeannot and become mute, myself, like a fish, on this unfortunate affair…. But you understand, Father Prior? Give and take…. What the Devil! the monks of Frontenac who are so rich, who own so much forest, fields, ponds, farms and chateaux, can easily give up several thousand crowns to provide an endowment to my daughter and assure my tranquility for my old age! One must have a conscience, and really when I think of the damage that my revelations could cause, I do not think that my conditions are so bad."

22   Gospels: Luke 17.1

The Prior appeared really tempted. He had enough worldly prudence to understand that the best way to avoid the scandal being menaced was to submit to the demands of Fargeot, to stifle with a miserable sum of money the slanderous allegations against him and his community. He shuddered, especially, thinking about how this might profit Baron de Laroche-Boisseau, the mortal enemy of the abbey. However, there were other considerations that asserted themselves into his thinking. After pacing the salon for a minute, he returned to his seat opposite the guard, who having seen him hesitate, was already smiling triumphantly.

"Whatever happens," said the Prior courageously, "I will not accept, neither for myself, nor for the sainted house that I represent, this abominable transaction. I do not want, through weakness, to reward slander, greed and falsehood.... Fargeot, the benefits that you and yours have received since the death of the Count de Varinas had no other justification, I repeat, than your role as old retainers of the family. As proof, I absolutely refuse to grant you what you are asking with such insolence. Do what you wish with the document you have and the testimonies you have been able to gather; neither the Prior, nor the priests of Frontenac will lower themselves to paying for your silence."

The guard was not at all expecting this refusal; his face took on a look of great disappointment.

"Come now, Father Prior," he replied, "this cannot be your last word! There must be other things of importance to you other than the lands of Varinas.... I have never heard about monks being hanged, except perhaps at the time of the Huguenots; however, you should think about it, I think...."

"I do not need to think about it; I reproach myself for having listened to you this long, and to have put up with the insults which my sacred duties should have rejected earlier. Now leave here, leave my presence immediately and never present yourself before me again!"

The Prior gave this order with so much energy that, despite his corpulence, Fargeot stood up without effort.

"That suffices, Reverend Father," he stammered, "I am leaving, but you will regret having treated me so badly.... I will go find Sire de Laroche-Boisseau."

Bonaventure turned his back to him. The guard acted as if he was leaving; but when he neared the door, he turned suddenly towards the Prior and resumed in an almost supplicating tone:

"Now, Reverend Father, I was perhaps wrong to speak to you without moderation. What can I say? I was never taught proper manners, and I say things bluntly as they come to me; however, I did not want a falling out with you. Would there not be a way to reach an understanding? I know well that you do not like me, and I must admit that I am not worth much; but if you do not wish to grant me anything, at least do not refuse what I ask for my daughter, Marion.... My poor child, as you said, is not happy with me; she is terribly bored at the lodge where one sees no one, and I leave her alone perhaps too often. To make matters worse, she has fallen in love with the son of Jean Godard, a handsome boy, an excellent person and hard worker, who would be a perfect husband, but Jean Godard would never let his son marry a woman who has nothing. Marion knows this and continues to cry in secret. This dismays me.... I am sometimes mean, even brutal, but I love this poor little one and I would like to make her happy.... There, all things considered, Reverend Father, do not think of me; perhaps I do not deserve your favors; but promise me that you will give a dowry of five hundred ecus to Marion so that she can marry the son of Jean Godard, and I will immediately tear up, before your eyes, Marguerite's note."

This new language seemed of a nature to change the Prior's resolution. It was no longer a despicable speculator but the father who was speaking, and one could, without risking one's dignity or moral standing concede something. However, Bonaventure did not judge this to be the case.

"The fate of this innocent child touches me," he said in an austere tone, "but I cannot accept an arrangement in any way that resembles a deal. I will not explain myself further regarding my beneficial disposition towards your daughter; however, know that I will make no formal commitment and I will not allow any conditions to be imposed on me."

Fargeot did not understand that there were perhaps secret promises within this apparent inflexibility, and he resumed with anger:

"Alright! Alright! By the Devil! I will take revenge. Sire de Laroche-Boisseau will straighten this out! I wanted to be easy on you; I was asking only for my daughter; so good, so devoted despite my faults, so unhappy.... You are without pity; well, he will cook your goose!"

"That is enough.... Get out!"

"We will see if you lower your tone when everyone knows..."

"Silence! and get out of here, I say! must I call someone? There are plenty of people here who detest you and will willingly rid me of you."

Fargeot left growling and with fury in his heart.

When he was at last alone, Bonaventure did not maintain the calm and firmness that he had just exhibited. Leaning his head forward on his chest, he remained plunged in somber thoughts.

"I had to do what I have just done," he murmured finally with a sigh while straightening himself; "but what misery and shame I foresee if that man carries out his menace!"

Chapter X

THE CHASE IN THE WOODS

Miss de Barjac, after the event at Creux-aux-Sangliers, had retrieved her horse, as we have said, and had launched herself haphazardly into one of the lanes in the forest. Hair flying, eyes glazed, she continually urged on her mount which devoured the space before it. Christine seemed to still have a need for movement which had devoured her that morning; but it was neither pride nor joy that motivated her flight; far from seeking the presence of hunters, she plunged further into the most deserted and quiet portion of the forest. Buch's black hoofs grazed the grass and they skimmed under the foliage like silent shadows.

Christine, indeed, in spite of her usual firmness of spirit, was deeply affected by the terrible events that had just occurred. At the thought of the murder that she thought she had just committed, she returned to being a normal woman; she felt the weakness, the craven terror of a woman. The wrenching scream emitted by the Baron was still ringing in her ears. The pale and bloody image of the victim appeared to her at the end of every path, grimacing in the obscurity of every thicket. Sometimes she would give a start and turn her head; but after a moment of stupor, she would again urge on her agile mount, which would spring forward at full tilt such that it seemed that it would only stop if it dropped dead of fatigue.

For some time now, Miss de Barjac had wandered in this manner, without worrying where she was, or towards what objective she should head. No human sound reached her in this immense labyrinth of trees and greenery. However, as she was crossing a clearing, she heard her name called out in a vibrant voice. Thinking that she was once again experiencing a hallucination, Christine was about to move on, but once again the voice repeated its call, but even louder.

Trembling, the young girl restrained her mount, which stopped, steaming and covered with lather. Léonce had just risen from the foot of an oak tree where he had been sitting and moved towards her rapidly.

We will remember that Léonce, driven by jealousy, had wanted to leave the chateau to rejoin the hunt in spite of his weakness, but he had also gotten lost in the forest, and soon exhaustion had forced him rest at this particular spot. Chance had brought to him the person he wanted the most to meet.

"Good Lord! Miss, how is it that you are here by yourself?" he exclaimed. "Where are you going? What has become of those who are supposed to watch over your security?... What has happened?"

At first, Miss de Barjac did not seem to hear what was being said to her; she remained still and silent. arms hanging down, her head bowed. Finally, some color returned to her cheeks and she sprang down from her horse, and moved to lean her head on the shoulder of the young man.

"Léonce, my dear Léonce," she murmured, "it is God who sent you to my rescue!"

And an abundance of tears flowed to relieve her fears.

Léonce, although he could not suspect the cause of this grief, did his best to calm the lovely chatelaine. As she was having difficulty standing by herself, he had her sit at the foot of a tree, and sitting down beside her, began questioning Christine with tender interest. She continued to cry and was not answering. The young man, surmounting his timidity at this moment of crisis, had wanted to take her hand, but it was stained with blood.

"What is this, Miss?" he asked in consternation, "Are you wounded?"

Christine let out a cry and hurriedly attempted to wipe her fingers against the moss that served as her seat.

"This is not my blood," she stammered distractedly, "My friend, do not push me away with horror.... I have just committed a crime!"

"A crime, you? That is impossible, your mind is troubled...."

"I am not delirious, and I am telling the truth.... Yes, a crime, an abominable murder. A man attempted to rape me, and I stabbed him, mortally undoubtedly.... Oh, Léonce, Léonce, can God forgive me?"

Léonce persisted in thinking that this confession was the result of a shocked imagination; however, Miss de Barjac briefly provided him with some explanations.

"Well, Léonce," she continued, "you who are so severe in your judgements, so unforgiving of weaknesses, why do you not heap reproaches upon me? This is the result of the nonchalance and deplorable imprudence of which everyone vainly tried to make me understand the risks.... Oh, speak, say something; I prefer your reprimand, your anger, to your somber silence!"

Léonce smiled sadly at her.

"Reprimand you, Miss," he replied, "reproaches when you are suffering, when I see you so distressed? I can only feel sorry for you!... Moreover," he added animatedly, "were you not acting in self-defense? And since the Baron turned out to be so contemptible and cowardly as to aggress you, why would you not have repulsed him and punished him?"

"And you are not telling me that it would have been better if I had not placed myself in such a situation? You are not saying that my reckless conduct might have encouraged this unworthy gentleman in his bad intentions, and as a result, the horror of his crime must be shared by me?... You are right, Léonce, since the most serious reproaches could add nothing to my remorse."

"Please, Christine, take courage, I beg of you! The Baron deserved his fate; and perhaps his wound was not fatal. Undoubtedly with prompt help…"

"Do you think so?" Miss de Barjac cried out impetuously, straightening herself. "Is it possible that he did not die? But, no, no," she continued immediately. "I heard his cry of pain, I saw him fall at my feet, I saw the blood flow from his chest. Now, Léonce, listen to my solemn promise; as of today, I will cease being the stubborn, opinionated child whose continual rebellions are the despair of her friends. I will enter the normal community of women; It has cost me too much to try to escape it! I will be reserved and timid like the others; I will no longer expose myself to potential dangers by ignorance or flippancy…. You, Léonce, you who have always been for me like a wise and devoted brother, you will help me with this transformation, will you not? Precepts, which from the mouths of others, wound or irritate my pride, seem to be full of good sense when they come from you. Listening to you, I feel a sentiment of admiration for your wisdom, recognition for your affectionate zeal and I think seriously about improving myself."

It is impossible to overstate the adorable naiveté, the chaste and confident simplicity that accompanied these words. Christine, until now so haughty, had been tamed by suffering.

"Oh! thank you for this resolve, my friend," exclaimed Léonce, carried away; "thank you for this good opinion you have of me!... Thus, Christine, dear Christine, you do not love Baron de Laroche-Boisseau, and the awareness of a defiled relationship is not the cause of your distress?"

"Me, love that lecher?" replied Miss de Barjac, blushing; "what are you thinking of, Léonce? I only saw in him an agreeable companion, whose simple and open manners reminded me of (may they pardon my error) those of my father and my uncle, so rich in honor and loyalty."

"Praise be to God that he did not allow this error to have graver consequences!... Well, Christine, since you are disposed to following my counsel, we must hasten to avert further consequences of this tragic event. As soon as you have recovered a bit from your emotions, we must return to Mercoire; we will explain in detail to my uncle what has happened, and he certainly will put things in their best light."

'Your uncle, the Prior of Frontenac?" asked Christine, whose expression had darkened.

Léonce noticed the change.

"Ah, Miss," he resumed vehemently, "I see that you have retained an unjust prejudice against this excellent priest, and that is ingratitude. Why do you persist in this inexplicable aversion to all those who can have some authority over you?... Christine, I assure you that you do not understand my uncle. He is not rigid, he is generous, full of Christian charity; his high intelligence understands and pardons faults when they are atoned for by the sinner. Confide in him; if you only knew how he finds the right words to reassure a troubled soul! I had the proof myself this morning; I went to him sad, desperate, and he left me strong, courageous and full of hope!"

"I have never doubted," replied Christine, coldly, "the eloquence of the Prior of Frontenac.... But," she added in a different tone, "how is it that you, Léonce, needed his consolation?"

"Miss, do not ask me.... I could not tell you.... Know that one word from my uncle suffices to produce miracles on me. In spite of reason, I had dreamed of a happiness that seemed unattainable, and a most somber depression had fallen upon me. The Prior has just informed me that my hope was legitimate, that my ambition was not unreasonable.... Now I can move forward with ardor and steadfastness; I feel strong and full of courage, and I will do everything to deserve the prize I dare hope for."

Léonce did not think that Miss de Barjac could suspect through the vague obscurity of his words what that prize could be; he forgot that the sparkle in his eyes, his tone, his gestures revealed the truth, and he did not realize that the most innocent of women are gifted with a marvelous instinct of penetrating love to which they had given birth.

Christine moved away from him with an abrupt, almost hateful motion.

It was indeed the perfidious insinuations of Laroche-Boisseau that came to her mind. She remembered that she had been told of a plot hatched by the monks of Frontenac to give her hand to the nephew of the Prior, and all her pride rose up against this abuse of power. Even though perhaps secret sentiments drew her towards Léonce, she could only feel indignation when the young man expressed in a thinly veiled manner, his innocent hopes. This expression of this chaste and honest love, that she could have perhaps listened to without anger a few hours earlier, now generated an extraordinary repulsion in her alerted mind.

She had risen to her feet, and without looking at Léonce, she said drily:

"Take care, Sire, that hopes, even guaranteed by your uncle, the Prior, might not come true. The world does not turn on the whims of the monks of Frontenac, as opiniated and as clever they might be; perhaps they will discover this soon.... But now," she continued, "I must return to the chateau; I am feeling better.... As for you, feeble as you are, you could not follow my horse on foot since it does not accept a slow pace.... We will find each other at Mercoire.... Oh, where is that cursed animal? Has it run off somewhere?"

She cracked her whip and called out for Buch, but Buch did not appear. The frisky animal, capricious and erratic, like its mistress, feeling the reins on its neck, had judged it appropriate to take a canter in the woods on its own. It had left during the preceding conversation, and ended up, as we know, showing up by itself at the chateau.

Christine frowned, tapped her foot on the ground, and gave all the signs of anger that could have a cause other than the caprice of her horse. Léonce, not understanding anything to explain the sudden change in the language and actions of the young chatelaine, had stood up and was timidly offering his services. Christine refused.

"No matter," she said, "I will go on foot, I know the way.... Do not bother yourself; I am big enough to walk alone, I believe., Upon returning, I have several orders to give.... You are ill and wounded; you can take your time returning to Mercoire."

Léonce was still searching in vain the precise reason for the cause of her irritation. He asked, almost trembling:

"Please, Miss, explain to me how I had the misfortune to displease you so... I do not understand...."

"Displease me, Sire Léonce? And how could you displease me? Your problems do not concern me; at this moment, I have enough of my own.... Rain is threatening. Return to the chateau. I will do so on my own."

"Christine, Miss, I beg of you, allow me to accompany you. These woods are not secure.... I will not speak, if you so order; I will only walk by your side and..."

"Ah, now is everyone going to try to keep me under his supervision? Ventrebleu! Have I not proven today that I am capable of protecting myself?... Leave me, Sire.... Do not follow me; I forbid you to follow me!"

She resolutely took the first path which presented itself, and departed.

Léonce did not dare move, but when she had disappeared around a turn in the path, he could not resist his concerns. He began to run as fast as he could to try to catch up to her, and he soon saw her as she was entering a smaller path bordered with holly and hazelnut trees. Miss de Barjac, realizing that she was being followed, suddenly turned around and made a such a menacing gesture that the poor boy stayed once more frozen in his tracks.

However, as soon as Christine disappeared from sight, the charm that kept him motionless in the middle of the path, was broken once again. He ran down this small path, but arriving at its end, did not find Miss de Barjac. He followed all the trails that cut back and forth in that part of the forest; in none of them did he see the svelte form of the young girl. In desperation he called out; a mocking echo was his only reply.

Then, the nephew of the Prior was overcome by a profound sense of discouragement, and leaning against a tree, he shed abundant tears.

"She flees from me," he murmured; "she prefers facing the dangers awaiting her in this solitude than accepting my help... Good Lord, what have I done to have so offended her? Undoubtedly, imprudent as I am, I let her see too clearly my secret hopes, and since she does not love me, and as she does not want to love anyone.... Ah! the Prior was right! I should not have been in such a rush to celebrate my joy, but should have considered the obstacles and how to overcome them. Now the worst.... She does not love me.... Woe is me, woe is me!"

He resumed, after a moment of silence:

"However, I cannot give up like this; I will watch over her from afar, without her knowledge.... And when I see that she is safe, well then, may our fate play out as it may."

And he plunged once more into the woods, forgetting that alone, without a weapon, weakened by his wound, and one arm in a sling, he could not have been much help to the person he wished to protect.

On her side, Miss de Barjac was not much less troubled. This new feeling, which added to all the other dramatic events of that morning, brought to a maximum the tension on her nerves, the stirring in her blood and the confusion of her thoughts. While she walked lightly on the grass, her head was spinning, her ears were ringing and the trees around her seemed to be dancing to an infernal tune. However, the persistence of being followed prevented her from slowing her flight. Her long silk dress tight against her body, her lips pinched, she ran along the trails, without thinking where she was going.

However, when she no longer could see Léonce, when she no longer heard his calls, when she felt completely alone in the immensity of the forest, her temporary over-excitation subsided suddenly and she felt the need to stop to catch her breath.

A few steps away from her was a boulder, standing alone on the side of a hill, covered with lichens and ferns and shaded by tufts of brier. At the base of the boulder was a small depression which made a perfect hiding place. Christine headed for this hideaway and panting, curled up inside it like a cornered deer.

At first, she closed her eyes and remained almost as in a faint; however, after a few minutes, she stirred, and lifting herself up on one elbow, she tried to determine where she was.

Below her was an enormous basin, almost circular, encircled by high mountains dominated by the majestic peaks of the Monadière. The forest occupied a great part of this sort of valley; however, the tapestry of trees was interrupted here and there revealing the softer greens of prairies or the deep purple of heather. Near the center of this basin, surrounded by reeds and marsh grass, was a pond, or rather, a large body of calm water. This pond was well known to the hunters of Mercoire; it was there that the deer and boar fleeing from the hounds usually stopped to refresh themselves before the inevitable hallali.[23] On the edge of the water, about a half league from the where Christine found herself, was a small isolated house, half hidden in a dense grove of leafy trees. As far as the eye could see, there was no sign of another dwelling.

This area, normally sad and solitary, was especially at this moment, particularly dismal and somber due to the state of the weather. Everything presaged that the storm which was forming since that morning over the summit of the Monadière was about to break with an indomitable fury on the neighboring countryside. The sun had disappeared. The dome of black and sinister clouds that covered the mountain had now largely spread. By intervals, a low rumble, similar to the sound of a chariot rolling on paving, emerged from the mass of menacing clouds. The craggy rock formations, which crowned the Monadière and the Creux-aux-Sangliers ravine as well as the slopes leading to the edge of the forest were now no longer visible. Nevertheless, below the murky veil which encircled the countryside like a shroud, was a point of light centered on the distant horizon.

Christine, in spite of her troubled spirits, could not misconstrue the signs, and awareness of her situation returned rapidly. It is certain that passions cooled down more easily in the face of overwhelming scenes of nature, as if she better understood their unrealities and weaknesses. This grandiose tableau affected Miss de Barjac more than any human words could have done; Her feverish ideas began to calm and she thought seriously about finding a shelter against the imminent storm. She now knew where she was and calculated that it would take her an hour of walking to reach the chateau; unfortunately, well within that hour, the rain, lightning and gale winds would be unleashed in the surroundings. The only resource remaining was to seek refuge in the small house which we had described, and which was the home of the guard Fargeot. Christine had just taken that decision when a new circumstance brought back all her anxieties.

Crouching in her hideaway, she had been hearing over the past few moments strange rustling sound in the nearby thickets. Someone, or something, was walking on the dead leaves and pushing its way through the brush. Such was the silence that Christine could clearly distinguish the crackling or dry wood breaking under the steps of this unknown being. Furthermore, there was noise coming and going as if a trail was being followed. The sound came sometimes from the right, sometimes from the left, and was coming closer and closer.

Still struck by the idea that Léonce was yet in pursuit, Christine thought

23 Hallali: the cry of the hunters as they moved in for the kill.

that chance had led her persistent protector in her direction, and she huddled back into the crevice in the boulder. But soon, a doubt entered her thoughts. Was it Léonce who was prowling around outside? Lifting her head with precaution she carefully spread the branches and looked.

An excess of fright kept her from screaming. It was not a human creature who was following her, but an enormous animal with bristling fur, a red tongue hanging over ivory fangs and glittering eyes. Christine, daughter and niece of the best-known hunters of the province, was too experienced in hunting to not recognize an enormous wolf; undoubtedly, she had before her the formidable beast, so fond of human flesh, that had escaped this very morning from the search of several thousand hunters, and that was called the beast of Gévaudan.

The poor child, in spite of the courage she had shown in normal circumstances, was shaking like a leaf. However, she still hoped that by remaining hidden, she might not be seen by the monster. Immobile, holding her breath, she anxiously watched every move of her terrible enemy. The wolf moved with little steps, muzzle close to the ground, like a well-trained bloodhound following game. Like a hound, it deeply sniffed the ground from time to time. Sometimes it would stop to catch scents in the breeze; it seemed that the air brought it fresher and more abundant emanations of the prey that it coveted. However, finally, with the marvelous shrewdness of its race, it returned to the slower but surer trail, lowered its muzzle to the ground and continued the trace with perseverance.

Now, it made exactly the same detours that Christine had made a short time earlier when she was looking for a spot where she could elude the annoying persistence of Léonce. It was she that the beast had identified! She was now the object of the terrible hunt where the roles were so strangely reversed. Fortunately, Miss de Barjac, while searching for a spot to hide, had retraced her steps a number of times. This confused the wolf which ended up going in circles without realizing its error and correcting it, while it could have taken only a few bounds to reach the poor child, its recompense for a cruel persistence.

Christine, always alert, saw with increasing terror the beast hesitate, reflect, compare, as if it were about to find the lost trace, when a new sound rose up from the bushes which seemed to worry the wolf itself. The thickets parted ceding passage to a man whose tattered clothing, bestial appearance, and especially from his multiple leaps using his hands, Miss de Barjac recognized as Jeannot Grandes-Dents.

In spite of her recent quarrel with the crazed vagabond, she could not help but invoke, in this perilous situation, the help of a fellow human, as degraded as this creature might be. She wanted to stand up, but strength failed her; she wanted to cry out, but the sound died in her throat. The ferocious beast that paced back and forth, with a gaping jaw, fascinated her, like a serpent fascinates a little bird, still in the safety of its branch above, but feels itself drawn by an irresistible force.

While the unfortunate Christine remained incapable of helping herself, Jeannot Grandes-Dents had arrived at the clearing where the wolf was constantly circling. Annoyed at being disturbed, it expressed its anger by a series of deep growls and gnashing of its formidable teeth. Jeannot did not seem bothered.

"Hum, hum! What are you searching for there?" he said in his guttural voice using the local dialect. "Do you not know that there are hunters everywhere today? One can smell their trace in all the thickets…. Come now, lift up your muzzle, what are you thinking, wasting all that time?"

Christine was too far away to hear the words distinctly, but she felt an immense surprise at seeing the apparent intimacy between the beast of Gévaudan and the vagabond. What affinity could bring together these two savage beings? Not only had the wolf not fled at the arrival of Jeannot and not only did it leap at him, but visibly it treated him like a companion and an ally. However, one could say that this alliance between the brute and the man could be subject to crises capable of jeopardizing her situation. Thus, the wolf, increasingly irritated by the intervention of Jeannot in its affairs, increased its growling. Jeannot, on his side, also began to display anger.

"I tell you that you are an idiot and that you are wasting your time!" he added in his hoarse tones, "but if you are so stubborn, go… search…. You will only find at the end of the trail a hunter who will put a bullet in your body, and you will deserve it!"

The wolf, as if it scorned these menaces, returned to its hunt, while Jeannot stepped back and shrugged his shoulders.

This time, the imminent danger allowed Christine to find both her strength and her voice. She sat upright and without knowing yet if the action she was about to take might be more disastrous than useful, she cried out in a heart-wrenching tone:

"Jeannot, Jeannot! Rescue me!"

The crazed man flinched, and the wolf suddenly stopped, a large paw mid-air. Vainly, Jeannot searched to find from where the cry had come; on the other hand, the piercing eye of the wolf travelled without hesitation toward the boulder and settled on Miss de Barjac with a menacing intensity. Jeannot Grandes-Dents, accustomed to depending on his companion's more reliable instincts, looked to it for confirmation, and finally identified the pale features of the young girl among the leaves.

About a half-minute passed as they mutually observed each other, and one could understand Christine's anguish during these moments of uncertainty. Appalled by what she has just done, she now neither dared move nor speak. On their side, the beast and Jeannot remained in place, as if each was evaluating their own situation.

The wolf was the first to decide. It let out a small yelp of pleasure, licked its jowls and happily prepared its attack.

However, it had forgotten about Jeannot. The latter, upon seeing this reaction, cut short his reflections, which undoubtedly worked their way more slowly to his brain, and he threw himself in front of the beast with a frenetic joy:

"The girl, the girl!" he cried out; you smelled her out all right, my comrade wolf!... But, she is mine; do not touch her.... I know of another one, I'll give her to you.... This one I want. She is mean, she mistreated me.... Now, she does not have a rifle; I will have her, you see, or we will have to fight!"

The wolf, motivated by the presence of Christine, moved forward with tenacity, sometimes to the right, sometimes to the left, to get around Jeannot, who countered each move and continued to block its path. The beast did not seem to want to use all its redoubtable strength; however, it might be imprudent to stretch its patience as it was starting to growl ever louder and casting looks at its friend that spelled nothing but trouble.

Jeannot finally began to get very angry himself.

"I tell you that you will not have her," he continued, with an imperious gesture; "I have been watching for her a long time because she has caused me many miseries; I'll give you another for you, for you alone.... As for this one, I will take her, even if we have to fight each other!... Ah! you growl!... Ah, you rebel against your father, your benefactor? Do you think you frighten me?... Well, I repeat, you will not have her, you will not have her!"

Christine could barely hear these words but it seemed to her certain that she could not expect any help from Jeannot; Already she feared one as much as the other. Therefore, taking advantage of the conflict that had just developed between the two ferocious companions, she nimbly launched herself from her hiding place and with surprising speed, headed for the plain below.

At the same moment were heard sounds of furious snarling and a terrible clamor which signaled that the struggle had ensued.

However, Christine did stop to make sure. The fight was a short one and calm was re-established. This silence redoubled Christine's fright. Undoubtedly, her persecutors, man and beast, were now going to unite their forces for the chase; she thought that she could already hear them in the thickets behind her, and she kept running, crossing the ravines, bushes, and rock formations at a vertiginous speed.

After a few minutes of this frantic dash, she felt that she was out of breath; her heart was pounding and the ground was giving way under her feet. She had to stop to rest at the foot of a tree.

Her fears were only too well founded; a perfect harmony now reigned between Jeannot and the wolf; both were pursuing with ardor. Jeannot was bounding down the mountain, his long arms flailing, and with the wind rising, his straggly hair askew. The wolf was a little further back, muzzle to the ground as though he had caught the trace of the fugitive; it moved a little more slowly, but with the certainty of attaining its prey.

Every second of rest that Christine could take would increase her chances of salvation, and moreover, she had to rapidly plan her next move. Therefore, in spite of the alarming noises coming from her persecutors, she did not hasten to depart; she had confidence in her agility and was reflecting on the fastest way to escape this danger.

The woods were still deserted. The threatening storm had encouraged the hunters who were in the forest that morning to take refuge in their homes; most probably, Léonce, discouraged, had made his way back to the chateau. Christine, therefore could only count on herself, unless she succeeded in reaching the lodge at the pond, that isolated house one could see at the bottom of the valley. This became her plan. Although she never had much affection for Fargeot, necessity obliged her to seek asylum in the home of her guard.

This decision taken, she resumed her flight. The others had made up lost ground during her short rest, but she soon succeeded in outdistancing them again, and plunging into the thickets, she attempted to change directions to keep them from knowing the true one she was following. Her strategy succeeded; from time to time, the man and the ferocious animal hesitated as if they had lost her trace. However, as they always finally solved the ruse, Christine imagined with terror the moment where, her strength gone, she might find herself at their mercy.

She reached the edge of the woods, at a hundred paces from the home of the guard. However, the lodge, as a have said, was built on a bare strip of land, and Christine while crossing it, could not help being seen.

Nevertheless, she could not hesitate; the wolf and Jeannot were not far behind, and at times she thought she could even hear the sound of their panting.

She therefore, had to spring out onto the plain in full view of her formidable enemies, who could catch her with a supreme effort. Just as she was about to leave the last bush, the sky came to her rescue.

A powerful blast of wind engulfed the forest, whose branches twisted in all directions, tree trunks cracked; layers of dust, moss, and dry leaves were lifted in the air. At the same instant, blinding flashes of lightning crisscrossed the sky, a thunderclap shook the countryside and large drops of rain began lashing the foliage of the old chestnut trees.

This sudden disturbance of nature must have struck all the nearby living creatures with stupor. However, Christine, obeying her instincts of survival, launched herself into it with courage; tossed around by the storm, blinded by rain, she managed to reach the guard's dwelling. She forcefully opened the door which was closed only with a latch, and entered the lodge accompanied by gusts of wind which threatened to topple the old structure. A cry of terror came from the interior; but Christine did not worry about it and used all her strength to close the door against the tempest outside. She succeeded, and thought at last that she was in security in the home of persons in her service.

Chapter XI

THE SIEGE

The pond's lodge, although inhabited by the chief guard of Mercoire, was as destitute and bare in its interior as the humblest dwelling of the most miserable peasant in the countryside. The furniture seemed old and dilapidated, although well maintained by a meticulous housekeeper. However, the obscurity was such at this moment that one could only see these details when lightning struck nearby.

The person who cried out when Miss de Barjac arrived was a thin and sickly young girl with a haggard look. Her clothing consisted of a short skirt and a long blouse made of a rough striped fabric; her head, legs and feet were bare. This poor girl, daughter of guard Fargeot, had nothing attractive about her, but her unhealthy pallor, her gentle and timid air and the melancholy look on her face inspired pity. When Miss de Barjac had arrived, Marion was working on her spinning wheel, and judging from her tired and bloodshot eyes, suffering had accompanied her bleak solitude. Standing, now, she contemplated, with a mixture of surprise and concern, poor Christine who had collapsed on a stool unable to speak.

Finally, Marion recognized the person who had entered so unceremoniously.

"Good Lord! it is our Mistress!" she exclaimed, clasping her hands; "who would have expected... Ah! Miss, what has happened to you?"

Christine was beginning to regain her senses and began mechanically to repair the disorder in her clothing, a first concern for women regaining consciousness.

"Yes, it is I, Marion," she replied in a hesitant voice; "the storm... and then they were following me.... Is your father here?"

"No, Miss."

"You are alone in the lodge?"

"Alone... as always."

This was said with a pathetic sadness; however, Christine was still too upset to notice the nuance.

"In that case," she continued, "hurry and lock every door of the house. They might come searching for me here.... Hurry, hurry!"

Marion, undoubtedly long used to blind obedience, hastened to execute the order. She went to slide the bolt on the main door, then moving to another room, she took the same precaution with the door leading to an enclosure in the back of the house. At that moment, the violence of the storm redoubled in intensity: the rain, thunder and wind raged outside; and, although well shuttered, the windows shook as if they were about to open.

Marion, returning, saw that her mistress was trembling.

"Excuse me, Miss," she said, "but you must be cold, your clothing is wet, and I was not thinking…"

She went to a corner of the room to get a small bundle of sticks which she threw on the embers in the fireplace, and soon a bright flame lit up the lodge. The poor girl resumed with embarrassment:

"When our good Mistress deigns to come to our home, I should perhaps offer her some refreshments: a little milk… some wine… something; but I have nothing… nothing!"

"Thank you," replied Christine distractedly, "a cup of water will suffice."

Marion took a pewter goblet from a shelf, which she rubbed for a long time with a cloth, then filled with water and presented respectfully to the chatelaine who emptied it in one swallow. This natural cordial succeeded in reviving Christine.

"Marion," she asked, "where is your father at this hour? I did not see him at the hunt today."

"He should be here soon, Miss, and probably the storm forced him to stop somewhere on the way back…. He went to the chateau to see the Reverend Father Prior of Frontenac."

"And what did he want from the Prior?" asked Christine, whose ardent sentiments were re-awakening; "if he had a favor to ask, he should have come to me!"

"Miss is too kind," replied Marion, making a humble bow; "my father is not in the habit in confiding his intentions to me."

Christine did not reply; she was no longer paying attention to the conversation, and was listening to the sounds outside.

"Miss," Marion timidly asked after a moment of silence, "you were saying a while ago that someone had frightened you in the woods; who would have dared, on your own domain, threaten you with violence?"

"A dangerous madman that I had thrown off my lands, and who had just suddenly reappeared…. But, you must know him, Marion. He is an old protégé of your father, and I suspect that Fargeot is still providing him with his protection, in spite of my forbidding it."

"My God, my good Mistress, did you anger Jeannot against you?"

"That is possible; today I chased him out of his hut at the Creux-aux-Sangliers; insane or not, no one defies my orders with impunity…. Tonight, as I was wandering alone in the forest, due to an event that you will learn about later, I encountered this man accompanied by a horrible beast.... They both pursued me until I reached this lodge."

Marion gave signs of great terror.

"You have irritated Jeannot," she repeated; and we are alone; and my father is not back!"

And she went to make sure again that all the doors and window shutters were hermetically closed.

"From where comes this fear, Marion," Miss de Barjac asked, now also alarmed; "what have we to fear in being here?"

"I do not know, but Jeannot is different than other men.... I wish that my father was here, and I wish that you were in security at the chateau."

"Has Jeannot ever hurt you or your father?"

"Never, Miss; he has known us for such a long time! But when this frenzy takes over him like today.... May God protect us; as if we did not have enough misery!"

"Admit it, Marion," resumed Miss de Barjac severely, "is it your father who has been protecting that old maniac and now allows him to remain in my domain against my wishes?"

"Well, yes, Miss! But I beg of you, do not chastise my father because of this.... Jeannot was one of our herdsmen when we lived in Varinas, when my poor mother was still alive; although he has lost his reason since that time, we cannot refuse him our pity. In addition, my father says he knows about some important things, and for this reason he has been handling him carefully. When this miserable lunatic returned here two months ago, my father did not have the courage to send him away, and he forbade the other guards to torment him. Jeannot is not mean when he is lucid, however he does not speak and he always wants to hide. Moreover, he lives in the wild, one is not quite sure how, and asks for nothing. We sometimes see him here, but..."

She interrupted herself. In the midst of the storm's fracas, she thought that she heard a distant savage clamor.

"What is that?" she asked.

"I thought... No, no, it is the wind blowing through the trees.... What horrible weather!"

They both fell silent, the house creaked and groaned as if it might collapse under the strain of the storm raging around it and blowing into the chimney.

"So," resumed finally Miss de Barjac, "Jeannot Grandes-Dents occasionally came to the lodge?"

"Yes, yes, Miss, and sometimes he leaves me in mortal fear. When he comes when my father is not here, I run to hide in the attic; because of the way he looks at me...."

"I know the look," answered Christine, growing pale herself at the memory; "but Marion, can you explain why Jeannot is accompanied by the wolf which we call the beast of Gévaudan, and why this animal not only does him no harm but seems to enjoy his company?"

"What are you saying, Miss?" said Marion in sincere astonishment. "In truth, Miss, Jeannot, in his excesses of folly, he sometimes thinks that he is a wolf himself; the idea came to him when he was guarding his flock in the mountains, and myself, I have seen him running on all fours in the forest, like the animals.... But, good Lord, who could think that a Christian could live with the beast of Gévaudan?"

"I too have seen him, Marion, and I will never in my lifetime forget that encounter.... Yes, yes," added Christine in a somber voice, "For many reasons, this day will leave indelible traces in my memory."

There was a new moment of silence.

"Miss," finally resumed Marion reflectively "I remember now that Jeannot, before totally losing his reason, was known in the countryside, as a sorcerer and as a *charmer* of animals. At that time, he had domesticated a wolf cub that he had found in the forest, and that cub followed him everywhere like a dog. My father and the other guards obliged Jeannot to get rid of his pet, and it was drowned, or shot, or strangled, I do not know which; but since then, Jeannot could have well *charmed* another wild beast."

"And who knows," resumed Christine, struck by another idea; "what if the cub was not really been killed, what if Jeannot had succeeded in fooling the other guards and what if the cub was now fully grown.... These suppositions could explain a number of strange things that have struck me, and I am almost sure..."

"Shh! listen again!" said Marion in a low voice, extending her arm to draw her attention.

This time, two distinct howls could be heard coming from some distance away from the house; one was clear, strong and domineering; the other was hoarse, less sustained and a rather poor imitation of the first one.

"We are lost!" murmured Marion, almost not breathing.

"That infernal beast found my tracks despite the storm and its torrents of water," resumed Christine, almost as affected. "Oh! if only I had a gun!"

Fargeot's rifle was hanging under the mantle of the chimney and Christine seized it eagerly. However, the guard had been lazy and careless and the rifle was rusty, in poor condition and not loaded. Vainly, Miss de Barjac asked for ammunition; poor Marion, terrorized, did not understand her.

In the meantime, the howls are gotten closer, and suddenly, there was loud banging at the door; at the same time steel-like claws buried into wood, undoubtedly removing fragments; as the heavy door was resisting, one heard a guttural voice saying:

"It is the wolves!... The wolves want to enter…. Open, Marion, open quickly or the wolves will eat you!"

Marion, incapable of answering, or even moving, was pressing herself against Miss de Barjac; the latter, mute, and trembling as well, soon gave up preparing their defense, which she felt was useless.

The banging and scratching continued with increasing ferocity; they were even trying to dig a passage under the door. They removed dirt and bricks and the poor besieged saw a large furry paw with its terrible claws. However, it seems that there was an unsurmountable obstacle and they were obliged to give up on this method of entry. At this point, the pair changed tactics and began circling around the lodge searching for a weak point where they might find another point of entry. They could be heard attacking the door at the rear of the dwelling, then each set of shutters. Their teeth and the claws continued to scape on the boards and each foiled attempt was accompanied by sinister howling.

The situation of the two unfortunate young girls was becoming desperate. A profound obscurity surrounded them now, barely interrupted by the strikes of lightning seen through fissures in the shutters. The fracas of the storm, the continual howling and on top of that, the successive attacks on various parts of the lodge, kept them both in a state of mortal terror. The building was old and poorly maintained; it seemed impossible that the two aggressors, man and wolf, would not succeed in soon penetrating the house unless rescue arrived. Moreover, at this hour of the night, and with this terrible storm, who would have the idea of coming to the pond's lodge? And even if a lost hunter came this way, or Fargeot, as Marion was hoping, came home, what could one man do against the beast of Gévaudan and a furious lunatic who was just as dangerous?

However, the assailants seemed to understand the futility of these superficial attacks on several points of the dwelling and changing their tactics, concentrated their efforts on the shutters of a ground-level window. They could not have chosen better; the wood on the shutter had been half decayed by the humidity; the rusty hinges would soon distort or break. A strong hand, undoubtedly assisted by a rock, banged against the shutter with increasing intensity. The entire house was shaking, and the planks seemed ready to split at any moment. During the short intervals of rest, a hoarse voice under the window was heard saying:

"The wolves want to enter…. The wolves will enter…. And they will eat everyone…. The wolves will enter!"

A blow more forceful than the others finally split a board of the shutter its full length, and a cruel laugh alerted the poor distraught women to the results.

They could not see each other, but automatically found each other in the dark and were now pressing together.

"We are lost!" said Marion in a faltering voice. "Oh, Miss! God is my witness that it is not for me that I tremble.... I have been so unhappy! Since losing my mother, I have not had a moment of joy; I have often lacked for food; alone and abandoned, I have shed all the tears my eyes have to give.... No, I do not fear death for myself, at least a less cruel one; and often I looked at the pond behind the house and thought about throwing myself in to end my miserable existence.... But it is for you that I fear, Miss; you who are so beautiful, so noble, so rich; you have everything to be happy!"

"Our situations will soon be equal," replied Christine distractedly: "but we cannot perish in this way! What? In all that crowd that surrounded me this morning swearing allegiance, is there no one to protect me?"

"Now, our only recourse is God, Miss."

"Even so, I had hoped that there was one person at least.... But no, no, I rejected his help, and perhaps even at this terrible moment, I might hesitate to accept it!"

"One person... who loves you?" asked Marion with a sentiment of infinite sadness. "Ah, Miss, all the joys of happiness were really there for you.... Me, no one loves me. No one will miss me after I have been devoured by this savage beast."

At this point in their conversation, the shutter completely shattered; a flash of lightening revealed, in the opening, the hideous features of Jeannot, dripping with water, and the large muzzle and flashing eyes of the wolf, standing on its hind legs and trying, with its teeth to tear away the fragments of the broken boards.

Marion hid her face in her hands resignedly and remained still. Miss de Barjac, on the contrary, could not bear this horrible scene. She retreated to the other end of the room while crying out:

"Help! My God, help!... I thought myself so strong, but I have neither strength nor courage.... Oh! whoever comes to help me in my profound distress, I will bless him for the rest if my life!"

As if this prayer had been heard, several human voices responded at some distance from the lodge. Jeannot and the beast stopped short just at the moment they were about to launch themselves into the house.

"Help!" cried Christine again, revived by sudden hope.

"Help!" repeated Marion in her high-pitched voice.

The four flashing eyes disappeared from the window. At the same instant, several persons ran up and began firmly knocking at the door, while someone was saying from outside:

"She is here, I recognized her voice.... I am sure she is here!"

Obviously, the danger was past, but Christine could not move. The guard's daughter, less troubled, went to unlock the door. Immediately, the new arrivals hurriedly entered the lodge.

A twilight glow still lit the countryside, but the dwelling's interior remained plunged in darkness. One of those who had just entered called out anxiously:

"Christine! Miss de Barjac! For God's sake, are you here?"

"I am here, Léonce, and I thank you, you and those who accompany you, for the service you have rendered me!"

"Praise be to God! Ah! Miss, you have caused me great concern!"

Marion lit a candle. Léonce had brought with him one of the guardsmen and a servant from the chateau that he had met in the woods while looking for traces of Christine. He had ordered them to come with him, and in spite of the driving rain, the three of them had searched the part of the forest that bordered the pond. Finally, assuming that the young chatelaine might have sought refuge in the lodge, the only dwelling nearby, they went to it to make sure and arrived there, as we have seen, just in time.

They appeared to be in a deplorable state, having suffered the ravages of the terrible storm, and their clothing was dripping with water. Léonce, in particular, was exhausted; his illness and his arm in a sling should have prohibited such an effort; the paleness of his face was witness to his terrible fatigue. However, he did not complain; far from it, he was radiant contemplating Miss de Barjac who was now safe. On their side, the guard and the servant were not worried about their appearance; they had the satisfaction of having found their young mistress, whom they adored despite her abruptness. In addition, there was perhaps the happy thought that a nice reward might await them upon their return to the chateau.

Poor Marion had hurried to throw a new bundle of sticks into the fireplace; it was all that she could do for her guests. While they were drying their wet clothes in front of the fire, Christine remained seated, slightly separated from them, repeatedly murmuring:

"Oh! what a day, what a horrible day!"

Finally, she turned toward Léonce, and asked in a tone which revealed a trace of bewilderment:

"A short time ago, when you arrived… you must have seen them?"

"Who, Miss?"

"Those whom your presence caused to flee…. That hideous maniac and that frightening beast who were about to devour us."

"I do not understand you, Christine…. We saw no one."

"What?" in front of this window! You saw no one?"

"We arrived from the other side; moreover, the rain blinded us and the sound of the wind was deafening…. But please, Miss, tell me what happened."

Christine recounted as briefly as she could her adventures since leaving him in the forest. Her audience listened with a combination of awe and incredulity. Léonce, himself, tended to believe that Miss de Barjac was still delirious with fever, and did not really hide this opinion.

"Morbleu! do you take me for a crazy woman?" exclaimed Christine in her usual impetuous manner. "Well! ask poor Marion; ask her what she has seen, what she has heard, here, just moments ago."

Marion, eyes lowered, timidly confirmed what her mistress had said.

"And if this testimony does not suffice," continued Christine, "examine this shutter. Those who broke it, were they imaginary?"

The guard went to pick up the fragments of the broken shutter. Although the wood was rotten on its surface, the center of solid oak retained a remarkable strength, and it would take considerable force to split it. Moreover, one could see grooves on the boards that went all the way to the hinges that could have been made by a steel instrument.

The fragments were passed from hand to hand; the guard and the servant examined them, shaking their heads in wonder. Léonce remained thoughtful.

"Pardon me, Miss," he resumed, "for having dared express a doubt on this extraordinary affair.... I now remember having read somewhere that certain men, used to a solitary life, notably mountain shepherds, were subject to a sort of folly which consists of believing they have been changed into wolves. This monomania, which the learned have named lycanthropy,[24] is fairly common, they say, in French-speaking countries and in northern Scotland; however, until now, I had not taken this very seriously, and the existence of men-wolves seemed questionable. Now, I do not have any doubts on this matter. It seems to demonstrate that Jeannot Grandes-Dents is suffering from lycanthropy. But what upsets my thinking and does not have a plausible explanation, is the relationship which seems to exist between this maniac and the veritable bloodthirsty wolf which is devastating the countryside."

Christine repeated the explanation that she had from Marion Fargeot concerning the wolf cub that Jeannot had domesticated in the past. As Léonce still did not see in this fact a motive sufficient to explain such a monstrous association, the old guard, who was warming himself in front of the fireplace, suddenly spoke up:

"With your permission, Sire, and also with the permission of the noble lady, our Mistress, there is nothing extraordinary in all this. If Jeannot has really raised this beast, it could easily have become attached to him, even

---

24 Lycanthropy: a form of madness involving the delusion of being an animal, usually a wolf, with correspondingly altered behavior. (Oxford dictionary of languages)

if it had returned to the wild. I can cite several similar cases. I once had myself the fantasy of raising a little wolf cub which had survived from a litter that had been destroyed by the hounds of Sire Count. I had it nursed by my hound which developed quite an affection for it, and breast-fed it like her own. When it grew up, I kept it carefully on a leash to avoid an accident, but one day it escaped. I was no longer thinking about it, but two years later, while hunting in the forest of Pouillac, I saw my hound suddenly start following a trail but without even making a bark and enter some thickets. Not understanding what this meant, I followed her and after a brief search, found her licking a she-wolf that seemed to return her caresses. The wolf leaped as I approached, and I, without reflecting, I automatically brought my rifle to my shoulder and fired. The poor beast fell, and when I approached her, she crawled forward, dying, to lick my feet…. It was the wolf cub that I had raised. My hound was crying, and I think I was too…. You see, beasts of prey can also show feelings…. Nevertheless, if that she-wolf had been protecting cubs, I do not think we would have been so well received."

"And similarly," resumed Miss de Barjac, "it seemed to me that harmony was sometimes troubled between that poor maniac and his horrible companion. In any case, we must rid the domain of these two inhabitants as soon as possible!"

"Is Jeannot Grandes-Dents really so dangerous when he is by himself?" asked Léonce, struck by a suspicion. "Tell me, guard, you can no longer deny that you have often crossed paths with Jeannot in the forest since his return to Mercoire, and that your chief, Fargeot, forbid you to tell anyone? I implore you to reply frankly: do you think that this lunatic, in his mania, is capable of attacking human beings?"

We have not forgotten that Léonce had been aggressed two days earlier in the heart of the Mercoire, and he thought he had been attacked by a man, rather than a wolf.

The guard replied that he hardly knew Jeannot, that he had only seen him two or three times and he seemed harmless. In addition, he tended to flee when approached. Marion confirmed this report.

"Never mind," continued Léonce, "I must be wrong. I had suspected for a moment… but, no, I am maligning the poor fool. He could not push imitation that far!"

During this conversation, the wind had calmed down and the rain had stopped. Storms in the mountains are of short duration, but all the more violent and destructive. The servant went to peek outside, and through the gaps in the black clouds that were fleeing but still rumbling, he could see parcels of blue sky sprinkled with stars. He returned to share the good news.

"Miss," Léonce said to Christine, still somber and pensive, "would it suit you to get moving? They must be very worried about you at the château. However, since the storm must have severely damaged the trail, perhaps we should send for a horse...."

"I will walk," replied Christine, hurriedly rising, "and I am anxious to get home and in security. We are perhaps still running a risk travelling through the woods at this hour."

The guard and the servants had guns, but the rain had surely dampened the powder and Christine ordered them to reload their arms in her presence. As for Léonce, he only had a cane to lean on to steady himself, but he counted on being able to put it to good use if attacked. When he assured Christine of this, she smiled sadly.

Once these preparations completed, Miss de Barjac approached Marion who had been watching with secret apprehension her upcoming abandonment.

"Marion, dear Marion," said Christine with fondness, "we have just spent together hours of anguish which we will never forget. You will always have, in me, a devoted friend. Words which escaped you taught me that you are not happy. I wish to know the cause of your miseries. Come to see me in the chateau tomorrow and explain your sorrows, and perhaps the two of us can find remedies."

Marion was touched to the point of tears.

"Oh, Miss! You are so kind!" she replied, "I am a poor creature, too unworthy to receive the attention of a noble and rich lady like yourself. However, if you have developed any interest in me, I beg of you to be indulgent with my father. He has made a number of mistakes, and probably will make more in the future.... Well, I just implore..."

"Now, now, we will discuss all this, and we will find solutions, I promise you. Come tomorrow to the chateau, and I will wait for you. In the meantime, take courage!... Sires, are you ready?"

Marion seemed increasing worried, and embarrassed.

"Miss, Miss," she finally stammered with an effort, "are you really going to abandon me?... And if they return?"

"Of course!" she exclaimed, "and I did not think of this; they are right; at times I am an egoist and mean.... Pardon me, Marion, I should have realized that we could not leave you here alone with that broken shutter.... Well, my dear, why not come with us to the chateau now?"

"Miss, I cannot. My father should return soon, and if he does not find me here..."

"Well, Grand-Pierre will stay here with you until Fargeot returns. He has a rifle and he knows how to use it; you have nothing to fear while under his protection."

"Ah! Miss, all my thanks!... This should not tire Sire Grand-Pierre too much; moreover, my father should be here soon."

Grand-Pierre, the servant, appeared very unhappy with the mission he had just been given, but he could not refuse it.

"Well, Morbleu! Marion," he resumed in a humorous tone, "if I have to wait for your father, I will probably have to spend the night at the lodge."

"And why is that, Sire Grand-Pierre?"

"Because this evening, before coming here, Jerome and I found Fargeot dead drunk on the side of the road from Cransac, about fifteen minutes from here. We tried to convince him to stand up, but he was unable to do so., and we would have had to carry him, which was impossible since he is so heavy. We were then able to push him under a rock overhang to protect him from the coming storm. He is surely still there, and most likely will not be back until tomorrow morning."

Marion's face reddened with shame, and tears flowed from her eyes. She spoke to Christine without daring to look at her:

"Forgive him, Miss; in spite of his errors, he loves me… yes, he loves me, at least as much as he is capable of loving. Further, my mother, on her deathbed, made me promise to look after him in all circumstances, and protect him against his own excesses. I will keep this sacred promise. My poor father cannot survive the night exposed to this foul weather, and the possible attack of ferocious beasts. I must go find him, but I cannot without help…."

"I understand; Grand-Pierre will accompany you to where your father is, and he will help you, if necessary, to bring him back. He will only leave you when you are back home and have nothing to fear…. Does that satisfy you?"

Marion multiplied her thanks and expressions of gratitude. During this time, Jerome repaired the broken shutter as well as he could. Miss de Barjac confided her protégé to Grand-Pierre and once again reminded Marion that she awaited her at the chateau the next day; then leaning on Léonce's arm and escorted by Jerome, who was ready to fire on anyone if necessary, she left the pond's lodge.

Chapter XII

THE DRUNKARD'S DAUGHTER

Left alone with Grand-Pierre, Marion hurriedly put on a puny wool cape, her best piece of clothing for the winter, as well as summer. She then went to an old chest and pulled out the heavy overcoat of her father, correctly supposing that the drunkard, numbed by the cold, could need it. The servant standing by the door and leaning against his rifle, watched her impatiently.

"By thunder! Will you soon be ready?" he asked brutally, stamping his foot; "are you going to keep me here until tomorrow, my pretty one?... The Devil with this task! It should have been for Jerome to go pick up his drunk chief rather than me. I am only a footman at the chateau who runs errands; but nasty tasks are never lacking!"

Marion interrupted her preparations; she spoke with a mixture of sadness and shame:

"If you have so much revulsion for accompanying me, Sire Grand-Pierre, then leave me. I shall go by myself. It is still easy for you to rejoin our Mistress; you can tell her that I sent you away, that your help was not necessary, and I swear to you that not a word of complaint towards you will leave my lips...."

"Let us get moving and not waste any more time; I have received an order, and I have to execute it.... What a malediction! On my feet the entire day thanks to that infernal hunt, soaked to the bone, dying of hunger and exhaustion, and now I have to run through the woods to find a drunkard, accompanied by a princess with bare legs and a skirt full of holes.... In the meantime, the others at the chateau will be putting on airs and bragging about having saved Miss de Barjac from a great danger; they will have acquired some ecus in their pockets and received compliments from Sister Magloire, the knight, and who knows? perhaps even the Father Prior himself. As for me, who the Devil will care tomorrow morning how I will have spent the night?... Well, the wine is poured, and I have to drink it.... Now, my girl, are you finally ready?"

"Here I am, Sire Grand-Pierre," said Marion softly.

She carried under one arm the overcoat of her father; the other arm was passed under the handle of a small basket containing strips of cloth and other items to bandage bruises or wounds; the poor child knew from experience that these precautions would probably be useful. As for herself, she had nothing to add to her own preparations other than donning her flimsy cape which covered her head and framed her thin face.

Marion left a candle burning, to find some light when she returned with her father; then she pulled shut the bolt on the door and left with her companion who was still grumbling under his breath.

The night was somber; the rain and the thunder had ceased but flashes of lightning could be seen in the distance. Moreover, the vague glow from the sky made it possible to travel as long one did not go under the dark cover of the trees. A majestic calm now reigned in the countryside; one could only hear the sigh of breezes in the depth of the forest, the isolated sounds of drops of water which were still falling from the leaves of the chestnut trees and the ripple of torrents of rain water streaming down the ravines.

The young girl and Grand-Pierre walked side by side without speaking. They had taken a trail which was in a bad state and crossed a moor; at any instant they would find pools of yellowish water which intersected their path. Marion, with her bare feet and legs, was not concerned, but Grand-Pierre was incessantly obliged to take detours which multiplied his cursing.

Poor Marion no longer responded; she simply sighed quietly. Sometimes she considered again suggesting to her guide that he return by himself to the chateau; but seeing the frightening solitude of the area they were crossing, she could not help but shiver, and the words died on her lips.

They finally arrived at the spot where Fargeot was supposed to be. There was a sort of shrub a few steps in from the path; beyond it rose a formation of volcanic rocks superimposed on each other in a strange formation: trees, bramble and rocks were melded in the darkness.

Grand-Pierre was having difficulties in orienting himself on this rugged terrain. He wandered through the thickets and he could not find where he had left the drunkard. As a last resort he called out to him as loudly as he could, but received no response.

"Good Lord!" said Marion, in terror, "could something have happened to him?"

"Bah!" replied Grand-Pierre, brutally, "accidents do not happen to fellows of his size. We will find him! Come, he is probably sleeping in his filth like a wild boar stuffed with fresh acorns…. Ah! now I begin to recognize where I am…. Come with me."

He headed towards two boulders that the darkness had at first hidden. They were roughly shaped like inverted pyramids and their positioning was unusual. The two were joined at their summit while leaving an open space at their base. It was into this open passage that they had carried the chief guard. Certain of his find, Grand-Pierre leaned into the opening of the passageway and unceremoniously called out in a loud voice:

"Hey, brother Fargeot, get up!... That is enough sleep. Get up, I tell you. Here is your daughter who has come to bring you back to the lodge."

"Yes, yes, father, it is I!" said Marion in her turn. "Please get up! You must be very cold in there.... Come now, let us not abuse the kindness of Sire Grand-Pierre."

A grunting sound came from the cavity in the rock.

"Saint Virgin! Sire Grand-Pierre," exclaimed Marion, increasingly alarmed. "Does it not seem to you that he is suffering?"

"He is drunk, and he is sleeping like a log.... Ah, that cursed Fargeot!" continued the servant with irritation; "must we smoke you out to convince you to leave your lair? Get up, by the Devil, and go sleep it off at the lodge!"

While speaking, he was now vigorously shaking the sleeper.

The latter seemed to finally hear the repeated calls. He stirred lazily on his bed of stones.

"Some wine, yes, some wine comrade Planchon!" he replied in a halting voice, revealing that he was still quite drunk; "pour me some wine.... But do not make me tell my secrets.... The affairs of these important persons concern only me!... Morbleu, some wine! and as a reward you will have a little song!"

And the drunkard laboriously sang the old Protestant refrain:

"The brother drank like four,
But the prior drank like ten."

"Never mind that," interrupted Grand-Pierre, shaking him once again; "on your feet! and come with us immediately!... You are no longer in Cransac at the tavern of that poacher, Planchon, but in a field of cracked boulders, and your daughter is waiting to take you back to the lodge."

"The lodge, my daughter," repeated the drunkard, without really understanding what was being said to him, though affected by certain words; "I do not want to return to the lodge; I am too bored there.... As for Marion, she will have a dowry.... Yes, a dowry, and as she is a good daughter, she will let me happily spend the money.... But who will pay this dowry? The Prior is a miser who did not want to take the bait; but he will regret it; I will tell the gentleman, and the gentleman will make life very difficult for that cursed monk."

"The brother drank like four,
But the prior drank like ten."

Grand-Pierre, infuriated by all these delays, was about to mistreat this depraved being, but Marion prevented him from doing so.

"I beg of you, Sire Grand-Pierre," she said, "do not harm him.... Let me speak to him. He will recognize my voice, and perhaps finally he will understand us."

The valet stepped back a short distance; Marion leaned in turn into the opening and resumed in a caressing tone:

"Well, dear father, is it not time for us to go home? I have much to tell you. During your absence, Miss de Barjac came to the lodge, and she had some adventures that will astonish you.... However, everything ended well, and Miss de Barjac ordered me to come tomorrow to the chateau. She promised me that we shall all be happy.... Wonderful news, I hope! But, do you not want to come with me now? I will tell you all about it on the way."

She waited for a response; it was only after a moment of reflection that it came with harshness:

"That Marion! How did she know that I was here?... Scamp, lazybones, what are you asking? Have I not told you never to bother me when I am with my friend, Planchon, in Cransac? I am my own master, am I not?... Turn yourself around and leave, immediately! I wish to spend the night singing and drinking."

> *"The brother drank like four,*
> *But the prior.........."*

The remainder of the song was an unintelligible stammering and the drunkard went back to sleep.

The patience of Grand-Pierre had reached its limits.

"To all the Devils both father and daughter!" he exclaimed. "That miserable bag of wine will not be in any condition to walk until tomorrow morning; what a lovely night we are likely to spend here; our feet in the water, with empty stomachs, soaked to our bones and in glacial winds!"

"Sire Grand-Pierre," said Marion humbly, "why would we not try to carry my father to the house? I am strong, really, stronger than you think."

"Hah! even if you had the strength of four men we would not succeed in carrying this enormous mass to the lodge. The only thing that we succeeded in doing, Jerome and I, was to drag him from the path to under this boulder, and that was hardly thirty paces.... He is not a Christian; he is a barrel, and a full one at that!"

"Well! Sire Grand-Pierre," replied the poor girl, crying, but in a resolute tone, "if this is the case, I do not want to retain you any longer; leave me alone here.... It is my duty to look after my father, to wait until tomorrow, if necessary, until he is capable of following me.... As for you, Sire Grand-Pierre, one could not ask more of you. Return to the chateau; I will be witness to your good services, and thank you with all my heart."

She sat down on a rock with an air of resignation, and placed her little basket next to her.

Grand-Pierre was more irritated than mean; he was touched by the devotion of the poor creature.

"Moreover, I cannot leave you here like this!" he said anxiously.

"God will protect me, perhaps," sighed Marion, wrapping herself in her small cloak which provided little protection against the nocturnal breezes.

Grand-Pierre reflected for a moment.

"I only see one way," he finally said.

"How, Sire Grand-Pierre?"

"By going to the village of Cransac to get some help; it would take about a half hour to get there. We will go to the tavern keeper, Planchon, the worthy friend of your father, and we will convince him, one way or the other, to accompany us to render a service to his best customer. Planchon has a vigorous donkey that we will bring with us; the three of us should be able to hoist our drunkard onto the back of the beast, and the trip to the lodge should be a trifling matter.... Well, my little one, what do you think of my plan?"

"It is excellent from all points of view; and you, Sire Grand-Pierre, are a worthy man.... However, I will beg you to go without me to get help in Cransac while I remain here at my father's side. I cannot leave him while he is incapable of defending himself; my conscience and my poor mother who is in heaven would reproach such an abandonment, and God would punish me for it, perhaps...."

"What! Marion, is it necessary that you remain in this terrible place alone during my absence? Think of that dangerous beast that lurks in the countryside. What need does Fargeot have of you? He is sleeping peacefully and we can be sure that he will not move."

"Sire Grand-Pierre, my decision is taken; I will not leave my father now. Leave as rapidly as possible; you will find us safe and sound as you left us."

Grand-Pierre insisted again that the young girl accompany him to Cransac, but she remained steadfast. Time was a factor, and perhaps impatience blinded the servant to the dangers of his conceding. Finally, he agreed to leaving by himself; after some encouraging words to Marion, he took the path leading to the village.

He had hardly taken a few paces that poor Marion felt like calling him back, but she blushed at her weakness and hid her head under her cape to resist the temptation.

A long time passed and Grand-Pierre had not returned. Marion, sitting on her damp rock, dared not move or even catch her breath. The least noise, a dry leaf falling from a chestnut tree, the tremor of the breeze in the brushes, the buzzing of the night insects, made her tremble. However, soon she did her best to reassure herself, and to occupy her thoughts, concentrated on the sounds of the wheezing respiration of her sleeping father.

Two or three times, however, her alarms seemed to have more serious origins. She thought that she heard furtive steps and crackling sounds in the neighboring thickets; also, there were moans, weak like sighs, coming from the depths of the darkness. At those times she would begin trembling, the hair on her head would stand on end and she would open her mouth to scream… then she would discover that the cause of her terror was an innocent deer foraging, or a timid stag exhaling as it gnawed the tender bark of the saplings.

Marion had no way to measure the time, but it seemed to her that the hour estimated by Grand-Pierre to go to the village and return had long passed. The poor girl was lacking in strength and courage. The violent atmosphere and continued anguish had exhausted her. She shivered under her light clothing; her bare feet were freezing, and little by little, the cold moved upward to her heart. A sort of numbness overtook her, and this numbness which seized both her body and her thoughts, resembled more closely death than sleep.

Nevertheless, a moment came when her blood rushed to her heart, where her arteries pulsed to the breaking point. While Marion surveyed the silence of the countryside, hurried steps that no longer had the capricious lightness of wild animals, could be heard successively in different parts of the woods, and were approaching steadily. Marion feverishly turned to look to the right and left to try to see the mysterious being that was prowling increasingly near her; but nothing detached itself from the dark uniformity of the night, and when her attention was drawn in one direction, the noise would start again from the opposite.

Suddenly, the horrible doubt that she already felt became a certainty. At less than twenty paces from her, shining in the darkness, two eyes, two burning coals which launched their devouring flame. She could no longer be mistaken; this enemy which multiplied its circling around her, which stalked her like its prey, was the beast of Gévaudan.

Marion had jumped up in a convulsive movement. Although the burning eyes had disappeared, she knew her end was near, if not sure, unless help arrived immediately. Crazed with fear, she leaned into the rock opening where Fargeot was sleeping and screamed out:

"Help! My father, help me!... It is the beast… the beast of Gévaudan! Wake up! Say something! If it hears your voice, perhaps it will decide to run away…. My father, my dear father, help me!..."

A muffled yawn, similar to that of a person waking with difficulty, was the only response to this plea.

But Marion did not give up. There was a continual sound of trampling in the brush and one could begin to hear menacing growls. She seized her father by one leg and shook it with all her strength, screaming in desperation:

"Help father, I beg of you!... Wake up or we will both perish.... My God, help me! I do not want to die now.... I was promised that I would be happy, that I would not cry anymore! Miss would make me rich, and I would leave that lodge where I had suffered all alone, and I would marry the son of Jean Godard whom I have loved so long.... No, I do not want to die.... My father, I beg of you.... Help ... me..."

Soon her voice made only inarticulate sounds.

The drunkard received a jolt, and in spite of his enormous weight, was dragged half out of the passageway where he had been laying. Either the abrupt movement awakened him, or the piercing cries of his daughter had stirred some paternal fiber benumbed by debauchery, he began to move about laboriously. However, as he no longer felt himself vigorously shaken, and he could only hear sighs and faint cracking sounds nearby, he simply turned on his side, humming his favorite refrain:

> *"The brother drank like four,*
> *But the prior drank like ten."*

And then he went back to sleep.... In response to his loud snoring, a sinister and cruel laugh came from the neighboring bushes.

Chapter XIII

THE PROPOSITION

The day following the tragic events just described, Miss de Barjac entered the small salon especially reserved for her use, where Sister Magloire and the knight normally came each morning to receive their orders. The young chatelaine was pale and visibly tired; but a remarkable change had occurred in her appearance. In place of the usual amazon outfit in green taffeta and a man's hat, which even yesterday she favored, today she wore a simple but elegant dress in the current style; her hair was coiffed upward and powdered under a lace shawl. Her slow movements and melancholic expression combined to make the transformation complete. In place of the proud huntress, whom, the preceding day, galloped through the Mercoire forest with a rifle on her shoulder, there was now a modest and reserved young girl, with the frailty of a woman who had recovered all her grace.

Neither the good Sister Magloire, nor the honest Knight de Magnac had expected such a metamorphosis. They had arisen to greet their young mistress, and remained dumbstruck as if they doubted what they had seen. However, their surprise was immediately replaced by delight; Magnac opened wide his eyes, forgetting his usual ceremonious greeting, spilling on his white frilled shirt a portion of the pinch of tobacco that was on its way to his nose, and murmured to himself:

"What poise…. Perfect decorum…. Noble bearing…. One could not ask for better."

However, the admiration of the royal valet was too respectful to be openly manifested. The nun was less reserved.

"Saint Virgin! my dear child," she said, clasping her hands, "how this dress becomes you! you are beautiful enough to thrill the angels. Will you finally give up that terrible riding outfit that makes me suffer?"

"I have, dear sister, as you see," replied Christine, with a gentle smile; "henceforth, I shall wear clothing that suits my sex and my age."

She let herself drop on a sofa, as if the trip from her room to the salon had used all her strength. Noticing the stunned expressions of her advisors, she continued wistfully:

"I see that I have surprised you; however, the change that has taken place in my mind is greater than the one that strikes you in my manner of dressing…. Ah! my good friends," she continued with emotion, "these lessons that you have taught me so many times, and to which I did not listen, reality has repeated in a cruel way!"

She hid her face in her hands. The sister and the knight exchanged looks; they began to fear that this transformation that delighted them was costing their young mistress dearly.

"My child," said Sister Magloire, kissing her forehead, "yesterday's events surely justify some painful soul searching, but you must not let it destroy you…"

"Yesterday's events, my good sister, are totally my fault," replied Christine dejectedly, "I have been trying in vain not to face it. If, by the thoughtlessness of my actions and words, I had not emboldened the attack, I would not have had to resort to such disastrous actions. If, a few moments later, I had calmed the agitation of my thoughts, if I had only simply returned to the chateau, as prudence required, I would not have exposed myself, and other persons, to new dangers…. All my grief comes from my pride, my violence, my obstinacy, but I will quell these unworthy inclinations; I promise it, I want it, I shall succeed!"

After a short pause, she continued:

"You will remove from my room the weapons, the clothing, and all this masculine paraphernalia that will henceforth no longer be suitable for me. In addition, Sire Knight, I invite you to sell Buch, or give him to someone: in fact, get rid of the stable, as soon as possible."

Magnac's more ponderous mind had trouble following the rapid evolution of his young mistress's still impetuous desires; each new phrase from Christine provided the brave gentleman with a new challenge.

"Sell Buch!" he exclaimed, dropping his long arms to his sides; "Is this possible? And if Miss wishes to go riding?"

"I will no longer go riding, my dear Knight, and since the state of the roads in this area makes it impossible to travel by coach, I will stroll on foot, accompanied by the two of you…. My good friends," continued Christine affectionately, holding out a hand to each of her two mentors; "Until now, I have been so ungrateful and so mean towards you; I have scorned your wise advice and often ridiculed it; forgive me…. In spite of my injustices towards you, I have never stopped admiring and loving you."

These affectionate words touched and brought tears to Magnac and the sister. The knight brought her proffered hand respectfully to his lips. Sister Magloire, carried away, exclaimed:

"My dear child, I am so happy to find you with these sentiments; Heaven has finally answered my daily prayers. However, beware my dear, of suddenly imposing on yourself sacrifices that could exceed your strength. I find these reforms very swift, and a bit harsh!"

"Alright, we will return to this subject, my sister," interrupted Christine distractedly; "but I would like to have some news about…"

She stopped short, embarrassed.

"How is the *wounded* one?" she finished her phrase.

"You must undoubtedly refer," continued the nun, "to that fine young man, Sire Léonce, who rendered you such a service yesterday, and protected you with courage and devotion? We hope that all the excitement and fatigue of that terrible day will not leave bad consequences for him. What folly to have escaped our vigilance and go running off into the forest before having regained his strength and his wound having healed! I saw him this morning; his shoulder is much better, and if he could calm down…"

"I am happy to learn that Sire Léonce will not have reason to regret his act of devotion to me," replied Christine in a somewhat cooler tone; "yesterday's events left me with sufficient remorse! However, I wanted to have some news about…"

"This must concern the gentleman who wounded *himself* through imprudence with his hunting knife?" asked the knight; "No one more than I hopes that the Lieutenant of the Louveterie makes a rapid recovery, and I have special reasons for this; however, the surgeon is not very optimistic about his wound."

"Oh! that God not allow him to die!" sighed Christine, lifting her eyes to the sky.

Soon, she began speaking again:

"Leave me for now, my friends; I will shortly come down to the salon, where we still have some guests…. Sister Magloire, the guard's daughter, Marion Fargeot, will undoubtedly be coming to the chateau this morning; you will give the order that she be immediately brought to me…. I wish to discuss at length with the poor creature; this will perhaps be a distraction from the sadness which overwhelms me."

As the sister was about to leave with the knight, she suddenly said:

"Ah! Miss, the joy of hearing your kind words made me forget…. The Father Prior de Frontenac requested the favor of a personal conversation."

Christine let escape a slight sign of impatience; nevertheless, she answered softly:

"I cannot refuse to receive the Prior; therefore, tell him to rejoin me, dear sister. I await him."

Magnac and the sister left the room. Each were pleased with the new qualities in the imperious young lady in their charge. However, while the knight was ecstatic about Christine's new docility and *decorum*, the sister, more clairvoyant, was shaking her head and saying:

"Patience Sire Knight, I do not like too rapid recoveries…. Beware of relapses, believe me…. Relapses in medicine are sometimes worse than the original malady."

Several moments later, Prior Bonaventure entered Christine's salon. Miss de Barjac, drawn and depressed, was seated on the sofa. Upon seeing the Prior, she rose and made a ceremonial bow, and pointed to a chair opposite her, but without saying a word.

The Father also seemed anxious and tired. After an exchange of greetings, he spoke in a serious tone:

"You have experienced some cruel sorrows in recent hours, my child, and I wish to believe that these were not deserved.... But I am not here to reproach you as you seem to already profoundly regret your errors. I prefer, if within my power, to help you recover from them.

Christine thanked the Prior for his past kindnesses, and expressed her firm desire to henceforth follow his wise advice. Prior Bonaventure smiled and his facial expression brightened somewhat.

"It is with great pleasure, my child," he resumed, "that I hear you speak in this manner; until now, I must say, you have often shown yourself to be ungrateful and rebellious towards those whom your father chose on his deathbed as your guardians. Their intentions have been misunderstood; you rebelled against the rules that they wished to impose in the interest of your happiness and your dignity. Your resistance has even been so unrelenting that I have asked myself if there might be another cause other than the ferocious independence of your character. The situation of a Catholic community in this half-Protestant country is particularly delicate. The prosperity of our abbey has drawn passionate irritation. Our enemies and the enemies of our sainted religion are heaping odious calumnies upon us.... Is it possible, my dear child, that some of these lies have reached your ears? Could this explain the estrangement, or even the hostility, that you have shown us at certain times?

Christine replied, in an embarrassed tone, that the rumors concerning the priests of Frontenac were based on allegations that were too vague to merit serious consideration.

"Nevertheless, you are aware of them, my child," replied the monk, bitterly, "and I have reason to think that they have made an impression on you! What would happen if these rumors were to become a reality for you, if they seemed to be based on unquestionable facts, and finally if they were openly supported by powerful individuals? Would you not be the first one to blame your benefactors, to curse the paternal care which has surrounded your youth? It is my duty, dear child, to arm you against false accusations; do not forget, whatever happens, whatever the appearances, the Fathers of Frontenac deserve your respect and your friendship."

Miss de Barjac listened somberly as though these insinuations increased her distrust rather than reassuring her. The Prior continued:

"Let us set aside these eventualities which may never happen; I have another reason for requesting this meeting…. I cannot extend my stay in Mercoire. Urgent matters require my return to the abbey where the frail health of the Abbot places on me the full weight of its administration. Unfortunately, as you know, my presence here could not prevent yesterday's deplorable events; Therefore, since there is no remedy, I plan to leave as soon as my nephew's health permits, which should be soon. However, before my departure, I wish to discuss with you certain matters of the greatest importance for your future."

"I am listening, Reverend Father," replied Miss de Barjac, with a mixture of curiosity and reserve.

"My child," he resumed, in an insinuating tone, "as seriously as we are committed to our mission, we cannot exercise the total vigilance required. The proof is yesterday's catastrophe for which we must now limit the damage and hide the truth about the real circumstances. These events, or others no less distressing can repeat themselves to your detriment. I therefore believe that it is urgent that we now act on a decision already taken by the Frontenac Chapter. You will soon be eighteen years old. This is an age when one must begin to consider what is just and good in our society. I must tell you, without detour, that the Fathers of Frontenac and I are determined to have you married as soon as possible."

Upon hearing this unexpected announcement, Christine's face flushed.

"In truth, Sire Prior," she said haughtily, "you and your Reverend Fathers are being too careful. If the task of caring for me seems today to be too distracting and troublesome, abandon it. I feel myself perfectly capable of managing and protecting myself. As for accepting the husband it pleases you to impose on me, I will not submit. I will never marry if I am not free to make my own choice."

The Prior smiled.

"Hmm!' he resumed, "I see, my child, that your will is far from being broken by your recent sorrows, as was being said!... But can you imagine that the Fathers of Frontenac, whom you have appreciated many times for their kindness and justice, would tyrannize your sentiments? That is not their thinking, as they only wish your happiness. Therefore, I beg of you to reply with sincerity: regarding your choice, have you not selected someone?"

Christine abruptly turned her head.

"No one," she replied.

"Think carefully, my child, and do not let shame stop you…. Answer as if you were speaking to your mother, or a Confessor…. Among the young people that you have seen here, or elsewhere, is there not one who has inspired in you some preference?"

"No," replied Christine.

"How strange! I had thought otherwise…. But upon reflection, my child, perhaps you are afraid to express this preference because it has fallen upon a person whose fortune and position in life is inferior to yours? Such a situation should not prevent you from admitting the truth; we are better judges than you regarding the distance that may separate you from the object of your choice…. I beseech you, to avoid all unfortunate results, to express yourself frankly."

He gave a penetrating look at Miss de Barjac who could not hide her discomfort. She replied with a degree of anger:

"I do not understand, Reverend Father, where this idea originates! I have too much pride to lower myself to that point; and if a sentiment unworthy of me had developed in my heart without my realizing it, I would have enough strength to remove it."

The Prior still gazed at her as if he doubted the energy she was displaying. Suddenly, he changed attitude and continued in a more relaxed manner:

"I am delighted that this is the case, Christine; I was worried, I must admit, that you might have some frivolous passion that young people sometimes fall into. Since I was mistaken, all will be well, I hope."

Miss de Barjac was at the height of astonishment.

"How so?" she asked.

"Because, your heart being free, you will have no reason to refuse the honorable match that the Fathers and I plan to propose."

"What! You wish to…"

"It concerns, my child, a match as brilliant as you could possibly desire. All our votes went to one young man; handsome, high-born to great wealth, learned, and well mannered. You will surely receive him with favor when he is presented to you."

Christine leaped to her feet.

"You are mistaken, Reverend Father," she said with agitation, "your handsome young man, so rich and perfect, perhaps might not please me…. And, to cut this short I will never marry him!"

"But why, my child?"

"Well, suppose that I just do not wish to get married, and that I wish to retain my independence. Your handsome pretender would not please me, I am certain."

"How can you know this. You have asked me neither his name, nor his position in this world, nor his character, nor anything that could determine a serious resolution."

"No matter! I do not want to know him, I do not want to see him…. Be advised, Father Prior, and forewarn the other priests of Frontenac, I will never marry the young man about whom you are speaking."

She suddenly collapsed in tears without apparent cause. The Prior had her sit down again and spoke to her in caressing tones:

"Come now, my child, be frank with me…. To reject without examination such an honorable candidate, you must be lying to me, or to yourself about the real state of your heart…. You have to admit it to your friend; you love someone, right?"

"No, no, a thousand times no!" exclaimed Christine, tapping her foot.

"Well, for what reasons…"

"Why do I need reasons? An unreasonable prejudice, or a whim, if you wish!"

"There must be a reason that you cannot admit, my child," replied the Prior severely, "because it comes from a feeling of shame. "In spite of your denials, the falsehoods of which I spoke about a short time ago, have penetrated your soul and filled it with rancor. If you reject in principle a plan that your tutors have made for your future, it is by hate towards them and contempt for their authority; anything that comes from them is suspect and results in your repulsion…. Strange recompense for so much care and effort!" added the monk bitterly; "a terrible ingratitude that we have not deserved!"

Miss de Barjac did not try to deny the sentiment, which was only too real.

"Miss," continued the Prior with a little dryness, "the Chapter of Frontenac and I will not cede to what, by your own admission, is an unreasonable whim…. We have always treated you with extreme indulgence, and you can see what our softness has produced! We have, through the wishes of your father, an absolute power over you until your marriage; this power we know how to use. Do not persist in this spirit of revolt which I thought had been tamed by recent events; it has caused enough misery; the time has come to end it. Prepare yourself to receive with propriety the pretender that will be presented to you in the near future. If, by one of those fantasies for which you are known, you attempt to circumvent our orders, we will find the way to have you regret it."

Perhaps the Prior, in using such menacing language with his pupil, had planned the effect that it had on her. Christine quivered with indignation; her brow was furrowed; her eyes were flaming and her nostrils were flaring. One could have thought for a moment that she was about to abandon herself to a release of her fiery nature; but her will finally dominated this interior tempest, and perhaps for the first time in her life, Christine de Barjac succeeded in moderating, if not conquering her temper.

"My Father," she said in a slightly trembling voice, "you have just shown yourself to me under a new light; fine! I prefer this aggressive tone to a honeyed and hypocritical one…. One did not mislead you in saying that I had changed since yesterday; yes, I have profoundly and completely changed, and you will soon have the proof. Do not fear from me an any act of new insubordination, or any direct affront. I have the firmest of desires to, henceforth, not exceed the limits of what you call duty and propriety: I will submit myself, without a murmur, to the sometimes childish reserve imposed upon girls in my situation.... However, remember well my words, Reverend Father, and transmit them to the Chapter of Frontenac; no law, divine or human, will force me to accept a husband that it has pleased you to select, and I will never accept him.... Never.... Never!"

She repeated these last words with an extraordinary vehemence. The Prior contemplated her with an air of pity.

"I must be satisfied for the moment," he continued, "with the assurance you give me that henceforth you will live a modest and reserved life; the rest will come later. You will reflect positively, and find reason in your thinking, and I am certain, that when you learn who is the husband we have selected..."

"I will receive him politely, Reverend Father; but expect nothing more.... Yes, I would prefer giving my hand to the worst villain in my domain than to this unknown whom I already detest!"

"Simply agree to see him," said the monk, smiling, "but until then, hold off any premature decision.... But, let us leave this subject, my child," he continued in a different tone, "and let us turn to another which may perhaps be just as painful for you. In spite of all our efforts, few persons, here or elsewhere, seem to believe that the Baron de Laroche-Boisseau had really wounded himself during the hunt; they connect the circumstances and compare them, and already suspect the truth.... Therefore, there is a danger for your reputation that this truth be known."

"Yes, yes, my Father," exclaimed Christine; I would die of shame if they knew.... But this man could not be so vile as to reveal his own infamy?"

"I hope not, my child; and I have confidence in those that know your secret. The most dangerous might be the little bourgeois, Sire Legris; but the knight assures me that he had given him such a fright that Legris would not dare whisper a word of what he had seen.... Nevertheless, many of the circumstances can put the idle and the curious on the path of discovery; and your natural horror of Sire de Laroche-Boisseau could add to their suspicions."

"What do you want me to do, Reverend Father? Was it not enough to have received that terrible man under my roof?"

"Prudence as well as humanity, my child, necessitated this action. How, in other people's eyes, would they have judged your refusal to receive a gentleman who had seriously wounded himself in your service? The interpretation would have been to clear, too easy. But, be patient, my child, the Baron will leave Mercoire as soon as his health allows him to be transported without danger."

"My Father, my Father, do you really think he will recover?"

"God only knows, my child, but in order to throw off public opinion, it is important that you hide, if this is possible, your legitimate anger against Sire de Laroche-Boisseau and that you even express the concern that an ailing guest would expect from the mistress of the house.... It would be prudent, for example, that you visit him in full view of all the strangers that are still in Mercoire; Those of malicious intent would be denied their argument."

"What? My Father, you wish me to... Well, even though I might have no reason avoid this man, the action you suggest, would it not be contrary to the social norm?"

"There are cases where humanitarian consideration overrides the norm.... This visit will seem natural; and why would one be surprised when you had been seen two days ago, almost carry Léonce, my nephew, in your arms; that poor obscure child who had no right to such attention."

Christine really blushed at this memory.

"Well! so be it, Reverend Father," she resumed; "if I plan to later refuse the sacrifices you are asking of me, I can at least satisfy you on this.... I will go to the room of Sire de Laroche-Boisseau; I will force myself to hide my aversion, my contempt, my remorse in his presence; I will oblige my mouth and my face to lie since it is necessary. It will be a first and harsh atonement of my past sins."

The Prior stood up.

"Come now! take courage, my child," he said with kindness; "I expect the best results from this action. You will find me in the room of the Baron, and I will make sure that there are a maximum number of witnesses.... Decidedly, Christine," he added, smiling, "your unfortunate spirit of insubordination is beginning to soften.... Several times during this conversation, you succeeded in controlling the disorganized impulses of your soul; these are favorable omens and I have the hope that you will finally accept the dearest wishes of your friends."

"My Father, do not count on my..."

"Alright, alright, leave me to my illusion, if it is one; and do not spoil the joy inspired by your current co-operation. I will see you shortly, my child. May God counsel and enlighten you."

At the same time, he left the room.

When he was gone, Christine remained plunged in thought.

"He seemed very satisfied with this conversation," she murmured defiantly; "has he set a trap for me? It is said that the Prior has a genius for

weaving a plot; and I... my God, how do I protect myself from his de-
vices?"

On his side, Prior Bonaventure was saying to himself while returning
to his room:

"Marvelous! Now, in one way of the other, she will have to decide, and
I am sure of success... unless there occurs one of these sudden events that
upsets the best laid human plans!"

Chapter XIV

THE OATH

The Baron de Laroche-Boisseau occupied, in the Chateau de Mercoire, a large room hung with tapestries with various personages and illuminated by two large windows in heavy frames, with diamond shaped leaded panes. He was lying in a four-poster bed whose curtains were half open, revealing his pale and distorted face. His friend Legris remained constantly by his side. Each hour, the doctor that had been summoned, due to the seriousness of his condition, came to check the Baron's pulse or listen to his labored breathing; and his prescriptions were carefully filled by Sister Magloire, who, confident of her own medical experience, did not hesitate to modify them at her discretion.

Since that morning, all the guests at the Chateau de Mercoire had sent their servants, or had come themselves, to obtain news regarding the Baron. However, with the exception of the persons we have mentioned, none had entered the room occupied by the sufferer; his condition was serious, and the continual movement around him had added to his fatigue. Therefore, masters and valets were grouped in an antechamber almost as vast as was the sickroom itself, and was always full. Among the visitors, some were discussing in low voices the probable malady and its mysterious cause, others were watching for the visits of Sister Magloire or the doctor to have fresher news; others, finally, remained near the door which remained open, in the hope of catching a glimpse of the Baron, who, at certain times, could not restrain plaintive moans.

When the young chatelaine entered, the antechamber was full of people. Christine arrived on the arm of her royal valet; she was accompanied by Prior Bonaventure and Léonce, who the Prior, for his own reasons, had wished to associate with this official visit.

There was a movement of surprise in the crowd as soon as Miss de Barjac appeared. Perhaps they suspected the truth and this visit upset the various versions which had been rumored on the origin of the wound of de Laroche-Boisseau. Christine had a calm demeanor; her facial expression reflected exactly the degree of friendship and concern towards a gentleman wounded accidentally on her domains. Her attire had the perfect *decorum* as the Knight de Magnac would have said. In any case, she did not give them time to make any observations. She acknowledged them graciously and rapidly entered the room.

All the necks stretched and all the ears strained to try to catch some words coming from the sickroom; however, all these efforts were thwarted; there was a noise of moving around of chairs and unintelligible whispering and that was all. Those who could catch a glimpse inside the room could see the persons who had just entered sitting around the bed speaking quietly with the patient. There were no raised voices or unusual movements during this conversation. It was simply noted that Magnac and Sister Magloire placed themselves obstinately between the curious crowd and the principals in the sickroom.

However, the emotions of the latter, though controlled, were no less strong. The Baron, in spite of his pain and fever, remained fully lucid, At the sight of Christine, he had Legris, who was at his bedside, help him sit up, and he spoke a few words in a low voice, while his discolored lips formed a feeble smile. On her side, Miss de Barjac could not help but wince when her eyes fell on this man so handsome, so proud, so joyous, just days ago in his rich uniform of the Louveterie, and who was now so pale, languishing, having difficulty breathing and seeming to have barely the breath of life. In reflecting that this terrible change was the result of her handiwork, the young girl forgot the offense and thought only about the severity of the punishment.

She seated herself in a chair which was hurriedly approached for her, and she stammered with lowered eyes:

"I am distressed, Sire, cruelly distressed to see you in this terrible state, but…"

"But I deserved my fate," replied Laroche-Boisseau, in a very low voice; "is this not what you meant to say? Also, Miss," he continued, becoming a little more animated, "I appreciate your visit, although perhaps concern for me is not your only motive. It gives me the hope that you can still see me without hate, without anger and that perhaps you might condescend to granting me your pardon!"

Christine looked away in confusion; tears were flowing from her eyes. After a moment of silence, the patient continued:

"Am I mistaken? I beg of you Miss, answer me…. All the persons who are listening, I know, are aware of the secret of my guilt. Tell me, can my suffering atone for a moment of madness? Must I die with your hostility?"

Miss de Barjac could not resist any longer.

"All right, I will pardon you, and may God pardon you as I do!... But you will not die, I hope; on the contrary, that you will live to…"

"To always be grateful for your generosity." the Baron finished by saying, and, exhausted, fell back on the bed.

Prior Bonaventure broke the silence; In his unctuous and penetrating voice, he urged the Baron to examine himself, admit his wrongdoing, and if necessary, die a good Christian. The patient, who had for a moment, closed his eyes, suddenly opened them, and said with a sardonic smile:

"You know, my Reverend Father, that we cannot agree on anything…. Thank you for your thoughts; but whether I live or die, I plan to live or die as my own man. However, if this wound turns out to be fatal, I will only regret leaving this beautiful and pure young girl, who has just pardoned me with such nobility, exposed without defense from the dark machinations to which she will probably become a victim."

"Machinations, Sire? What machinations?" said Léonce in a shocked tone, half rising.

However, he did not need the severe look from his uncle to realize the inappropriateness of his intervention, and he sat back down blushing.

The Baron, in spite of Legris who was begging him to calm down and stop talking, said with irony to the Prior's nephew:

"I understand the virtuous indignation of Sire Léonce for the vile schemes to which I refer; but that will undoubtedly change. How could they be seen in the same light by those who are victim and the one who perhaps reaps the reward?"

This poisonous remark thrown in the direction of Christine and Léonce appeared to strike them both brutally. The features of Miss de Barjac took on an expression of anger, and that of the young man, one of surprise, doubt and concern. Pleased with the effect he had obtained, Laroche-Boisseau was about to launch a few more treacherous words when the Prior suddenly got up:

"A longer visit could tire Sire Baron; it is time for us to leave…. I truly hope that our guest recovers, as, if I am not wrong, the pardon of his offenses and Christian charity have not yet sufficiently prepared him to meet his maker!"

Following the example of the Prior, everyone was now standing. Christine, at the moment of leaving, approached the patient, and offered her hand, which he pressed to his lips.

"Get well soon, Sire Baron," she said with emotion, "and no one, I promise you, will greet your recovery with greater joy than I."

"I will recover, Christine," replied Laroche-Boisseau; "yes, I will recover to love you always… and to protect you from your enemies."

The young chatelaine withdrew her hand quickly stammering:

"I cannot accept in these terms… I cannot leave you thinking…"

A sound of voices and steps, which came suddenly from the antechamber, prevented her from finishing her phrase. It appeared that something serious had occurred there; in the middle of a murmur of confusion came the sounds of moans and sobbing.

The knight and Sister Magloire moved towards the door to ask what was the cause of the sudden tumult, when the crowd from the antechamber flowed into the room.; among them were Chief Guard Fargeot and the valet Grand-Pierre.

Fargeot, completely sobered, had greatly changed since the previous evening. In spite of his great corpulence, his movements had a feverish intensity. His face was pale, distorted and streaked with tears; his clothing was covered with mud, and still damp from the latest storm. Grand-Pierre, similarly disheveled, seemed equally upset and terrified. Behind them pressed all the persons from the chateau, all appeared stunned.

Miss de Barjac, annoyed by this invasion, ran up to the crowd that was entering.

"What do you want? How dare you enter this way…"

"Ah, Miss, my good Mistress," said Fargeot, falling on his knees, "avenge my daughter, my poor daughter! They say that you were good to her last evening, while I, bad father, a drunkard without a soul, was the cause of her misfortune… But since you can do nothing for my poor Marion, at least avenge her, I beg of you."

And grief, shaking his robust body, tore heartrending wails from him. Christine began to suspect that something really terrible had happened.

"Now, calm down, Fargeot," she resumed, "what are you saying about your daughter? Where is she? Why did she not come to see me this morning at the chateau as she had promised?"

"She will never come back… never!" cried out the guard.

Christine awaited anxiously for an explanation of these words; her eyes turned towards Grand-Pierre.

"It was not my fault, Miss, I swear," said the valet in desperation, responding to her questioning look. "I exactly followed your orders; but my absence took much longer than I thought. The night was particularly dark, and I tripped several times in the ravines; I had to swim across the Plein-Val creek. Once in Cransac, it took a long negotiation to convince that cowardly tavern keeper to accompany me with his son and donkey…. While retuning, we were held up by a thousand obstacles; when we finally arrived where we were to find the guard and his daughter, it was dawn, and it was much too late."

"Too late? are you telling me that something happened to Marion? Where is she? Why do I not see her?"

"Dead," murmured Grand-Pierre.

"Dead and devoured by that accursed animal, the beast of Gévaudan, may the Devil take it!" cried Fargeot.

Christine's legs gave way under her and devastated, she collapsed in her chair.

Then, Grand-Pierre began recounting in detail how Marion had refused to leave her drunken father in the rock formation, while he, Grand-Pierre went to get help in the neighboring village, and how upon his return he had found Marion dead and half devoured, not far from her sleeping father.

"Yes, yes," said Fargeot with dismay, "I was there, only a few steps away, and I could not even stretch out my arm, or cry out to protect her! I have a vague memory of her having called out to me for help, but a profound sleep numbed my limbs and my damned drunkenness... Oh! I am indeed punished. My wife died of sorrow, and my daughter, my dear Marion... Why did that ferocious beast, instead of taking her from me, not take me, who is of no earthly use?"

This man, so vulgar, so ridiculous even under normal circumstances of life, was sublime in this moment of paternal sentiment. The belated recognition of his wrongdoings, the horrible circumstances which accompanied the death of his daughter, gave his despair a most heartbreaking character; his cries and sobs made the witnesses shudder and drew their tears.

Miss de Barjac, more than anyone, was accessible to such feelings. Her suffering, still contained by her desire to know all the particulars of this dismal event, would surely translate into an impetuous tempest.

"Is it certain, at least," asked Christine, "that is was the beast alone..."

"Oh! this time, Miss," said Grand-Pierre, who guessed her thought, "the beast is the only culprit. This morning, when we discovered the body, we explored the surroundings. The soil was humid and we had a good visibility; on all sides we could identify the imprints of a large paw, and none from a human being. At a hundred paces or so from the catastrophe, we did find traces of a bare footprint next to that of the wolf. We followed these for a moment, but lost them in the forest. The man and wolf seemed to be moving with certainty, as if they had taken a decision, or were even preparing to leave the domain."

Fargeot was listening to this explanation with a somber air.

"Miséricord!"25 he cried, "what human creature would have wanted to hurt my dear Marion? She was so sweet, so gentle! Everyone loved her.... They speak of Jeannot, my old valet; but Jeannot is completely harmless; his only obsession is that he thinks that he is a wolf; I handled him as I wished by speaking to him softly and flattering his folly; Jeannot knew Marion since her earliest childhood, and he would have protected her from that terrible animal.... Yes, yes, it is the wolf who is the only culprit in this disaster.... Miss, you who are so rich and so powerful, will you do nothing to avenge my daughter, to rid your domains of this scourge which is destroying us?"

25 Miséricorde: divine mercy, indulgence—often used as an exclamation.

These last words seemed to excite to a frenzy the anger and suffering of Miss de Barjac.

"Oh! what do you want me to do?" she exclaimed, stamping her foot in frustration; "my friends and my servants are constantly being attacked all around me; every day, every hour I learn about a new tragedy, another loss. Even yesterday, I found myself in the greatest danger, and thought myself in my last hour. This morning I am told that this generous child in whose home I had found safety has just perished in the cruelest manner.... And I could do nothing.... Nothing! All the efforts to free the countryside of this enraged beast have failed miserably; it eludes its pursuers, bullets seem to bounce off it, hunting knives cannot pierce its hide; one would think it has supernatural powers which render it invulnerable. It has once again escaped a hunt by several thousand men; it is true that there were disastrous circumstances.... But good Lord, what can I do, a poor woman who is distraught, terrified, and at the end of my patience, strength and courage?"

She reflected for several seconds. Suddenly she raised her head. Her eyes: had cleared, an energetic resolution glowed on her face.

"Yes, yes!" she repeated with emphasis, "I can do something, and I will do it.... It will also serve to disconcert the unwanted and tyrannical influences which torment me.... Everyone, therefore, listen to me," she continued in a solemn tone; "the government has promised honors and sums of money to the person who kills the beast of Gévaudan; well, I, I swear to give my hand and my fortune to any man, not in a servile situation, who comes to claim his rights, having proven in an irrefutable manner, that he has killed this terrible beast!"

This oath had been totally spontaneous, and Christine, in pronouncing it, had obeyed only her impetuous nature. However, the words had hardly left her lips that she seemed to realize herself their numerous and terrible consequences. She grew pale and fell back, hiding her face.

The witnesses, at first speechless with surprise, raised their voices to express their reactions to this extraordinary solution. The Prior's words dominated the noise:

"Christine, poor child, what have you done?" he exclaimed. "Revoke this absurd vow, this indiscreet oath; there is still time! Think of the inevitable problems...."

But the monk's comments seemed only to harden the heart of Miss de Barjac.

"I will not revoke it!!" she cried out with obstination; "I maintain it, with all my strength."

"Ah! Christine! Christine!" said Léonce in, in his turn, with hopelessness, "so you do not love me? You have never loved me?"

This simple question troubled the young girl more than anything else;

however, she remained silent.

Meanwhile, the whole assembly had become quite agitated; who knew how the words of the rich and beautiful chatelaine awakened ambitions, initiated rivalries and opened brilliant new horizons for those who were listening? In the middle of the uproar, one voice rang out from the far end of the room.

"And I, Miss, and I? Will I be allowed to aspire to the precious reward which awaits the conqueror of the beast?"

It was Laroche-Boisseau who had just asked the question; one could see him leaning over the edge of his bed, a concerned look in his eye and his chest heaving.

"I have excluded no one!" replied Christine in muted tones.

"Then I want to recover…. I will recover!" exclaimed the Baron.

The Knight de Magnac sidled over to him:

"Before you resume your pursuit of that cursed wolf," he said in a low voice, "remember that you have promised me the favor of a meeting…. I am counting on it, I assure you."

However, Laroche-Boisseau was not listening.

"If I have understood you correctly, Miss," said someone next to him, "your vow does not exclude the bourgeois…. I mean someone who is not of the nobility… but honorable?"

"I exclude, Sire Legris, only persons in a servile situation."

And then, Christine fainted in her chair. As persons were pressing around her, Magnac approached Legris in his turn:

"You are aware, Sire," he said, still in a low voice, "that as soon as your friend no longer needs your care, I intend to erase your presence…. You are not yet Lord of Mercoire."

Miss de Barjac was transported to her apartment. The Prior, who followed with Léonce and Sister Magloire, was appalled.

"What a disaster!" he was saying; "just when I thought I had anticipated all the obstacles, all the risks, that cursed oath completely upsets my plans."

"I expected a relapse, my Reverend Father," Sister Magloire, now in tears, was saying, "but who could have predicted that?"

Léonce, on his side, murmured, with despair:

"No longer any doubt: she does not love me…. I have lost her!"

Chapter XV

THE RECOVERY

For two months following the events reported in the preceding chapter, the beast of Gévaudan continued its ravages, although it had changed the location of its attacks. Indeed, it had abandoned the forest of Mercoire; the incidents and the killings were increasing in number but were occurring in neighboring counties. But it appeared that the monster, now more prudent from experience, did not dare stay in one place for long, and remained constantly on the move to throw hunters off its track. One would learn that in the morning it had spread terror in a village in Rouergue, and that evening it had devoured some women or children at a hamlet in Auvergne, fifteen or twenty leagues away from there.

The tales that were circulating regarding the monster's exploits were certainly of a nature to generate great fear, even if one discounted some exaggeration. One time, five unfortunate children from the Chanaleilles parish, guarding a flock in the mountains, were suddenly attacked by the ferocious animal. It had carried away the youngest child when the others, armed only with knives strapped to the end of their staffs and led by Portefaix, one of their group, resolved to rescue their companion. They pursued the wolf and succeeded in tormenting it sufficiently that it released its victim and fled into the neighboring woods. On another occasion, one recounted the story of a woman from Rouget, Jeanne Chastan, at her door with her three children, found herself in a fierce struggle with the beast of Gévaudan, which had tried, one by one to drag away each of her little ones; but the mother, furious, threw herself on the monster, clawed at and fought with it, and in spite of many bites she received, succeeded in making it flee. However, the cost was high. One of her sons, the youngest, and perhaps the most loved, was dead when they came to the aid of the poor family.

In all these stories relating the misdeeds of the beast, there was no mention of Jeannot Grandes-Dents. Perhaps the lycanthrope had found himself unable to follow his tireless companion; perhaps there had been a falling out between them; or perhaps Jeannot had finally understood, in spite of the malfunctions of his mind, the dangers of such an association. However, the few persons who were familiar with the events in Mercoire, thought they recognized in certain adventures of the beast of Gévaudan, the possibility of human intervention, notably, in its manner of escaping capture.

The desperation of the provinces exposed to the ravages of the beast was at its peak. Since the unfortunate hunt which had been organized by the Baron de Laroche-Boisseau, other hunts followed without interruption, sometimes in one place, then another. Often, twenty or thirty parishes united to besiege a Canton where they knew the wolf had taken refuge; the most capable huntsmen of the kingdom came to help the unfortunate inhabitants of the Gévaudan. The king himself, had sent the Baron d'Enneval, gentleman from Normandy, reputedly the best wolf hunter in France. The country was rising en masse against the common enemy. On one occasion, twenty thousand hunters[26] came to surround the Prunière forest, where the wolf had settled. This army did not do any better than the less numerous troops that had preceded it.; the wolf escaped once again with infernal ease. On different occasions, it was thought that they had it trapped in a narrow enclosure surrounded by excellent shooters; each time it disappeared as if it had turned to smoke. Hounds refused to track it and would run away howling at the sight of the beast. Some hunters said that their lead bullets bounced off its hide or were flattened and fell off. Others, who had shot at almost point-blank range, using silver bullets, claimed to have mortally wounded the beast and shown traces of its blood. In spite of this, two or three days later they would learn that it had miraculously recovered and once again had devoured a victim. The discouragement became generalized. The most sceptic finally believed in magic or sorcery. They resorted to prayers and processions. According to one mandate from the Cardinal of Mende, the Blessed Sacrament was to remain exposed in all the churches of Gévaudan, as in the times of the pest, or public disasters. Populations in distress, having tried all other ways to halt a scourge, seemed to have no other hope than in God.

This was the state of affairs when we bring the reader back to Langogne, to the inn of the widow Richard where Laroche-Boisseau had been transported once the state of his wound permitted it. This wound, despite the doctor's pessimistic expectations, had rapidly healed, and the Baron, feeling that his situation in the home of Miss de Barjac was awkward, was eager to leave the chateau. Moreover, he left it with all the honors of a war hero. As he was on a stretcher, the chatelaine, accompanied by Sister Magloire and her principal servants, came ceremoniously to curtsy and wish him safe travel. Magnac had accompanied him on horseback to the limits of the domain, where, after an exchange of words in subdued voices between the two, they separated with all appearances of most cordial relations.

From that day onwards Laroche-Boisseau had taken up residence in

---

26   *Twenty thousand hunters*: French author's note: These facts are not an exaggeration. They are historic and can be verified in memoires of that time.

Langogne, where thanks to the care of Madam Richard, de Labranche, his tracker and valet, and finally, Legris, his friend and financier, he was able to pursue his recovery. In truth, Legris absented himself a number of times to visit his father who lived in a town some distance away, but he would rapidly return to the patient's side, and their intimacy appeared even greater than ever. Perhaps the desire to frequent the local nobility which gathered around the Baron to help him support the boredom of his confinement, was a key to this diligence. Madam Richard's inn now became a center for festivities and pleasure; they drank, they laughed and they gambled continually, and the young bourgeois must have eagerly seized upon this opportunity to slip in among this exalted company.

One morning, Legris entered the room that the Baron occupied on the upper floor of the inn. The resourceful zeal of Madam Richard had assembled everything needed for his comfort. Double curtains garnished the windows; a carpet covered the floor; a folding screen protected him from drafts coming from the door, and as it was the end of autumn, a warm fire of chestnut wood glowed in the chimney. Laroche-Boisseau, wearing a magnificent dressing gown, freshly shaved and powdered, appeared totally recovered from his wound, except for a slight paleness hardly noticeable on his male features. He was in the process of counting a large number of gold coins spread on the table, which did not prevent him from listening to Madam Richard, who, standing before him, always radiant and smiling, entertained him with gossip.

"Delighted to see you up and about, my dear Baron," said Legris cheerfully; "Morbleu! this cheers the soul after all the worry you have caused us!"

"Thank you, Legris," said the Baron carelessly while still aligning his pieces of gold; "Yes, things are going well this morning; I have never felt as joyful or free."

"I understand," continued Legris, winking, "how your present occupation gives you a rosy outlook on life."

"Well! what are three or four hundred miserable Louis that I won recently from the Marquis de Castillac and at Vaupillière? My convalescence should be of some use. However, you know, Legris, that I am a great consumer of money; these coins will not take me very far."

At the same time, he let the gold pieces drop in a brilliant cascade into a drawer.

"By the way, Madam Richard," he continued, addressing his hostess, "the man from Mercoire, Fargeot, who has been coming every week on behalf of Miss de Barjac, has he arrived?"

"Not yet, Sire Baron, but he should be here soon, as this is his day. My word," continued the pretty widow, with a knowing air, "you must have made quite an impression there! A week does not go by that someone sends a messenger from Mercoire to find out how you are; there are an infinite number of questions regarding your health and your activities.... They even carefully inquire about Sire Legris, which must flatter him, I suppose!"

This observation was greeted by an equivocal smile from the Baron, and a grimace from Legris.

"Indeed," replied Laroche-Boisseau, "we have some friends there, but friendship is so fragile, Madam Richard!... Well, when Fargeot arrives, let us know right away; we need to speak with him."

"As you wish. Will Sire Baron need anything else?"

"Certainly, my dear," answered Laroche-Boisseau.

He suddenly turned and planted a kiss on each of the hostess's plump cheeks.

"There!" he said; "now think about my lunch.... Some Saint-Péray and a trout omelet, like old times."

"Decidedly," responded the widow as she left, "Sire Baron is cured.... He has returned to his old habits."

As soon as the door had closed behind her, Laroche-Boisseau suddenly became very serious.

"Sit down, Legris," he said to his confidant, pointing to a chair. "Yesterday evening, when you arrived from town, I had just finished fleecing these country bumpkins, who dared challenge me at gambling, and I have not yet had time to chat with you. However, you must have many things to tell me.... Well! what news from your father, that intractable Croesus?[27] Will he provide me financial support for the new lawsuit that I will launch against the Frontenac Abbey regarding the Varinas domain?"

To tell the truth, my dear Baron, the *old man* is still hesitating; you already owe him so much money! Moreover, those Frontenac monks are very powerful and there is fear in attacking them.... However, perhaps I can arrange things to your satisfaction.... You have never doubted my friendship or my devotion, I hope!"

"A thousand thanks for your friendship, Legris; but by the Devil, your father does not take a great risk in advancing me a few thousand Pistoles, if, as one can imagine, I succeed in imposing reason over those rascal monks. The lands of Varinas, with their revenues over the past sixteen years, can, according to my calculations, be worth over five or six hundred thousand ecus.... A nice prize, Legris! And your father should take that into consideration. But, the most pressing is for us to make an arrangement with Fargeot.... You are certain, are you not, that this man holds an important secret concerning the death of my young cousin de Varinas?"

"I have told you, Laroche-Boisseau, everything I know about this

27 Croesus: Was the king of Lydia 595 BC—renowned for his wealth.

affair. My valet had been drinking, some time ago, in Cransac, and had learned from the tavern keeper that Fargeot had drunkenly boasted that he could ruin certain highly placed persons; he insinuated that you would pay a fortune to have a small note that was in his possession, as that note could help you regain the Varinas domains."

"That is clear," said the baron pensively. "Well, Legris, take care of receiving this man when he presents himself today. You are not lacking in finesse when you want. Another favor which you will not regret. Take Fargeot aside; have him drink, promise him anything, give him what he wants.... I will make available to you all the gold that I have just won; I will find more if necessary.... Oh! what I would not give to have in my grip, under my boot, those accursed monks!"

"Frankly, Baron, this is not an easy mission. Since the tragic death of his daughter, the Chief Guard has become gloomy and uncommunicative; he no longer drinks and has stopped going to taverns. My valet was not able to get a word out of him concerning the affair which interests us."

Your valet is an idiot, and you are a creative spirit, my dear Legris. I do not believe in these sudden transformations. Scratch the skin of. a convert, and you will find a rogue.... He who has drunk will drink, an old proverb says. See for yourself. I am counting on your friendship, and I am sure that you will succeed.... Now, on another subject.... What news concerning our lovely friend, the chatelaine of Mercoire?"

"To my great satisfaction, Miss de Barjac's wishes are not known to the general public. You will remember that Prior Bonaventure had recommended secrecy to all of us, saying this would limit the number of pretenders. Consequently, few persons are aware of the magnificent prize that awaits the conqueror of the beast, or it may be mentioned as a vague rumor that does not merit credibility. I do not expect more than three or four persons..."

"Among whom you are counting yourself, naturally; is that not so, Legris?" asked the Baron with a hint of irony; Indeed, why would you not be, like anyone else, Lord of Mercoire. Your father could buy you certain rights which can ennoble you and that are called savonnettes à vilain[28]. Then you could rejoin the gentlemen, and after two or three generations, no one would suspect that you were the son of a simple prosecutor. However, do not let it go to your head, my poor Legris, as there will be some formidable competitors who will present themselves to challenge you for the hand of the lovely damsel!"

---

28 *savonnettes à vilain*—in English: *Villainous Soap*: Under the Old Regime, this was a procedure allowing a commoner to buy land (i.e. a Barony) allowing him to be ennobled. The soap is a reference to washing one's hands of one's background.

"This is true, Baron, and including yourself, who has all the chances of winning, it is said that someone we know has also entered the competition. It is a young man who until now we have judged only as having his head in the clouds and breathing out maxims and morals...."

"Yes! you are speaking of the *lamb* of the Reverend Fathers?" replied Laroche-Boisseau bitterly; "to the Devil with me if I did not think him more capable! That youngster is not lacking in energy or courage, and, if he succeeds in finding his independence.... Thus, Sire Léonce is also in love with Miss de Barjac? I had guessed it from the first moment."

"It is said that he has turned everything upside-down at the Frontenac abbey to which he returned with his uncle, the Prior. He now has hounds and horses; they have just bought for him the best arms from Liege and Saint-Étienne; he continually practices to become a first-class shooter. He brought in a former tracker from the Royal Hunt, who is highly regarded, and they travel the forest together, either on foot or on horseback. The monks refuse him nothing, and complacently pay all his expenses. In spite of all this, I strongly doubt that Sire Léonce achieves his goal."

"Who knows?" said Laroche-Boisseau with a worried air; "all he might need is a moment of luck.... But then again, that moment might never come. By the time this novice hunter is able to enter the fray, the beast should be already dead. We will see to it, unless that wolf hunter from Paris gets there before us."

"Now, now, Laroche-Boisseau, can you not forgive that poor Baron d'Enneval who arrived here, so confident and so proud of the commission he had received from the King? Now, he is beginning to understand that the task is perhaps beyond his abilities. After ten formidable hunts, he is no further advanced than the first day. The beast is playing a game of hide and seek with him. He continues to chase after it without ever catching it. D'Enneval is under tremendous pressure; his hounds, his horses and his valets are begging for mercy. He is speaking of returning to Paris and leaving the task to anyone who wishes to rid the Gévaudan of this scourge."

Laroche-Boisseau pensively took several paces in the room.

"What you are telling me, Legris, confirms an idea that I have developed since the unsuccessful hunt which I led in the forest of Mercoire. These hunts with deafening noise never succeed with an animal as defiant and cunning the wolf in question. The sounds perturb it and keeps it constantly on alert. What is needed is two determined individuals, excellent marksmen armed with rifles, with complete confidence in each other, such as you and I, and followed by a maximum of two or three valets. It would be totally useless to encumber ourselves with howling and cowardly hounds that flee as soon as the animal shows itself. I would only want my bloodhound, Badineau, with me to follow its trail and a good large mastiff to release at the right moment. The wolf, according to all reports, is coura-geous. It would not refuse combat against so few enemies, and as vicious as it is supposed to be, we may find the occasion to be done with it. I know exactly where to obtain the kind of dog I need. There is one that has already merrily attacked the beast of Gévaudan. It is the mastiff of Jean Godard, the chief herdsman of Mercoire. Jean Godard will cede it to me, even if I have to pay him a thousand ecus…. Thusly accompanied and equipped, I will be on my way as soon as my strength has returned, which should be the case in only a few days from now. Well! what do you think of my plan, Legris?"

"It is excellent, and it has all the more chance of working since it is completely different from the ones which have failed up to now. There-fore, Baron, you are willing to associate me with its execution, even if, by chance no doubt, it might be me that might earn the prize."

"Remember our agreements: equal chances for both you and me. If fate favors you, I will be the first to congratulate you. If luck turns my way, you will have to take your loss graciously…. I am being as fair with you as I would be with myself, Legris; the most demanding of friendships could not ask for more."

"That is true, my dear Baron, and I thank you. However, this expedition with only two or three persons against such a formidable animal presents certain dangers…."

"If you are afraid," said Laroche-Boisseau, in a mocking tone, "remain by the fireside; in all probability, fatigue and dangers will not be lacking."

"Neither frighten me, if I were certain… No matter what you say, Bar-on, the chances for you, and for me, are far from being equal. You are an experienced hunter, and in this domain, as in many others, I feel a great inferiority compared to you. Is it possible that after having shared in your efforts and your perils, that I would not have any part of the reward?"

"Indeed, that is a strong possibility, my poor Legris," replied Laroche-Boisseau with a warmth which hid a lot of malice. However, what to do? I am loyally offering you the opportunity to win the announced reward, all the while trying to win it myself; do not expect more."

Legris did not seem satisfied with the unpredictable chance he was giv-en in this shared enterprise. He had perhaps an uncertain faith in the gen-erosity of his friend; and being an excellent schemer himself, he dreamed of a finding a way to assure some positive advantages. After a moment of reflection, he became bolder and firmly asked:

"Come now, Laroche-Boisseau, let us discuss frankly…. Do you re-ally love Miss de Barjac, who does not love you, and has already seriously proven it?"

The Baron's eyes flashed upon hearing this question, but suddenly re-membering his interest in managing his confidant, he replied with a feigned cheerfulness:

"Do you know women so well, my dear Legris, to believe that such an act rigorously proves an aversion? Do you not know me well enough to believe that a knife wound from the charming chatelaine would be more apt to excite my passion rather than to subdue it?... But why such a question and where are you going with this?"

"Like this, Baron: the moment has perhaps arrived to ask you to pay the price of my past services and those of my father. Over the last few years, you have drawn liberally on our fortune. At this hour, the sale of all your properties would hardly reimburse one half of your debt. However, my father has a very specific idea on the value of money: if it had been any other person than the friend of his son, he would have called in the debt long ago, and you can imagine the inevitable result. Furthermore, you are embarking on a lawsuit against the richest and most powerful religious house of the province and you have need for considerable financing…. Well! everything could work out very well if you do not love Miss de Barjac."

"How do you come to this conclusion, Master Legris?"

"Listen to me, Baron, and I beg of you to not take offense…. My father won a great fortune in a number of ways, and like many newly rich bourgeois, has the ambition of ennobling his race, of seeing his only son becoming a gentleman. Perhaps, indeed by acquiring one of those rights which you so disdainfully called *savonnettes à vilain*; you know as well as I do that a number of families, considered honorable today, became so in this manner. Nevertheless, our project of elevation in status could have been slow and uncertain, until the bizarre wishes of the heiress of Mercoire came along to change things. My father became fired up the first time I mentioned this event. He sees this as a sure and rapid means to achieve our goals, and he would make the greatest sacrifices, even his entire fortune, which is immense, to see me marry Miss de Barjac."

"Well! my dear Legris, succeed in killing the beast of Gévaudan, and Miss de Barjac is yours."

"However, I cannot succeed in this enterprise without your help, and your antagonism leaves me very little hope…. This is why I implored you to tell me if you really loved the lovely chatelaine."

"Perhaps yes, perhaps no…. Again, what is it to you, Legris?"

"No, you do not love her; you could not love a woman who had treated you so cruelly, who put your existence in such danger! She must despise you, and you must hate her; any marriage between you is impossible. If you desire her hand with such ardor, it is, without a doubt that you are doing so for one of three reasons, which are: that you wish to take revenge for her disdain and past violence against you, or that you wish to thwart the monk's project of marrying off their pupil to the Prior's nephew, or finally, that you have no other reason than increase your fortune by becoming Lord of Mercoire…. Come now; answer with your normal honesty, Laroche-Boisseau, am I not correct?"

"There is perhaps some truth in your suppositions," answered the Baron laconically.

"I can therefore," continued Legris, with extraordinary agitation, "openly ask you to make some sacrifices. From all appearances, you will come into possession of the Varinas domains, much larger than those of Mercoire; but if you want to wrest this rich prey from the clutches of these greedy monks who have been holding it so many years, you will need new funds; funds which my father is disposed to provide. Further, in case the lawsuit fails, you will find him very flexible on the history of your past debts; he might even go as far as returning to you title of all your properties. Finally, we would give you full satisfaction on all the issues."

"And what do you ask in exchange, my dear Legris?"

"Very little: if the beast of Gévaudan was to be killed by either one of us, it would always be me who profits from that exploit."

"Marvelous; and since one must plan for all possibilities, what if neither one of us succeeds in this endeavor?"

"Then we will owe you, in good form, for your generous intentions…. But you will make every effort to make this work, and you will succeed. You would have too much displeasure at seeing Léonce, or any other adventurer, steal the hand and the lands of Miss de Barjac. Yes, we will succeed. You will have the patrimony of Laroche-Boisseau and the domains of Varinas; and I will have Mercoire and that capricious lady who despises you…. Well, Baron, give me your answer; is it agreed?"

Laroche-Boisseau, in his life of adventure and debauchery, had lost long ago the touch of finesse, the personal sentiments of dignity that characterizes the wholesome side of the nobility. However, either he indeed loved Christine, or he was outraged by the insolence of this upstart who cynically proposed such a deal; he suddenly straightened with a menacing air. He was perhaps about to explode, when the door half opened and a servant announced that the "man from Mercoire" had arrived and was waiting in a reception room.

This news brought Laroche-Boisseau back to himself; controlling his temper he resumed an ostensibly benevolent air:

"Now, now, we will return to that subject later! Let us not count our chickens before they are hatched…. The most urgent, my dear Legris, is to see Fargeot and discover his secret and take advantage of it; until we are enlightened on this point, we should postpone any final decision."

Legris feared that he had wounded the gentleman's pride and this current mildness surprised as well as delighted him. He hastened to stand up.

"You are right," he replied, "I will take the old scoundrel in hand, and wily and timorous as he may be, I will know how to bring him to reason. However, I would be much surer of success if you would promise me…"

"What can I promise before having a greater certainty relative to the Varinas domain? Bring me good news and we will come to an understanding. Now! get to work, my dear Legris! You have to win your spurs. It appears that Fargeot is not easy to handle; you will have all the more merit in conquering him…. I could have taken care of this myself," continued Laroche-Boisseau, "but it suits you better than me; There are things that I do not know how to do, after all."

Legris pretended not to notice the barely hidden contempt expressed by his patron concerning the mission he had been given. Laroche-Boisseau opened the drawer where he had crammed the pieces of gold that he had won gambling.

'Take them," he said, "and do not jeopardize the negotiation with your usual stinginess. Give Fargeot all that he demands, even up to the last piece of gold. You must dazzle him; make promises as if you had at your disposal all the treasures of Peru…. Have you understood me?"

"Yes, yes," replied Legris while collecting the coins in the drawer; "I hope to succeed without having to throw all this money out the window. Until things change, you will not have too much, my dear Baron…. Now! I will leave you, but I will return soon to announce my victory!"

He gave a sign of encouragement, and went out. As soon as the Baron no longer heard the sound of his steps, he gave vent to his frustrations:

"What impudence! what stupidity! what brazenness; to dare make such a proposal… to me! Purport to marry Miss de Barjac, him, the son of an old penny-pincher, this narrow-minded, evil-thinking, stingy coward! I do not know what kept me from exploding and telling him so…. However, the situation is too serious, and I must handle him with care… as long as I need him!"

Chapter XVI

THE AGREEMENT

Fargeot, since the tragic death of his daughter, had left the lodge by the lake and relinquished his position as Chief Guard for Mercoire, a function, moreover, in which he had always poorly performed. The general opinion there was that he had been the primary cause of the gruesome event, and in spite of his apparent repentance, they made no attempt to hide the loathing that he inspired in them. Nevertheless, either Miss de Barjac had followed Marion's last wishes, or a mysterious influence had intervened in favor of the former Chief Guard, as he was not ingloriously dismissed for his disgraceful conduct as he deserved. Far from it. He was granted a pension at the chateau; he had a sort of supervisory role over the other servants, and he was given the least arduous tasks. His life was therefore very comfortable in his new position, unless the disdain that they showed him at all times, and perhaps secret feelings of remorse, troubled his thoughts.

Even physically, Fargeot had undergone a complete change. His formerly florid complexion had become normal, his luxurious portliness had subsided; his cheeks were flaccid and sagging, his eyes lackluster and empty. In place of his handsome guard's uniform, he wore a sort of grey livery which floated on his emaciated body. Everything about him illustrated the withering effect of humiliation and the loss of self-esteem. However, it did not require long observation to realize that grief did not make him a better man; his temperament seemed to have embittered further, and his hatred towards others increased with the contempt and the hate towards himself.

When Legris entered the kitchen, Fargeot, who was sitting by the fireplace, got up and greeted him somberly. The young bourgeois took a familiar and protective tone with him, as he had learned from his patron, LaRoche-Boisseau.

"Good day to you, Master Fargeot," he said with enthusiasm, "delighted to see you!... But let us go into the salon; we will be more at ease there to chat.... And Madam Richard will be happy to have us served two bottles of her best wine.... Immediately; is that not so, Madam Richard?"

The hostess was quite surprised. Normally as arrogant with inferiors as he was servile and indulgent with gentlemen, Legris was not in the custom of treating persons with Fargeot's status in this manner. However, the

Baron's friend did not appear to notice the effect produced by the dispensation of his usual haughtiness.; he moved to the next room, and Fargeot automatically followed him. Soon they were each seated across from each other at a table where the two requested bottles had already been placed.

Legris began by overwhelming the messenger with questions about all the inhabitants of Mercoire, for whom he expressed great affection. The replies were laconic and cold, spoken as if on the defensive. Tired of this irritating reserve, Legris seized one of the bottles and filled the glasses with a golden liqueur which released a delicious aroma throughout the room.

"So, friend Fargeot," he said in an engaging tone, "you must be tired by this early morning errand. You will certainly accept my invitation."

"Thank you, but I promised myself to no longer drink wine."

"That can apply to the poor wine of the village tavern, but this is Saint-Péray, and Madam Richard's Saint-Péray is reputed in all the Province. Taste it, I insist; just this once will not hurt. What the Devil!"

Fargeot turned his head away, repeating his refusal.

"As you wish," said Legris.

He brought his glass to his lips and appeared to slowly savor the precious nectar. The former drunkard remained impassive.

The conversation continued: one not letting himself be questioned, the other, answering briefly and with monosyllables. In this way, Legris learned that Miss de Barjac, true to her resolutions, had not once worn her amazon outfit since the last hunt in the forest of Mercoire., that she no longer went horseback riding, that she never went out without being accompanied by de Magnac and several servants, that she lived by herself, that she seemed sad, etc. So, while these details were interesting, he was no further advanced as regards the mission he had been given. He sought some way to astutely broach the issue; however, either by chance, or by plan, Fargeot never gave him the opportunity, and time was passing without a result.

"We have to find the way," Legris thought to himself, "or he really did become a convert…. The Devil if I know how to handle the old goat!"

Fargeot, undoubtedly annoyed by this useless chatter, finally got up.

"I have replied to all your questions, Sire Legris," he continued; "On your side, allow me to accomplish my mission; may I advise my masters that Sire Laroche-Boisseau is still well on the road to recovery?"

"You may even announce that he has completely recovered; my noble friend is even speaking of riding his horse!"

"That will certainly please Sire de Magnac who is very impatient to hear that Sire Baron's wound is completely healed."

"And why is that, Fargeot?"

"I do not know…. And you also, Sire Legris, you are refreshed and ready for action. Sire Baron must no longer need your daily care as it is said that you often travel outside the area?"

"Ah," Legris asked uncomfortably, "is the knight also inquiring about me?"

"I believe so; he is concerned as much about you as Sire Laroche-Boisseau himself, and asks about every little detail about one as much as the other."

"That is too kind…. The truth is, my dear Fargeot, that the Baron does not rest enough and that his strength is returning very slowly. If I was not here to watch over him and prevent him from acting recklessly… Do not be in too much of a hurry to give favorable news to that worthy knight. For example, I hope that in two or three weeks, Laroche-Boisseau will be able to stand and that I will no longer have to worry about him."

Legris was undoubtedly counting that by that time he and his friend would have left Langogne and the Mercoire area.

"That suffices," resumed Legris, "I can now make my report."

He was about to leave. Legris, momentarily disconcerted by the Knight de Magnac's high degree of interest in him, was suddenly reminded of the urgency of the current situation.

"A moment, my dear man," he resumed affectionately; "I remark in you a great sadness, which distresses me. I am aware of your misfortunes, and although we are of different circumstances," (he emphasized those last words,) "I would like to give you some comfort…. Come now, Fargeot, what has changed you to this point? Are you not happy in Mercoire? Are they not giving your tribulations the respect that you deserve?

These friendly overtures were of a nature to make quite an impression on Fargeot, still somber and constrained, and plagued with remorse, was not used to hearing himself addressed with words of sympathy. However, he answered with bitterness:

"Respect! Sire; and what respect do you think they have for me? Everyone, over there, blames and despises me. I was re-admitted to the chateau, but that was out of pity, and perhaps in consideration for the deceased…. They do not like me; I could die like a dog behind some bushes, no one would regret it…. Finally," he continued in a fierce tone, "perhaps I deserved it, or worse?"

"And for what reason? Was it your fault that the poor child insisted on running off to find you in the forest in spite of the entreaties of Grand-Pierre? Had you done or said anything to push her to act so imprudently? This was simply a deplorable accident that was unjust and absurd to blame on you."

"Do you really think so, Sire? Is this really what you believe? resumed Fargeot, straightening himself with an indescribable expression of joy. "That is what I told myself, but the others, especially the priest of Mercoire, think otherwise."

"Sit back down, and let us chat like good friends. Those who wish to torment you have perhaps their own reasons for acting this way. But less critical persons, like myself and my worthy patron, Sire Laroche-Boisseau, can only have pity. The only culprit is that cursed animal which we are going to hunt down and destroy when the Baron has fully recovered."

"Oh! allow me to assist you…. I will help you!" exclaimed Fargeot, with warmth; "I can provide you with the means to surprise that accursed beast…. Thus," he continued in a different tone, "Sire Baron finds that I have no reason to reproach myself in the terrible event that deprived me of my poor daughter?"

"One would have to be stupid or very mean to think otherwise; or I repeat that someone purposely working to inspire these ideas in you to gain some advantage…. What were you saying about the priest from Mercoire who was trying to trouble your conscience with undeserved reproaches?"

"Ah! you are right, Sire," said the guard, with a hateful expression. "That priest was expecting something from me, and now I am certain that this was at the instigation of the Frontenac monks…. But although I was half mad with pain, I proved myself as cunning as he, and he did not obtain what he coveted."

"And what did he covet, dear Fargeot?"

"Nothing, nothing, Sire."

Legris understood that he could not go too rapidly, and that he would most surely attain his goal by redoubling skill and patience.

"I conclude from all this, Fargeot," he resumed carefully, "that they are not treating you well over there in Mercoire, and I would counsel you to leave the chateau as soon as possible. By my faith, they will end up by driving you crazy!... Already, you are unrecognizable. Formerly such a good companion and merry company; now you live like a wolf; you do not laugh any more, you do not speak, you are pale and hollow-cheeked. Come now, Fargeot, are you a man? Cheer up, morbleu!... Here," he added, filling up the glasses, "I propose a toast that you will not refuse this time: to your charming Mistress, the noble Damsel de Barjac, and to the disarray of the schemers that surround her!"

At the same time, he presented the glass to Fargeot, who accepted it.

"I cannot refuse such a toast," he replied. "Miss de Barjac had excellent intentions for my poor daughter, and although she does not like me…"

"She would feel sorry for you if she was not continually besotted by those creatures from Frontenac; and may God or the Devil confound them!"

"Amen, with all my heart," replied Fargeot.

And he emptied his glass.

From that moment on, it seemed that Marion's father became another man. The treacherous capabilities of the tempter had finally triumphed over his regrets; balanced until now between good and bad, Fargeot fell back headlong into the bad.

A conversation in low voices, but quite animated, had now been established between the two friends. Fargeot, renouncing his taciturnity, seemed to have recovered his old instincts for astuteness. But if certain proposals startled him and awakened his scruples, then Legris redoubled his wit and eloquence, and Fargeot could not resist. Moreover, one drink followed the other; Fargeot, after the first glass was emptied, did not stop searching in the excellence of the wine compensation for his long abstinence of all alcoholic spirits. The two bottles of Saint-Péray having been emptied, more were ordered; and once again, more were ordered. The generous host led by example and did not spare himself, such that by the end of their session, he was almost as drunk as his companion.

One can guess the results of this conversation. Little by little, a complete harmony reigned between the two drinkers. The gold that filled the pocket of one, passed, by stages, to that of the other. Soon, Fargeot, in his turn, took out of his vest pocket a greasy wallet, and out of the wallet a paper which he gave to Legris. The latter, after a brief look, expressed an extraordinary level of joy. Finally, Fargeot stood up tottering.

"Marvelous! What will be will be!" he exclaimed; "Morbleu! I do not want to be sad anymore. I want to have a good time again.... Sadness would kill a cat, by thunder!... Well! Sire Legris, it is agreed, I will return to Mercoire and give them my leave; then I will enter the service of Sire Baron, and we will all begin looking for my old valet, Jeannot, whose testimony is so important in this affair. I will charge myself with making him talk, despite his folly, and furthermore, he will help us find that infernal beast of Gévaudan which devoured... but one must not think of that... One word, however, Legris. Are you sure that Sire Baron will agree to all this?"

"He will keep all my promises, dear Fargeot, I assure you; but I must add that I was acting in his name, and it is his gold that is now jingling in your pockets.... Leave, then; and hasten to return.... In the meantime, let us have one more toast to the health of your new master, the Baron Laroche-Boisseau!"

"Yes, yes, to the health of Sire Baron!" exclaimed Fargeot, resolutely emptying his glass, "and may he confound all those villainous monks, including that hypocrite Prior who took those arrogant airs with me! Now they shall see what sort of a man I am. And the others, over there in Mercoire, how I will put them back in their place! And as for that attention-grabbing knight, with his nu-cracker jaw, that old prudish nun, Sister Magloire and those shiftless lackeys, how I will rebuff them and make them envy my gold! I cannot wait to see that!... Right, I am leaving."

They were both standing: Fargeot threw himself into the arms of Legris, who not steady on his legs either, almost fell over from the shock.

"Ah! Legris!" he exclaimed with affection, shedding winey tears, "you are my benefactor, my comrade, my best friend.... I was blind, stupid and miserable. You opened my eyes and spirit. You put joy back in my heart.... This will be between us for life unto death! We must separate now, but I shall return tomorrow, and we will never be separated again.... What good times we shall have together.... Now, come with me; I want you to see me mount my horse; One should never have to leave one's friends, my dear Legris!"

While speaking, he had passed his arm under that of his drinking partner and was dragging him towards the door. They crossed, in this manner, the main hall of the inn where the widow Richard and her service staff were working. Legris, as we knew, was very elegantly dressed: hat embroided with gold, silk suit with lace trimming and epaulettes; made him look like a real gentleman. Fargeot, on the contrary, with his common look, dreadful face and drab clothing, presented a typical drunk in his final stage. The fact that both were wearing outfits which were disheveled and that their faces were flushed, inspired a maximum of disgust in the lovely hostess and her servants.

Without worrying about this silent disapproval, they reached the courtyard of the inn where Fargeot had left the old wheezy horse that had brought him there. They again exchanged friendly words and advice, then the traveler laboriously mounted his steed and departed, singing his favorite refrain:

> *"The brother drank like four,*
> *But the prior drank like ten."*

A minute later, Legris ran with staggering steps to report the results of his mission to Laroche-Boisseau.

The Baron, who was just finishing his lunch, frowned when he first saw the condition of his confidant; however, when Legris recounted the details of his discussion with Fargeot, and especially when he had shown him the important note that the guard had refused to give up until now, Laroche-Boisseau could not hold back his enthusiasm:

"This time, I have them!" he cried out impetuously; "I now have the means to bury those insolent monks! An accusation of assassination! What luck! The threat of announcing this abomination alone will suffice to decide them to restore the Varinas domains to me.... And what a great role this gives me! I will appear to be simply seeking vengeance for my young cousin who had been assassinated. My anger and my loathing for those people could not ask for more…. Divine maneuvering, Master Legris! You did not spare yourself in this battle, it seems; so much courage disarms me, and you shall have your share of the victory, I promise you. Now may Fargeot give us the opportunity to kill the beast of Gévaudan, so that the beautiful chateleine becomes yours with all her riches…. You see that I do not haggle over your services!"

Perhaps there was some irony in the Baron's promise; but Legris's usual perceptiveness had been blunted at this moment, and he did not notice.

"That is splendid, Laroche-Boisseau!!" he said warmly; I fully recognize your usual generosity! You will soon have all of your wishes fulfilled, I so predict. Entrust this affair to my father, and you will see what he achieves. Success is certain, and he will provide you with the necessary funds, I guarantee…. When I told you, Baron, that I would succeed!… In addition, see how well I managed your wealth. Here are a dozen Louis d'Or that I protected from the greed of Fargeot."

At the same time, he presented in his trembling hand, the mentioned pieces of gold. Laroche-Boisseau turned away.

"I do not want them!" he replied with disdain; "you will give this money to Fargeot! It belongs to him!"

"You do not want them?" resumed Legris; "Only a few days ago, Baron, you did not have enough, and you will be happy to find them when needed… Therefore, I will keep them for you…. You must not be so lavish!… Ah! my dear Laroche-Boisseau," he continued, abruptly changing his tone and sitting back in an armchair. "You cannot understand what sacrifices are imposed by friendship! Would you believe that I had to lower myself to the point of drinking with that peasant and treating him like a friend? And all this in front of Dame Richard and her servants, who were mocking me!… Can one debase oneself in such a way?"

And in a continued reaction, he burst into tears.

"Sometimes in debasing oneself, one raises oneself," said the Baron; "you will put him in his place when you are chatelain of Mercoire."

Chapter XVII

THE CONVENT

The Frontenac Abbey, as we have said, overlooked the small town of Florac a short distance below it in one of these picturesque and perfect locations that the monks had a talent for finding when selecting a site for their dwelling place. It was situated in a fertile valley, and its climate was far different from the inhospitable harshness of the northern part of the Province. The fruit trees and vineyards were known only by their names in the highlands but prospered around the monastery, along with cereals that nourished people and fodder crops which fed the livestock. The Frontenac valley was part of the blessed region which is called the Midi[29] of France; already known for its blue sky, blazing sunshine and warm gusts of wind of the Sirocco[30]. Undoubtedly, the long chain of mountains which extended over the horizon like blue barriers, sent it, by intervals, stormy clouds, devastating torrents and whirlwinds of snow; however, nature was so powerful and fertile in this privileged area that damage from disasters were rapidly repaired, and each year brought its own abundance and riches.

The founders of the religious institution established in this valley, as we know, were of ancient origin, and a number of its monks played an important role in the history of the Languedoc provinces. The monks of this monastery were erudite collectors of information, renowned under the names of Bollandists[31] and Benedictines, who dedicated themselves to historical and literary works. A good number of these powdery parchments that yet today overload the shelves of our public libraries came from the work cells of Frontenac.

Moreover, the elevation and size of the buildings bore witness to the importance of this illustrious Abbey. One found there the architecture of many eras, from Gothic in the XIIth and XIIIth centuries to the flat surfaces and right angles of modern times. This and some damaged portions of walls and stones charred by fire evoked the revolutions and disasters that had

---

29   Midi: defined as the south of France bordering Spain to the south and Italy to the East.
30   Sirocco: a hot wind that blows from the Sahara Desert to southern Europe.
31   Bollandists: scholars and historians who since the 17th century have studied the cults of the saints in Christianity

occurred around it. However, the overall construction which encompassed a number of courtyards had a majestic aspect; the cloisters, in particular, were magnificent, and an immense park, shaded by centuries-old trees, provided the monks with long alleys favorable for meditation.

Outside this collection of buildings was an isolated house with a private garden and a special entryway; this was, for practical purposes, the secular area of the Abbey; it was called the *Guest Pavilion*. It was used to house persons involved with the convent; such as relatives and friends of the monks, or simple visitors; all of whom were received with sumptuous hospitality. It was there that Léonce also lived, his close kinship with the all-powerful Prior of Frontenac, having qualified him for such a favor. This cherished student at the monastery occupied a small apartment that consisted of a bedroom and a study. When he was a child, an elderly nurse had taken care of him with motherly tenderness. Later, a lay brother had performed the functions of an attentive and devoted servant. As for the education and instruction of Léonce, this was in particular the handiwork of his uncle, the Prior, but the other priests of Frontenac had all played their own part. Each of the Abbey's collection of linguists, historians, mathematicians and theologians were delighted to contribute to the intellect of the best loved pupil of the convent. In summary, never did a young man have as many eminent experts as teachers in the various branches of human knowledge. In this manner, Léonce became scholarly, but at the same time had contact at the pavilion with many guests, distinguished for the most part, who imperceptibly put him at ease in the environment he would join one day.

However, since Léonce had returned from Mercoire with his uncle, following the events that we know, much had dramatically changed at the peaceful Guest Pavilion. Our young resident, formerly sedentary, quiet and studious, became raucous and dissipated. He came and went at all hours of the day and night; he surrounded himself with outsiders to the convent, went hunting on horseback, and his hounds' barking sometimes disturbed the services of the neighboring church. In his work study, his mathematics instruments began to rust, and his globes were covered with dust; the books borrowed from the rich library of the Abbey lay scattered on the floor, while the furniture was covered with whips, spurs and rifles. In other words, the pavilion's resident had suddenly veered from a studious contemplative life to an active and turbulent one, which heralded an age of passion.

However, these changes did not appear to surprise or upset the Prior or the other dignitaries of Frontenac; far from it, they smiled with indulgence at Léonce's dissipation, and his uncle, with a complacency which seemed to border on weakness, allowed him to continue without constraint. Certain monks of a lower rank sometimes muttered about the young man's noisy lapses, but no one listened. The Prior's nephew retained a total independence of conduct, and although he was a subject of surveillance, a surveillance ever so discreet, this would not trouble him.

That was the situation as we entered the winter season. On a lovely morning in November, Léonce left for a hunt accompanied by his trackers. Impatient to see him again, Prior Bonaventure had the idea of going to meet him on his return. He therefore left the Abbey, opening his prayer book, and slowly walking down the well-kept path that led to the area where Léonce was hunting.

Although the cold had already exercised its rigors on the surrounding mountains, the happy valley of Frontenac had not yet suffered too cruelly from its effects. The grass was still green, and the chestnut trees had not yet lost their leaves. Moreover, the warm, though pale, sun brightened the surroundings and encouraged the birds to sing in the shrubbery. The Prior, after having finished reading his scriptures of the day, sat on the parapet of a wooden bridge where one could discover the vast countryside below; the bridge being the limiting point of his walks, and where his nephew usually rejoined him. Once again, Prior Bonaventure's wait was not in vain; soon the sound of a gunshot and distant barking announced the return of the hunters; then Léonce himself emerged from the thickets, rifle on his shoulder, followed by his trackers and his hounds.

However, while waiting for his nephew to rejoin him, the monk mechanically glanced in the opposite direction and noticed an object that did not fail to draw his attention. It was a closed litter carried by two mules, since the use of wheeled carriages was impractical in these mountainous regions. In addition to the mule driver who walked in the lead, there were four lackeys on horseback who escorted the litter. This little caravan was descending one of the hillsides that dominated the valley and was heading towards the Abbey.

The Prior became pensive.

"Who could this be?" he asked himself; "we are expecting no one at the convent, unless it is one of those poor gentlemen in the vicinity who greatly appreciates our wine and our food…. But, no, those gentlemen would come on horseback; it would be a woman or a cleric who would travel in this fashion. A woman would not be admitted to the Abbey; then is must be… However, a cleric accompanied in this way must be of high eminence."

He fell silent and again studied the travelers.

"Bah!" he eventually continued, "what I fear is unlikely to happen, at least not so soon. The rumors that I have heard do not seem credible. I suppose that it is some Reverend Father from Sainte-Énimie who is coming to visit our Abbey!"

He was interrupted in his reflections by Léonce who, preceding his helpers, came running up accompanied only by a beautiful black bloodhound with tan spots.

The Prior's nephew seemed to have grown and attained a new level of vigor over the past three months. His complexion was now tanned by the sun and exercise. He had a more masculine appearance and an assured composure that did not resemble the clerical timidity of the past. He was wearing an elegant green hunting outfit with gold braid, and he now resembled more a young and brilliant gentleman, friend to raucous pleasures and worldly joys, rather than that studious pupil raised in the shadow of the cloisters who recently asked to be allowed to pronounce his vows at the Frontenac Abbey.

Nevertheless, Léonce had not lost his respect for his uncle and benefactor. He approached him, doffed his cap, and kissed the hand of Father Bonaventure; it was only after having acquitted himself of this duty that he exclaimed joyously:

"Wonderful news, my uncle! it was a magnificent hunt!... One fox and two hares, killed at more than twenty paces, and each time with a single shot. Denis, my tracker and tutor in hunting, is delighted with me. As for myself, I do not yet dare brag about my achievements; I attribute them especially to the excellence of the rifle from Liege that you gave me, and also the marvelous instinct of this bloodhound that you found the means to somehow kidnap from a royal pack of hounds."

And he distractedly caressed the handsome animal which was bounding around them wagging its slender tail.

"Less modesty, my child," said the monk kindly, "your successes are due, in particular, to your dexterity. However, I am delighted that your tracker is conducting himself so well, and to complement your hunting staff, you will find at the Abbey Jean Godard's dog, the courageous mastiff that was the only one in the Province that dared pursue and attack the beast of Gévaudan."

"Is that possible, my uncle? I had heard it said that Sire de Laroche Boisseau..."

"The Baron, like yourself, understood the importance of such a creature, as it seems that he was planning a campaign similar to yours. He had therefore offered Jean Godard twenty Louis d'Or for his dog; but I had already given him forty, and he has just sent me that vigorous animal which you will find on a leash in the Pavilion's stable.... It was to announce these happy results of my efforts that I had come out here meet you."

Léonce was overwhelmed with joy, and he warmly expressed his appreciation to the Prior.

"Well, my dear uncle, what prevents me from beginning my pursuit of the beast immediately? My education as a marksman and hunter is completed; my assistants are ready. Denis and Gervais, my second tracker, are equally devoted; they would follow me anywhere; why would you not give me permission to go? According to recent reports, the beast is known to be in the mountains of Mézenc though they have not been able to force it out into the open; we will undoubtedly find it there, and with the help of God…"

"Léonce, my child," said the monk, giving a sigh, "why be in such a hurry to risk the dangers of such a task? I hate to expose you to… And I am still hoping that a new event will dispense you from going to this extreme."

"Oh! my uncle, how can one change what has already happened? I beg of you, do not hold me back any longer. I have been told that Sire de Laroche-Boisseau has completely recovered from his wound; he could take advantage of my tardiness to win the promised reward; and if this misfortune occurred, I would not survive it.!"

"Do not say that, Léonce, you have no idea how such an eventuality would sadden me! And reflect that you will not be the only one to suffer!... She also, this proud young girl, she would die of grief and shame if she found herself obliged to accept a husband not worthy of her…. Ingrate and imprudent! In a moment of madness, she disconcerted the wisest plans. Truly, since she pronounced that disastrous vow, I have proposed to her to have her released from her vow by the authority of the Church. In spite of the gentleness and submission she exhibits today, she refused to consent, and she replied to me, with her usual pride that a daughter of the House of Barjac, should not, under any circumstances, disavow one's words."

"And perhaps, dear uncle, she is right," said Léonce, with sadness; "no-one more than I will regret that fatal oath; but it seems to me that the best way to atone for her error is to honor it."

During this conversation, the Prior and his nephew were slowly returning to the Abbey. They were rejoined by Denis and Gervais, one carrying the rifles, and the other the game shot by their master. Denis was a man in his sixties, with an honest expression, and despite his age, was in robust health and had tireless legs. Gervais, much younger, was simple in nature, but at the same time, had the straightforwardness of the mountain people. The monk stopped and smiled at them.

"Good day, my brave people," he said with his usual benevolence. "I am very happy to see you so that I can thank you for your affectionate care and devotion for my dear nephew…. You have an excellent student, Denis, but do you really think he is ready to confront the terrible beast of Gévaudan?"

"With all due respect, my Reverend Father," replied Denis with enthusiasm, "our young master would be capable of confronting the Devil if the Devil's skin could be pierced by a bullet! I wish that your Reverence could have seen how he had killed that fox only an hour ago. A shot in the head at sixty-two paces away. One could not ask for more from gunpowder and lead. I am amazed myself. I have never seen such dexterity, sharp eye and rapidity.... And how well Sire Léonce handles a hunting knife! He never misses the heart of a deer, I guarantee. One should never glorify oneself, but considering I have been his only teacher..."

"You are right, Denis," replied the Prior cheerfully," one must always be just, even with oneself.... Well, you will go ahead of us and return to the Abbey to rid yourselves of your burdens as rapidly as possible; then you will go, on my behalf, find the Father treasurer, and you will tell him to give you, Denis, twenty Louis d'Or, and to you, Gervais, ten Louis d'Or.... Continue to serve my son faithfully, each of you, and you will be compensated."

Denis and Gervais, besides themselves with joy, wanted to thank the Prior for his generosity; but the Father made them a sign that he wished to remain alone with Léonce; therefore, they contented themselves with a bow and resumed their path to the convent.

Once they had travelled some distance away, Léonce spoke timidly:

"I admire your liberalism, my uncle, but sometimes I fear that it is sometimes expensive for you.... My fantasies are costing you large sums."

"Is the cause of your scruples the donation I just gave those poor souls?" asked the Prior, smiling. "Do not let that worry you, Léonce; you can remunerate with dignity all the services which are rendered to you... And for this purpose, I placed this very morning on your table a roll of one hundred Louis d'Or for your use as you see fit."

"I am overwhelmed by your kindness, my uncle, and I do not know if I should..."

"Accept in all good conscience, my child, as these riches are really yours. You were too young until now to inquire about your heritage; however, it is considerable, and when I have explained this to you, which will be soon, you will realize that they have been administered wisely. So, take these coins; since your childhood, you have learned with us austerity, prudence and moderation in your desires; you will use it within measure of your wealth, I am sure."

Léonce was about to reply, when the principal bell of the abbey began clanging like on the days of religious events.

"What is happening, my uncle?" he asked, giving a start.

"I do not know; there are no services at this hour; the ringing must be to announce the arrival of a high-ranking church official, or a call for an immediate meeting of the Chapter, or perhaps both. Also, since the Abbot is suffering at this moment from gout and rheumatism, it might be because he needs help.... Therefore, Léonce, we need to hurry."

"Of course, dear Father; but you cannot guess the reason..."

"I still hope that it is only a formal visit. His Lordship the Bishop of Mende began his pastoral rounds a few days ago. However," continued Bonaventure seeing a priest who was hurrying towards them drenched in perspiration, "what does the good Father Anselme want of us? There must extraordinary circumstances to have him decide to run."

Indeed, a stout monk, usually happy and smiling, but at this moment breathless, and looking very worried, was about to join them.

"Ah, dear Father Prior," he exclaimed, "hasten to return…. Never has our Sainted house been in such a disarray. We are in a panic, we have been looking for you everywhere: only your presence can reassure us."

"What is happening then?" asked Bonaventure, keeping pace; "the guest who has just arrived, is it not His Lordship the Bishop of Mende?"

"Alas no, Father Prior. It is indeed a Bishop, but not the one from Mende…. It is His Lordship Bishop of Cambis, *titular* Bishop of Alep, and he comes as the King's Commissioner over the Abbey and the Frontenac Chapter."

"The King's Commissioner?" repeated Bonaventure, who could not keep himself from turning pale; and why would the secular powers intervene in the affairs of our peaceful community?"

"That is something that you should know better than I, Father Prior, but His Lordship de Cambis speaks to all of us in severe tones which we are not used to. He claims that he has formal orders from the King and His Lordship the Bishop of Mende to whom we belong…. Barely arrived, he refused all offers of refreshments and ordered the assembly of the Chapter; not the general Chapter which includes all the priests of Frontenac, but the senior members of the Chapter which includes only the dignitaries of the convent. We obeyed, as we are already trembling in his presence, and the senior members are already gathered in the room of the Abbot. However, what will surprise you the most is that the Bishop first asked about you…."

"About me?"

"Yes, and when he learned of your absence, he appeared worried that you had left forever, which greatly angered him; he calmed down only when he learned that you had gone out for a simple stroll. The Abbot is extremely agitated and ordered me to run to get you and beg you to hasten to return."

"Well, your task is completed, Father Anselm, and we have arrived…. May God protect us from all harm!"

They were entering the first courtyard of the Abbey. This courtyard, usually quite calm, was now, very animated. The litter that the Prior had noticed was still attached to the two mules in a corner; the four lackeys of the escort had dismounted, but were standing still, their arms intertwined with the reins of their horses, as if awaiting orders. Some monks were wandering around them reciting their rosaries which were being agitated loudly in the folds of their robes. Some priests gathered at the entryway of the corridor that led to the apartment of the Abbot, were discussing heatedly, while the large bell of the monastery continued to shake the old edifice with its clanging sounds.

All eyes turned at the arrival of the Prior; however, the rules of the house may have prohibited questioning a superior, or they were already aware of some rumors unfavorable to Father Bonaventure; no one dared speak to him and simply bowed as he passed.

The Prior, on his side, had recovered his serenity. After having crossed the entryway of the Abbey, he said amicably to his guide:

"Thank you for your trouble, dear Father Anselme; since you are not a senior member of the Chapter, we must separate here. I will go up to the rooms of our Reverend Abbot; you, dear Father, pray to God."

"For what reason, please?" asked the monk, with ill-concealed curiosity.

"So that God give us the strength to accomplish a painful duty and help avoid a scandal."

And he redoubled his steps, leaving Anselme completely intrigued by this answer.

As he was about to cross the threshold of the building occupied by the Abbot, Bonaventure felt a discreet tug on his sleeve, and Léonce, who had not left his side, asked him with a worried air:

"My uncle, please, what is going on? One would say that some misfortune menaces you. Could you tell me…"

Bonaventure smiled calmly at him.

"Nothing, there is nothing, my son," he continued; "you are wrong to be alarmed. It probably concerns some old disciplinary affair that will be easily corrected by His Lordship Bishop of Alep…. Return to the Pavilion, Léonce, and do not think any more about it… And listen," he added as if it were an afterthought, "since you have such an ardent desire to start your campaign to hunt the beast of Gévaudan, I do not see why I should continue to resist granting your wish…. Following the meeting of the Chapter, I will come to see you at your apartment and we will agree on the final arrangements."

"What! My uncle," exclaimed Léonce joyously, "you finally agree to…"

"I must, wicked child, since you are impatient to leave…. I am not totally decided about this separation. I want to clarify certain points before definitively releasing you. However, go ahead and make preparations as if you were leaving the Abbey this very evening…. Go now, my dear Léonce; they are waiting for me…. May God protect you."

He smiled once more, waved his hand and entered the convent.

Léonce had the presentiment that his uncle was not as calm as he wanted to appear; but his joy prevented him from noticing a number of circumstances, which at any other time, would have awakened his suspicions, and he returned to Guest Pavilion.

Chapter XVIII

THE CHAPTER

The room of the Abbot of Frontenac was a dark one, with chestnut wall paneling, decorated with sculptures and paintings representing subjects taken from the lives of Saints. The deep-set stained-glass windows projected strange colors upon the five or six elderly bald-headed monks who were the senior council of the convent. These clerics were seated in wooden armchairs around the Abbot, a venerable old man, whose mind had never been strong, and whose infirmities weakened it further with each passing day. Half-lying in a large arm chair, the leader of the Community had his legs and feet enveloped in blankets. However, in respect to the illustrious visitor who had arrived in Frontenac in such a brusque manner, he had hurriedly donned his monastic vestments which he wore over his bed clothes. He had replaced his normal head covering by a golden mitre[32] and had ordered that his golden pastoral staff be attached to the arm of his chair. Thus surrounded by all the symbols of his ecclesiastic dignity, he did his best to take on a cool and serious air that did not entirely hide his inner anguish and physical suffering.

Across from him, sitting on a chair higher than his, sat, as if on a throne, the Bishop who was charged with a royal mission concerning the Frontenac Abbey. The small size and paleness of Monsignor de Cambis contrasted with the formidable powers he was said to have. It had been necessary to place a velvet cushion under his feet so that they could touch the floor. His thin and bony figure appeared endowed with exceptional mobility; his eyes were bright and piercing, his voice harsh and dry, and his words voluble. He wore a purple cassock without a tunic; and his head which had little hair, was covered with a simple purple skullcap. Despite his stunted appearance, there was an element of pride which was imposing. On the oak table near at hand were papers and parchments, several of which bore large wax or lead seals.

When the Prior entered, the Bishop was speaking to the members of the Chapter in a muffled voice, but with extreme vehemence. The Fathers and the Abbot listened in modest silence with heads bowed, their hands

---

32 mitre: a liturgical headdress worn by Roman Catholic Bishops and Abbots, developed from the papal tiara.

hidden in the ample sleeves of their robes; one would have said like statues. However, at the sight of Prior Bonaventure, the wisdom and strength of the convent, the statues awoke; everyone straightened and seemed to breathe more easily; a flash of hope illuminated their austere expressions. The Abbot, in particular, appeared relieved of an enormous weight; he lifted his hands towards the sky, and spoke to the Bishop with vivacity:

"Excuse me, Monsignor; here is our worthy Father Prior, who can best reply to all the queries of your Lordship."

And he added, addressing Bonaventure:

"Ah! dear Father, what is this situation you left me in? May God help me! My strength abandons me!"

And he passed a handkerchief over his face bathed in cold sweat.

The Bishop of Alep had fallen silent and was examining the Prior of Frontenac with avid curiosity. The latter did not react when he felt this inquisitive look fall upon him. He calmly took some holy water from the font placed near the door, made the sign of the cross, bowed deeply before the Abbot, and then knelt humbly on the cushion at the feet of the Bishop.

"May your excellence," he said, "grant me your pastoral benediction."

There was nothing in that exchange that did not conform to normal ceremonial procedure in use at that epoch by the clerical hierarchy. However, the Bishop suddenly drew back.

"One moment, Father Prior," he replied drily, "we shall soon see if I must…. You have certainly made us wait!"

Bonaventure arose, bowed once more, then went to an empty seat next to the Abbot.

There was a moment of ominous silence.

"Father Bonaventure, Prior of the Frontenac Abbey," continued the Bishop of Alep, pointing to the papers scattered on the table, "I have already communicated to the members of the Chapter the powers by which I must inquire about certain already ancient events, both spiritual and temporal, relative to the succession of the estate of the Count of Varinas. These powers give me unlimited authority to evaluate the facts concerning this affair…. Would you care to also look at these documents?"

The Prior did not leave his seat, and modestly replied that he had no intention of questioning the authority of the Monsignor; as for his part, he would submit himself, without a murmur, to all the decisions of His Excellence. This response softened the prelate a bit.

"That suffices," he replied, "and in particular, Father Prior, you have an interest in that we follow scrupulously the formalities of justice in this affair. At this point, I will not hide from you that you are seriously incriminated in a manner that not only compromises your sacred character as a priest, but also your reputation as an administrator of worldly goods. We have been assured that you are innocent of the monstrous crime for which you have been accused, and that a word from you will suffice to justify your actions. Can you agree to provide that word? I will facilitate as much as it is my power to help you prove your innocence. However, if you are not able to do so, you will find that I am unrelenting in my judgement."

Bonaventure bowed once more. The good Abbot, who had found his courage, dared make a tentative effort to support his old advisor:

"Monsignor," he said softly, "our beloved Prior, I repeat, is for us a model of wisdom and piety. All the Fathers here present are guarantors of his innocence!"

"This is true, Monsignor, this is really true," said the other monks respectfully.

"Peace! My Fathers," resumed the Bishop drily: "the spirit of religious solidarity is carrying you too far, and perhaps I should place blame on your entire Community.... If one has committed crime, have not all the others profited? However, it is time to leave the generalities. Listen now, and learn why I have been sent here with the task of linking or absolving, of rewarding or punishing."

He then began to expose the details of his mission. The events referred to are already known to the reader, and we will summarize the actions that created the storm which suddenly burst upon the Abbey of Frontenac and on its Prior.

We know how the purported written proof of an act that Fargeot had at first tried to sell to Father Bonaventure had fallen into the hands of Laroche-Boisseau. The Baron then used this note to force the monks to restitute to him the Varinas domains as he was the direct heir since the death of the last member of that family. Skillfully counseled by the elder Legris, he submitted a petition to the King in which were registered the facts against the Abbey and its Prior. This petition, along with supporting documents were immediately forwarded to Versailles. Laroche-Boisseau, in spite of the state of disdain in which he was held within his province, had retained a number of friends at the Royal Court. His title as Baron of Gévaudan and Lieutenant of the Louveterie gave him status with persons of influence who warmly pled his cause. His petition was therefore submitted to the King and passed on, approved for further action, to the Chancellor[33] of France.

The circumstances were favorable for a legal proceeding of this nature. Philosophism was making continual progress. Voltaire was a power; the works of Jean-Jacques Rousseau were already shaking the old world. The Duke of Choiseul, then Minister of the Chancellery, was very conscious of public opinion. He had recently banished the detested order of the Jesu-

---

33 Chancellor: under the Ancient Regime, the Chancellor was responsible for the judiciary.

its. The accusations in the petition against the opulent Abbey of Frontenac seemed to merit serious attention. They wished to give themselves an air of impartiality by showing themselves severe with the clergy as well as their enemies. There was the issue of the estate of the Count de Varinas, especially the mysterious death of his child and the abandon of his fortune to the religious Community, all that was needed to excite public indignation; it was important to bring justice as soon as possible, without creating a scandal that could have unpleasant consequences. To that end, the Royal government had decided to secretly send a Commissioner to Frontenac with full powers to investigate this unfortunate affair and terminate it without noise. They had chosen for this delicate mission Monsignor de Gambis, a passionate and violent man, but of an integrity above reproach. The Bishop, by his zeal and tireless actions, had shown himself worthy of this lofty mission. He had left Paris before any notice had been transmitted to Frontenac; he had travelled night and day without stopping except to have his powers verified by the Bishop of Mende, and he landed like a clap of thunder on the Abbey, with an authority all the more formidable in that it had to be exercised in the shadows and without limitation.

The prelate, picking up the papers that he had brought, among which was the declaration of Fargeot's wife along with the Baron's petition, enumerated at length all the charges which were being brought against the Fathers of Frontenac. He brought up the lawsuit that had been initiated long ago by the Laroche-Boisseau, father and son, close relatives and legal heirs to the Varinas family. He affirmed that the decision of the judges regarding the will of the deceased Count would have been quite different if they had known then about the strange revelations which came out later.

"However," he continued, "it is not initially on the affair of the succession of the Varinas that I wish to draw your attention, Reverend Fathers. That your Community, in its desire for gain and temporal goods, convinced a sick gentleman whose spirit had been weakened, that they had found an excuse in the almost admitted Protestantism of the Barons Laroche-Boisseau to have themselves bequeathed a heritage which was rightfully theirs, these are undoubtedly wrongs, but that can be repaired. I have the power to demand restitution in favor of the current Baron, and will do so as justice serves heretics as well as the orthodox…. But what really upsets the Royal Court, and generates both horror and indignation, is that a priest of this Community can be reasonably suspected of complicity in the assassination of a poor little child…. This appalling accusation must take priority over all the others, and it is to this, my Fathers, that I urge you to answer first. Speak without fear; nothing which is said here must reach the exterior, and absolute secrecy will protect your confessions; but the entire truth must come out."

Monsignor the Royal Commissioner stopped speaking, tired by this long harangue. To his great surprise, the listeners expressed more sadness than fright. The Abbot himself, in spite of his suffering, did not look downcast, but straightened himself and spoke with nobility:

"In the name of God, the Virgin and all the Saints, I protest against the bad intentions, the scandals and the crimes of which the Frontenac Community is accused, and in particular our dear and venerated Father Prior; these charges are false and slanderous. The respectable prelate who is listening to me will regret one day having been the echo of it."

Monsignor de Gambis frowned.

"Very well, Reverend Abbot," he replied, "but I can no longer accept simple denials. I am alleging facts, and it is with facts that one must respond…. Father Prior of Frontenac," he continued, addressing Bonaventure, "you have the heaviest role in the charges against the Abbey. What do you have to say in your defense?"

"Monsignor," he replied amidst a profound silence, "before bringing these accusations against an institution as ancient and illustrious, one that has produced so many renowned defenders of religion, so many confessors of the faith and which today, contains so many individuals eminent for their science, their virtue and their piety; it would have been just perhaps, and in conformity with the spirit of the Church, to verify the testimony of our detractors. Therefore, who are, according to the papers that you have just indicated to us, those who dare bring upon us this odious slander? I can, while keeping in moderation, characterize them thusly: the wet-nurse of the young Viscount, a weak and timid woman who perhaps was searching in the guilt of others an excuse for her own negligence; then the guard Fargeot, her husband, who tried to sell me, for a sum of money, the paper which is the primary evidence of this accusation, an offer which I rejected with disdain; then finally, the Baron de Laroche-Boisseau, a heretic, a libertine, who after having spent all his money on debauchery, had wanted to take revenge after the failure of his claim to the heritage of his uncle. As for Jeannot, that old farm helper, whose testimony could have some importance concerning my role, has been suffering for a number of years from a form of madness called lycanthropy, and his testimony could not merit credence."

"Very well," said the prelate nodding his head, "I understand your system of defense. You wish to place your high reputation of wisdom and piety compared to the unworthiness of your adversaries; however unworthy people, by themselves, can tell the truth, and once again, simple denials do not suffice to destroy a collection of material proofs. As for the monomaniac Jeannot, the former Chief Guard of Mercoire affirms, with the guarantee of the Baron Laroche-Boisseau, that this man, in spite of his current handicap, has moments of lucidity. Therefore, Sire de Laroche-Boisseau and Fargeot have set out to search for that unfortunate, and they are doing their best so that in a few days…"

"I can spare them that tiring and perhaps dangerous effort," replied the Prior calmly. "You have not understood me, Monsignor. I have no intention of denying certain testimonies, and to prove it to you, I admit that Jeannot told the truth. All the Fathers here know, indeed, that on the evening of the disappearance of the little Viscount, I was in the vicinity of the Varinas chateau with… with an unknown person."

Monsignor de Cambis leaped up from his chair.

"You admit it?" he exclaimed. "What? Shameful priest, sacrilege, you dare claim…"

"Allow me, Monsignor, we still do not understand each other…. Yes, I was at Varinas at the time of the tragedy; but I reject with all the strength of my innocence the crime I am accused of, if there was a crime."

"So, how do you explain yourself?"

"I do not explain, Monsignor…. A solemn oath that I took, and that all the Fathers here took as well, prevent us from saying what I was doing there in Varinas, and that oath obliges us to maintain an absolute silence on this for about two more months."

The prelate was struck with astonishment.

"An oath… which commits all the members of the Chapter?" he resumed with a smile of disbelief; "that is a strange excuse! And you will permit me, my Reverend Fathers, to find it… hardly admissible."

"Nevertheless," said the Abbot, "our worthy Prior has never lied."

'In any case, I can release you from your vow by virtue of the spiritual powers with which I have been vested."

"With your permission, Monsignor, only the Pope can annul a vow, and you did not come with a Papal brief."

"Then I shall write to the Court of Rome in order to obtain the brief; then you will no longer have a pretext to maintain silence."

"Indeed, Monsignor, but Rome is far from here and the response from His Holiness would not arrive here before two months, and in two months, nothing would oppose our secret to be known."

"Marvelous, my Fathers; This way I can wait peacefully for two months until it pleases you to justify yourselves? However, there is another way to convince you to speak…. Like yourselves, I am a priest, responsible for souls…. Therefore, I order you to reveal, under the seal of confession, the events that are within your knowledge."

This proposal produced a certain effect on the members of the Chapter. Their eyes turned towards the Prior, who showed no hesitation and said firmly:

"This was foreseen, my Reverend Fathers, remember the meticulous conditions which were imposed on us.... As for myself, I refuse to betray, even under the seal of confession, a secret which was confided in me as a man of property, and as a man of faith and minister of the alters."

"And we too! And we too!" repeated the other monks.

This obstinate resistance to his wishes and the absolute confidence in the Prior, succeeded in bringing to a maximum the displeasure of Monsignor de Cambis. He arose, and despite his small size, he had such an expression on his face of contempt, indignation and menace, that all the Fathers trembled.

"There is no longer any doubt," he resumed with a constrained voice, "this is a concerted effort to elude spiritual and temporal orders; it is open rebellion against everything that is respectable on earth and in heaven; it is a ruse to escape the punishment you deserve! If I were to grant you, my Fathers, the delay that you ask, who knows what machinations you would invent again to escape my justice? You are under a bad influence, and this influence is that of an audacious and clever monk who reigns supreme; but I will succeed in destroying his pride!... Come now, my Reverend Fathers, there is still time.... Will you answer my questions? Will you finally resist the temptations of this evil spirit who is inspiring your revolt?"

The monks were dismayed and trembling, but they remained silent.

"Monsignor," said the poor old Abbot painfully, "what you interpret as a revolt is merely the awareness of a great sense of duty. Once again, the day that the truth is known, you will bitterly regret your severity and your haste!"

"That is enough, Reverend Father, I am accountable to the judge of judges. Well, since all the convent has sinned, all the convent will share in the atonement.... I will settle here until I have succeeded in taming your senseless stubbornness; I will occupy one of your cells and the meager fare of your brothers will suffice me. I will immediately take over the governance of this monastery. I am closing down the monastery as is within my power. All its functions are suspended; there is no longer an Abbot, nor a Prior, nor dignitaries of any sort; but only unworthy monks in rebellion against their God and their King. The bells of the Abbey will no longer sound and the lamp of the sanctuary shall be extinguished; Religious services will not be held in a desecrated church. We shall fast every day: the meals will consist of bread and boiled vegetables. The community may not assemble, and no one may leave the convent without specific permission. Three times per day, the professed and the novices will recite the psalms of penitence.... This state of things will continue as long as you have not answered my questions concerning the succession of Varinas and the murder of the child. Anyone who transgresses these rules will risk excommunication, whoever he is."

Tears and sobs erupted from all sides. Bonaventure, distraught, threw himself down at the feet of the Bishop.

"Oh! Monsignor, Monsignor," he exclaimed, I beg of you, do not treat with such severity a Sainted house where the laws of God and men have never ceased to be obeyed. If there is a guilty person, it would be me, and me alone who is charged with the worldly affairs of the Abbey...."

"You admit it again?... Well, have the courage to admit your sins, and my justice will spare your brothers, more astray than guilty, undoubtedly, to concentrate on you."

"However, to obey would be sacrilege.... It concerns interests which are dear and sacred and which are for me more precious than life! I swear it, Monsignor, I swear it on my eternal salvation...."

"You dare speak of your salvation, cursed false priest provocateur? If I listened only to my legitimate anger, I would remove you from the Holy Orders and deliver you to the secular authorities.... However, since the fear of scandal prevents me from going to that extreme, do not think for a moment that I will reserve a punishment any less painful; the day that your crime is definitely proven, you shall be thrown into a dungeon where you will never again see the light of day.... In the meanwhile, return to your cell; you will be restricted to bread and water of penitence; you will not communicate with anyone and the keys will only be given to me. Anyone who attempts to speak to you without my specific permission will be struck by excommunication."

This terrible sentence was received with renewed sobbing. However, Bonaventure, who had so deeply felt the pain and shame of the punishment inflicted on the community, showed himself completely resigned when it concerned only himself.

"Monsignor," he said, crossing his arms on his chest, "we are perhaps each doing our duty.... May God pardon and enlighten you! I submit myself humbly to the penitence which you see fit to impose upon me!"

"And we also, Monsignor," repeated the members of the Chapter, one after the other with humility.

The Royal Commissioner finally appeared to experience some doubt on the guilt of these poor monks. He was a severe judge, but his piety was sincere and profound. He paced pensively two or three times around the room; then he went to kneel in silence before an ivory crucifix that decorated a wooden panel. After a few moments of prayer, he arose and spoke to the monks who had resumed their attitude of silence and mediation.

"Pardon me, my Fathers; I have sinned by an excess of zeal and human presumption; up to now, I have not brought to this affair the patience and moderation that you have a right to expect from a judge.... My Fathers, I will suspend the effects of my threats for one hour, starting now; in that interval, perhaps God will inspire in you repentance and confidence: but if your hearts remain hardened, you will take upon yourselves the results of your obstinacy. Deliberate calmly; I will await in a nearby cell the result of your reflections, and when the hour is up, I will come to learn your answer…. May peace be with you, my Reverend Fathers!"

And he went out with measured steps, leaving the monks free to communicate among themselves on their fears and hopes.

After his departure, the lamentations continued, however, no doubt, no uncertainty was expressed as to the direction to take. The members of the Chapter were unanimously in agreement that it was better to suffer the humiliation and rigors than to betray a secret confided to their conscience, and Bonaventure, with a few heartfelt words, confirmed them in their resolution.

"My dear Fathers," he had said to them in an emotional voice, "it would be easy for us to tear down this construction of calumny that they have brought against us; but we cannot do so without violating sacred scruples. We must therefore accept, with resignation, the ordeal that the heavens have sent down on us: we will come through it even stronger and purer! Let us avoid blaming the hand that strikes us; the most faithful servants of God are sometimes subject to error! The day, and it is not far away, that our innocence is revealed, we will be raised in our strength and our dignity!"

All the monks embraced each other: then Bonaventure seemed to ready himself to leave.

"Ah! Father Prior,' said the old Abbot with concern, "are you going to abandon us again? Monsignor de Gambis will soon return, and I feel too weak to support the weight of his anger!"

"I will be absent for only a few moments," replied Bonaventure, "I wish to take advantage of this short respite which we have been given to carry out a project, the postponement of which could later create certain problems."

And he spoke in low tones to the Superior to explain.

"Good, good, dear Prior; you are always right!" replied the Abbot; "go and hasten to return to give us the benefit of your prudence and courage."

The Prior bowed, and went out.

He hurriedly crossed the silent corridors, cloisters and courtyards and headed towards the Guest Pavilion. Everything on his way was calm; the convent had its normal aspect; there was no sign of the impending execution of the sentence planned by the Bishop against the unfortunate Abbey. The portals were all open, everyone could come and go freely. Bonaventure thought only that the Fathers and Brothers who passed near him, giving him the customary bow, appeared sad and downcast, as though they had a presentiment of the cruel change which was about to occur.

Léonce, in his small apartment, had just finished having his arms and other effects that he wanted to take with him packed. At the sight of the Prior, he ran up to him and asked anxiously:

"Well, my uncle, are you coming to give me a counter-order?"

"On the contrary, my child," said Bonaventure; "Having reflected on it, I no longer wish to oppose your desires. As you said yourself, time is passing, and you might miss an occasion to succeed in your enterprise. Therefore, I am here to give you leave and bid you farewell... You shall leave immediately."

"Immediately, my uncle?" exclaimed Léonce in astonishment.

"Why not? You will sleep in Mende tonight with your people and early tomorrow morning you will take the road to the Mézenc mountains. In this manner you will save a day, and it could be important in this affair... My friends," he continued, addressing Denis and Gervais who were closing the suitcases, "load this baggage on the horses and on the mule which belongs to my nephew.... Now hurry, and make sure that all is ready in ten minutes."

"My good uncle, what is going on? Your sudden determination and eagerness to see me leave, when only this morning, you seemed to still feel hesitation for this journey, makes me think... And then you are so pale, and there are traces of tears on your cheeks.... What has happened to you?"

"You would not expect, my child, that this separation could be accomplished without deep regrets on my side.... But let that be, my dear Léonce, and listen to my advice, the last you will receive from me for a long time."

In few words, he gave his nephew wise and prudent instructions, to which the young man promised to conform. Then he continued with emotion:

"And now, my son, another recommendation, mere important than you can imagine.... I have tried to warn you a number of times against certain calumnies that powerful enemies have been spreading against the Fathers of Frontenac and myself. Do not listen, I beg of you, to these detestable lies. Even if the whole world turns against us, allow me to hope that you will keep piously in your heart sentiments of respect and gratitude."

"How could you ever doubt this, my uncle?" interrupted Léonce, warmly. "If someone had the audacity to claim..."

"Do not even try to fight this scandal mongering, my child, they will fail on their own; it suffices to me that you not give them any credibility. And by the way, my son, during your coming adventures, you may encounter Baron Laroche-Boisseau: I insist that my young relative, my beloved pupil, give me his solemn word that he never quarrels, under any pretext, with the Baron.... Can he do this?"

"I do not see, my uncle, why I should have any consideration for that unworthy gentleman who has so seriously offended Miss de Barjac, and who has also insulted you.... "

"Miss de Barjac has taken her own revenge, and I, I am a Christian; I know how to forgive. I have strong reasons, my child, to request of you this commitment.... Dear Léonce, would you refuse to make it?"

Léonce gave his word, but with visible repugnance. Then, the uncle and nephew embraced cordially; each had their eyes full of tears.

"Alright! It is time," the Prior courageously resumed. "Come! I will transmit your farewells to the Fathers with whom you were particularly close as a student and friend.... They will pardon this unexpected departure.... We have only a few minutes left...."

While speaking, he was leading his nephew towards the courtyard.

"But why, my uncle," asked Léonce, "does my departure from the Abbey, which I consider to be my paternal home, have a furtive appearance, like an escape?"

"I will explain this later.... But they are waiting for me.... Come, come!"

At the portal of the convent, they found Denis and Gervais, who had completed their task. The two horses were saddled, and the mule loaded with baggage. The tracker had the bloodhound as well as the mastiff on leash, the latter growling at being so close to the other.

Bonaventure warmly recommended Léonce to the two valets, promising them magnificent rewards if they brought him home safe and sound. They renewed their promise to protect their young master with their lives; then they took their leave first, as Léonce, with a better horse, would catch up rapidly.

Left alone, uncle and nephew embraced once again, and Léonce mounted his horse.

"May God bless you, my child!" said the Prior; "may He protect you from all dangers, and have you succeed in your enterprise.... Above all, that He bring you back soon among your friends!"

The traveler departed slowly, looking back frequently; and the monk, in tears, returned to the Abbey murmuring:

"May my fate be done! At least one major problem has been averted.... It would have been too painful to have this noble child witness my humiliation; moreover, he might have compromised everything by some imprudent action.... Ah! he will never know how much my bringing him up will have cost me!"

And he ran up to the Abbot's room, where he arrived only a few minutes before the time fixed by the Bishop.

Chapter XIX

THE FÉRÉOL FAMILY

At some distance from the city of Langogne, also situated on one of the highest plateaus of the Lozère, begins a chain of mountains which connect, at different points, with the Alps and the Cévennes; it is called the Mézenc.

Like other mountain chains in the Velay and the Vivarais, it is made up of volcanos which have been extinct for thousands of years. It would be impossible to find a landscape more rugged and bristling with natural obstacles; in other words, far from easily accessible. One finds arduous peaks, jagged ridges and lava flows from which the cooling process had left strange formations; add to this chasms, boulders, roaring waterfalls and lakes formed in ancient volcano craters. Apart from the valleys and certain privileged slopes, the countryside was bare and sterile; its richness consisted of pastureland on which grazed numerous flocks, and chestnut trees the fruit of which furnished the only resources of the inhabitants. Consequently, the mountain dwellers of Mézenc lived in extreme poverty and in a semi-savage state. Hardship and isolation had rendered them mistrustful, quarrelsome and unsociable. Even to this day, when so many outside issues could influence their traditional character, they remain jealous, vindictive and always ready for a fight at the mildest offense. In summary, one could say that this untamable spirit was in harmony with the menacing nature and rugged countryside where they were born.

In one of the most solitary valleys of the Canton, was located an isolated tenant farm whose inhabitants' sole activity was caring for livestock, as none of the land around them was cultivable. It is in this sad and miserable dwelling, surrounded on all sides by pine trees and basaltic masses, that we will soon rediscover certain important characters in this story.

Towards the evening of the third day after Léonce had left Frontenac, the tenant farmer and his family were seated on a bench outside the door of their home; they were having their supper which consisted for each of a wooden bowl containing a porridge of chestnuts with milk. The father was dressed in a large cloak made of local cloth with a jacket and pants of the same material, and wearing a cap with its side brims folded upwards. His feet were shod in wooden clogs. He was about fifty years old, had a morose expression, a cold manner and was taciturn in appearance. His family included his wife, a vigorous peasant woman, whose laced bodice and disheveled hair did not give an impression of cleanliness nor freshness; then a daughter, an uneducated and unattractive twelve-year-old; and finally, two tall sons; eighteen and twenty years old, dressed much like their father, and already somber like him. All this crowd were not saying a word, and the only sounds heard were those of spoons against the steaming bowls.

In another season one would have thought that these people were just outside their door to breathe the fresh air before a good night's sleep; however, the cold was piercing and a stinging wind was blowing down from the mountain. A light layer of snow had already covered the countryside which had prevented the livestock, which one could hear moving about in the stables, being sent to pasture that day. Therefore, these mountain dwellers had another motive for neglecting the warm fire which brightened the interior of their home while they dined outside in spite of the cold.

Indeed, on the slope of the hill which was opposite the dwelling, four mounted travelers were following a path that had been irregularly traced by the flock. The path led to the farm, and did not go further; thus, the travelers were by necessity coming to the farm, and considering the solitude in which lived this family of shepherds, such a visit must have generated much curiosity.

Of the four persons that we have mentioned, the two that were leading seemed to me the masters, while the two others appeared to be of inferior status. However, all were well dressed in city attire, well-armed with rifles and hunting knives. Meandering around them were several large dogs whose colors stood out against the snow.

It was a spectacle of great interest to these coarse people who, from time immemorial, had not seen such an affluence of city-dwellers in their wilderness. They waited, therefore, wooden bowls in hand, not daring to turn their eyes away, for fear of losing one detail of what was about to happen.

They did not have long to wait. A horseman, perfectly mounted, who seemed to be the head of their group, preceded his companions and came by himself towards the farm. In a moment he had rejoined the mountain people still motionless, on the threshold of their home.

"My friends," he said in the Gévaudan dialect, which differed little from the one used in Mézenc, "is this not the farm of the Motte-Rouge, occupied by the tenant farmer Guillaume Féréol, also known as *Épée-du-Juste*?[34]"

It was the head of the family who replied with stiffness:

"You are at the Motte-Rouge, and I am Guillaume Féréol…. As for the sobriquet Épée-du-Juste, that was given long ago to my grandfather, and I

34 *Épée-du-Juste*: in English—Sword-of-the-Righteous

would consider myself unworthy of using."

The traveler did not seem to notice these last words.

"Fine! Well friend Féréol," he resumed, "grant me and my friends your hospitality for this night…. I come on the recommendation of your master, Sire de Langeac, who I have known for a long time; moreover, I shall pay generously for your trouble."

"I do not have a *master*," replied the mountain dweller with a sort of fierce pride, "and my door is open to anyone, rich or poor, who presents himself in the name of God…. Therefore, enter, there is room in my home for you and yours; your animals will find bedding and hay in my stable. I cannot receive you in the style to which you are accustomed as we are very poor, but the little I have belongs to the guests that God sends me."

"Excellent, my friend," said the traveler; we are hunters and we will not be difficult. Moreover, we brought some provisions, so we will not deprive your family."

At the same time, the Baron Laroche-Boisseau, who the reader had undoubtedly recognized by now, dismounted and signaled his companions to rejoin him. They finally arrived; these were Legris, Fargeot and their tracker, Labranche; all were famished and exhausted by their long journey in the mountains.

The Féréol family did not show any signs of courtesy, but at a signal from the father, they each put themselves into movement to receive the new arrivals and prepare the honors of the house. The horses were led to the stable where they had plenty of forage. The dogs, which had already begun to quarrel with those of the farm, were enclosed in a pig shed, except for the favorite bloodhound. The quarreling dogs were given a coarse but abundant soup to compensate them for their captivity. As for the guests, Féréol introduced them into the house; several pine logs were thrown into the fireplace; then, while the travelers were warming themselves, the mother and daughter actively prepared items for their supper.

These items were modest, the provisions consisted of bacon, cheese and chestnuts with water as the beverage. Fortunately, Laroche-Boisseau, and especially Legris, had come prepared. Some cold meats and assorted items, more appealing than those of the household, were taken from the saddlebags and spread on the table. Soon, all the travelers, masters and valets, were fraternally partaking in the feast, seasoned by fatigue and appetite.

In the meantime, night had fallen; a small iron lamp added its light to that of the hearth. The door was shut and the wind whistled around the roof. While the travelers ate, the various members of the Féréol family finished their farm chores, which put an end to the infernal noise of their clogs and they came to sit down behind their guests. They were invited, without ceremony, to partake of the good food; they refused somberly; only the father accepted a glass of wine, as a sign of hospitality; but he set it back on the table after only wetting his lips.

These strange manners had several times provoked hilarity from Legris; however, Laroche-Boisseau suppressed by a piercing look those reactions which might indispose their host, who undoubtedly did not have much patience.

After the meal, the Baron wished to initiate an intimate conversation with the inhabitants of the farm.

"Well, Master Féréol," he asked in an informal and friendly tone; "you are here only one or two leagues away from Bois-du-Saut, where that terrible beast of Gévaudan was last seen. Could you tell me if it has left the area recently?"

"Not as far as I know, Sire."

"It is said that it has been wounded," continued Laroche-Boisseau, "and this might give us a more favorable opportunity, as you have undoubtedly guessed that we have come to Mézenc to hunt the beast of Gévaudan."

Something resembling a smile crossed the lips of Féréol.

"It is true that I have been told," he resumed, "that it had been shot by a guard at Langeac; however, whether it was wounded or not, Sires, you would be better off abandoning your project."

"What? my dear fellow," asked Legris in a mocking tone, "are you among those who believe that the beast is invulnerable?"

"I do not believe it to be invulnerable, Sire," replied Féréol becoming animated; "because I have seen for myself traces of its blood in the snow at the Margeride; many shooters have seen it fall under their fire and thought they had killed it; however, two or three days later it would reappear, seemingly more vigorous and dangerous, its wounds no longer visible. It would have shaken off the bullets that had struck it like gravel. It had regained its strength and ferocity. What more does one need?" he continued with vehemence. "Does not the finger of God appear here? Is it not evident to mortal eyes that this formidable beast has been sent as chastisement for our sins, that it has been unleashed like a plague to punish us for the incredulity, half-heartedness, vices, and abominations of this wicked generation? In truth, I say to you: it is not with your bullets and rifles, with your hunting knives and your swords that you will kill this emissary of divine justice, but with fasting and prayer.... Return to God, impious men, and the beast will be hurled back into the depths from which it came!"

The family received this almost biblical homily from Féréol with a respectful inclination of their heads. Legris, stupefied for a moment, was about to release a peal of laughter, but a gesture from Laroche-Boisseau stopped him just in time.

"Sire Féréol," resumed the Baron, "your words confirm a suspicion I had after seeing the golden crosses worn at their necks by your wife and daughter; you and your family, are certainly followers of the Protestant religion?"

The master of the household straightened proudly:

"What is it to you?" he said. "When I received you in my home as my guest and my friend, did I ask you if you and yours belonged to the arrogant Church of Rome or to the poor and dispersed members of the Protestant Church?... However," he continued with harshness, "I will never disavow either my faith or my God. My peers attended the preachings, their rifles at their shoulders and their hands on the hilt of their swords.... My sons and I would be ready to do the same!"

His enthusiasm was reflected in the eyes of his sons, and even in those of his wife and his daughter, who were listening in silence.

They were obviously in the home of descendants of the terrible sectarians who, sixty years earlier, under the name camisards[35], bloodied the Cévennes region. Obliged to avoid large population centers, where the Royal edicts prohibited them from publicly observing their religion, their followers took refuge in the most inaccessible parts of the country and established themselves in isolation. Government tolerance had been extended to them since that epoch, and despite the severity of the decrees still in effect, no one was concerned about what was happening in those solitudes.; therefore, those Protestant mountain dwellers had maintained their indomitable fanaticism of those times, a fanaticism all the more exalted due to the fact that persecution could, at any moment, be renewed for them.

"You are mistaken, Master Féréol," resumed the Baron, gravely, "there are no stupid judgements in my words.... But now that I think of it, the surname of Épée-le-Juste that was given to your grandfather and that you still have today, was it not also held by a brave partisan who shared the suffering of the pious and loyal Pierre de Varinas in the days of Berwick and de Villars?"

The farmer raised his head.

"As you have said, Sire," he replied, "my grandfather was precisely the loyal retainer who never abandoned the Count, his Lord, during the persecution, and who lived a long time with him in the Grotto de Varinas. They lived on roots and wild fruit; they slept leaning against their rifles. Twenty times the soldiers were sent to capture them, but they always escaped them

---

35   Camisards: Camisards were Huguenots of the isolated Cevennes region in southern France in the early 1700s who raised a resistance against persecution, following the revocation of the Edict of Nantes.

thanks to their skill and audacity…. My grandfather, Épée-le-Juste, who I knew during my childhood, enjoyed telling me about the events of those cruel times, and myself, I recounted them many times to my own children…. Because we, poor people, have remained loyal to the faith of our martyred fathers in place of the Lords of Varinas…."

"You must be speaking," said the Baron, "of the last Count de Varinas, who after having converted to Catholicism, died miserably at the Frontenac Abbey? He was cruelly punished for his apostasy, Master Féréol, and the extinction of his branch was perhaps a chastisement from Heaven…. However, you must be aware that a minor branch of the Varinas has scrupulously kept its faith, and to this branch, Féréol, I am a proud member; as I too am a descendent of the audacious Varinas you were speaking of a short time ago; I am the Baron de Laroche-Boisseau!"

This revelation did not appear to have the effect on the sectarian that the Baron perhaps expected; on the other hand, his wife and the children could not help showing their surprise and respect. However, Féréol stood up:

"I will not hide from you, Sire Baron," he said with reserve, "one has spoken to me of you as being a gentleman who is luke-warm in his faith, as a worldly person who has squandered his fortune on women…. But, no matter! It is a feast when the house of Épée-le-Juste receives a descendent of the Sainted martyr, the Count of Varinas…. Blessed be the day!"

He kissed the hand of his guest, and each member of the family in turn went to render the same tribute. This ceremony was accomplished with the same puritan rigidity that characterized all the actions of Féréol; however, Legris no longer thought about laughing; and he remained stupefied by the new seriousness that his patron had assumed.

Laroche-Boisseau, indeed, seemed to patiently adapt himself to the mood of his co-religionists.

"You must not, my dear Féréol," he resumed, "show yourself too severe with city Protestants. The Royal edicts are not to be taken lightly, and if we lack prudence… However, I see that you are already frowning…. Let us drop a subject on which we perhaps do not agree…. I wish to live peacefully with you, Master Féréol, as befits brothers in religion; and first of all, I must ask if we can count on your help tomorrow. I will need a guide who perfectly knows the area, to take us to Bois-du-Saut, where it is said that the beast of Gévaudan has taken refuge."

"Hence, Sire, you persist in this senseless and perhaps sacrilegious project? I repeat that no physical weapon will prevail against this monster; the bullets will be powerless, the iron will flatten against its skin, as it has received the mission from God of vengeance and extermination…. But, so be it," continued Féréol in a different tone; "you will be served in accordance with your wishes…. Here is Ruben, my oldest son, who will take you tomorrow morning to Bois-du-Saut, and perhaps I may even decide to accompany you myself."

Ruben, a handsome boy, almost of colossal height, gave a sign that he had heard the order and would execute it punctually. The Baron thanked both the father and the son.

"That is not all," he continued, "I am searching for a person whose discovery is almost as important to me as finding the beast, and this person may also be nearby. It is a person originally from here but who has lived for a long time in the Varinas domain and that of Mercoire; however, it seems that he has returned to Mézenc only a short time ago. He has lost his senses and now prefers living in the woods. His name is Jean Peyra, but he is better known by the name of Jeannot Grandes-Dents…. Would you be able, dear Féréol, to provide me with any information about him?"

This request made a certain impression on the Protestant family. Only their chief maintained his composure.

"Sire Baron," he said, after a short silence, "prior to coming here, did you not stop at the sheep farm at Grandsaigne located about a league from here on the other side of the mountain?"

"Certainly not, we came in a straight line from Langogne, where we had been told that your place was the closest to Bois-le-Saut…. But why this question, friend Féréol?"

"Well, the fact is that this morning, at Grandsaigne, a troop of hunters who announced, precisely as you have, their intention of hunting down the beast and finding the traces of Jeannot Grandes-Dents. Martin, the tenant farmer at Grandsaigne, came to warn me less than two hours before your arrival here, and at the same time asked for my advice about… things that concern me only. Thus, you did not stop at Frémin's place?"

"Not in the least," said the Baron, agitatedly, "and I would really like to know who are these insolent hunters who dare compete with us!"

"What! you do not guess?" exclaimed Legris; "it is the nephew of the Prior, the *lamb* as you like to say…. I had told you that he was he was about to set out. He did so!"

"Are you sure of this, Legris? Indeed, it seem possible…. Yes, I can well understand his interest in hunting the beast, but I do not understand his motives in looking for Jeannot."

"Bah! since the word had gotten around of the close relationship between the beast and the lunatic, one could have inquired about one to find the other."

"That is possible," said the Baron pensively, "here is a competition that displeases me, although Sire Léonce does not seem very redoubtable…. He undoubtedly intends to start the hunt tomorrow morning; we have to prevent that."

"We will leave before daylight if necessary."

Féréol had listened quietly to this conversation.

"Well, my dear host," resumed the Baron, "do you know anything about this Jeannot, who I fervently wish to locate in the interest of our mutual faith?"

Féréol hesitated for a moment.

"Sire Baron, Jean Peyra is my second cousin, and I know of a place where we might find him…. But I would let myself be torn to pieces before betraying his hiding place, unless I know what one is expecting from him!"

Laroche-Boisseau explained to him the dispute concerning the Varinas inheritance and tried to prove to him that it was of the utmost importance to the Protestant cause that this fortune returns to the legitimate heir to the detriment of the grasping monks of Frontenac; All the fanaticism of the mountain dweller was aroused by this cleverly presented narrative.

"Shame and abomination on the Church of Rome!" he exclaimed. "Since when must the assets of the children of God pass into the greedy hands of the children of Israel? I will commit my life and that of my family, Sire Baron, to helping you obtain justice in this beautiful cause…. Unfortunately, I fear that my cousin no longer has the capacity to provide testimony in your favor; his reason appears to be gone beyond remedy. He came here about a month ago, and sat in front of the house, where he had frequently visited a long time ago. My children were afraid of him and did not dare approach. When I returned from the pastures, I found him in the same place, and I recognized him immediately, in spite of his rags and miserable appearance. He recognized me as well, however all that I could get out of him were meaningless phrases followed by idiotic laughter. He refused to enter the house, but when I brought some food out to him, he threw himself upon it and devoured it in a blink of an eye. Afterwards he left, and since then, has been wandering around the countryside, living off who knows what. We cross paths with him often, but when we approach, he flees into the brushes where we cannot follow. However, because of our kinship, I had deposited, from time to time, in the locations that he frequented, bread or chestnuts; these provisions always disappeared the next day. You see, Sire Baron, it will not be easy lay a hand on poor Jeannot; moreover, I have reason to think that at certain moments, it could be very dangerous to approach him!"

"However, I intend to try, friend Féréol," resumed the Baron; "over there is someone who not only promises to be able to approach the unfortune maniac, but also to tame him completely as soon as we locate him…. Is that not so, Fargeot?" he continued, speaking to the former Chief Guard, who had returned to the fireside immediately after supper.

"Yes, yes, Sire Baron," replied Fargeot confidently; "that poor devil and I, we have known each other for a long time, and I know how to appease him…. In truth, he was not as savage then as he is today but I am sure that he will not flee if he is close enough to recognize me or even hear my voice."

The mountaineer, in his exaggerated respect for the bonds of kinship, insisted that the Baron promise that he would never harm his cousin, Jeannot, and that they would let him go free after they had obtained his testimony. Then it was decided that Féréol and Ruben would accompany the hunters the next day to Bois-le-Saut, where the madman seemed to be living, as in the past, in harmony with the beast of Gévaudan.

"It is wonderful," resumed Legris, "that we were able to agree on certain details of action; but what we must do, Baron, we must do as rapidly as possible. The proximity of Sire Léonce and his people begins to worry me greatly. If the wolf is really wounded, it should be easy to get him, and it would be inexcusable to miss the opportunity."

"Well, Legris," said the Baron, "we will leave with the first light of dawn. What would you want more?"

"I want nothing, Laroche-Boisseau, nothing at all," replied Legris with humor, "but now that certain projects which are important to you seem to be close to success, I find you cool about one of them; you seem to be much more pre-occupied with Jeannot than the beast."

The Baron spoke several words to him in a low voice to appease him.

"Alright, alright!" said Legris, "but tomorrow it is I that must kill the beast of Gévaudan… We will then see how your word can be judged."

And he went to sit near the fireplace with a sullen air, while the Baron disdainfully shrugged his shoulders.

Moreover, the evening was not prolonged. The travelers were exhausted, and they needed to regain their strength for the next day, which threatened to be a difficult one. Thus, Laroche-Boisseau expressed the desire to retire. However, prior to deferring to his wish, Féréol coldly invited him to join the family prayers which were about to take place in accordance with their custom each evening.

Laroche-Boisseau was well aware that his refusal might upset his host; however, his deference could not go so far as to put up with at least an hour of recitation of psalms in French. Therefore, he excused himself from this obligation by saying that his overwhelming fatigue would prevent him from attaining the necessary level of meditation. Féréol frowned, but contented himself by murmuring:

"It is written that prayer soothes and meditation invigorates the spirit. May God forgive the sinner and the man light in his faith."

Several moments later, the travelers were slumbering, some in the beds of their host, others on hay in the stable, where the breath of the livestock maintained a mild temperature. During a part of the night in the middle of the howling of the wind outside, could be heard the solemn and monotonous voice of the head of the family as he gave religious instruction to his children.

Chapter XX

THE BOIS-DU-SAUT

The next morning, at the first light of day, as had been agreed, the hunters, led by Féréol himself and his oldest son, left the farm of Motte-Rouge, headed for Bois-du-Saut where they hoped to find Jeannot and his horrible friend, the beast of Gévaudan. All were on foot, the difficulties and dangers of the paths not permitting the use of horses in the region they were entering. Laroche-Boisseau and his companions had their rifles; however, Féréol and his son, still convinced of the uselessness of these against the beast, were carrying only their iron staffs.

The sky was a somber grey; none of the brilliant hues which normally accompany a sunrise in the mountains colored the high peaks. A fresh layer of snow, which had fallen during the night, hid the irregularities of the terrain under its white uniformity. Thankfully, the wind had died down, and it looked as though it would be a calm day.

The travelers followed exactly in the tracks which their guides left in the snow. In spite of this precaution, they stumbled at almost every step and had great difficulty in avoiding falls. Moreover, a fall here could be mortal; they had left the cleared paths; sometimes they descended steep slopes bristling with sharp-edged lava or shards of granite, or sometimes they skirted chasms whose depth they did not dare judge. The tenacious snow which enveloped their feet seemed to enhance the peril.

A dismal silence reigned in this solitude, and all the living creatures seemed to have abandoned them. Not one bird of prey was to be seen swooping around the bare peaks. The dogs, upon leaving the farm, were running joyously ahead of them, but soon fell back; either the hidden crags were hurting their paws, or perhaps the absence of any trace of game had caused them to decide to conserve their energy for another day.

They had been walking for about an hour and they had covered about one league. However, they could not yet see Bois-le-Saut, and Legris, less robust than his companions, began to suffer.

"We are approaching," said Féréol with grave serenity; "but if you complain now about the difficulties of this trail, what will you say when we get to Saut?"

They needed another hour of walking before they reached the designated spot. A deep muffled sound, caused by a waterfall became increasingly louder as they moved closer; and when they finally reached the summit of a craggy rock formation that they had been climbing with difficulty, they suddenly found themselves in the presence of a view which was both forbidding and grandiose.

What one sees is four mountains of differing heights grouped in a square, such that at first glance. their bases seemed joined. However, at the foot of this gap plunged a hollow valley, like an abyss, where clumps of trees, peaks of basalt and blocks of rock, strangely superimposed, presented an impression of chaos. One's gaze loses itself in this terrible disorder, where everything seems mingled due to the layer of snow which covered the countryside. Most of the trees, uprooted by landslides, avalanches, or even the maelstrom of winds that engulfed these fearsome canyons, were bent, twisted, entwined around each other and linked by creeping vines. Enormous fern plants, gorse and a thousand thorny shrubs produced an impenetrable copse.

Several torrents streamed from the heights of the mountains down into the valley. The most important one came down from a mountain just opposite the hunters and formed a waterfall in front of them. The cold had not been too rigorous so the streams were not yet frozen; they charted a black or grey trail across the white base of the snow. The abundant waters which flooded from all directions were supposed to come together in the center of the valley; but here were lost underground as often happens in lands ravaged by volcanos, or perhaps did they flow into a subterranean canal? These were unknowns; the trees, the rocks, the large plants all seemed to have the mission of hiding from man the secrets of God.

Such was this formidable area that the hunters had to search with great care. In its first aspect, even the most confident began to have doubts about the success of their enterprise. However, they followed the fringe of this irregular forest, and they visited places where the traces of Jeannot and the beast had been seen several times. The most intensive investigations failed to produce results. Neither footprints nor paw prints were outlined in the snow. The dogs, discouraged, had no thoughts of pursuit, but were wandering around morosely, their snouts in the air, as if they were worried by the difficulties of their task.

They called a halt near one of those enormous boulders of basalt, which came from God knows where, but which one finds quite frequently in these burned mountains.

"May God help us!" said Féréol; "I do not understand a thing, any more…. It is very doubtful, however, that the man and beast have left the area."

'Indeed," resumed the Baron, "they could not find elsewhere a better place to hide, and more inaccessible…. However, Fargeot," he continued, addressing the guard, "the time has come for you to keep your word; it is your turn to track down this terrible Jeannot Grandes-Dents."

"My dear Baron," said Legris excitedly, "would it not be better to first take care of finding the wolf, and…"

"Corbleu! Legris, must one repeat it a thousand times that if we find Jeannot, the wolf will not be far?… Well, Fargeot," continued Laroche-Boisseau impatiently, "what are your thoughts? Have you been boasting about a power that you do not have? I thought that you were very impatient to revenge the death of your unfortunate daughter, Marion."

Fargeot, who appeared distracted and irresolute, jumped at the name.

"My daughter!" he repeated, rapidly lifting his head, "yes, yes, you are right…. I hesitated to betray that poor devil who had placed his confidence in me; but if he is really protecting that accursed animal that devoured my daughter… My conscience will be clear…. I will put myself to the task, and if Jeannot is near, we will see him soon."

"That is fine, Fargeot, do not lose any time…. Remember my promises, and remember yours!… Well, while you go off on your own, what should we be doing?"

Fargeot reflected.

"Wait here for my return," he resumed; "avoid showing yourselves on higher ground, and speak in low voices, as these customers have fine ears and piercing eye…. You must also attach the dogs, and they are not to be unleashed until further order. As for me, I do not need this rifle as the sight of it will immediately cause Jeannot to flee if we meet; the small pistols that I have in my pockets will suffice if needed."

He handed his rifle to Labranche and made sure that his pistols were operational. Then, tightening his clothing around him, he set off into the thickets.

Suddenly, at exactly the same spot where he had just disappeared, came an appalling howl that dominated the fracas of the waterfall. The dogs perked their ears; the hunters could not help giving a reaction of dread.

"The beast! the beast!" murmured Legris, cocking his rifle.

However, the practiced ear of Laroche-Boisseau had discerned the truth.

"It is Fargeot himself," he replied, laughing; "he has not forgotten that one must be able to howl with the wolves…. But, shh! Let us see if he gets an answer!"

During the several moments of waiting, the only sound to be heard was the muted sound of the torrents.

It seemed that Fargeot had changed his location, as soon a new howling was heard from a new location and with renewed vigor; however, this time, it had barely ceased that it was feebly repeated from a long distance.

Fargeot emerged from the woods and rejoined the hunters.

"He is here," he said animatedly, "and he recognized my signal…. He must be over there, near the large waterfall…. You must work your way around the woods and station yourselves on the other side, taking maximum precautions, while I cross back through the thickets. When I shoot one of my pistols, you must all come at once, after having released the dogs…. Is that well understood?"

They rapidly agreed on the various maneuvers; the hunters headed towards the waterfall following the mountain ledges, while Fargeot returned into the forest, where he began again his howls and calls.

We will follow first Laroche-Boisseau and the other hunters.

As we have said, they followed the edge of the forest as rapidly as they could, taking advantage of the irregularities of the terrain to hide their movements from the enemy. They maintained an absolute silence, and the sound of their steps was muffled by the snow. However, they had to make a long detour, and they were still a long way from the designated position, when the Baron, in spite of the orders that he had given to keep silence and hasten the march, suddenly stopped and gave out an exclamation of surprise and anger.

"What is it?" asked Legris, who had immediately rejoined him.

"Look!" said Laroche-Boisseau.

On the incline of the principal mountain, not far from the waterfall, appeared several persons also resembling hunters. Two vigorous dogs came and went in the snow as if they had discovered the trace of those that the Baron had searched for in vain. These unknowns constituted a group slightly more numerous than that of Laroche-Boisseau, and they all appeared well-armed.

"By the Devil! it is the Prior's nephew!" said Legris worriedly.

"Yes, it can only be he," replied the Baron, frowning. "And does it not seem to you, like myself, Legris, that these people are precisely positioned to reach our quarry before us, either the man or the wolf, that the imbecile, Fargeot, was to find?"

"Indeed, and this is an outrage…. But we will not allow it, is that not true, Baron? Let us meet up with them as rapidly as possible; we will give them the order to leave or…"

"In case of a conflict, we might not be the strongest, Legris; but in spite of your aggressive methods, you will be the first to recognize that it might best to react with cunning, if possible."

"I find you strangely tepid and patient, Laroche-Boisseau," said Legris disgruntledly.

They were rejoined by Féréol, who had stayed back a bit to study the other group of hunters.

"Those are the people who had stopped at Grandsaigne, and who I had mistaken you for," he said animatedly; "I recognize Martin, the tenant farmer of Grandsaigne, who is acting as their guide…. The hypocrite! the liar! he had promised not to betray my cousin, and he undoubtedly sold him out for a few ecus…. But, by the soul of my father! I will take blood revenge if some misfortune befalls Jeannot because of Martin!"

The puritan had disappeared at this moment and given way to the Mézenc mountain dweller, vindictive and indomitable in his fury. Laroche-Boisseau, despite his irritation, could not help smiling; it seemed to him strange that Féréol would show himself so terribly angry against someone for an action that he was guilty of as well; however, the Baron spoke to him with authority:

"No conflict with these people, do you hear me Féréol?… Let us go move toward them, and may no one dare disobey me!"

And he resumed his route with rapid steps, without noticing the gestures of revolt and the wrathful looks of the old sectarian, reluctant to concede to any other authority whatever it might be.

Finally, they arrived at the place that Léonce and his people had last been seen. During a portion of this travel, Fargeot had made himself heard from the middle if the brush, and he had been answered in the same manner; however, towards the end, the howling was no longer to be heard; either the two howlers had met, or the rumble of the waterfall drowned out their voices. Moreover, the sound of a shot which was to be a distress signal had not yet been heard, so they advanced carefully, taking care not to be discovered.

In spite of their precautions, Léonce and his companions had definitely seen their competitors advance towards them, and their hunt had been disturbed. They had stopped at the edge of a wooded precipice, unwilling to enter it until the other group made their intentions known. Léonce, upon sighting Laroche-Boisseau who was walking in the lead, made a move placing himself on the defensive, but immediately remembering that his uncle had asked that he avoid any quarrel with the Baron, he adopted a peaceful mien and prepared to act with friendship or as an enemy, depending on the circumstances.

On his side, Laroche-Boisseau had been thinking. The idea had come to him that it would add spice to the situation if he could use the Prior's nephew to help him succeed in his plan, which the inexperience of the young man might facilitate. He counted on being better able to counter Léonce's plans if he could gain his confidence; and perhaps he hoped to cleverly torture his detested rival. He therefore approached him with a smile on his lips and greeted him politely.

"Sire Léonce…. I believe?" he said in an almost friendly tone; "I have already had the honor, if I am not mistaken, in Mercoire?"

Léonce coldly returned his greeting.

"This is true, Sire, but our relations were so short, so lacking in warmth, that it would be perhaps better…"

"To not extending them? Allow me to disagree…. Come now, Sire Léonce," continued the Baron with an apparent friendliness, "I do not wish to remind you of my claims against the Frontenac Abbey, although you are now perhaps aware that they are legitimate; but why would a gallant gentleman like yourself take sides in that affair? You have become a hunter, it would seem, since our previous encounter, and I remember that you wish to take revenge on that cursed beast of Gévaudan…. The same reason brings us both here. Since circumstances bring us together, why not work together in mutual trust and fraternity that characterizes fellow huntsmen?"

This deceitful proposal was aligned with Léonce's secret intentions; nevertheless, he replied with an air of reserve.

"Perhaps I will find other grievances than those of the Fathers of Frontenac to bring against Sire de Laroche-Boisseau…. But, so be it. I prefer to forget these for the moment. I will not oppose anything that the Sire Baron wishes to attempt, providing that he also commits to not impede my projects during the brief time that we will be together."

"Accepted, Sire; each of us will retain complete independence; this is agreed."

They were interrupted by the sounds of a violent altercation between Féréol and the other tenant farmer. Féréol was energetically reproaching Martin for what he called his *betrayal*, and Martin, on his side, was reaching for his *coutelière*, the terrible hunting knife that the Mézenc mountaineers always carried with them. In addition, Léonce's dogs, emerging from the brush, were baring their teeth at the hounds of Laroche-Boisseau, and a conflict seemed inevitable between the beasts as well as the men.

The heads of the two groups hastened to intervene. Some firm words from Léonce and the Baron brought to a halt, in appearance at least, the dispute between Martin and Féréol, who moved away from each other throwing each other somber looks. As for the quadrupeds, several well-placed whip lashes sufficed to make disappear all inclinations of insubordination.

"Morbleu! Sire Léonce," said the Baron cheerfully, after all had calmed down. "Harmony is not that easy to establish between us. However, we will succeed if you wish it as much as I do…. And to begin with, I would ask you where that superb mastiff comes from that is over there snorting in the bushes. It must have cost you much, and by my faith, these days, a Prior's nephew seems to do better than a gentleman…. But let us forget that…. The actual circumstances oblige us to combine our resources. I will therefore not hide from you my plan of action; that insane fellow they call Jeannot Grandes-Dents is hiding in the forest; and it is in my greatest interest that I lay hands on him; one of my people who know him is already on his trail…"

"What!" exclaimed Léonce, as if relieved of a great weight, "it is only Jeannot that you are looking for here? I had thought… but," he continued, "if Jeannot is really in this Canton, he is accompanied by the beast of Gévaudan…. Look here!"

And he designated in the snow large footprints which followed the edge of the precipice. The Baron recognized everything first, but he feigned indifference.

"Decidedly," he replied. "one does not travel without the other, and this explains, Sire Léonce, certain circumstances relative to this famous wolf that really surprise the profane. As for me, I will not hesitate to send a shot its way if it crosses my path, as I am not unaware of the prize that can be claimed by the conqueror of the beast; however, above all, I wish to capture that cursed Jeannot for a reason that you will understand later…. On the other hand, Sire Léonce," he continued, pointing to Legris, who was observing them with irritated air, "over there is a hunter who intends to be your real competitor."

Legris, seeing that they were speaking of him, approached them, and after a brief greeting, addressed the Baron will ill-concealed anger:

"Must we renounce our project, LaRoche-Boisseau? I would think so seeing the new allies that you are adopting."

A frown from his patron warned him that he should take a calmer tone.

"One no longer hears Fargeot," he continued, "and I do not know what to think of his silence…. Why not search for a slope less steep to descend into the chasm?"

"Myself, I will go down from here," said Léonce firmly; "my dogs have found his trail again, and I must encourage them…. My hunting companions are free to follow if they wish."

And he moved towards the narrow ledge that bordered the precipice; it was the only path that could reach, from this side, the large waterfall. A crust of hardened ice and snow, thirty to forty paces in length, increased the perils on this frightful foot path.

"But that is folly!" exclaimed Legris, turning pale.

"Listen to me, Sire Léonce," said the Baron in his turn, "as I have promised to be a loyal adversary to you; that path is impractical to anyone but a mountain goat…. Besides, no signal has been given, and you have just as much chance staying here…."

"Remember our agreement, Sires," said Léonce with vivacity; "I do not intend to hinder your actions, do not hinder mine."

At that moment a shot was heard coming from the direction of the waterfall. Then were heard piecing screams, which were mixed with incredible howling.

"It is Fargeot!" exclaimed Legris.

"It must be Jeannot," said the Baron.

"I recognized the howling of the wolf," said Léonce.

He jumped, supple and light, onto the perilous ledge, lifting his rifle over his head, and moved towards the waterfall. The other hunters followed him with their eyes, expecting him at any moment to plummet into the abyss. However, this temerity remained unpunished; Léonce reached the other extremity of the ledge which led behind the waterfall itself, and passed under the arch formed by the tumbling water itself, and reappeared safe and sound on the other side. At the same instant, one could see him approaching two human forms which had suddenly appeared on the slope of the mountain.

The spectators were stupefied by this unexpected success. Legris was the first to regain his presence of mind.

"That trail is practicable? he exclaimed, "we must not hesitate; if we do not hasten to rejoin Sire Léonce, he is capable of winning the reward…. Remember your word and come with me."

"In fact," replied the Baron, "it would really be a shame to lose such a lovely match to that galantine. He will boast afterwards that he performed an action that made us hold back…. Let us do it, then, and the Devil with it!"

And in turn he launched himself onto the dangerous ledge, when his companion, who had preceded him by several steps, suddenly disappeared, letting out a cry of distress.

Laroche-Boisseau halted. Legris had just fallen from a frightening height. Fortunately, a mass of shrubberies appeared to have cushioned his fall, and soon one could hear him call from the bottom of the precipice. The Baron at first hesitated; then thinking that the mountaineers would be sufficient to provide the appropriate aid to his unfortunate friend, he continued to follow his path on the ledge.

Chapter XXI

THE LYCANTHROPE

Let us return now to Fargeot whom we left in the densest part of the forest. He could not go very far without being stopped by serious obstacles. Sometimes it was a rock that had to be pushed aside, sometimes a cavity full of melted snow to cross, sometimes a thorn bush it would take a fire to conquer. Fargeot, as we know, still retained enough corpulence to make these difficulties seem doubly difficult to surmount. However, he continued, from time to time, to repeat his howling which would serve as a means of recognition with the lycanthrope, and as he regularly received a response, he did not get discouraged.

A time came, however, when he found himself in a particularly difficult situation. He had arrived next to a slippery boulder, under which one could hear the rumble of a subterranean stream. The thickets and the brushwood that Fargeot had passed through had closed back up behind him, such that it seemed impossible to advance or to back up. Even in his bewilderment, the stout fellow continued his usual howling; however, this time the response was not in the same tone; only a mocking laugh, idiotic, bizarre, could be heard from a short distance away.

Fargeot looked carefully around him without seeing a thing; however, the menacing laugh resumed, but with an even more ironical and joyfully evil tone. He finally perceived, at the foot of bramble bushes which seemed to form an unsurmountable barrier, a hideous bearded head with long protruding teeth and with piercing bloodshot eyes fixed on him. The rest of his body remained hidden; only the horrifying head was visible just above ground level between roots and the brambles.

Perhaps Fargeot felt a moment of panic, but he prevented himself from betraying his unease. On the contrary, putting on an expression of confidence and unnatural graciousness, he said in honeyed tones:

"Good day wolf…. It is a wolf who has come to see you! Would you help me to get out of here?"

However, the lycanthrope continued his strange laugh, as though the quandary of his old friend provided great entertainment for him.

"Ah! is this the way that you receive me?" said the poor Fargeot. "Well, listen wolf, you must be famished, as usual…. I have in my pocket a large piece of bread which I kept just for you!"

The bearded head shook its straggly mane, and responded with an almost unintelligible voice, but with evident anger:

"Wolves do not eat bread, but the flesh of sheep… and of other things!"

This was said in such a manner that Fargeot shuddered.

"Now, now, do not be angry," he resumed. "In your activity as a wolf, there are days of fasting, where one eats what one finds, and you must fast often around here!"

This reasoning seemed definitive to this deranged man; he enlarged, with his two callused and hairy hands, the passage he had created in the brush, then he said in his hoarse voice:

"Come to the den of the wolves; you will give me your bread and we will chat like friends; there is another one I do not like…. I will explain; come with me."

And he entered the thickets.

Fargeot did his best to follow. Slipping himself in to the gap made by the lycanthrope, he advanced, like him, on his feet and on his hands. Undoubtedly, this manner of walking must have seemed very tiring, but it was really the only feasible way in this almost impenetrable forest. Unfortunately, the guard's clothing did not have the practicality of the simple rough cloth smock that constituted the clothing of the madman. At any moment, Fargeot was stopped by low hanging branches and thorny undergrowth that seized him like tenacious hooks; necessity and a secret desire for vengeance gave him the necessary strength to overcome these obstacles.

However, he would have had a difficult time following the man-wolf, who romped in this manner with an inconceivable ease, if the latter had not stopped from time to time to listen. It seemed that something unusual awoke alternately the curiosity and the distrust of Jeannot, and the poor guard took advantage of these moments to catch his breath. However, soon the maniac, undoubtedly reassured by the belief that he was unassailable in this labyrinth of rocks, bushes and chasms, let his mocking laugh be heard and continued his way.

They finally left the deeper part of the forest and began climbing the slope of the mountain. As they reached greater heights, the forest became less dense. Although Jeannot persisted on leaning on his hands, a habit adopted over a long period, Fargeot took advantage of the situation to straighten up and walk normally on his two feet like a human being. Moreover, his clothing was now in shreds; his breath wheezed from his chest and large drops of perspiration fell from his brow onto the snow.

They continued to climb for a while, and in spite of the steepness of the incline, the path no longer presented insurmountable difficulties. Fargeot still needed to hang on to clumps of ferns to maintain his balance, but he was no longer being pierced by a thousand sharp thorns. They were now quite near the waterfall and they were being soaked by the freezing mist it exhaled. It even seemed at certain moments that they would have to pass under torrents of white foam from the cliff above, which left a narrow space between them and the terrifying ledge which we already know.

At the area on the mountain where the shrubs became sparse and stunted, Jeannot, who was advancing in the lead, finally stopped. He turned to await his companion who rejoined him in a breathless state; then, the maniac spread apart several shrubs, and slipped into a cavity in the rock formation that was almost invisible from the exterior.

Before risking entry into this dubious lair, Fargeot took a rapid look around him. Not a hunter was in sight, and if a problem occurred, from all appearances, he could count only on himself. Nevertheless, he did not worry about this eventuality, and resolutely entered the grotto.

This sort of natural subterranean tunnel was very dark, and a strong odor of wild game bore witness to the likelihood that he did not receive only human guests. Soon, Fargeot's eyes became used to the darkness, and he could begin to examine his friend's hideaway.

This cavity, the ceiling of which did not exceed the height of an average man, was eight to ten feet in depth. Its temperature was relatively mild and the foliage at its entry way did not let in the humidity. One could not see any clothing, utensils, or provisions; a thick layer of leaves and moss formed a soft bed indicating intelligent foresight.

However, Fargeot did not have the time to make any long observations; his companion had sat down at the back of the grotto, and said with savage eagerness:

"The bread! the bread… quickly!... the wolf wants to eat… the wolf is hungry!"

The guard drew from his pocket a large piece of bread, which Jeannot seized with his two wretched hands and began devouring with voraciousness.

In a couple of swallows, it was gone, and the lycanthrope's appetite seemed far from satisfied. Fargeot said to him softly:

"It seems to me, wolf, that you have been fasting for a long time…. You must find meat difficult to find in this lost countryside! I would wager that you have not eaten in at least three days!"

'This is true," replied Jeannot, blinking his large fierce eyes; "the *other* one treats me badly! *He* goes far and has a good meal, then he only comes back to me when he has been hurt…. Then I have to take care of him…. He is an ingrate, a villainous ingrate!"

"The *other*!" repeated Fargeot, although he understood full well, "who are you speaking of, Jeannot?"

Upon hearing his name, the maniac had a fit of fury.

"Ha! Are you now also going to pretend that I am a man and that my name is Jeannot? If I believed…"

He suddenly stopped speaking, and his look became fixed; one would have said that the presence of his old master awoke in his mind some vague and ancient memories.

"There are moments," he replied pensively, "that it seems to me that I could have been a man and was named Jeannot… at least I lived among men and I ate bread and slept in houses…. But perhaps I dreamed all that."

Fargeot saw in these words the beginning of a return to reason, and he wanted to take advantage of this interval of lucidity to obtain the information that he came for.

"Certainly, you have been a man," he said affirmatively. "Do you not remember having been my valet at the Varinas farm? Have you forgotten my wife Marguerite, the wet-nurse of the little Viscount, and my daughter, Marion, as well as your friend, Simon Granget, with whom you fought so often because he lost his sheep and then accused you of stealing them?"

Each of these names made a marked impression on the man-wolf; his bestial features revealed reflection. Encouraged by this success, Fargeot continued:

"By the way, there is another situation that you may have kept in your memory; do you remember the evening that the poor little child, the Viscount de Varinas, disappeared? It was always believed that he had perished in an accident, but you knew… you had seen…"

"It was neither I, nor the *other*, who devoured the child!" said Jeannot as if carried away by his memories; "the wolves were not there… there were not any wolves yet…. But I did encounter that night the monk who was coming up to the chateau with another man; it was the monk who took the child, I am certain!"

"Aha! here is an admission that is important!" exclaimed Fargeot, forgetting all reserve. "Well, listen, Jeannot; agree to repeat to certain persons who are not far from here; what you have just said about the monk, and as a recompense, you shall be well treated; you will have as much bread and meat as you want; you will no longer suffer from hunger or cold, you will have a home and clothing…"

He stopped, noticing that he had been too hasty in counting on the intelligence of the lycanthrope. The latter, tempted for a moment by these seductive promises, had suddenly resumed his savage attitude.

"I am not a man," he said in a furor; "I am a wolf…. Look at my claws, look at my teeth…. Must I slash and devour you to prove that I am a wolf?"

At the same time, he stretched out his hands with its sharp nails, worthy of a ferocious beast, he clacked his long and pointed teeth together, from which he got his sur-name. Fargeot felt for the pistols in his pockets, just in case; however, he answered while hiding his fear:

"Well, well, who said anything to the contrary? One can see that you are a wolf… and the most dangerous one at that! Are you not the one they call the beast of Gévaudan who makes the whole country tremble?"

This bizarre flattery deliciously tickled Jeannot's mania.

"No; no," he replied he said with a tone of false modesty while swinging his large head on his scaly neck, "it is not I, it is the *other* one…. However, where would he be without me, I ask myself? Who would open doors so that he could enter houses? Who would help him avoid the traps they lay for him everywhere? Who would find the tricks to help him hide during the great hunts? Who would treat his wounds when he lets himself be surprised by the hunters? He is so obstinate and imprudent! Without me, he would be dead twenty times over…. And yet, if you knew how badly he treated me! We argued constantly; he only thinks of himself…. He is an ingate, I tell you. However, I fed him, I raised him, I can almost say that I am his father!"

"Well, if he is so nasty, wolf, why do you not leave him?"

"I cannot," replied the lycanthrope, in a melancholic tone, "it is stronger than me…. We have been friends for such a long time. I used to have family among the humans; I even remember meeting some in this area…. But I hate them so much. But you have to love someone, so I became attached to him…. Is it not shameful to act so badly? For instance, he is out right now; but he will return soon because a little while ago I heard near the edge of the woods some hunters who continually search for us. Well, you will see, he will not bring me piece of lamb, hare or rabbit like another would. Moreover, he will probably be in a bad mood because he probably has received bullet, or a dog bite or even a knife slash…. On top of which he has still not recovered from the other day…. I will have to treat him, take out lead shot, and avoid his bites because he does not treat me any differently than another!"

While expressing these complaints in a tone of surprising fondness, the somber maniac's eyes were full of tears. This unbelievable aberration of human sentiments appeared not to affect Fargeot who continued feigning indifference.

"Well, wolf, my friend, you speak of lamb, hare and rabbit. Are these the only things you enjoy here?"

Jeannot smiled mysteriously.

"Do not tell anyone," he replied in a low voice, "all the hunters would chase after me like they chase after him; instead, the idiots take me for a man and leave me alone when we meet during their hunts. Is it not amusing that they take me for a man?... Yes, yes," he continued confidentially, "we often make a feast of these cursed persons; but you must not say anything…. It is a secret!"

"And is it not you," asked Fargeot, trembling, "who devoured my daughter in the Mercoire forest, my daughter, my poor Marion?"

"No, it was not me, I swear!" replied the maniac; "once again, it is the *other*…. Myself, I just wanted the young lady who is so mean, the one who always has a rifle. It was only for a laugh that I promised him the little one; but he has no sense of humor; he took it seriously, and as always, he was the strongest."

"You should have torn out his tongue, pierced his eyes, called for help…"

"Well, if I had been a man; but we wolves, we do not react that way, you know it well."

"You should have at least awakened me," exclaimed Fargeot energetically, abandoning his prudence, "you should have warned me, me, miserable father, who was there, drunk, asleep, while that infernal beast was tearing apart my daughter…. I will avenge her, poor innocent child, who I rendered so miserable all her life!... I will not leave here before she is avenged! So, call him, that cursed monster who took my dear Marion! Where is he? I await him; why does he not come?"

The lycanthrope perhaps did not fully understand these words, but a glimmer of suspicion began to appear on his bewildered features. Fargeot was not concerned as he was now lost in his defiance.

Suddenly, as if the heavens wanted to fulfill his ardent desire, a light brushing sound came from the shrubs which protected the entryway of the grotto. An enormous animal furtively slipped through the foliage; but it stopped after its first steps and began growling as if something new had awakened its distrust and anger. Its powerful silhouette detached itself from the luminous entryway of the cavern and its eyes glowed like two coal nuggets in a furnace.

Fargeot's excited state deflated and he remained immobile and silent. On the contrary, the madman seemed to forget everything else, and; crawling on his hands and knees towards the beast, said in a jovial tone:

"Well, runner, where have you been? By any chance have you again received some blows?... However, you seem hearty and fit as if there were no more hunters in this world. I wager that you have been laying in the snow to treat your latest wound! It is amazing how the snow is good for you…. But why are you growling and bristling your hair? The one you see here is a friend; he is a wolf like us. Come in! There is nothing to fear!"

Despite these urgings, the ferocious beast did not move forward, and its flaming eyes seem to illuminate the interior of the grotto.

Meanwhile, Fargeot was slowly recovering from his shock, and anger and the desire for revenge soon overcame his fear. He furtively took a pistol in each hand.

"Jeannot," he stuttered, "is that the monster that… is that really the beast of Gévaudan?"

And without waiting for a reply, he aimed at the ferocious animal. However, Jeannot, overcoming his fear that the sight of firearms normally created in him, jumped on the distraught guard; when the pistol fired, the shot lodged in the wall of the grotto.

The beast seemed more irritated than alarmed by the sound of the explosion; his growling became a formidable howl, and it sprang forward, either to protect its companion, or to avenge the attack. The maniac was still clinging on to Fargeot, preventing him from using the second pistol.

"Help! Wolf," he was yelling in his hoarse voice, "we are betrayed!... He is not a wolf, he is a man, he is a hunter! He has *little rifles*... Avenge us! We must destroy him, tear him to pieces. He is ours!"

The cavern was full of smoke and it was impossible to see anything; there was a terrible struggle in the obscurity. Fargeot felt as if steel spikes had pierced his body. Was it the beast, was it Jeannot who was devouring him alive? He did not know but he resisted with all his strength, and, as he was robust, they had not been able to force him down. He headed for the entryway to the grotto, in spite of his enemy's efforts, and cried out:

"Somebody, help!... Hunters, help me!... The beast is here!... Jeannot is here!... You must help me!"

However, it is doubtful that Fargeot, covered with bites and losing blood from his many wounds, could escape carrying the weight of his adversaries, His survival instinct and his need for vengeance provided him with one solution in this terrible moment. He still had one pistol, the hand that held it was firmly constrained. His finger, however, pressed on the trigger and the shot was fired. The bullet, like the first, hit no one; but the flame from the gun powder singed the wolf's fur, which caused it to momentarily let go. Fargeot felt one of his legs released as if from a vice. He took advantage of this to shake loose from the lycanthrope, whose long fasts and way of life rendered much less dangerous, and he was able stagger outside, continuing his cries for help.

Although he could see daylight, he was not yet out of danger. He found himself on a sort of platform, only a few paces wide, just in front of the grotto. Below him was the thorny forest, inextricable, where his enemies would not take long to reach him; above was a rock face, perpendicular and inaccessible. However, the situation did not permit long reflection; The man and the wolf would soon be coming to renew the battle. Then, Fargeot noticed the ledge that led under the falling water. At any other moment, he would have backed away from the difficulties of this unique path to safety;

but necessity said otherwise, and he ventured out, tottering, on the rock ledge.

He had taken only a few steps when he saw under the sort of archway formed by the waterfall, Léonce coming towards him, followed by Godard's mastiff.

"Help! Help!" exclaimed the miserable guard who, losing his strength, collapsed on the humid rock.

However, help had arrived too late. Fargeot remained prostrated at the edge of the precipice, when he felt a heavy body fall on top of him; it was Jeannot who had caught up and was grasping him with renewed rage. Just behind him, the beast of Gévaudan was showing its large shaggy head.

A desperate thought reanimated the guard. Instead of pushing away the lycanthrope, which was furiously biting him, he put one arm around him, while with the other hand, he was trying to seize the ferocious beast. He, indeed, succeeded in grabbing the monster's leg, and immediately began twisting convulsively to drag the two enemies towards the edge of the chasm.

"Ah!" he said in a faltering voice, "we shall perish all together, and my daughter will be avenged!"

But the others had understood his plan; they stiffened in an attempt to maintain themselves on the narrow protrusion which was the theatre of their struggle. A powerful effort of the wolf broke the unfortunate Fargeot's hand and liberated the beast. However, the guard wrapped himself even more firmly around Jeannot; the latter attempted to cling to the rocks with his robust nails scratching the humid surface. Suddenly, there was not enough ground beneath them. They remained several seconds, attached together, suspended over the abyss; but soon the lycanthrope weakened and suddenly released his hold; they both plummeted into the precipice, and disappeared into the turbulent foam of the waterfall.

These events, the struggle and the calamity, took less than time than it took to describe it.

At that moment, Léonce was arriving, accompanied by the loyal Castor, and followed in the distance by the Baron Laroche-Boisseau, who had crossed the dangerous ledge with more prudence. Léonce had indeed seen from the other side of the torrent those two men struggling together, but concentrated on his own safety, he could not follow the result. When he reached his present position, he was astonished that they were no longer in sight. He thought that they were hidden by the terrain or by groupings of brush, and would soon reappear. Moreover, something else immediately drew his attention: at only a few paces from him, an enormous wolf was leaning over the abyss, looking into its depths and emitting plaintive howls.

One can easily understand that Léonce lost some of his presence of mind. He hesitated to recognize that this animal which appeared so unexpectedly was the terrible beast of Gévaudan, whose death would be so handsomely rewarded. Perhaps this was also the inevitable reaction of a novice hunter that contributed to his inaction. However, he rapidly recovered his composure.

"It is he!" Léonce thought, "it is definitely he!"

And he brought his rifle to his shoulder to fire.

However, the beast, which due to the extraordinary circumstances that had neutralized its vigilance, had finally become alarmed. It turned its head towards the motionless Léonce, sending him a piercing look that few persons could support; then ceasing its howling, launched itself down the grassy incline leading to the forest, where it would find its security assured.

Léonce still had it in his sights, but unfortunately, it used its cunning to hide behind shrubs and in the contours of the hills with a talent honed over the years. The hunter could therefore not shoot with hope of success, and it had distanced itself, almost to the edge of the forest, when he finally pressed the trigger.

The bullet traced a groove on the impenetrable hide of the animal; tufts of fur flew in the air. The wolf growled and sent another furious look towards the young hunter; however, after an imperceptible halt, it entered the thickets and disappeared.

Castor had seen the beast and chased it with fervor.

"I think I hit it," Léonce exclaimed with emotion, "I am sure of it!"

"You may have hit it, but you did not kill it," replied the Baron de Laroche Boisseau, who had just arrived; "the bullet just creased its thick fur. However, considering the distance and the difficulty of the shot, it was perfect…. Morbleu! how well you move, young man! What boldness, what ardor, what a sharp eye, what steel legs! You leap like an antelope in the middle of rocks and ravines. If pride had not been involved, God bless me, I would never have tried to follow you."

However, Léonce was not listening to these ironic compliments.

"I hit it," he repeated excitedly. "Wounded, it cannot fight off Castor. I will go down to the forest to assist Castor, and perhaps…"

"Go down to the forest!" repeated the Baron, shrugging his shoulders; "and how will you defend yourself if the beast attacks you? As for your dog, it is strong and courageous, I agree; but you will see in a while what happens to it!"

"No matter, I want to enter the thickets."

"As you wish, Sire," said the Baron with unconcern; "however, believe me, you had better not go down there without reloading your rifle."

This time Léonce understood that the Baron was right, and he went about the task of reloading it. While he was hurriedly doing this, a howl of pain could be heard coming from the woods; at the same instant, Castor was hurled over the bushes by a violent shake of the wolf's head.

"As I was saying!" resumed the Baron, laughing, "your dog was just given its notice.... The beast is not worried by such enemies, no matter how much they cost their masters! So, here comes your mastiff, limping back, and in a piteous state.... Now that our valiant wolf has rid itself of its adversary, it will lose no time in leaving for distant places, otherwise, it would ruin its reputation for prudence."

He had hardly spoken these words that the wolf, as if it wanted to confirm the predictions of an experienced hunter, came out of the woods at the opposite side of the valley and rapidly entered a neighboring canyon.

"Well, do you still have any doubt?" said Laroche-Boisseau to a dismayed Léonce. Our friend has taken its pace and is fleeing nicely, although you have slightly damaged his fur coat.... Come now, Sire Léonce, just a lost match.... However, really, I believe you capable of taking your revenge! Zounds; amazing how you hunt the wolf for a peaceful student from the Frontenac Abbey!"

Léonce, disheartened, tapped his forehead.

"It flees! it flees!" he said with a sort anger against himself. "and to think that I had it here, in front of me, and that I could have... However, I will leave in his pursuit," he continued, excitedly; "I will track him, which should be easy with his traces in the snow."

"In that case, you will track him by yourself, because your poor dog will not soon be capable of accompanying you," said the Baron. "Listen, Sire Léonce, believe me; do not be in a hurry to chase after that vigorous animal. Judging from its appearance, it will not stop until is twenty or thirty leagues away from here.... Moreover, humanity requires that you do not leave us so soon. You see over there poor Legris who they are in the process of pulling out of the precipice, and I like to think that thanks to the brushwood that broke his fall, he has no broken ribs or limbs.... However, I fear, Sire Léonce, that this not the only misfortune that we will have to deplore.... When approaching here, you must have seen the two men who were at the place we are now. Do you not suspect what could have happened to them?"

Léonce, absorbed until now by the emotions of the chase, seemed to awaken from a dream.

"Indeed," he said, shuddering, "they were right here a while ago, and I could not understand.... Do you know these men, Baron?"

"From all appearances, one was Fargeot, the old Chief Guard of Mercoire, and the other is that unfortunate maniac, Jeannot Grandes-Dents.... I have the greatest interest in knowing what became of them...."

"Well, let us search for them as rapidly as possible. Truly, their sudden disappearance could not be explained… unless an accident…"

They called some mountaineers, who decided to approach by the perilous path on the ledge. Then began a minute search of the surrounding locales. They visited the grotto where the discharged pistols still lay; they followed the traces of Fargeot's blood to the spot where the final struggle took place; There, the Baron, with the wisdom of a skillful hunter, studied the terrain, and had little trouble in determining precisely what had occurred. However, their visual search of the bottom of the chasm revealed only dark rocks and foam.

"Whatever were those men," said Léonce warmly, "we must not overlook anything to try to save them if they did not perish, or at least find their bodies to give them a Christian burial…. Therefore, I renounce my plans for the moment of pursuing the beast of Gévaudan; later I will find its traces; in the meantime, Sire Baron, my people and I are at your disposal."

Laroche-Boisseau accepted this generous offer with an air of cordiality, although his mocking smile betrayed a hidden agenda. A few moments later, the group split up to descend into the abyss by different paths. As for Legris, the mountaineers had already retrieved him from the precipice, and except for numerous contusions which should oblige him to remain in bed several days, his fall appeared to not have had any serious repercussions.

Chapter XXII

THE CONFIDENCES

Towards the end of this same day, the Baron and Léonce, with the hunters and the mountaineers of their group, returned, exhausted to the farm at Motte-Rouge. Their energetic and dangerous search proved to be useless. They examined at great risk the caverns and the brushwood at the foot of the waterfall; the bodies of Fargeot and the lycanthrope were not found. However, they no longer doubted that the two unfortunates had perished; and, indeed, several months after these events, a shepherd discovered in the torrents, far below the waterfall, two hideous skeletons, broken and crushed by the shocks against the rocks, but still so interlaced with each other that it was difficult to separate them.

Night was approaching; large flakes of snow were falling, though this time without wind or tempest. These circumstances rendered impossible Léonce's plans to immediately resume the pursuit of the wolf; the new snow would cover all its traces. Moreover, the young man, despite his vigour and courage, had not had any respite during this eventful day, and his fatigue was such that he had difficulty in returning to the farm where he was to rejoin a part of his group.

Léonce and the Baron were walking side by side, a little behind the main group. An attentive, if not cordial politeness had been maintained between the two, despite their latent rivalry. The Prior's nephew, by plan and by character, did not want to see himself overcome by this assault of courtesy, and was being careful to avoid any mention of the past that could offend his companion whose presence was imposed by necessity. However, perhaps he was secretly impatient to leave him and regain his liberty of action.

Laroche-Boisseau, having ironically complimented Léonce at length for the energy, zeal and skill he had shown in the search for the missing victims, had now become anxious. Léonce, in turn, spoke to him with civility:

"You seem sad, Sire Baron.... I hope that the state of health of your friend is not alarming in nature and that when we reach the farm there will be satisfying news about him."

"My friend?" said Laroche-Boisseau with disdain; "Legris is not my friend, he is the son of one of my financial advisers, and as such, I was willing to help him in society…. His contusions do not appear to be serious; some rest and a few cups of vulnerary[36] will put him back on his feet…. However, I thought, Sire Léonce, that you knew how important it was to me that we find those two poor devils who seem to have gone up in smoke?"

"One of the two, if I am not mistaken, was for a long time in the service of Miss de Barjac before entering yours; as for the other, one speaks of him as being a dangerous maniac…."

"Is that so, Sire?" asked the Baron looking at him fixedly; "What? you are not aware of what powerful interest I have, as well your own, in the fate of these two men?"

"I, Sire? Once again, I did not know them, and it was only in the interest of humanity that I…"

"When you showed yourself, a while ago, so ardently interested in searching for those unfortunates who might have only been hurt, I attributed your zeal as being of another nature; for instance, the desire to throw light on the affair that affects both of us, but in different ways."

"Upon my soul! Sire, I still do not understand you."

"It seems to me impossible that you; the student of the Fathers of Frontenac and the nephew of its Prior, have no knowledge of the criminal lawsuit that I have brought against the Abbey as well as your uncle personally concerning the disappearance of the young Viscount of Varinas, my relative…. However, the former Chief Guard of Mercoire and Jeannot were the only witnesses that I could present in support of my evidence; and their death may be the ruin of my accusations. These events are fortunate for your friends, Sire Léonce, and you can congratulate them."

Poor Léonce was trying in vain to understand these semi-confessions deviously calculated perhaps to torment him.

"These, Sire, are veritable enigmas for me…. I have of course heard speak of the ancient rights of your family over the Varinas domain; but those right were rejected a long time ago by a decision of the courts, and one could not revise this today."

Laroche-Boisseau adopted a serious look.

"You may have," he said, "the most honorable motives in pretending ignorance on what is public knowledge, and these motives are none of my business…. However, Sire Léonce, you must admit that you are aware of the arrival of Monsignor Bishop of Alep, the Royal Commissioner, at the Frontenac Abbey. The suspension imposed on the entire convent, and finally, the commitment to forced confinement of… a person very close to you?"

This time, Léonce began to have a glimmer of the terrible truth.

"Wait!" he said agitatedly, "I indeed remember that the day I left the

---

36 Vulnerary: Any preparation, plant or drug used for treating wounds.

Abbey, an ecclesiastic official had just arrived.... Then there were the mournful expressions of the Fathers, the obvious concern of my uncle, and especially, his eagerness to see me leave.... Oh! please, Sire Baron, what motives could have decided the Bishop to punish the good Fathers so severely, and in particular my beloved uncle.

"I have perhaps said too much," replied Laroche-Boisseau, sighing hypocritically; "I would not want to distress you, Sire Léonce, as you are decidedly, a brave young man, and I am not including you in my legitimate hate for those despicable monks.... Let us leave this subject please; it can only be painful for both of us. In addition," he continued, but this time with a real sadness; "the death of my two witnesses will probably change the face of things; the accusation has not been sufficiently proven, the charges may be dropped, and I might be accused in turn of fraud and slander.... Mordieu! we shall see."

"Sire Baron," resumed Léonce with increasing anguish, "I am not your judge, nor anyone's judge; but I beg of you to tell me what has happened in Frontenac since my departure."

"I would have preferred that anyone else but me would have provided these details," replied Laroche-Boisseau with a tone of repugnance perfectly delivered; "but if I offend you, please remember that you obliged me to make these revelations. Then learn that monks of Frontenac are accused of having assassinated my young relative, the Viscount of Varinas, to appropriate his rich heritage for themselves."

Léonce was terrified by the seriousness of this case, but he stammered: "Such an accusation is so unbelievable, so absurd..."

"You are free to think so; but it is supported by considerable evidence; and undoubtedly it did not seem absurd to everyone since the King judged it appropriate to send an eminent prelate to launch an inquiry at the Abbey, and the Royal Commissioner placed a ban on the monastery and condemned the Prior to solitary confinement."

"My uncle!" resumed Léonce in a choked voice; "my uncle is really implicated in this affair?"

"It would be useless to hide it from you, dear Léonce; that the Prior of Frontenac is compromised in the strongest manner. It appears that he was the principal actor in the death of the young Viscount of Varinas; and how could it be doubted since Jeannot, one of the two unfortunates who have just perished, encountered Father Bonaventure in disguise near the Chateau de Varinas a few moments prior to the tragic disappearance of the poor child?"

"This is false, Sire, it is certainly false!" exclaimed Léonce, growing pale, but responding with energy; "the good, wise and generous Prior guilty of such a crime?... This is insane, I tell you! Your hatred towards the Fathers of Frontenac, and in particular against my venerable uncle must have blinded you completely for you to be adding credence to these slanders!"

This heated protest could not help but awaken the anger of Laroche-Boisseau, but he controlled himself and replied with a tone of indulgence:

"I will not get angry with some ill-advised words which just escaped your lips, Sire Léonce; it is absolutely natural for you to defend a close relative who fed and raised you; even if he was guilty in the eyes of the rest of the world. Besides, perhaps soon you will have good news; as I had been telling you, my inability to provide two important witnesses may change the situation; and the good Fathers, who are not lacking in either skill or funds, may come out as white as snow… although I do not yet consider myself beaten!"

These last words were said in a menacing tone; Laroche-Boisseau, while pursuing his cruel intent of torturing the Prior's nephew, could not resist revealing some of his true feelings. Moreover, he had succeeded only too well in his secret project; the unfortunate Léonce had been devastated by the atrocious revelations. Nevertheless, he suddenly raised his head:

"Sire Baron," he resumed with vehemence, "I persist in thinking and saying that this accusation is false, dishonest and slanderous…. And when justice has been pronounced, I hope in my turn to demand accountability from the slanderer!"

And he ran off like a madman to rejoin the group that preceded them, while LaRoche-Boisseau smiled with an air of satisfied vengeance.

In the meanwhile, they were approaching the tenant farm whose buildings could now be seen ahead in the evening mist. As soon as the hunters could be seen, a man came out of one of the buildings and hurried towards them. It was Labranche, Laroche-Boisseau's trusted personal valet, He approached his master and spoke with him eagerly:

"Some letters have just arrived for you, Sire Baron. They were brought here by the Madam Richard's stable boy in Langogne; the poor lad has been following our trail for the past two days, and had the greatest difficulty in finding us. Knowing how impatient you were to have news, I hurried…"

"You did well, Labranche; your vigilance will merit you a Louis d'Or as soon as I have the funds…. But where are the letters?"

"The messenger insists on giving them to you personally. One comes from Florac, the other from Mercoire."

"From Mercoire?" repeated Laroche-Boisseau, with astonishment, "who the Devil would write me from there?... As for the other letter, it is most certainly from the elder Legris, my attorney, and must contain important information…. Let us go retrieve them immediately."

He redoubled his pace and soon found himself side by side with Léonce, who was walking somberly, his head down and eyes brimming with tears.

He rejoined him affecting a great sympathy for his sadness; the young man turned away from him with an abrupt movement.

"You are angry with me, Sire Léonce," resumed Laroche-Boisseau in a tone of friendly reproach, "but I have not given you a reason to be so. Listen; a short time ago you questioned certain facts that I brought to your attention, and I insist on proving to you their exactitude. I have just been advised that letters have arrived for me from Florac and Mercoire; agree to stop for a moment at this tenant farm and I will communicate to you the portion of this correspondence that pertain to these events. Unless I am very mistaken, you will have here the proof that all that I have said is true."

Léonce did not lack reason to question the sudden confidence expressed by Laroche-Boisseau. However, he had an ardent desire to know the news that had just arrived; the letter from Mercoire in particular aroused his curiosity as it would certainly mention Christine de Barjac, whom he had not seen for a long time. Therefore, after a brief hesitation, he replied in a strained voice:

"So be it, Sire Baron, I will receive the information that it please you to give me…. Nevertheless, God is my witness that I would give my life willingly to have the certainty that you have deceived me."

They reached the tenant farm. Martin and the other mountaineers refused to enter Féréol's home, since he was now their enemy; they preferred waiting for Léonce in front of the door, exposed to the night chill and their feet in the snow. Féréol, on his side did not invite them to come in and rest in front of the hearth, and just gave them somber looks. Since he knew of the tragic results of his plan concerning his cousin Jeannot, he was tormented with secret remorse. Too proud to acknowledge his personal guilt, and not daring to attack the Baron as the primary cause of the accident, he kept mortal grudge against Martin, his neighbor and his equal. This affair, after the departure of the strangers, would certainly be at the origin or a long and fierce dispute in which the *coutelières* and rifles would play an undoubtedly bloody role.

The main room of the farm was already lit, although the glow of dusk still came in from the sky. The messenger was warming himself in front of the fireplace. In a large bed situated in a corner of the room was Legris, bundled in sheets and compresses. The farmer's wife and her daughter came and went around the patient; A strong medicinal odor indicated that all the family recipes against contusions had been put to good use.

Laroche-Boisseau walked directly up to the messenger, who upon seeing him, hurried to rise and give him the dispatches. He avidly seized them, and was about to read them when Legris, lifting himself up on one elbow, asked him in a pathetic tone:

"Ah, dear Baron, you are finally here; is the beast of Gévaudan finally dead?

Without answering, Laroche-Boisseau tore open one of the letters. Suddenly, he let out a cry of joy.

"Victory!" he said, waving the paper which he held in his hand, "I did not dare expect such a result…. Congratulate me everyone…. I am as of now Count and Lord of Varinas!"

Everyone looked at him in astonishment.

"What are you saying, Baron?" asked Legris, "if this so, knowing you, you will abandon me without pity!"

Laroche-Boisseau turned towards Léonce:

"You asked for proofs," he said, "you will be served. Come with me."

He picked up a torch from the table and pulled the Prior's nephew in to a small adjoining room where they had some privacy.

"Read this, Sire," he said with a malicious joy while handing Léonce the opened letter.

This letter, dated from Florac, was from Legris' father, who as we know, was acting as Laroche-Boisseau's attorney.

It was written as follows:

"Sire Baron,

"Your affair is going well. It is no longer necessary to chase over hill and dale for this Jeannot Grandes-Dents, whose testimony, by the way, would not have been very useful considering his known madness. The affirmations of Fargeot are no longer indispensable; the Prior, our most dangerous adversary HAS ADMITTED EVERYTHING to his Highness, Monsignor Bishop of Alep. This fact is capital, and I cannot believe that the wily Bonaventure would have let escape such an admission if Monsignor, whom I have just seen in your defense, had not HIMSELF given me confirmation.

"You can easily guess, Sire Baron, the consequences of these new facts. The Bishop, convinced of the guilt of monks of Frontenac, is absolutely disposed to restore to you the lands of Varinas as soon as I have furnished him with the proof that you are the closest relative and direct heir to the defunct Count and the little Viscount. I am searching for these documents and should find them in your family papers, and will prepare them in a legal form as soon as possible. However, your presence here will soon be necessary, and, if you give us a few more days I have no doubt that your interests will be in perfect order.

"In the meantime, the Royal Commissioner is greatly irritated against the monks of Frontenac and treats them with an iron rod.

As you can imagine, there is a lot of chatter in the countryside; however, it is believed that for the honor of the clergy, the Abbot and the Fathers will be exonerated; all the punishment will fall on the Prior, who is, indeed, the guiltiest in this affair, and he will probably be quietly committed to one of those underground dungeons to be found in these convents, *etc. etc.*"

The remainder Legris's letter concerned other details already known to the reader, along with some recommendations for his son.

One can judge Léonce's suffering! Doubt was no longer possible; the Prior had admitted his crime, and the prelate in charge of the inquiry was convinced of his guilt. The poor young man dropped the paper and hid his face in his hands, sobbing.

In the meantime, the Baron had opened the dispatch from Mercoire and had glanced through it rapidly. Undoubtedly the contents were less serious as Laroche-Boisseau was expressing great hilarity, when Léonce's distraught reaction drew his attention.

"Now, now, courage my friend!" he resumed sweetly, "being obliged to hate, even despise a man who raised you and inspired so much affection and respect is indeed cruel, I admit…. However, do not despair. Monsignor de Alep will not want to push things too far; On my side, if I peacefully obtain possession of my family's heritage, I will not pursue this affair too rigorously. It is so ancient that I am willing to be reasonable on a number of points; and the affection you inspire in me will certainly dispose me towards clemency."

These consolations, supposing that they were sincere, produced on Léonce an effect diametrically opposed to what the Baron seemed to expect.

"Of what importance, the punishment?" resumed Prior's nephew with despair; "it is the crime, only the crime that concerns me…. The more I think about it," he continued, becoming animated, "the more I believe that this odious, revolting, terrible crime is totally impossible! The appearances lie, the proofs are false, everyone is wrong. At the base of all this is a mysterious misunderstanding that will be understood later. I am sure of it."

"Let us leave this subject which distresses you so, Sire Léonce; you are free to consider as reality the suppositions that please you…. But to distract you from these ideas, would you not like to take a look at this letter that comes from Mercoire? It is quite entertaining, I assure you."

"From Mercoire?" repeated Léonce who had forgotten that fact.

"Yes, read it; it does not contain anything that you might be expecting, perhaps…. But it will cheer you up, I hope."

This second dispatch was signed by the Knight de Magnac, and its style had all the formality of this solemn character.

"Sire Baron,

"I have been advised that you recently took into your service a former guard of the chatellany of Mercoire, named Fargeot. However, since you did not judge it appropriate, in this affair, to obtain the approval of my noble mistress, the high-born and powerful Miss Christine de Barjac, Countess of Mercoire and other lands, I, Antoine Léonard, Knight de Magnac, Squire of honor to Miss de Barjac, assert that you have not acted as a real gentleman. If you are of a different opinion, Sire Baron, I request that you summon me as soon as possible to a place where we can meet and I will hasten to rejoin you accompanied by a discreet friend, and we will settle this matter in the manner that suits persons of quality.

"You might think that the motive of this dispute is trivial, and in requesting the favor of this encounter, I remember older and more serious wrongs; that is not the case, Sire Baron. During your too brief stay at the Chateau de Mercoire, you were careful to always meet the obligations required of you by hospitality, and if foolish persons were to say otherwise, I think that, like myself, Sire Baron, you would be ready to impose silence in the proper manner.

"In the hope of a prompt reply, I am, Sire Baron etc.

ANTOINE, Knight DE MAGNAC

This singular epistle, riddled with many spelling errors, ended with a post-scriptum which read as follows:

"I have been assured that you have been assisted in this rude diversion of a Mercoire servant, by a Master Legris, your supposed friend. Since it is not necessary to spare the feelings of this sort of person, I would ask, Sire Baron, that you tell Master Legris that I will thrash him wherever I find him."

After having read this letter, Léonce remained pensive.

"What do you think of this quaint duel invitation? Said Laroche-Boisseau roaring with laughter; "have you seen anything more amusing?"

"The knight does not mention Christine," murmured Léonce distractedly.

But immediately, ashamed of having expressed his thoughts aloud, he resumed with an effort:

"Well, Sire, have you the intention of responding to the Knight de Magnac's invitation?"

"Me? fight a duel with that grim buffoon, that moronic righter of wrongs? I would be as ridiculous as he. Moreover, I have other things to do; you saw that my attorney believes that my presence is necessary; I will leave tomorrow morning for Florac…. I am obliged to abandon poor Legris in this house waiting to be thrashed by our valiant knight…. And you, Sire Léonce," he continued, "do you not plan to return to Frontenac? We could travel together."

Despite the Baron's apparent kindness, Léonce finally realized that since they have been together, each passing minute brought him a new torture. He arose abruptly:

"I do not know yet what I want to do," he said vaguely; "I have reason to think that my poor uncle, in sending me away with such haste, wished to hide from me his mortal humiliation, and perhaps my presence might only increase his suffering. Thank you for your offer, Sire Baron, but I will not accept it…. We must now go our separate ways, for a long time, no doubt, as our paths cannot be the same!"

"As you wish," replied Laroche-Boisseau with a mocking smile, also standing up. "I see, Sire Léonce, that the reward promised to the fortunate hunter who will kill the beast of Gévaudan concerns you more than the fate of your beloved uncle. Go, then, and take courage. However, do not be too hopeful that we will not meet again, in spite of the difference in our paths; on the contrary, I imagine that you will find me again soon."

They exchanged parting phrases, ironic on one hand, glacial the other, and Léonce went out. A few moments later, one could hear him leave with his people.

Chapter XXIII

THE VISIT

Winter raged in the mountains of Gévaudan and affected in particular the area surrounding Mercoire. It was not that the temperature was particularly harsh as in certain years, notably 1709, which left terrible memories in all of France; a continual alternation of cold, storms, river floods and snowmelts had completely upset the country and rendered communications difficult. To make matters worse, a great number of wolves, whose hunger increased their ferocity, infested that part of the province. More than all the others, the beast of Gévaudan, recently returned to the forest of Mercoire, for which it seemed to have a predilection, had begun again to prove its terrible prowess in the neighborhood.

One can understand that under such circumstances visitors and guests were not flocking to the chateau; therefore, nothing troubled the calm of that ancient abode. Since the beginning of winter, it had taken on the air of solitude and sadness; the shutters remained closed, the snow piled up in the courtyards, birds of prey nested in the crevasses and one could have thought the place uninhabited. Individual hunters that necessity obliged to stop there for one night had been received with meticulous politeness by the Knight de Magnac, in the name of the lady of the house, but left without having seen the Chatelaine herself. Christine, formerly so active, who one regularly saw riding on horseback on the avenue of the chateau or the long alleys of the forest, now rarely left the confines of the dwelling she occupied, and all her outings consisted of short strolls in the garden.

On a somber day in January, Miss de Barjac was with Sister Magloire and the Knight de Magnac in the main salon of the chateau. Although an entire tree trunk was burning in the massive fireplace, frigid drafts of air traversed the vast room. The window drapes, open to let in the light, allowed one to see a low and hazy sky, clouds in bizarre forms that trailed heavily on the slopes of the mountains and the old bare trees, hideous skeletons of the forest.

Christine and the nun were seated on opposite sides of a work table on which one saw smocks and shirts made of a rough cloth, destined for the young children of the village. The nun had found nothing better than manual work to occupy the spare time of her young mistress, and Christine lent herself with good will to this activity all the more that while manipulating the needle in the service of the orphans of her fief, she could abandon herself without constraint to her secret thoughts. The tireless pair had been so productive during the long days and even longer evenings of this dreary winter, that the poor people were thanking God in the poor thatched cottages of the surrounding villages.

Christine's exterior had not changed less than her character over this period. The tanned and vigorous child no longer existed; the glow had disappeared from her cheeks along with the colors of health. On the other hand, her paleness and slight weight loss had given her features an extraordinary fineness. He facial expression was pensive and melancholic, although her dark eyes, soft and velvety, sparkled with a live flame at brief moments. The elegance of her clothing contrasted with her former indifference for her appearance. In the deep solitude of her manor, her hair was coiffed with white powder, as was the style of the time, and her magnificent hoop-skirted dress with half-bared arms shrouded in lace. In spite of all this, she maintained an air of sadness and despondency which revealed in the lovely and rich young lady secret suffering.

However, at the moment we are finding Christine de Barjac, her appearance seemed to have regained that animation, that passionate mobility that distinguished her in the past. She had just interrupted her sewing, and needle in the air, frowning, she was listening to her squire of honor who was giving her important news. Magnac, standing before her, legs stiff, one hand on his hip, the other toying with his collar, was noting with chagrin those signs of irritation that his young mistress had shown in the past. Perhaps he regretted the admissions which were making such an impression on Miss de Barjac, although his scrupulous honesty and pride could not allow him to retract.

"Once again, Sire Knight," Christine was saying, in a tone that made Sister Magloire wince, "that is one of these ridiculous stories told you by servants to whom you always give credence…. This is not possible, I repeat, and if it were…"

She stopped, and breaking into tears, she stammered:

"I would die of sorrow!"

Upon seeing Miss de Barjac in tears, Sister Magloire felt a sentiment that, in such a holy person, more closely resembled anger. She set down her sewing and said with acrimony to the unfortunate knight:

"Jesus, my God! What are you thinking, Sire? Why do you need to come and tell such poppycock to our dear damsel? They were mocking you, and you could have dispensed yourself of repeating that twaddle."

She embraced Christine and lavished upon her the most affectionate consolations. However, certain expressions that she had used had wounded the fastidious gentleman. He threw his head back and said in an emphatic tone:

"Poppycock, my sister! twaddle; Madam?... Nom de Dieu, If I did not take into consideration that you are a woman, and a nun.... Nevertheless, know and understand, and be convinced... one NEVER mocks me, do you hear? And if anyone dared, peasant or gentleman, I have a sword to obtain satisfaction from a noble, and a cane to chastise the naughty.... Be so kind as to remember that, my very dear sister!"

Unfortunately, this lovely tirade was not heard; the two ladies, quite occupied by their grief, did not seem to be concerned by the poor Magnac., whose extravagant remarks on his honor, and whatever were his other good qualities, were already well known to them. In the meantime, the knight, self-satisfied, had now abandoned his attitude of braggart, when Christine, disengaged herself from her governess, and resumed in a calmer tone:

"Pardon me, my good friends; it is not in denying the danger that we can reduce it.... Come now, Sire de Magnac, repeat to me the serious news which perhaps should make me rejoice, but which strikes me with horror.... Is it true that the beast of Gévaudan was killed yesterday evening in the forest of Labeyssère, three leagues from here?"

I cannot guarantee my word as a gentleman for a fact that I had not witnessed. I am simply repeating exactly what was said to me by the guard Jerome. This morning at the tavern at Cransac, a guard from Labeyssère came and announced in a positive manner the death of the beast. It was felled, last night, by a gunshot from a hunter tracking it for several hours, and its heart was pierced by the shot. It was really dead, and they cut off its right paw and its head as a trophy.... That is exactly what I was told. Furthermore, Miss can ask Jerome and question him herself."

"That will not be necessary, Sire Knight; and do we know the name of the hunter?"

"The Labeyssère guard was unable to give any information on this point; he remarked only that the happy huntsman was followed by persons who seemed to be under his orders, which probably means that he is a person of quality."

"Well! my dear Knight," asked Christine with a strained almost unintelligible voice, "do we have any reason to think that he might be aware of the disastrous oath, the stupid vow..."

She could not finish the phrase.

"I do not wish to deceive you, Miss; however, the precaution he took in cutting off the head and paw of the beast is not a good sign."

"Oh! do not say that! do not say that!" exclaimed Christine with despair; "God would not want to punish me to that extent for my folly, my recklessness!"

After a pause, she resumed with an embarrassed air:

"My friends, would there be any hunters that we know in this vicinity that could have achieved this exploit?"

"Yes, yes, indeed.... There are several," replied Magnac.

And he began to name several gentlemen in the area that had set out in search of the ferocious beast. Miss de Barjac listened attentively and she seemed to be waiting for a name which did not come up.

"And that is all?" she asked impatiently; "do you wish to kill me with your absurd restraint?... I know that there are hunters that you do not mention."

"Well, Miss," replied Magnac, with a sort of military brusqueness that he assumed when he was pushed to the limit, "it is said that the Baron de Laroche-Boisseau and his friend Legris returned to the Mercoire area a few days ago; however, I do not believe it"

"Therefore, it is not possible that the odious Baron has killed the wolf?"

As the knight was about to reply, Sister Magloire prevented him:

"Certainly, it is impossible," she resumed with vivacity; "you should be aware, my dear child, a messenger from His Reverence Sire Abbot of Frontenac, stopped at the chateau to rest recently, and also to obtain information on the subject of his message; he had been tasked by His Reverence and by Monsignor the Bishop of Alep, the Royal Commissioner, to locate Sire de Laroche-Boisseau and to invite him to come immediately to Frontenac, where the opening of the codicil of his relative, the late Count of Varinas, is scheduled to take place. As the messenger did not come by again, one can surmise that he found the Baron, and they left together to go to the Abbey. Since the event was set for yesterday, Sire de Laroche-Boisseau should have been in Frontenac when the beast was killed in the forest of Labeyssère."

"Fine, my sister," Magnac said drily; however, as I had myself given the messenger a letter which should have had the Baron coming here at all speed, if he had a drop noble blood in his veins, I must assume that he did not find him. Nothing should have kept a gentleman from responding to my last challenge.... Moreover, as you well know, my sister, the messenger was tasked with a commission for another person who also did not respond to this invitation, because..."

The knight stopped speaking when he saw Sister Magloire make him a mysterious sign.

"And that person," exclaimed Christine, breathless, "was Léonce, was it not?... Do not try to hide it from me.... He is nearby; I know it.... I saw him!"

"You, Miss?" asked the nun in astonishment.

"There.... There.... On that mountain opposite us, when I am strolling in the garden, I have often seen a hunter who stops at the crest of a rock formation, his gaze towards the chateau.... I guessed it the first moment, in spite of the distance.... But if it is he, why does he not come? What does he have to fear from me?"

"Perhaps he is seeking justice, Miss," replied Magnac stiffly; "since you are aware of his return, you must know that the terrible crime committed by his uncle prevents him..."

"Fie on you, Sire," interrupted Sister Magloire with indignation, "Do you dare believe this slander, you who has received so many benefits from the Prior? As for Sire Léonce, who would want to connect him to the fault of another, even if the fault is real? He is so gentle, so good, so generous! Recently, upon learning about the accusations hanging over his uncle and the severe treatment he is receiving, Sire Léonce hurried to Frontenac to console and defend him. They did not allow him to see Prior Bonaventure who is in his cell under absolute secrecy. So, the courageous young man resolved to organize his uncle's escape, and everything had been prepared when the plot was discovered. He refused to be discouraged and would have confronted all the temporal and spiritual powers to come to the aid of his unfortunate uncle, if the Prior himself, warned about these audacious attempts, had not sent him specific orders to remain calm and await the will of God."

"Yes, Léonce must have reacted this way!" exclaimed Christine warmly; but please, my sister, give me more details."

"I do not know much more, my dear Miss, as nothing transpires on what is happening over there since the ban was placed on the Abbey. I obtained this information from the most recent messenger from Frontenac, a lay brother who is quite timid, but whom I tried to get talking while he rested in the kitchen. However, I had to tear the words out of him one by one.... The fact remains that Léonce had to renounce his desperate attempts; and ceding to the wishes of the Prior, he returned to Mercoire to hunt the beast of Gévaudan, while the trial continues at the Abbey."

"Ah!" said Christine with a bitter smile, "the Prior, even in the mortal embarrassment in which he finds himself, has not given up on his old projects.... But he does not matter, Sister Magloire. Would it not be strange if Léonce was the conqueror of the beast of Gévaudan?"

"And why would it not be so, Miss? He is skilled, courageous, untiring..."

"What? you think.... And you, Knight, you are more competent than we in these matters; my supposition seems to you inadmissible, then? "

Magnac reflected.

"Unfortunately, no, Miss," he replied, but with an evident regret. "Sire Léonce, I am certain, did not go to the Abbey, in spite of the invitation he received; he remained at the farm in Cransac where he has established his residence, and I do not see any reason that he might not have found the beast in his path…. Once again, it would have been a great misfortune, as finally, a commoner… the nephew of a monk who had committed a crime…"

Miss de Barjac had not heard this last observation; she had stood up impetuously:

"Oh!" she said in a trembling voice, "if that had happened, if it could happen… However, if that was the case, he should have presented himself here! Why did he not come?"

Just as she finished speaking these words, a servant came running in, obviously stunned:

"Miss," he said, "Sire Léonce has just arrived, and has requested permission to come and bid you well."

Had the chateau been suddenly lifted up in the air by a supernatural power, the three persons in that salon would not have been more surprised. None thought of replying to the valet; finally, Christine murmured in an inexpressible haze:

"Him? Is it Léonce, then?… Thank you, dear God, you have not punished me for my imprudence and folly!"

"Miss, I beg of you to reflect…"

"Christine, dear child, consider that you can be mistaken again!"

Miss de Barjac, regaining her composure, thanked her two advisers with a smile; then, seating herself again, she said to them:

"Remain next to me…. I will receive him as befits a lady of Barjac…. François," she added, addressing the servant, "bring in Sire Léonce."

Several minutes later, timid steps crossed the antechamber, and Léonce entered.

He was dressed with extreme simplicity; there was something about him that was sad, constrained, humiliated. However, at the sight of Miss de Barjac, a flush colored his cheeks and it seemed that a great astonishment mixed in with the tumultuous feelings he was experiencing. He had always imagined Christine proud and fearless, in her riding outfit, as in the past, and one would have said that he had trouble recognizing her in this elegant and gracious person, seated modestly between her governess and her old squire. In any event, none of the phrases that he had undoubtedly prepared produced themselves in his mind at that moment; he halted, silent and trembling, a few steps from the chatelaine, and simply bowed profoundly.

Christine, on her side, did not know how to maintain the cool dignity that she had hoped to display. Giving in to a driving force stronger than her will, she ran up to her childhood friend, her hand held out towards him, and said in a soft tone:

"Léonce, my dear Léonce, you are most welcome to Mercoire."

This affectionate reception released an explosion in the broken soul of the poor young man; he seized her hand and murmured in a voice interspersed with sobs:

"Ah! Miss, you are so kind!... You do not despise me, you do not hate me, then?"

"Hate you, despise you, my friend? do not even think it…. Poor Léonce! I know your sorrows, and I share them…. But where now is that strength of character, that intelligence and that confidence in God that I admired in you in the past?"

They sat side by side. Sister Magloire kept bowing to the Prior's nephew, while the knight, more reserved, addressed him with stilted compliments. Léonce soon calmed down.

"Forgive me, Miss," he resumed, "my emotions which you can well understand…. Could I imagine that you would receive me this way, in spite of the depths I fell into, when not long ago, you treated me severely in the middle of my joys and successes."

"This is a reproach, Léonce, and perhaps it is partially deserved. However, if my eccentricities sometimes attack those who are happy and proud, they always spare those who are feeble and unfortunate…. As for you, forgive my past faults; I have atoned for them more cruelly than you can imagine!"

This conversation, once established on a basis of friendly intimacy, Sister Magloire and the knight soon joined in. However, Léonce remained somber and restrained; Christine observed discreetly, and seemed to express increasing impatience. Finally, she interrupted Magnac in the middle of a long tirade, and suddenly asked:

"I know, Sire Léonce, that you have been for some time searching for the beast of Gévaudan; do you have many competitors in this dangerous hunt?"

"Too many, Miss!... The reward to the winner is so great!"

"However, among these competitors, are there any that are aware of my insane vow, pronounced in a moment of folly…."

"I do not know, Christine; but what well-born man would take advantage of such a dubious promise and impose a choice not worthy of you? To deserve the hand of the beautiful and noble Christine de Barjac, it does not suffice to have had a life without reproach, one must have a good name, high birth and exterior advantages that merit the admiration of all. Anyone not having these qualities who wishes to take advantage of a rash vow would be a wretch that all good-hearted persons would reject with indignation. Your free and judicious choice could only give value to such a victory."

Listening to these words pronounced in such a passionate tone, Christine could not help feeling a shiver of joy. Evidently, Léonce must be the conqueror of the beast, but a sentiment of delicacy coming from the dishonorable status of his uncle prevented him from declaring such. Miss de Barjac resumed, her eyes lowered:

"I made no reserves, Léonce, when I took this formidable and solemn engagement…. Whoever meets the condition imposed will have the right to claim the implementation of my promise; however humble and low be his origins, I will resign myself to my destiny, if with regret, at least without complaint or murmur."

Léonce dreamed for a moment.

"That will not suffice," he resumed finally, "for someone who will love you with a profound and selfless love…. He should also assure himself that you feel for him respect and affection…."

"Well, he will be free to inquire," said Christine, with a form of anger.

As Léonce did not reply, and remained plunged in his reverie, she asked, affecting a tone of indifference:

"Have you heard it said, Sire Léonce, that the beast of Gévaudan was killed yesterday evening in the forest of Labeyssère?"

The young man straightened quickly.

"What say you, Miss?" he asked; the beast of Gévaudan killed in the forest of Labeyssère!... But that is impossible!"

"And why is that, Léonce?"

"Because at the moment that I am speaking, my tracker, Denis, is in the process of following the wolf in the depths of the Monadière, less than a league from here, and has the hope of *diverting* it soon."

Christine did not know at first whether she should be alarmed or rejoice at this news.

"You have heard him, Knight?" she resumed; "what were you telling us, then?"

Magnac repeated point by point the account he had from the guard Jerome; Léonce listened an extreme attention.

"It is inconceivable!" he finally said with an anguished air; "Denis, always so prudent, so experienced in his art, could he be mistaken? Could he have taken the track of one of those large wolves which abound in the nearby woods for that of the beast? But then, Miss, if they have said the truth, you could have appear here, at any moment, some insolent hunter claiming the prize of his victory?"

"I fear so, Léonce, I fear so! Seeing you arrive a while ago, I had hoped…. But if it was not you who had killed the beast, for heaven's sake, what motive brings you now to Mercoire, after having remained so long in the vicinity without deigning to come to this friendly home?"

Léonce slapped his forehead.

"Of course! thank you for reminding me why have come, when the awareness of my disgrace perhaps prevented me from crossing your threshold…. You will now learn that the Bishop of Alep wrote to me recently to invite me to come to Frontenac 'where they will inform me, the missive said, of things of the greatest interest.' I have become very indifferent as to my own destiny for which I despair; moreover, I did not want to obey the orders of that arrogant priest, that relentless persecutor of my friends; I therefore had a reply sent saying that it was impossible for me to come to the Abbey. Since that day, I was sent another notice, coming this time from a person that I still love, despite his apparent guilt. This notice engages me to come to the Chateau de Mercoire this very day, where I am to await certain communications. I have never disobeyed the person in question, and I will not start now, especially when he is suffering…. I therefore hurried here, in spite of the bad reception that I feared, and which your goodness spared me, Miss; and I will now ask you if some letter or message has arrived for me?"

Christine gave a questioning look to her two advisors.

"No one," said Magnac.

"Nothing," said Sister Magloire, "but it is still early and perhaps…"

"In that case," resumed Léonce, "if Miss de Barjac would be willing to give me a little corner in her home where I can wait until tonight the news which have been announced for me. I do not need much room, and as soon as night falls, if nothing has arrived for me, I plan to leave with apologies for bothering you."

This humility dismayed Christine.

"Léonce, my friend, my brother," she resumed, "can you speak to me this way?... Stay in this salon, with me. We will chat about our childhood memories; it has been such a long time since I have had that satisfaction…. And then" she said in worried tone, "in spite of myself, I cannot get this stupid story that the Knight told us out of my mind. If my fears, undoubtedly absurd, became reality, it would be a consolation to have near me a devoted friend to support me and feel sorry for me!"

"Miss, does she not have," said Magnac, with the air of an aggrieved victim, "her squire of honor who believes himself quite capable of protecting her against all dangers?"

Christine leaned towards Léonce and began speaking to him in a low voice. The young man, embarrassed perhaps by this reversal of the roles, responded with monosyllables; however, Christine, alternately smiling and melancholic, was not discouraged and imperceptibly Léonce forgot about his painful preoccupations. Soon they began to be, one with the other, in unison; they spoke in even lower tones, but with increasing vivacity, and sympathetic tears dampened their eyes.

These murmurs of an innocent love impressed differently the knight and Sister Magloire. The good sister, who had perhaps loved in her youth, smiled indulgently. On the contrary, the knight squirmed on his seat, taking dose after dose of tobacco and making sounds like hmm, loudly, which everyone ignored.

Perhaps the poetic memories of the past had drawn the poor children towards vague hopes for the future; Perhaps this future began to seem less laden with clouds and somber colors, when suddenly one heard in the main courtyard the sounds of horses. Almost immediately the fanfare of the hunt awoke in a formidable manner the echoes of the old manor.

The young people trembled; they listened to the sounds which prolonged themselves, menacing and dominating, in the hallways and in the courtyards.

"My Lord, what is this?" exclaimed Sister Magloire, clasping her hands.

"Who dares," said the knight, "declare themselves with such insolence in the Chateau de Mercoire?"

Rapid steps echoed in the hallway; then the door was brusquely opened and the servant announced:

"Sire Count de Varinas!"

The Baron de Laroche-Boisseau entered.

Chapter XXIV

THE COFFER

Laroche-Boisseau was wearing his rich Lieutenant of the Louveterie uniform. He walked in proudly, head held high and a smile on his face, like a man very sure of himself. Behind him came one of his trackers, who after having deposited a tightly closed coffer on the floor near the door of the salon, left after a sign from his master.

All three were astounded by the boldness with which the Baron presented himself in a place where there were so many reasons for him to be hated and despised. Sister Magloire was purple with indignation, and the shallow cheeks of the knight had taken on a greenish pallor. Léonce, torn by conflicting sentiments, was incapable of movement.

Only Miss de Barjac, perhaps by the excess of her emotions, recovered her dignity which had failed her moments earlier with Léonce. She arose, and while the Baron was bowing, said, with irony;

"Count de Varinas, what is the meaning, Sire, of this manner of having yourself announced in my home? Did you hope that by taking a new name, that you would erase the memories that you left behind using the old one?"

Laroche-Boisseau, despite his self-assurance, was disconcerted by the harshness of this rude remark.

"Ah, charming," he said forcing a smile, "is it generous to remind me of faults which you had forgiven me, and for which I had been so cruelly punished?... As for the title and my new name, they belong to me by birthright and no one can deny them to me."

'Consequently, Sire," demanded the Chatelaine, whose feminine curiosity quieted for a moment the sentiments of another nature, "you are already in possession of the Varinas domains?"

"Not yet, my lovely, but only a simple formality remains, as I have the promise of Monsignor Royal Commissioner. Perhaps the transfer would have already taken place yesterday if I had gone to Frontenac, as I had been invited to do; however, other important business kept me in this region, and I preferred sending my attorney, who could defend my interests better than I against those unscrupulous monks.... In the meantime, I have reclaimed, as you can see, the title and name which are my legitimate family heritage."

Léonce could not contain himself.

"It seems to me, however," he said drily, "that you are in a hurry to adopt a status that you do not yet have a legal right to."

Laroche-Boisseau swiveled around and looked at Léonce as if he had seen him for the first time.

"Ah! is it you, my happy hunting companion?" he asked with a disdainful familiarity. "I could reply that your opinion does not have any importance in this affair; However, I wish to be indulgent towards you as I can guess why you are intervening in this manner.... In your opinion, undoubtedly, my present status is proof of the crime by those who's dark machinations had succeeded in depriving me of my rights. Perhaps you are right, and moreover, I pardon much to a friend whose grief embitters..."

"A friend, Sire? I did not know that I had the honor of being yours."

"Is that so? When our relations were so intimate and confidential?... But after all, it will be as you wish; I am not for it, I assure you."

And he began to snicker; Léonce trembled with anger, but he remembered again his promise to his uncle, and he said to himself:

"No, I will not add to my uncle's grief.... I will keep my promise, no matter what happens!"

Laroche-Boisseau was perhaps about to launch some new sarcasms at Léonce, when the knight diverted his attention:

"Sire de Varinas," said Magnac, addressing him with a great bow, "seems to have forgotten the invitation to a duel he received under the name Laroche-Boisseau. It is certainly for this reason that he did not receive my messages and did not reply as befits a gentleman in good standing.... However, now I have him, and, Varinas or Laroche-Boisseau, I will not leave him until I have obtained some words of explanation."

The Baron began laughing louder.

"Morbleu! my wonderful errant knight, my handsome defender of beauties, my valiant paladin[37] of oppressed women," he exclaimed; "you are devilishly tenacious in your ideas! Is this because of the guard Fargeot, or my hunting in the Mercoire forest without your permission, or what? Well, well, we will certainly get back to this, and then, when we will have settled the matter with wooden sabers and gingerbread swords, you will have received satisfaction, I promise you.... However, for the moment, other more important matters require my attention, and I will first explain to your mistress the motive of my visit... which appears not to be to her liking."

"If Sire Laroche-Boisseau thinks this is so," said Christine stiffly, "it is inexcusable to prolong things."

---

37   Paladin: one of the twelve knights in attendance of Charlemagne; (774-816) As time went on, the meaning of the name grew to be any chivalrous or heroic person.

"You are treating me very cruelly, Miss; in presenting myself here, I had complete faith in the pardon you had so generously accorded me."

"My pardon did not authorize your presence. However, hasten to explain to us the purpose of your visit; you are right to believe that this meeting is very painful for me."

Laroche-Boisseau, due to his singular ideas about women, was perhaps not expecting an aversion as pronounced and obstinate; as he remained silent, Magnac said in his stolid and cold manner:

"Well, Sire Baron… or Sire Count, as I am not questioning your title, have you not heard? Miss de Barjac, my noble mistress, wishes that you inform her as rapidly as possible the object of your visit, and then…"

He pointed to the door with his finger. Laroche-Boisseau jumped with anger.

"By all the Devils, you old rascal, are you now going to take your role of valet seriously? If I thought so…"

"Sire," interrupted Léonce in his turn, "are you forgetting that you are in the presence and in the home of a lady?"

Laroche-Boisseau looked with flaming eyes at Christine's two defenders, and suddenly, he broke into peals of laughter.

"By Sambleu, Miss," he resumed, "I must congratulate you…. It would not be prudent to disobey your orders in this chateau! You have here two valorous protectors who would not hesitate to throw the audacious person out if they were allowed to do so…. But it is time for me to explain, and to try if I can finally reverse the roles…"

Miss de Barjac, who had remained standing until now, sat down trembling. Magnac and Léonce, forgetting their personal grievances, waited with great apprehension for what the Baron was going to say.

The latter seemed to get great pleasure in prolonging their discomfort; finally, he said, weighing heavily on each word:

"You remember, Miss, that you committed yourself with a vow, to marry the hunter who succeeded in killing the beast of Gévaudan, provided he is not in a servile position?"

"I do remember," replied Christine feebly.

"And that vow," continued Laroche-Boisseau, "are you still prepared to honor it? Would you refuse the hand of a gallant man who had taken your promise seriously and confronted fatigue and dangers to fulfil the conditions imposed?"

"Such a doubt is an insult, Sire."

"Well, then!" exclaimed the Baron triumphantly, "I claim for myself all the privileges promised to the conqueror of the beast…. I had the pleasure of killing the ferocious animal yesterday in the forest of Labeyssère…. Here is the proof."

He went to get the coffer that his lackey had placed near the door, opened it, and displayed the bloody head and one paw of a wolf.

However, Christine did not have the courage to look at the hideous trophy; she had collapsed in her chair.

The other witnesses were no less affected, although they should have expected such an eventuality. Léonce remained stunned. The knight, always slow to assimilate, seemed to be considering the situation, whereas Sister Magloire had her eyes and her hands reaching for the heavens while muttering prayers.

None of these details could escape Laroche-Boisseau.

"Well," he resumed in a mocking tone, "one would say that my victory does not evoke great transports of joy!... However, the Baron de Laroche-Boisseau, Count and Lord de Varinas is not a draw to be disdained when chance might have brought you some sinister poacher to become Chatelain of Mercoire."

There was once again silence.

"Sire Baron," Léonce finally said with desperation, "Miss Barjac's friends cannot accept without examination all your assertions. One must first establish without question that the animal whose remains you brought here is that of the beast of Gévaudan, and I have reason to believe…"

"Any person of good faith only has to look at this evidence," resumed Laroche-Boisseau pointing to the objects in the container. "Could any other animal than the celebrated beast of Gévaudan have such a monstrous head, dreadful fangs, robust claws…"

"And what proves to us," continued Léonce, "that you, Sire, you alone, mortally struck the wolf whose remains you present?"

"You will hear from Master Legris, my protégé. Although he is annoyed with me at this moment, and refused to come with me here, he could not avoid being witness to the truth. You will also hear from my lead tracker, Labranche, and the numerous peasants who were serving as beaters when I when I fired the fortunate shot with my rifle…. You may put your mind at rest, Léonce, we can furnish all the guarantees necessary to those who have the right to ask…. For the moment, it is important to know if Miss de Barjac will keep her word… even towards myself."

Poor Christine replied with difficulty;

"I will keep it, Sire… even if it kills me" This form of consent did not seem to be to Laroche-Boisseau's taste and he grimaced. Léonce exclaimed forcefully:

"Sire Baron, you are a gentleman, you cannot accept such a sacrifice! You should be too proud, too refined to abuse the advantage given you by a happy chance over a young lady worthy of great respect!... She does not love you and you know it; she will not place her hand in yours except to fulfill her reckless vow. Could a marriage created under these conditions assure happiness for one or the other? Would this not be a shame, a mockery for you? Renounce nobly as this is a thoughtless promise. The dignity of your name, your loyalty and your honor require it also!"

"Yes," finished Laroche-Boisseau with irony, "and leave the place free to a certain would-be lover, languishing hero of one of these flirtations that exist sometimes between a schoolboy and a resident, right Sire Léonce? In truth, if someone conceived similar expectations, one could not find an advocate more incapable of proving it to me."

This time, Léonce's resolutions, the recollection of his promises to his uncle, could not hold back the furor that suffocated him.

"Baron de la Roche-Boisseau," he said in a firm voice, "you are despicable.... Love plays no role in your intentions for a noble young lady who hates and despises you. What you desire is her fortune, her beautiful domains and the means to restore your image, tarnished and stained by your debaucheries."

The Baron, in turn, could not contain his disdainful cold-bloodedness in the presence of such a direct and violent affront.

"By the Devil! Sire Adventurer," he exclaimed, "that is pushing insolence too far.... Even if you were ten times worse, I would force your insults back down your throat. "

"They will not go back in, Sire; on the contrary, everywhere I go, I plan to say them out loud...."

"That is enough, Sire; through an excess of insults, you hope to bring us to the same level.... You have succeeded; let us go outside, Sire, immediately!"

"Finally!" said Léonce.

They were already heading towards the door, without Christine, who was still in a near-faint, being able to intervene, when the Knight de Magnac suddenly barred their passage with a vivacity that was not expected of him.

"One moment, Sires," he said with solemnity, "things are not going to happen this way.... Sire Baron, or rather Sire Count is not in control; I have long ago established my rights or priority over him, and these rights have been fortified by all the unseemly epithets that Sire de Laroche-Boisseau, I mean Sire Varinas... has just been using. I insist upon my rights; and, since Sire de Laroche-Boisseau, Count of Varinas is so available, I pray that he reserves me the honor..."

"Sire de Magnac, I beg of you," said Léonce energetically, "allow me to avenge the affronts against me and those who are the dearest to me in the world! You have no idea how much this unworthy gentleman has filled my heart with venom and bitterness!"

"With my deep regrets, Sire Léonce, I cannot cede to you on this. It is up to me to punish the insults to my young mistress; this is a part of my responsibilities; the grievances of a woman must pass before yours and mine; Sorry to refuse…"

"Oh, Morbleu!" interrupted Laroche-Boisseau in a paroxysm of furor, "come outside, both of you…. Do you think that I am worried by a young birdbrain, brought up with pincers by cowardly monks, and an old toothless fellow who fantasizes about drawing his rusty sword one more time from its scabbard? Come, I tell you! together or separately, I will teach you a lesson, both of you, I promise."

"Very well, let us go out first," resumed Léonce; "this issue will not be handled in the presence of a lady."

"Yes, yes, let us go out," said the Baron.

"As you wish, Sires," said Magnac, bowing.

Miss de Barjac was finally able to shake off the effects of these tumultuous events. She arose brusquely, pushing away the sister who was trying to hold her back, and exclaimed with authority:

"Stay, Sires, I beg of you…. No, I order you, if my orders here can still carry any weight!"

The three men stopped; after a moment of hesitation, they slowly approached the young chatelaine.

"For the love of God, Sires, listen to me," she resumed; "it is to you especially that I speak, Léonce, the companion of my youth; and to you also, my dear knight, you have always provided me with so much care and respect…. As much as I am against it, I cannot support the idea that you have a quarrel with Sire de Laroche-Boisseau because of me. Sire Baron seems to have exactly met the conditions imposed by my vow; the prize that he has come to claim cannot be denied him. I cannot permit that my retainers and my friends intervene to protect me from the consequences of a reckless commitment, as one could accuse me, with reason, of using unworthy subterfuge to elude my word. Anyone who does this would become my enemy."

"Christine," replied Léonce, "this man has used against my unfortunate uncle and myself the most outrageous expressions."

"He has insulted the honor of house of Magnac," said the knight.

"And you may add, Sires," resumed Laroche-Boisseau arrogantly, "that I retract nothing."

Christine continued, addressing the knight and Léonce;

"Do not try to deceive me, my good friends, it is my cause, not yours that you want to defend; renounce your efforts, I beg of you. The terrible situation in which I find myself is entirely of my own doing; my imprudence, my haste, my selfish stubbornness, all played a role; it is I who must pay the penalty of my error!"

Directly afterwards, she took each of the Baron's adversaries aside and appeared to be giving them the most pressing reasons to divert their project. One and finally the other seemed to cede to her entreaties; however, it was easy to guess that they would take advantage of the first opportunity to renew the quarrel.

Laroche-Boisseau had regained his composure; when he saw that Miss de Barjac appeared to have succeeded, he said, while smiling:

"Thank you my charming one; you have loyally kept your word! Allow me to hope that this good faith is a prelude to sentiments less hostile towards... the future chatelain of Mercoire."

And he kissed her hand.

"Chatelain of Mercoire!" repeated Léonce; "you do not have that title yet, Sire.... Miss de Barjac is still a ward of enlightened and severe turors, whose duty is to protect her from the dangers of her own generosity. And, if I am not mistaken, there is sufficient wisdom, power and energy among the fathers of Frontenac to render this marriage impossible!"

"Do you think so, my friend?" asked Christine quickly.

Léonce repeated his assertion with even more warmth.

"Well, Morbleu! we will see about that," replied the Baron with his disdainful smile; "this brave young man, in his great affection for the monks of Frontenac, forgets that they have a rather low standing right now, and that a certain Bishop has been trimming their nails very short recently.... I will be ready and waiting, and we will see which one of them will dare to attack me. Will it be the poor old Abbot, almost imbecile, crippled with his gout and rheumatisms, and who already has one foot on the grave? Or could it be the valorous champion of the convent, the headstrong one of the community, capable, prudent, eloquent Prior Bonaventure? Unfortunately, this star of the monastery finds himself at this hour placed in obscurity; the sainted man, accused of assassinating a poor child, is locked up in a cell, which he will soon exchange for a darker and deeper dungeon..."

"Are you so sure, Sire?" asked Sister Magloire in an unusual tone.

"Over the past few minutes, the noise of voices and horses had renewed in the manor's main courtyard. The sister, always concerned, or perhaps pushed by a secret presentiment, had gone out to determine the cause of the commotion. From a window giving on the large courtyard, she could see two litters mounted on donkeys and several servants on horseback. One glance at the interior of the litters was all she needed, and she returned to the salon quivering with hope and joy.

The others, noticing her agitation, wanted to question her; however, she did not have time to respond. The door suddenly opened and the servant announced in a voice choked with respect:

"His Lordship Monsignor the Bishop of Alep... His Reverence the Prior of Frontenac."

At the same time, the Bishop and the priest entered, leaning on each other in the friendliest manner.

Chapter XXV

THE REVELATIONS

Monsignor de Cambis, despite the smallness of his size, maintained a majestic poise and a dignified air which he imposed upon everyone that approached him. He was wrapped in a violet travelling cloak, and wearing a round cap of the same color under which one could see the sparkling of his grey piercing eyes. Walking next to him with humble steps, was the Prior Bonaventure, always simple, calm and smiling as before; a bit thinner and paler, the only witness to the ordeals which he had recently suffered.

"My uncle, my benefactor," exclaimed Léonce, besides himself, "you have been returned to me?"

"And breaking into tears, he threw himself into the arms of the Prior. The Prior Bonaventure, no less touched, returned his caresses, and murmured softly:

"And what, Léonce, so much tenderness for a sacrilegious priest, for a criminal?"

"My uncle, I never believed those calumnies, although they tore at my heart…. I am sure that you had no difficulty in clearing your name…."

"Child, do you think that I would accept your signs of affection if I did not believe myself worthy of them? But shush!" he continued, designating the Bishop, "we are in the presence of a Prince of the Church."

During this time, the lady of the chateau, assisted by Sister Magloire, had run up in front of Sire de Gambis. The nun prostrated herself, while Christine bowed and stammered:

"Monsignor, I am overwhelmed with gratitude, for the honor…"

Then, no longer able to contain herself, she fell also to her knees exclaiming:

"Oh, Monsignor, it is Heaven that sends you to rescue me at this moment…. You are all-powerful; protect me!"

And her tears fell in abundance. The Bishop assisted her to her feet with an air of kindness.

"May the peace of our Lord descend upon this house!" he continued in a serious tone; "and you, my daughters, humble yourselves only before the Lord. Even those who believe they are acting in His name are feeble creatures and subject to error…. I have recently had the cruel experience!"

Then, turning towards the Prior who was approaching with Léonce, he studied the young man for a moment, and said:

"Dear Father, is this... h?"

"It is he, Monsignor."

The Bishop made the sign of the cross on Léonce's forehead.

"May God bless you my child!" he said in an affectionate tone, "and always cherish the pure and venerable man from whom you have received precious lessons!... You did not wish to come to me, in spite of my pressing invitation; I have come to you, and I arrive for the joy of some and for the confusion of others.... And you also, Sire Baron," he continued, addressing Laroche-Boisseau who bowed with reserve, "you did not present yourself at yesterday's meeting at the Frontenac Abbey?"

"An important affair retained me here, Monsignor; however, you must have seen my attorney, the elder Legris?"

Sire de Gambis acknowledged this with a nod of his head.

"It is of no importance," he replied; "you will learn what happened, and it is again Providence that brings you here again in this house to witness a great act of justice."

He sat down, and they all took seats around him, except for Sister Magloire and the knight, who stood a little aside with a respectful attitude. Léonce and Christine, not understanding what was going on, alternately moved their eyes anxiously from the calm face of the Prior to the severe features of the Bishop. Laroche-Boisseau, less patient, or perhaps sensing some unpleasant developments for him, could not restrain himself.

"Ah, Monsignor," he asked with his usual confidence, "what has happened then since our last meeting in Frontenac? It seems to me that there have been some dramatic changes! You appeared to be horrified by those odious monks who had put to death a young child to obtain his heritage; you crushed them with all the weight of your anger; you announced openly that you would repair the injustices that had been committed and chastise, without pity, the guilty. However, now you are treating most favorably the principal author of this terrible assassination, the monk whose dangerous ploy perverted, it seems, the rest of the community...."

Monsignor de Cambis interrupted sharply.

"Sire Baron," he said, "cease insulting a good man who is listening to us and the Sainted house where he is the glory and the model. As you said, things have dramatically changed in the past few hours; truth manifested itself in a sensational manner, God permitted me to recognize the error in which I fell through an excess of zeal and also perhaps through an excess of human presumption.... The fathers of Frontenac, when I persecuted them, made themselves martyrs of their duty. The good Prior, who in my blindness I overwhelmed with unjustified severity, had not ceased to merit my respect and my admiration."

"Ah, I was sure of it, my uncle!" murmured Léonce, bringing to his lips the hand of Bonaventure who was seated next to him.

"Ah, my Reverend Father," asked Christine, "will you pardon me for having believed…"

The Prior imposed silence on one and the other by a gesture of kindness. Laroche-Boisseau resumed vehemently:

"Monsignor, Monsignor, one has deceived your religion and it is undoubtedly the work of this devious monk whose language has all the subtlety, all the venom of a serpent…. However, it will not be as easy to deceive me; even before learning through what tissue of lies he used to ingeniously mislead you, I declare that I will pursue my efforts against this assassin of my young relative; I will not fail, as the head of the family to meet that imperative and sacred duty. Did not Prior Bonaventure, by his own admission, the evening of the crime, accompany a mysterious man who addressed Madam Fargeot, the wet-nurse, in the gardens of Varinas? The Prior must identify this wretch and explain…"

"We know who he is now, Sire Baron," replied the prelate coldly.

"Well then, who was he?"

"Your uncle, the Count of Varinas, the actual father of the child who disappeared."

Laroche-Boisseau remained stunned as if he had received a blow to his head.

"You doubt," resumed Monsignor de Cambis, "however, you will doubt no longer when you will have seen the codicil of the late Count; by express order of its writer, the codicil was read yesterday in the presence of the senior members of the Chapter of Frontenac. The Count explained in great detail that on the night in question, he slipped into the Varinas gardens by a small door for which he was the only one to have the key; using a pretext, he was able to send the nurse away, giving him free access to the child…."

"Once again, Monsignor, he is deceiving you," interrupted the Baron; "a father, even if his mind was deranged, as was perhaps the case with my uncle de Varinas, would he have been sufficiently barbaric to become the assassin of his young son?"

"And who says, Sire, that the child perished?... The child is alive."

"That is impossible!"

"He is alive, I tell you…. And the proof is that we all know him, and he is here in front of you."

"What? he is…"

"The supposed nephew of the Prior, the supposed Léonce, who will finally take his true name and title as the Count de Varinas."

Exclamations of surprise and joy greeted this unexpected revelation.

Léonce, as we will continue to use this name, had suddenly stood up and was looking at the Prior as if asking him for confirmation of Bishop's words.

"Monsignor could not affirm anything that is not absolutely true, my child," said Bonaventure; "here is the secret that I have been hiding from you with so much care, all of this while preparing you for your present grandeur. You are not related to me by any other means than our mutual affection...."

"And that, my Father, will never be broken!" exclaimed Léonce, hugging him.

Everyone's eyes, except those of the Baron, were brimming with tears. Léonce received the congratulations of Christine, the knight and Sister Magloire. While he abandoned himself to these pleasant emotions, Christine leaned towards the Prior:

"My Father," she asked, "is he the rich pretender of high birth..."

"Whom you have rejected, my daughter, whom you sacrificed to an ill-considered emotional outburst.... Unfortunate child! Unfortunate child!"

Christine fell back in her chair and hid her face in her hands.

Laroche-Boisseau had not made a move to approach his young cousin. Recovered from his stupefaction initially created by the revelation, he resumed with irony:

"All this is quite touching, no doubt, but do not expect that I will accept without proofs such romantic assertions! I must see more clearly into this new kinship which deprives me from an important heritage...."

"The proofs will not be lacking, Sire Baron," replied the Bishop; "they are clear and decisive. The Father Prior has authentic documents that you have the absolute right to examine."

Indeed, Bonaventure laid out on the table a batch of papers which the Baron immediately began to carefully study, while the Bishop explained the events that established the filiation with Léonce. We will summarize in a few words these events.

We know that the Count of Varinas had renounced Protestantism; from there was born a disunion between him and his younger brother, the Baron of Laroche-Boisseau, father of the person who plays a major role in this story. However, the Count, in embracing the Catholic religion, had not ceded to purely human considerations that sometimes affect changes in religion. His conversion, the handiwork of the monks of Frontenac, and in particular, that of Prior Bonaventure, was frank and sincere; even more so, his religious sentiments, exalted by solitude and mediation, had progressed to a point approaching asceticism and mysticism.

Struck by the languor disease, which he knew to be fatal, the Count had retired to the Frontenac Abbey, and there, he had fallen under the influence of a fixation. The future of his only child, then three or four years old, constantly preoccupied him. With him dead, the guardianship of this beloved child would naturally transfer to his brother, Laroche-Boisseau, who was Protestant. Yet, would not Laroche-Boisseau take advantage of his authority over the young pupil to bring him back to Protestantism? This thought obsessed the sick man day and night. Undoubtedly, by naming another legal guardian for his son, he could protect him from this dreaded influence. However, the Count, extremely timid, overestimated the powers of his brother. He feared that Laroche-Boisseau, active and rambunctious, might succeed in breaking the will which removed him as guardian, or that if he failed, avenge himself by secretly diverting the boy from Catholicism. All these difficulties continually rattled his brain, and the Count imagined, to surmount all this, a very bizarre plan.

This consisted of kidnapping his son, who was then living at the Chateau de Varinas, and make it seem as though he was dead. The land of Varinas not being subject to substitution,[38] the Count could bequeath it to the monks in the form of a trust, and it would remain in their charge for a fixed period. As for the young Viscount, he would live at the Abbey under an assumed name and would be passed off as a close relative to one of the Reverend Fathers. He would be brought up carefully in the Catholic religion. His real name and status would be hidden from him. It would only be when he reached the age of twenty years that the truth would be revealed to him, which would be without dangers thanks to the excellent teachings he would have received.

The first time that the Count de Varinas shared this project with his friend and confidant, the Prior Bonaventure, the latter tried to explain its risks, even its impossibilities. The Count at first seemed to accept the Prior's reasoning; however, soon he came back to it; he had long meditated on all the eventualities, he had foreseen everything and planned every move; he used presentations of his plan alternately with prayers to obtain its acceptance; the feverish exaltation of his ideas was such that a prolonged resistance could be fatal to him. Ceding to his exhortations, Bonaventure finally consulted with the Abbey's Chapter on the Counts proposal, and, after much hesitation, they agreed to try to implement it, and would abandon it only if unsurmountable obstacles were encountered.

Everything succeeded beyond their expectations. The Count, despite his weakness, wanted to take charge himself of the operation. He secretly left Frontenac with Prior Bonaventure and two faithful servants. He arrived during the evening at the door of the Varinas garden, and, after having sent away the nurse with a clever lie, he seized his son, who, having recognized him, let himself be taken away without resistance. They carefully left the

_____

38   Substitution: refers to a pre-Revolution French law procedure sometimes used by the nobility to assure heritage rights.

little Viscount's cap on the ground; and, a few hours later, went so far as to throw into the precipice the corpse of a child they had obtained from a nearby village and had dressed in the clothing of the young Varinas. All these arrangements, coldly planned for a long time, had as their objective to distress the poor wet-nurse and give her the certainty that the child had perished. In the mind of the poor sick father, what importance were the tears of a simple peasant woman against the future and eternal salvation of the future heir of the Varinas? Moreover, Marguerite Fargeot had been recommended to Prior Bonaventure, and, in compensation for her anguish, she and her family, thereafter benefitted from a constant protection.

Thanks to all this foresight, no one suspected the truth; judicial authorities remained convinced that the young Viscount had fallen accidently into the abyss next to the chateau.

Then, the Count, who was feeling the end approaching, thought of nothing else than completing his work. Fearing that later someone might contest against his son the name and the title to which he had a right, Varinas took the most detailed precautions in order to render all doubt impossible. He had prepared three copies of a detailed transcript of the kidnapping operated by himself; two copies were deposited with different solicitors, and the third conserved in Frontenac. Each was signed by him, the two solicitors and the six principal fathers of the convent as well as the Abbot and the Prior. Then he prepared the two codicils, one of which was to be opened upon his demise and the other the day that his son had attained the age of twenty years. In addition, the Count insisted that the fathers who had knowledge of his secret take an oath to reveal nothing until the date specified for the name and rank of their pupil. These arrangements made, he died quietly, assured that all his wishes would be honored.

We know, indeed, with what diligent exactitude the Frontenac monks, under the influence of the Prior, had kept their vow; they allowed themselves to be treated with contempt and be persecuted rather than divulge the secret of their deceased friend; however, since the previous day, the prescribed delay had expired, the codicil had been opened, and the truth was no longer a secret for anyone.

Such was the narrative of the Bishop. Léonce, while listening to him, had given numerous signs of emotion. Monsignor de Cambis said to him at the end:

"You see, my dear son, that your pious and sound education had cost in sacrifices to your father and friends. Do not permit the good qualities of your generous soul to be smothered, and may the brilliant life that awaits you not allow you to forget the modest simplicity of your early youth. Above all, never cease to cherish your Frontenac benefactors, and in particular the worthy Prior who took such care of your childhood...."

"Ah! Monsignor," interrupted Léonce, carried away, "my unfortunate father himself, if he were still alive, could be jealous of the respect, gratitude and boundless affection I feel for this incomparable friend."

And he once again pressed his arms around the Prior, whose eyes were filled with tears.

"I have therefore been the only guilty one in all this," continued the Bishop, "I, who could believe for a moment that these peaceful monks, renowned for their wisdom and piety, had committed such a horrible crime. From the first days, seeing the simple and touching resignation with which they supported their bad treatment, I had doubts about the legitimacy of their severity; later, when Sire de Varinas attempted to have his supposed uncle escape from the Abbey, and the Prior refused, these doubts became stronger; however, it was not until yesterday, upon the opening of the codicil of the late Count, that I truly realized the immensity of my errors. I did not hesitate to recognize them in the presence of the entire assembly of the Chapter, and I asked the forgiveness of the excellent Prior, as I am doing again at this moment...."

"Ah! Monsignor," interrupted Prior Bonaventure, with humility, "can you debase yourself this way?... All appearances were against us, and you treated us with indulgence when one considers the enormity of the crime of which we were accused."

"However, I should not have judged you based on simple appearances," said the prelate stiffly; "the scandal that I provoked will henceforth be the shame of my life.... In any event, I wanted to repair my errors, and in spite of the terrible weather and the dangers of the trip, I wished to accompany the Prior myself to this house where the scandal caused so much damage, although perhaps nowhere else should the name of the fathers of Frontenac be more honored."

During this conversation the Baron was alternatively distracted and attentive. However, he had been carefully examining the documents brought by the Prior, as if he was searching a pretext for contestation which he did not find.

"Well now!" he said with an air of philosophic joviality, "my Earldom has decidedly gone to the Devil! But, no matter! I am still Laroche-Boisseau, and that is still something.... Dear little cousin," he continued ironically, "accept my congratulations.... Morbleu! a while ago when I invited you to the honor of having your throat cut, I did not think that the honor was so well shared."

"A duel, Léonce!" said the Prior; "is that what you promised me?"

"Pardon me, dear Father.... I understand now why you recommended so warmly that I avoid a quarrel with Sire de Laroche-Boisseau!... However," he immediately added, "this will not require that from now on I live in close relations with Sire Baron as normally befits such close relatives, and as a pledge I offer my hand..."

The Baron shrugged his shoulders.

"This might shock your friends," he said, laughing; "the infected hand of a heretic might be contagious, which your father so feared for you. It would be better that we each lived on our own side.... Glory and prosperity to the new Count of Varinas!... As for me, thanks to a fortunate shot of my rifle yesterday evening, I have no reason to envy him."

"Ah! you are right" exclaimed Léonce, "I would gladly exchange my fortune and my title against..."

"What are you talking about?" asked Bonaventure in astonishment;

Léonce explained to him in a few words how Laroche-Boisseau had killed the beast of Gévaudan. This news dismayed the Prior and the Bishop as well since he knew of the favorite project of the fathers of Frontenac. However after reflection, Sire de Cambis resumed firmly:

"This marriage cannot take place, and the Church will never agree to sanction.... Miss de Barjac, a good Catholic, could never marry a Protestant. The indiscreet vow must be declared null and void."

"Well, here are some monastic subtleties!" exclaimed Laroche-Boisseau with anger; "they had not planned for that; Protestants and Catholics were supposed to have the same privileges.... And as proof," he added, turning towards Christine, "I summon, once again, the loyalty of Miss de Barjac. This loyalty, I know, will not fail me."

Christine said nothing.

"Speak, my daughter," said Monsignor de Cambis; "we will release you without a problem from this disastrous vow."

The miserable child felt an inexpressible anguish. Finally, she replied:

"I belong to a family where good faith and fidelity to one's word has been the tradition for centuries.... I will not lift a finger, I will not say a word to remove myself from the consequences of my deplorable vow!"

A bleak silence followed this declaration.

"Morbleu!" Laroche-Boisseau finally said, rubbing his hands, "I can console myself for many disappointments.... Keep your titles and your riches, Cousin Varinas; I will have better than that.... And it seems to me that I could not be more timely in killing the beast of Gévaudan!"

"Unfortunately, you have not yet killed it, dear Baron," said a mocking voice behind him.

Two persons had just slipped into the salon without being noticed. One was Legris, the Baron's confidant, and the other was Léonce's old tracker.

The curiosity aroused by the assertion of Legris who had just spoken kept them from considering the impropriety of such a brusque intervention.

The Baron, his face crimson with anger, ran up to his friend.

"What do you want?" he said in hushed tones; "you dare show yourself here…"

"It is with your permission," resumed Legris out loud, and without worrying about his patron's threatening gestures. "You have not killed the beast of Gévaudan and I hurried here to prevent any misunderstanding or precipitated action."

"How, Sire, you who saw me yesterday place a bullet through the heart of the cursed animal, how can you put in doubt…"

"Ask this brave man," said Legris, with confidence. "Well, Denis," he resumed, addressing the tracker, who, without worrying much about all the eminent persons present, had begun examining the paw and the head deposited next to the door, "were you mistaken?"

"On the contrary, Sire," replied Denis; "what I suspected is perfectly true… this paw and head never belonged to the beast of Gévaudan."

A general exclamation greeted this decision. They overwhelmed the tracker with questions, and he did not know to whom to reply. The voice of Laroche-Boisseau dominated all the others.

"What is the meaning of this foolish jest?" he asked; "Who is this old ruffian that comes here to give lessons to a gentleman in a salon of a lady?"

"This is not my place, Sire Baron, I am well aware," replied the tracker, "however, with all due respect, I will only say what I am sure is true and concerns my profession. The wolf whose remains are here is not the beast of Gévaudan, but that of another large old wolf that prowled recently in the neighboring woods and that we had named the black wolf. It was extremely ferocious and had committed many misdeeds that we often attributed to the beast. Several times I had found its trace in the forest, and I was almost fooled myself, but its paw has two indentations less than that of the beast, and Sire Léonce, my master, will remember that I had shown him the difference in the paw prints."

"This is true, this true!" exclaimed Léonce; "moreover, now that I look at it, I do not see on the head of the wolf the scar from the bayonet slash it received from the little Chanaleilles boy; and that scar had been seen by other hunters."

"And what is more," said Legris, "I, who the beast had knocked over on a certain day in the ravine of the Creux-aux-Sangliers, I can affirm that its pelt was much tawnier."

"This is true!' said the knight.

Laroche-Boisseau remained speechless after this unanimity of testimony.

"Thus," asked Miss de Barjac breathlessly, "there is an error or fraud? It is not the beast?... Then the imposed condition has not been fulfilled, and I am still free…."

"Not yet, Miss," interrupted the Baron, violently agitated; "I maintain that the animal whose remains I have presented is indeed the famous beast of Gévaudan; and, to oblige me to recognize my error, you must furnish more positive proofs...."

"More positive proofs? Do you want some, Sire Baron?" Denis asked in a slightly sardonic manner; "well an animal that I have been tracking since this morning has finally been *diverted*; I maneuvered it so well that that it is entrapped in the large quarries of Montfichet at the foot of the Monadière. Pressured by our being too near, it made the blunder of entering this sort of cul-de-sac that has no exit. So, I left Gervais and some determined peasants to guard the narrow entrance and I hastened here to alert Sire Léonce.... This animal, which finds itself in a trap, is the one and only beast of Gévaudan."

"What are you saying, Denis?" Léonce exclaimed impetuously; "will it now be possible?"

"Sire, upon arriving here, I ordered that they prepare your horse, your rifles and all in your team. Agree to follow me and in less than half an hour, I will have placed you in the presence of the beast."

"Let us leave!" exclaimed Léonce; "God undoubtedly does not wish that my joy be incomplete.... Let us not lose any time.... The animal could escape!"

"That is not likely; but you must be ready for a real struggle, as..."

"No matter! Let us get going.... My horse, Denis.... My horse!"

And he approached the Prior and the Bishop.

"My Father, Monsignor," he said with exaltation, bless me... pray for me!"

Then, turning towards Christine:

"Miss, I will fulfill those required conditions to have you, or die in the process."

And he launched himself towards the doorway which the tracker had already reached.

"Courage, Léonce, courage," exclaimed Miss de Barjac, "and may Heaven assure your success!"

Then, faltering under the weight of her extended emotions, she fell in a faint in the arms of Sister Magloire.

While they hastened to revive her, Laroche-Boisseau remained somber and pensive in a corner of the salon, next to Legris who seemed to enjoy his consternation.

"By the Devil!" finally said the Baron, lifting his head; "all the joy is for that handsome flower, today!... But why would I not take advantage of the opportunity which presents itself? I am a hunter also, and not the least capable; my horse and my people must be waiting for me in the courtyard…. Perhaps the game is not lost!"

He made a sign to Legris to follow him.

"Leave me alone," Legris said brusquely; "you have deceived me…. Everything is finished between us."

"Aha!" said the Baron with disdain, "your father has already written you that my ruin is complete along with all my hopes?... But come, I tell you…. We will discuss this elsewhere. Do you think that they will accept you in that salon when I will no longer be there? Look, you will see that the eyes of the knight are already upon you!"

This last assertion convinced Legris, and they left together.

Soon, the Prior and the Bishop found themselves alone.

"Monsignor," said Prior Bonaventure, "this is a solemn moment…. Perhaps our efforts, our sacrifices to assure the happiness of some poor creatures of God may result in a catastrophe!... Léonce requested it; let us pray for him!"

Chapter XXVI

THE QUARRIES OF MONTFICHET

Laroche-Boisseau and Legris, while moving towards the main courtyard where they would find their horses, continued their conversation in low voices.

"Sambleu! Legris," the Baron was saying with a feverish agitation, "a quarrel between us! It does not make sense. You need me like I need you.... What are you thinking of in joining forces with my enemies? The day that they will have crushed me, they will make short work of you."

"Baron, I repeat, you have deceived me.... I almost ruined my father to satisfy your lavishness, and to please you, I resigned myself to the most humiliating actions. And now, you are not keeping your word in the most shameful manner when I claim the reward which I was promised and is my just due!"

"And what reward!" said Laroche-Boisseau, "the hand of the chatelaine of Mercoire, only that.... Block-head! Remember our agreement.... In the case that I kill the beast (and you have just finished proving to me, as clearly as can be, that I have not killed it!) I had promised that I would substitute you for my rights on the young lady provided that I had already obtained possession of the Varinas heritage. However, presently, I can no longer be the Count de Varinas... unless somehow, my dear beloved cousin, who just galloped away from here to go to the quarries of Montfichet, has the good taste to break his neck or get himself devoured by the wolf!"

"Your cousin?" asked Legris opening wide his eyes. "What are you saying? I do not understand you."

Laroche-Boisseau informed him about Léonce's history and without stopping during the exclamations of his confidant, he continued:

"My situation seems desperate but I need revenge, and I shall have it, by all the Devils of ell, if necessary.... You see, Legris, I would prefer a thousand times more seeing you marry the rich damsel than leaving her to that insolent relative. Unite with me, as in the past, and perhaps things will turn your way. By going immediately to the quarries, where they say the beast is at this moment, a favorable opportunity may present itself.... You know," he added darkly, "at a hunt, extraordinary and strange accidents occur....'

"For the love of God, Baron," asked his frightened confidant, "what do you intend to do?"

"Coward, idiot," said Laroche-Boisseau, tapping his foot.

Finally, he resumed.

"We will act in accordance with the circumstances. We will take advantage of the first opportunity that presents itself, and perhaps… Look, since you absolutely insist, I promise you again that I will make every effort to have you marry that seductive creature, whom I must now renounce in my own interest."

"Is this promise really sincere, Baron? If I believed it so…"

"I give you my word as a gentleman, and as low as I have sometimes gone, I never broke my… But you will obey me, will you not," he added with a violence that was barely constrained; "you will obey me no matter what I say or what I do?"

"However, Baron, I have to know…"

"Peace! Let us go… We are losing time!"

Legris did not dare reply.

They arrived in the courtyard. On a word from Laroche-Boisseau, they were brought two horses, saddled and bridled. Legris did not seem entirely decided to engage himself in the enterprise; dangerous certainly, shameful perhaps, and he hesitated to mount his horse. As Laroche-Boisseau, on his side, was placing his foot in the stirrups, someone, who had been calling him for several moments without obtaining a response, touched him lightly on the shoulder. The Baron, furious, turned and saw the Knight de Magnac.

The old squire was hiding under his coat two swords of even length. He had an cavalier and deliberate air which was not usual for him, and he kept his cap on his head.

"Ah! Sire Baron" he said in a light and impertinent tone, "one does not leave in this manner…. I did not become your cousin a few hours ago, did I? And on the contrary, I have more than ever the right to invite you to accompany me for a short stroll to a clearing on the edge of the woods…. I know a place that is perfect."

The Baron did not reply and remained still, his eyes fixed, as if he did not know what was expected of him. Finally, me made a brusque movement.

"Go to the Devil! you old fool," he said; "I do not have time to listen to nonsense; we shall see about satisfying you another time."

He attempted to mount his horse, but Magnac retained him by the tail of his coat.

"I may be a fool, Sire," he said with that cold fury of a bilious temperament, "but I still have a good eye, and my hand does not tremble. Now I invite you again…"

"Let go of my coat, you crazy old man; let go of my coat, or despite your old age and grey hair…"

He raised his hand; the other did not move.

"Now, Sire," he said, "you can no longer refuse me the satisfaction that is due me."

This last statement seemed to impress Laroche-Boisseau. He reflected several seconds.

"He has gone mad," he finally said; "so be it, let us be done with it…. I would not hold back for long…. Legris, leave your horse here and come with us."

"And where, my dear Baron?"

"Where it pleases Sire de Magnac to lead us…. And you, Sire Knight, do you have a second?"

Magnac removed his cap.

"Sire Laroche-Boisseau is most kind,' he said suddenly recovering his fastidious politeness; "I intended naming a gentleman as my second, and I could send for the Marquis de Gaillefontaine, but this would greatly delay us…. If you permit, I will call the master of the hounds from Comtois, who you see over there; he was a soldier, and considering that Sire Legris is only a bourgeois, Comtois is better than nothing.

"Bring whoever the devil you wish," said the Baron impatiently, "but let us get on with it."

The knight, quite happy, hurried to warn the hound master, who was rather flattered, and without worrying about the comments from the servants milling around the courtyard, the adversaries and witnesses set out.

"Keep the horses ready," said the Baron to his people upon leaving the chateau, "we will be back in five minutes."

They reached the nearby forest, and at the first clearing, the knight stopped.

"Does it not seem to you, Sire Baron, that we will be fine here?"

"Absolutely."

Immediately, the old gentleman threw off his cloak and his vest; then he offered Laroche-Boisseau the choice between two swords which he had brought. The Baron selected the first one which was offered and in turn began his preparations for combat.

The moment that the Knight took his stance, Legris, astonished by his presence and his martial grace, murmured to himself:

"Hmm! the soldier from Fontenoy has style, and while Laroche Boisseau is a refined duelist, he might find someone of his mettle. By my faith! I am not too sure for which of the two I should wish the best; the oldster has a grudge against me, however Laroche-Boisseau is becoming a very poor companion, not to mention that one cannot expect much from him….

Let us see! May God or the Devil chose between them. Myself, I am ready for anything!"

As he finished his charitable wishes, the two swords met with a sinister clicking sound.

We will know a little later the results of this duel. We must now return to Léonce and Denis whom we left galloping in the forest.

The quarries of Montfichet where the formidable wolf was blocked was located in the center of the mountainous and wooded region that was called Fond-de-la-Monadière, where Léonce had faced great dangers at the beginning of this story. However, that memory did not cool the ardor of the impetuous young man, and in less than a quarter of an hour after their departure from the chateau, the two cavaliers, breathless and covered with perspiration, as were their mounts, arrived at the entry of the quarries where Gervais and several peasants armed with rifles and staffs were standing guard.

This entry was a narrow gap which had been made earlier in the rock to give access to wagons. This was flanked by two blocks of basalt, one on the right, and the other on the left. Through this opening, the eye could plunge into a circular space, rather vast, surrounded by pointed rock formations spiked with stones and undergrowth. Gervais and his companions, always alert, held on leashes two dogs that growled intermittently, their eyes turned towards the quarry.

The sight of Léonce and Denis seemed to greatly please Gervais.

"I was waiting for your arrival most impatiently, Sires," he said, as they dismounted their horses. "That cunning beast approached us several times, and I feared that it might try to force its way out…. Moreover, daylight is beginning to fail and if the wolf is not killed before nighttime, we can be sure that despite all our precautions, it will escape us."

"However, in the meantime, you can assure us that it is still in the quarries, correct?" asked Denis.

"Certainly, you can see how the dogs are pointing with the wind and pulling on their leashes…. The cursed animal is not more than fifty paces away from us."

"That is good," said Léonce. "Denis, you will stay here with your brave people, and stand ready to stop the wolf if it tries to escape. On my side, I will enter alone with Castor; I have my rifle with its bayonet and my hunting knife. These will suffice."

The tracker listened with an air of astonishment mixed with fear.

"My young Master will pardon my boldness," he said respectfully, "but he would not have the temerity to confront such a formidable and desperate animal in that sort of pit by himself…. With your permission, I will accompany you, and perhaps the two of us…"

"That is what I cannot accept, Denis," replied Léonce firmly. "My intention is to not be assisted by anyone in this battle that I must face; No one is to penetrate into the quarries, no matter what happens.... You have well understood me, have you not? Woe be to the person who transgresses my orders! I will never pardon him in my lifetime. In case the animal does force its way out, then, and only then you may shoot it; Otherwise, simply stay where you are and remain alert."

Léonce normally spoke to his inferiors with cordiality; but this time his tone was dry, curt and resolute. However, once again, the tracker was not discouraged.

"Sire," he said with warmth, "I am an old hunter, and it is my duty to warn you of the dangers..."

"Enough," interrupted Léonce, "is my rifle loaded?"

"I loaded it myself a short while ago.... Two charges of powder and two iron bullets."

"That is fine."

He made sure that the primer of his weapon was not damp, passed his thumbnail over the flint; then after having half-pulled his hunting knife from its sheath, he appeared ready to get started.

"Do not forget my orders, my friends," he resumed in a tone that was softer and almost gay; "maintain your position, that is all I ask."

He was about to pass through the entry of this sort of stadium, after having released Castor, Godard's mastiff, when Denis said to him in a pleading tone:

"At least, my good Master, take also the bloodhound.... Even though it is cowardly, it will warn of the approach of the wolf, and will save you from being surprised."

Léonce agreed, although he did not expect much help from the hound, and, preceded by the two dogs, he entered the quarries.

A profound calm reigned, a deathly silence. Nothing moved in the middle of the sterile rocks and the dried brushwood that covered the ground. On all sides, the mountain raised its smooth vertical rock face like a rampart; one would have described it as a closed field where all retreat was impossible for the vanquished, where death would inevitably follow defeat. In places, drifts of snow, half-melted, detached themselves on the dark surfaces of the heather. In the center of the basin was a pond formed by the rainwater; it was frozen and white ridges drew lines across its bluish crust. Above this stark landscape, the misty sky, darkened by the approaching night, extended like a dismal shroud.

Léonce advanced, step-by-step, eyes and ears alert, his finger on the trigger of his heavy rifle. He scrutinized every indentation of the terrain and each tuft of brambles. The beast could, indeed, leap upon him and tear him to pieces before anything signaled its presence. He stopped at intervals, holding his breath. His dogs prowled around him in silence. The blood-hound in particular seemed worried. It frequently interrupted its wander-ings and returned to its master in fear. Then, it would be necessary to caress it, encourage it in a low voice to convince it to return to the trail. The other dog, robust and courageous, showed less hesitation; however, its dim sense of smell obliged it to rely on its companion. Moreover, the trail was fresh, and as the huntsmen say, all *bloody*; In places, one could see large and deep paw prints, which seemed to have been made only minutes before.

However, the beast did not show itself, and if the walls of the enclosure had not been almost perpendicular, one could have thought that it had suc-ceeded in getting out over the natural barriers. However, such was not to be feared. For this, it would be necessary to bound twenty or thirty feet in height, and the wolf, as agile as it might be, did not have the prodigious elasticity of tigers, panthers and the other ferocious animals of the feline family. Therefore, the beast was certainly still in the quarries, and at any moment, it might appear ready for its attack or to launch one of its own.

Léonce had been roaming among rocks and thickets when suddenly the bloodhound rushed back to him showing more terror than it had so far, looking for protection between the legs of its master. The mastiff Castor, on the contrary, stopped; and stretching its vigorous neck, protected by a collar with steel spikes, let out deep growls. All these signs indicated that the ferocious animal was near. Although the young hunter redoubled his attention, he still saw nothing.

Finally, however, he succeeded in identifying the position of his ter-rible enemy. At about thirty paces from him was the pond that we have mentioned, and on the edge of this pond emerged a large clump of dry and yellowing reeds; Now, Léonce discovered, through the stalks of the swampy grass, two points fixed and so brilliant, that even in the light of day they launched a menacing flame. One could not see more, but the hunter knew enough. The beast was there, undoubtedly prepared to hurl itself on him as soon as he came close enough.

Léonce had stopped, and was placing very slowly the but of his rifle at his shoulder, but did not shoot. His heart beat violently, clouds passed before his eyes; vertigo was beginning to have an effect on him. Perhaps he was remembering that this monster, which was only a few paces from him, had devoured eighty-five persons and had severely wounded another twenty-five or thirty; that it had confounded the pursuit of two or three thousand hunters, and that the entirety of France was on alert because of it. Fortunately, the lovely smiling image of the woman he loved appeared in time to divert the dismal thoughts in the young man's mind; immediately, his blood circulated more calmly, the vertigo disappeared and, in a few seconds, the objects around Léonce had regained for him the proportions of reality.

Either he was too far away, or he did not feel that his adversary was sufficiently visible. He began moving forward, the rifle at his cheek. The dogs followed, still growling, one in anger, the other in fear. However, this maneuver produced no result; the wolf did not move and one could only see its mesmerizing eyes. Finally, Léonce, impatient with this immobility, aimed precisely between those luminous points; but the roles suddenly changed.

The ferocious animal, knowing it was discovered, took its chance. Its powerful head, with ears erect, its enormous body with a fawn-colored pelt and heavy tail in the air, surged out of the reeds; then its large chest brushing aside all obstacles, it charged its enemy with fury.

Léonce did not let himself be intimidated by this sudden attack. When the beast was ten paces from him, he aimed at the head and fired.

The explosion of his large rifle, that reverberated with a thousand echos, produced a sound comparable to thunder, which had not prevented him from hearing a savage howl. Through the smoke from the powder, Léonce saw the beast had been hurled onto its back by the force of the shot, as if struck dead. Léonce was already opening his mouth to give a cry of joy and call to his companions. However, he did not have the time to do so.

The beast had just gotten up, all covered with blood, more frightening than ever. The pain, the desire for vengeance, had doubled its strength and courage. In an instant, it was on top of the hunter. Vainly, he attempted to use the point of his bayonet. The bayonet, although made of tempered steel, broke like glass; the rifle itself, was twisted, and Léonce, brutally knocked down, rolled stunned on the ground.

He appeared to be doomed, as he was incapable of protecting himself, but his faithful allies did not abandon him. The mastiff Castor, which we will remember had to avenge its defeat of Bois-du-Saut, threw itself on the beast and bit it with fierceness. The bloodhound, either because the sight of its enemy's blood revitalized it, or the danger to its master enabled it to surmount its timidity, lunged without hesitating at the throat of the wolf. The latter then had to quell its new adversaries.

The task did not take long; one lone slash of its fang sufficed to break the spinal column of the unfortunate bloodhound, while a cruel paw opened its stomach and sent its entrails flying. The poor dog emitted a lamentable cry and died.

Which left Castor, having also seized the throat of the beast, and was holding firm. The wolf attempted get rid of it by a massive shake of its head, which was its custom; however, the mastiff, no doubt educated by experience, was able to evade the blows. So they tumbled one over the other, tearing and biting with inexpressible rage. However, the beast, in spite of its wound, retained an advantage that soon became a complete victory.

This horrible struggle took place over the body of Léonce; The perpetual trampling and perhaps the imminent danger, brought Léonce back to his senses. Bruised by his fall, blinded by the dust and the icy snow which flew in his face, he lifted himself on an elbow and drew his hunting knife. At a moment when the two combatants were again rolling over him, he opened his eyes with effort, and gathering all his strength for a final effort, plunged the knife to the hilt into the hairy mass which was stifling him.

At the same instant someone near him cried out: "Courage, Sire.... Hold firm!... Castor... we are here!

But Léonce could no longer hear; something resembling points of steel was tearing at his chest, and a crushing weight fell on him; he could no longer breathe and lost consciousness.

A sensation of freshness and well-being reanimated him. Denis, Gervais and several other persons surrounded him and were treating his wounds. They had sprinkled some icy water from the neighboring pond on his face and loosened his garments.

Léonce instantly recovered his senses and the memory returned.

"The beast!" he asked, "where is the beast?"

"Dead, Sire," replied the old tracker, "really dead, for once, and, by my faith, very hard to kill!"

At the same time, he showed the formidable wolf, soiled and bloody, laid out dead next to the sad remains of the poor bloodhound; a little further, Castor, panting and broken, was sadly licking its wounds.

A painful suspicion crossed Léonce's mind.

"Denis," he resumed, lifting himself up with an sudden movement, "you disobeyed my orders; you came to my rescue.... It was you who killed the beast of Gévaudan!"

The tracker smiled.

"Look at my rifle, my good Sire," he said, presenting his rifle clean and still loaded; "truly, it was not the desire to send a shot into that monster that was lacking, but you were holding it so close that this was not possible.... Moreover, why waste good powder? You settled the old devil's account.... See for yourself!"

In lifting the gigantic body of the wolf, he showed Léonce's knife was entirely embedded in the inner part of its shoulder. The blade was so firmly entangled in bone and muscle that it took great effort to pull it out. Death must have been instantaneous; the gashes on Léonce's chest that caused him to lose consciousness were probably caused by the convulsions of the dying beast.

In accepting this incontestable proof of his triumph, Léonce was carried away by pride and joy.

"Thank you, dear God!" he cried out, "it is then true that I killed the beast of Gévaudan!"

An hour later, the victorious hunters were arriving back at the Chateau de Mercoire. Léonce, disheveled and covered with contusions, walked supported by Denis. The formidable wolf had been draped over the back of a horse. The large head, which still looked menacing, and the long legs, with their sharp claws, hung over each side of the saddle. Then came Gervais carrying in his arms the poor Castor whose pain still had it howling plaintively, although the sight of its enemy dead, and tossed around on the horses' back, seemed to occasionally raise its furor. Finally came the peasants who were expressing their joy at seeing their countryside liberated from this scourge.

They arrived in this manner at the chateau, and as they approached the main entrance, they ran into another group as sad and silent as the other was joyous and turbulent. It consisted of several valets who were carrying on a stretcher a body wrapped in a coat. Behind them came a different group whose faces, darkened by the dusk, were not recognizable.

Léonce asked his people to stop and maintain their silence. When the valets were near him, he asked in a low voice, pointing to the body:

"My God, who is that? What tragedy have we to deplore this time?"

It seemed that the valets did not hear the question, or did not care to answer; they passed with their mournful burden and disappeared under the arch of the entryway.

Léonce hardly dared renew his question, when a voice familiar to him came to his ear; at the same instant, he felt himself being pressed into the arms of the Prior.

"My dear Léonce, is it you?" asked the monk emotionally; "may God be praised! You…at least you, returned safe and sound!"

"And this was not my only blessing from God, good Father, as He has given me victory over the monster that was devastating the countryside…. But, please tell me, who was the unfortunate that passed a minute ago…"

"A man whose life was shameful and who died unrepentant, I fear. I was warned too late; he had already breathed his last when I arrived at the place of combat…. May God forgive his sins."

"But finally, Reverend Father, you have not given me his name…."

"Is it necessary to name him? My son, you are now the last representative of the old and noble family of Varinas!"

Léonce remained pensive for a moment; in spite of himself, he could not help but have great pity for the fate of this relative whose life and its end were deplorable. While he was thinking about this, two persons passed by him, and he heard one saying to the other:

"I have accomplished only half of my task, Master Legris; I have pun-

ished the main offender of my mistress, but I do not intend to stop there....
You have three days to arrange for the funeral of your friend; beyond that
delay, expect to be thrashed wherever I find you, as I promised."

The knight bowed deeply to Léonce, and walked away.

Bonaventure took the arm of the young Count and led him into the chateau. As they approached the inner courtyard, someone exclaimed:

"Léonce, my dear Léonce!"

And Miss de Barjac appeared on the front steps; the young man rushed
towards her.

"Christine," he exclaimed, "God has gas given me victory and I come
to claim the prize."

As a response, Miss de Barjac, overcome, let herself fall into his arms.

* * * *

Two months later, the Count of Varinas, Baron of Gévaudan, Lieutenant of the King's Louveterie for the Province of Gévaudan, married, in the
Mende cathedral the high and powerful Christine de Barjac, Countess de
Mercoire and other lands. The people greeted with their acclamations the
intrepid hunter that had rid the country of the formidable wolf, the ravages
of which would be recorded in the history of the kingdom. This marriage
was celebrated by his Lordship Monsignor de Cambis, Bishop of Alep,
assisted by his Reverence *Dom* Bonaventure, thirty-fourth Abbot of Frontenac, the poor old Abbot that played a role in this story having recently
passed away and the former Prior having been named in his place. Sister
Magloire, in her vestments of a nun, accompanied the bride to the altar, and
acted as her mother. As for the Knight de Magnac, the unfortunate fact that
he had killed in a duel the closest relative of the groom, prevented him from
officially taking part in the celebration, although a large pension placed him
henceforth free from any needs. However, as he watched at a distance his
young mistress with an immense joy, he murmured:

"It does not matter, I nicely made sure she was respected while she was
under my protection.... I killed one, and I thrashed the other.... May God
do the rest!

THE END

Made in United States
Orlando, FL
21 July 2023